THE NAQIB'S DAUGHTER

Also by the Author

The Cairo House

SAMIA SERAGELDIN

The Naqib's Daughter

FOURTH ESTATE • *London*

First published in Great Britain in 2008 by
Fourth Estate
An imprint of HarperCollins*Publishers*
77–85 Fulham Palace Road
London W6 8JB
www.4thestate.co.uk

Visit our authors' blog: www.fifthestate.co.uk

A catalogue record for this book is
available from the British Library

HB ISBN 978-0-00-718217 6
TPB ISBN 978-0-00-722539 2

Typeset in Minion by Palimpsest Book Production Limited,
Grangemouth, Stirlingshire

Printed and bound in Great Britain by
Clays Ltd, St Ives plc

For Kareem and Ramy

ACKNOWLEDGMENTS

No acknowledgment can do justice to Susan Watt's infinite patience, invaluable insight, and essential input in shaping this book. Warm appreciation is due to Toby Eady and Laetitia Rutherford at Toby Eady Associates; Pria Taneja and Anne O'Brien at HarperCollins. Finally, my family's unstinting support is a blessing I do not take for granted.

CONTENTS

Prologue

'Soldiers! You are about to undertake a conquest of incalculable consequences for civilization and commerce! You will deal the English a blow to the heart.'

Napoleon Bonaparte exhorting the army before the invasion of Egypt

'Egypt was once a province of the Roman Republic, it must become a province of the French Republic.'

Minister of Foreign Affairs Talleyrand to the Directoire,

14 February 1798

Quartidi, 4 Messidor, Year 6 (22 June 1798)
On board L'Orient

Ah, but they were a brave sight upon the sea! Nicolas Conté's lungs swelled like the sails ballooning in the wind above him. Their ships covered the horizon: thirteen warships, six frigates, a corvette, and over three hundred cargo ships. And what precious cargo! Such as never accompanied an armada in all of history – even a printing press with Arabic characters.

For it was to be Egypt, after all. After all this secrecy and all these months of rumours, after all this talk of India, it was to be Egypt, definitely. Bonaparte had just announced it officially, after weeks at sea. Even so, in spite of all the secrecy, Nelson might well have caught wind of their destination and might even now be chasing the French

1

fleet around the Mediterranean. But Conté trusted in the destiny of their mission; they could not fail. In Egypt they would bring the light of Liberty to an ancient civilization buried in the sands of ignorance and Oriental despotism.

For this expedition was surely unique in the annals of history: Bonaparte's Army of the Orient was accompanied by over one hundred and fifty savants, scientists and artists, including Nicolas Conté and his corps of military engineers. They were overwhelmingly young, the members of the Scientific Commission, and Conté sometimes felt quite the elder at the command of his balloonist brigade, many of whom regarded him with the unflattering awe normally reserved for a relic. Perhaps, he thought ruefully, it was his eye patch that impressed them so. But then again, he reminded himself, our General Bonaparte himself is not quite thirty!

Bonaparte, it was known, had read every treatise he could lay his hands on about Egypt's religion, history, philosophy and science; he had even found the time to pen a novella called *The Mask of the Prophet*. Never, Conté marvelled, had an enterprise been undertaken in such a lofty spirit, or a campaign so carefully prepared, or a dream cherished for so long.

Now Bonaparte was exhorting his men from the deck of *L'Orient*: 'The people among whom we will live are Muhammadans. Their first article of faith is that there is no God but God and Muhammad is his prophet. Do not contradict them . . . Show the same tolerance for the mosques and the rituals of the Koran as you did for the convents and synagogues, for the religions of Moses and Jesus Christ. You will find different customs, you must get used to them. Their way of treating women is different. But in any culture he who rapes is a monster.'

Conté had no doubt they would be welcomed by the Egyptians, to whom they would come as liberators rather than conquerors, bearing the incomparable gift of the Rights of Man. As for the vaunted Mamlukes who oppressed the people of the Nile, favouring English merchants at the expense of the French, the blood had run thin in that warlike race. All they knew was cavalry, and the age belonged

2

to cannon and musket. Foreign-born, strangers in their own land, they lived as parasites on the natives. Nothing should be easier than to turn the people against them.

And what incomparable discoveries awaited the French Scientific Commission! The Sphinx itself would no longer have any secrets for them. Conté chafed with impatience to see the coast of that ancient land appear over the horizon. What a long way he had come from his humble little village of St-Céneri-le-Gérei, Nicolas-Jacques Conté, the self-taught son of peasants, promoted rapidly in the Republican ranks by the sheer merit of his genius, the Director of the first Engineering School in France; and here he was now at forty, launched on the adventure of his lifetime, of all their lifetimes – an expedition for the ages.

'Land ho!'

Conte's heart leapt in his chest. Egypt, at last! The great adventure had begun.

PART I

The First Hundred Days

ONE

The Enemy at the Gates

For only the second time in her forty years of life, Lady Nafisa the White dreaded the dawn. Sleep had eluded her all night, but she lay quietly in order not to disturb her maids in the adjoining room. They would have risen, bleary and heavy-limbed with sleep, and hovered around her bed, offering to bring mint tea, or to massage her feet.

Nafisa knew where her husband was tonight, and wished it were with another woman.

She glanced at the gold-mounted ormolu clock with the rose faience face that she could not make out in the dark. It had been a present from the French consul, Magallon, in happier times. The irony struck her: how the world had changed! But she did not need a clock to tell the time; she could smell the dawn in the air before the first bird stirred, before the muezzin cleared his throat to chant the call for prayers; long before the watchmen unlocked the heavy wooden gates that secured each neighbourhood for the night against robbery and mischief. She knew the exact order in which the gates to the quarters were drawn back: first the Moroccan quarter, then the Jewellers Lane, then the Nasiriya quarter where most of the European merchants lived, then the Ezbekiah Lake and the Alley of the Syrians, and finally the gates to the Citadel. Cairo was her city; she could take its pulse at any moment.

The first time Nafisa had lain sleepless had been her wedding night – her first wedding night, thirty years ago now, to Ali Bey. Her awe of her husband-to-be had been complete. As a child she had seen his image struck on coins: Ali Bey the Great, sole master of Egypt. She had watched from the latticework shutters of the harem windows as he rode past at the head of his army, on one campaign or another, to Syria and the Sudan and the borders of Egypt. When his choice had fallen on her for his second wife, the honour had been overwhelming.

Her hair had been long and thick like a curtain then, the colour of light molasses where it sprung at the roots, grading down to the clearest honey where it slapped against the back of her knees. The first time she had undressed before Ali Bey, she had shaken her hair about her in a shudder of modesty, cloaking herself with her own tresses. He had thrown his head back and laughed, and her dread had begun to melt around the edges.

She had been little more than a child at the time. Over their long years together she had grown from child-bride to trusted consort, consulted and cultivated by the powerful in Egypt and abroad. Until the day Ali Bey had been betrayed and assassinated. Nafisa tensed and held her breath, listening for the clatter of horses' hooves, for the night watchmen dragging open the heavy wooden gates that closed off her neighbourhood. But it was only her overwrought imagination, and she lay back, winding a thick strand of hair around her palm. When the muezzin called for dawn prayers she would clap her hands and her maids would bring the mint tea she drank first thing every morning to keep her breath sweet all day. Even when she had gone on the pilgrimage to Mecca, two years ago, one of the camels in her caravan had carried nothing but pots of live herbs: mint, but also caraway for digestion, basil to stimulate appetite, and chamomile to rinse her hair. A cow plodded along, ensuring her diet of fresh milk and cheese. The Prince of the Pilgrimage leading the caravan from Egypt that year had made sure her every whim was accommodated.

Nafisa threw off her bedcovers; she was naked but for her fine silk shift. She was still beautiful, and still desirable. Was she not the same age as Khadija had been when she proposed to the Prophet Muhammad, and he a young man fifteen years her junior?

Like Khadija, Nafisa had chosen a husband. A widow as young and wealthy as she could not remain without a husband and protector, and so she had opted for Murad, with his curly red bush of a beard heralding his choleric temperament like a banner. Among the senior Mamlukes, Murad had stood out by his ambition, but it was her status as the widow of Ali that raised him to the rank of co-regent of Egypt.

Today, Murad would be tested as no one could have imagined.

Until a week ago, her world had turned steadily on its axis. Her days were spent supervising the trading operations of her wikala, the caravanserai at Bab Zuweila, and overseeing construction of the charitable waterworks she was erecting nearby on Sugar Street. And along with the rest of Cairo she followed avidly reports of the rise of Elfi Bey's new palace on the Ezbekiah Lake, and gauged the rise of his ambition as warily as the city leaders watched the peaking of the Nilometer before the summer flood.

Then came the news that English warships had dropped anchor off the port of Alexandria, looking for the French fleet. They had left, not finding their prey, but Egypt held its breath, waiting for the other shoe to drop. It had not been long in coming. The French fleet landed at the Bay of Alexandria two days later.

Last night her husband had gone to the judge's house with old Ibrahim Bey and Elfi and the senior Mamluke commanders to devise a strategy. And Nafisa had lain awake, unable to sleep for only the second time in her life.

Nafisa started at the clatter of horses' hooves followed by a shouted command and the scramble of the night watchmen to unlock and open the gates to the lane as her husband and his retainers approached. The servants bestirred themselves and fumbled to light torches with the haste bred by dread of their master's temper. Nafisa's maids hurried to her and she motioned for her Damascus silk slippers and robe. She slipped from room to room down the narrow, winding stone staircase, her robe sweeping the steps behind her, till she reached the mezzanine gallery with its arcades where, standing behind the wooden latticework mashrabiyya, she could look down on the central hall without being seen.

Murad had not come alone, there were two Mamlukes with him. As the servants scurried about, torches in hand, to fetch cushions for the wooden banquettes, Nafisa recognized Sennari, her husband's right-hand man, by his great height and his ramrod posture, even before she caught a glimpse of his coffee-brown face with the tribal markings of his native Sudan etched deep into the cheek and chin.

The other Mamluke commander had his back to her, but something about his bearing, arrogant and wary at once, struck a familiar chord. At that instant he glanced over his shoulder and she recognized in his gesture that sixth sense that alerted him that he was being watched. It was Elfi himself.

The first time she had laid eyes on Elfi, Nafisa had been standing in this very spot. All of Cairo had buzzed about the peerless young Mamluke her husband had paid an extraordinary price for; it was said there was none to rival him for beauty or spirit, so wilful he had forced his first master to part with him, although no one knew exactly what he had done. She had waited behind the filigreed mashrabiyya for Murad to arrive with his latest acquisition, and peered down at the handsome blond Circassian. Murad had looked up at her triumphantly, and the blond head had tilted up, following his gaze. The Circassian had shot her a sharp glance from hard blue eyes, then faced forward again, impassive.

Murad had looked into the unflinching eyes of the young Mamluke and seen in him the prize racehorse of his stable; perhaps he had even seen in him his heir-in-arms, the heir he would never have from his own loins. For what Mamluke would wish upon a son of his flesh and blood to live by the sword and to die by the sword? For that they bought Mamlukes and trained them. Was it any wonder if they sometimes grew closer to them than they were to their own kin? Closer, sometimes, than they were to any woman.

Murad had looked into the hard eyes of the young Circassian and seen courage and intelligence. Nafisa had looked and seen a disquieting ambition. She had recognized a kindred spirit, she who had once been, like him, the possession of others, depending on beauty and wits for the favour of those who held her fate in their hands.

Twenty years later, Elfi Bey had earned envy and enemies with his fearsome reputation, his thousand Mamlukes and his half-dozen homes. The latest palace he had just completed on the Ezbekiah Lake was the talk of Cairo, with French chandeliers, an Italian marble fountain in the courtyard, and a library bidding to rival that of the venerable Azhar University itself. Nafisa had been proved right about Elfi's ambition; she hoped Murad would be proved right about his loyalty.

Murad ushered his guests up the steps to the loggia with its arched colonnades, where the servants were laying out cushions and setting up round brass trays on wooden tripods. The men seemed to be arguing intensely, Murad's blustery voice rising above Elfi's deeper tones and Sennari's laconic interjections.

Nafisa clapped her hands for the chief eunuch, and gave orders for breakfast to be prepared. The big brass pot of Yemeni coffee was to be brewed stronger than usual, as she suspected no one had slept that night. The cook was to begin baking the flaky butter pastry right away; if he had any sense, he would have lit his oven an hour ago. As she gave the eunuch the keys to the larder to bring out the day's allotment of honey, butter and spices, she asked him, in an offhand tone, as if it were an afterthought, to report to her on the state of household stocks: how many sacks of wheat, rice, barley, lentils; how many jars of oil and clarified butter; how many bags of coffee, tobacco, sugar, nuts, spices; how many days' worth of fodder for the horses and mules. Later she would send her chief eunuch to check the larder stocks in Murad's three other houses around the city, and the Giza estate. Discreetly, of course; any rumours of a possible siege of Cairo would set the shopkeepers to hoarding goods and the residents to panicking.

Nafisa rather welcomed these mundane details; they would occupy her restless mind till Murad's guests were gone and she could find out what course of action had been decided against the French advance.

*   *   *

Seventeen days. Elfi counted them. Seventeen days since he had occupied his brand-new Ezbekiah palace, and not even as many nights. He walked out on the terrace in the tepid morning breeze and inhaled the sharp scent of lemon trees mingled with the softer perfumes of jasmine and apricot. In a month the Nile would flood, and the parched lake basin before him would rapidly fill with water, and the Ezbekiah would come alive every night with torchlight and music, the boats gliding back and forth, the shopkeepers' kiosks doing a bustling business in iced syrups and stuffed pancakes. Only seventeen days ago it had given him satisfaction to think that none of the houses around the Ezbekiah could compare, indeed no house in all of Cairo. Not one of the mansions of the great old man, Ibrahim Bey, nor those of Murad Bey, the master of Cairo, and his grand Lady Nafisa with her French friends and fancy furniture.

Elfi turned back to the downstairs hall and slipped off his shirt. He splashed his face repeatedly in the large marble fountain with its brass jets, trying to clear his head. Looking at his reflection in the water he saw a face he had not seen in many years: a boy called Shamil.

Growing up in a stone hut on the side of a mountain in the Caucasus, the boy he had once been could no more have imagined this Ezbekiah mansion than he could have dreamed of the Sultan's Top Kapi Saray in Istanbul. But tonight, Elfi was blindsided by a stab of homesickness for the sharp, clean mountain air of his native Tcherkessia. He longed for the taste of snow in summer, for the echoing silence, for the horizon that stretched on and on at a dizzying distance. Yet as a boy he had felt hemmed in by the vast emptiness of those mountains, and spent his time peering into the distance for a glimpse of the glittering Black Sea, dreaming of the ship that would one day carry him away.

Then, one summer day, as he watched his mother ladle yogurt into squares of cheesecloth that she hung in the sun to drip into soft balls of cheese, something in him turned. He went into the hut and threw his sheepskin-lined winter cloak over his shoulder, and stood for a moment at the door till his mother raised her worn face, tossed her long blonde plait over her shoulder, and put down her ladle. Then he turned away and jogged down the mountain, never looking back. He was fifteen years old.

The boy Shamil was buried in him now; there was only Muhammad Bey Elfi. Elfi thought of the first master who had bought him in Egypt: the Majnoon – the crazy one – had brought him home to a large, pleasant mansion with running fountains in the courtyard. That very evening he had invited a score of revellers to a lavish banquet. One of the servants had brought perfumed ointment and silk garments for Elfi to wear, and motioned for him to follow the sound of raucous laughter to the central hall where men lounged on cushions smoking long pipes and downing goblets of wine. His entrance had been greeted with a moment of admiring silence, then bawdy remarks in an Egyptian dialect he could not follow. The Majnoon had beckoned him and, removing a finely wrought gold chain from the several around his own neck, had tipped Elfi's head forward and slipped the chain over his head, patting the links flat against his bare skin with a smile.

That night Elfi had carried his drunken master to his couch, then taken up vigil in front of the window open to the night air. At dawn he heard the muezzin's chant, followed soon after by the desultory calls of the night watchmen across the city as they dragged open the gates of the neighbourhood alleys. From the stables across the lake there rose the mingled shouts and laughter of young voices, the sounds of horses neighing and rearing, of swords clashing: the young Mamlukes-in-training were engaging in their morning exercises in the horse ring across the way.

Elfi had walked over to the Majnoon's couch and, coming behind him, had lifted his slack body into a half-sitting position, supporting him against his chest, an arm drawn across the man's neck. His master had snorted awake, eyes wide with alarm, and Elfi had given him a moment or two to gather his sodden wits before whispering: 'By law, either the master or the slave has the right to take the other to court to rescind the contract of sale within the first two weeks. I did not become a Mamluke to be the house-pet

13

of a buffoon. Sell me now, or you will wake up one night to find your throat slit.'

The Majnoon had been so terrified he could not sell Elfi fast enough; he had given him to Murad Bey in exchange for a thousand ardabs of wheat – an unprecedented sum – and from that moment on he was known as Elfi, 'he of the thousand'. Murad Bey had taken him into the greatest Mamluke house of them all, and had trained him well. He had been taught to think of his master as his father, and of Murad's other young Mamlukes-in-training as his khushdash, his brothers. Recognizing Elfi's merit, Murad had manumitted him in record time. Elfi had risen rapidly in the ranks from kashif to amir, commander. Today he owned a thousand Mamlukes of his own and commanded forty kashifs under him with a militia of thousands more. He owed much to Murad, and tonight he needed to remind himself of that debt.

Elfi ducked his head under the water and held his breath. As a boy he had trained himself to hold his breath in the cold, pure streams of his mountains, for as long as it took a hawk to circle seven times. From time to time he still practised this skill; he did not know why – only that it might come in handy, one day. He timed himself, counting.

The first house Elfi owned he had bought from the Majnoon, his former master. Then he had built the mansion at Old Cairo opposite the Nilometer, and one between the Gate of Victory and the Damurdash, in addition to the two houses he had bought in Ezbekiah. But this palace he had just completed was the culmination of his heart's ambition. He had had it built from the ground up, razing the site, and sketching out the plans himself on a large sheet of paper. Day and night, kilns fired stones and churned out lime, and mills turned to crush gypsum, and large stones were quarried and transported by ship down the Nile to be sawn into slabs for floors, stairs and courtyards. Various kinds of woods, of marbles and columns, were imported, as well as the chandeliers and the indoor and outdoor fountains. The French had given him an enormous marble fountain with carved figures of fish that sent out jets of water, and that he had put in the garden, under the long vaulted roof he had built for shade and privacy.

He had installed latticework screens with inlaid coloured glass on the windows overlooking the lake, the gardens and the square, so that his women could enjoy the views in privacy. There were two bath halls with pools, one upstairs and one downstairs. He had the house built on different levels, with courtyards, doors and steps separating his private apartments from the apartments on the outer periphery of the courtyard where his Mamlukes would live.

He thought he had rid his nostrils forever of the sour smell of the goat cheese his mother made in that hut on the side of the mountain. But a hunger still gnawed in him, a hunger he could not satisfy with fine houses or sensuous women or hordes of servants or great power. He had grown up illiterate, but in his prime he discovered in himself a hunger for knowledge. Now he bought every book he could, even in languages he did not speak, and sought out the company of scholars and historians. His pride in the new mansion was the library, stocked with books on history and the sciences, particularly those that fascinated Elfi: astronomy, geometry and astrology. Were it not for the unassailable reputation for hard living he had earned in his youth, he would have lost face among his peers.

The first week after Elfi moved in, the house blazed every night with chandeliers and the courtyard and gardens sang with lanterns to greet the throngs of visitors who came to congratulate and envy. He owed it all to Murad. But on this day Elfi felt his loyalty tested as it had never been.

Elfi whipped his head out from under the jets of the fountain, taking in big breaths, and splashed the water under his arms and over his chest. He shook himself like a dog emerging from a pond. He could still hold his breath for as long as it took a hawk to circle seven times.

He had spent the night in council at the judge's house, with the assembled Mamluke amirs and the civilian notables. Old Ibrahim Bey, the senior Mamluke and Prince of the Pilgrimage; Murad, Master of Cairo; Elfi, Tambourji, Bardissi, and the two other Beys who

15

governed the main provinces of Egypt – the seven of them were the ruling Mamlukes. The senior kashifs immediately under their command were also present, along with Papas Oglu, the Greek captain of Murad's river flotilla. The leading scholars and clerics of the Azhar University, headed by the judge, represented the notables. The heads of the guilds and the chief merchants rounded out the council and represented the commercial interests of the city.

Before them all, Murad had laid out his strategy: to split their cavalry forces in two, with Ibrahim Bey and his men camped on the east bank of the Nile and Murad and Elfi on the west. This plan had immediately seemed disastrous to Elfi. In vain he had argued that they should mass all their forces on the far bank of the river, where they would have the advantage of forcing the French to cross over to meet them. Murad had dismissed this on the grounds that the French might advance along either bank or both at once. Elfi countered that any doubts regarding the direction from which the French were advancing could be settled by sending out Bedouin scouts. But Murad had remained immovable and maddeningly dismissive of the enemy's forces. Elfi had even ridden back with Murad to his house at dawn to try to change his mind, but Murad had refused to see reason.

And this morning, as Elfi gave the order to his Mamlukes to prepare for battle and to gather at the Citadel, he was thinking that his oath of fealty to his former master might never cost him, or the city, dearer.

Sitt Nafisa heard Murad's heavy tread on the stone steps leading to her rooms and dismissed her maids with a quick flicker of her fingers. Murad was in full battle regalia, splendidly attired in vivid tunic and pantaloons, his chest festooned with gold chains, his fingers encrusted with precious stones, bejewelled sword hanging at his side and burnished pistols tucked into his scarlet sash. Nafisa guessed that his shaved head must be perspiring under the turban, and that the sable-lined cloak over his shoulders must weigh on him unbearably in the July heat. The French consul Magallon – in the days when he and his wife used to call on Nafisa regularly – had once asked her why Mamlukes made themselves such a rich prize in battle, giving the enemy incentive to kill them expressly to pillage the corpses. 'Truly, *à la guerre comme à l'amour*, hmm?' Magallon had smiled quizzically. It was just the Mamluke custom, she had explained; they were a military caste. Perhaps it was their way of defying fate.

To a casual observer, Murad might not appear to be a man preoccupied by thoughts of an imminent meeting with destiny, but Nafisa could read him under his bluster. The scar from a sword slash across his face had turned livid, as it did whenever he was in the heat of argument or battle.

'We set off from the Citadel at noon, and we will cross the river and wait for the French at Imbaba. Ibrahim Bey has already made camp on the eastern bank.'

Nafisa nodded. All morning she had heard the kettledrums booming and the shrill pipes playing as the cavalcade of horsemen pranced through the winding streets on their way uphill to the Citadel.

'The French won't reach Cairo.' Murad's red beard bristled like a burning bush. 'They may have taken Alexandria, but they won't reach Cairo, nevertheless you may leave if you wish. Ibrahim Bey is evacuating his women; you can join his train. I can spare a small Mamluke escort for you, and of course you can take your maids and eunuchs.'

'I won't leave Cairo, whatever happens. Who will be left if I do?' She had been brought to Cairo as a two-year-old and sold into a great house; she remembered nothing else. 'I know Ibrahim Bey's daughter Adila will stay also, and many of the other women. Don't worry, about us – this is not the Mongols sacking Baghdad. But I'll move some of the coffers of coins and jewels to our other houses in Cairo for safe-keeping, just in case there is any lawlessness – or if we need to pay a ransom.'

He nodded. 'Send some valuables to the Giza estate,' he said, turning to go.

'Wait. What about the European merchants? A mob might attack them; people are restless in the streets, and fear makes them dangerous. We should take the Europeans into our houses for protection.'

'You and your precious Franj! It's your friend Magallon who has been agitating for this war against us.' He turned on his heel. 'Take the Europeans into our houses if you want – you won't have room for all of them.'

'I'll ask Sitt Adila to open her doors to them also; between us we can try to accommodate anyone who seeks refuge.'

'Do as you please.' Murad was already at the door, his mind on other matters. 'May I next see your face in good health.' He raised his hand in farewell.

As she heard the familiar formula of leave-taking, Nafisa shuddered with a premonition that she would not see his face again. She dismissed it instantly; she was not the type to heed such intuitions and she had much to do.

'Bilsalama. Go with God, and return safely.'

Outside the window the murmur of the city was turning to a dull roar of alarm.

T W O

The Battle of the Pyramids

'This was the first year of the fierce fights and important incidents, of the multiplication of malice and the acceleration of affairs; of successive sufferings and turning times.'

Abdel Rahman El-Jabarti's Chronicles of Egypt,

15 June, 1798

'Are you writing, child?'

Zeinab raised her head from the page and looked up at Shaykh Jabarti. How old was the venerable historian, she wondered. At least as old as her father, Shaykh Bakri, and he was two score years; she herself, at twelve, was her parents' second youngest child and only unmarried daughter. As she was serving her father pomegranate juice one evening last month, he had suddenly looked at her and turned to her mother. 'Is she a woman yet?' he had asked. And her mother had blushed and murmured that she was indeed, had been for four cycles of the moon now.

'Then we should get her married,' her father had pronounced, pinching Zeinab's cheek where it dimpled. 'Let me think on it.'

Zeinab had wondered whom he might have in mind, and hoped it would not be someone as old as the man her sister had married. But of course her father had not had time to think on it, with the news of the English ships off Alexandria, and now the French advancing to the outskirts of Cairo.

Shaykh Jabarti's dictation trailed off; he was staring out of

19

the window and stroking his beard, a world away. Zeinab waited quietly, chewing on the end of the ribbon tied around her thick, long black plait. She bent over the silver bowl of rose-water set on the table in front of her and studied her wavering reflection. Like the princesses of fairy tales, her face was as round and white as the full moon, but her eyes were large and dark and her fine black brows arched over them like birds winging over a still pool in moonlight. She blew at the rose petals in the water and the image dissipated.

'Are you writing, child?' Shaykh Jabarti said again, absent-mindedly, and she picked up her quill and waited. She had a fine hand, and for that reason, and because he had tired eyes and preferred to dictate his chronicle, Shaykh Jabarti tolerated her presence as his pupil and scribe. It was very unusual for a girl to be so honoured, and in fact it had been her younger brother, originally, who had been sent to learn at Shaykh Jabarti's feet, but her brother was only interested in spinning a wheel around a stick, as he was doing right now outside the window. It was Zeinab, sent with him as an afterthought, who had proved an apt pupil. She wondered how much longer her father would allow her to receive instruction from Shaykh Jabarti. Once she was married, of course, it would be out of the question.

She had heard that the French had brought a new invention that could make calligraphy and scribes obsolete, a machine that could make many, many copies. As they advanced south towards Cairo, they had distributed countless thousands of copies, in Arabic, of their chief general's proclamation. Shaykh Jabarti was holding a copy at that very moment and snorting as he parsed the words for hidden meanings and for lapses in Arabic grammar and syntax.

'Egyptians, they will tell you that I come to destroy your religion; it is a lie, do not believe it. Answer that I have come to restitute your rights, punish the usurpers; that I respect, more than the Mamlukes, God, his prophet Muhammad and the glorious Koran . . . Tell the people that we are true Muslims.'

'Who translated this?' Jabarti grumbled as he peered at the sheet in his hand, and continued reading.

Zeinab ventured a question. 'My esteemed teacher, do you think these French are Muslim as they say?'

'They say they agree with every religion in part, and with no religion in the whole, so they are opposed to both Christians and Muslims, and do not hold fast to any religion. In truth some hold their Christian faith hidden in their hearts, and there are some true Jews among them also. But for the most part they are materialists. They say the creed they follow is to make human reason supreme; each of them follows a religion which he contrives by the improvement of his own mind.'

Zeinab was distracted by a sudden swell of noise and ran to the window: a procession of dervishes and men in the robes of the Sufi orders were piping and drumming their way down the street. 'Look, my teacher, they have brought down the Prophet's banner from the Citadel!'

'It is all done to calm the fears of the common people. Many were so alarmed they were prepared to flee, had the amirs not stopped them and rebuked them. The rabble would have attacked the homes of all the foreigners and Christians if the amirs had not prevented them; Sitt Nafisa and Sitt Adila took them into their houses.'

'Surely the French will not reach Cairo?' Zeinab was alarmed.

'God alone knows. Murad Bey has had a heavy iron chain forged; it is stretched across the Nile at the narrowest point, to prevent the French ships from passing, while his own flotilla is moored below the chain. Ibrahim Bey and Murad Bey have assembled their troops and now sit in their respective camps across the river from each other, waiting for the French to arrive. Immovable as the Sphinx! Blinded in their arrogance!' Suddenly aware of her alarm, the old man attempted to reassure her with a verse from the Koran: 'Yet thy Lord would never destroy the cities unjustly, while as yet their people were putting things right. Amen.'

'Amen,' Zeinab repeated under her breath.

*   *   *

21

Nicolas Conté squinted in the sun as the Army of the Orient came to a halt along the western bank of the Nile and prepared to engage in the battle for Cairo. Ten thousand Mamlukes faced them on horseback, in full battle regalia, turbaned or helmeted, blazing in the sun with their muskets and lances, their splendid Arabians as richly caparisoned as the riders. The commanders flew back and forth along the lines, turning and wheeling their mounts on a hair, and brandishing their glittering sabres at the heavens.

'There can be no finer animal than a Mamluke-trained horse,' Dr Desgenettes observed, reining in his mount abreast with Nicolas.

'A brave sight indeed,' Conté concurred. 'Let us take a moment to admire them before we cut them to pieces.' He spoke with more bravado than he felt; the siege of Alexandria had been harder than anyone had anticipated, but it was the terrible, four-day forced march south across the desert with its sun of lead and its intolerable heat that had sapped every man's strength and spirit. And the Bedouin! Even the most romantic among the French, thought Nicolas, even Geoffroy St-Hilaire, had lost all illusion about Rousseau's Noble Savage. Like vultures, the Bedouin hovered on the horizon, ready to swoop down on stragglers who succumbed to heat, thirst, sunstroke or despair. There were many among the troops who took their own lives.

But now the ordeal of the desert march was behind them, and the great Army of the Orient was camped before the Nile at Imbaba in preparation for the Battle of the Pyramids, as Bonaparte referred to it.

'Can one even see the pyramids from here?' Dr Desgenettes remarked wryly to Nicolas. 'But I admit it sounds a good deal more memorable than the Battle of Imbaba; our general ever has his eye on the history books.'

Ah yes, thought Conté, but what the history books would record about the French expedition to Egypt was yet to be written. Would this battle go down as the great triumph of the Army of the Orient? And what of his own epitaph, Nicolas-Jacques Conté, Chief Engineer and Commander of the Balloonist Brigade? Would it say that he had survived to see his native shore again one day, to be reunited with his sweet Lise, and his three children? He was a true son of the Revolution and the Republic, and as such he was not a praying man, but at times like these he almost wished he had faith.

'Soldiers!' Bonaparte raised his arm and every ear strained to hear him. 'Go, and think that from the height of these monuments forty centuries observe us.'

At these words a great shout rang from the ranks and Nicolas' heart leapt in his chest. As if at the signal, the Mamluke cavalry charged at a full gallop against the stationary and unshakeable square formation of the French infantry. The fantassins held their ground with supernatural discipline till at twenty paces Bonaparte gave the order to fire cannon and musket, and the first wave of the fine cavaliers fell. Amazingly, the next wave charged right behind them, but the *carré* held again, and the cannon fired again from the corners, and the Mamlukes were cut down again, and this went on until those that survived threw themselves in the river and tried to swim back to the opposite shore, where their confreres were massed, helpless to come to their succour. The French then turned their fire on the eastern bank.

Elfi felt the horse buckle under him as it was hit, and leapt free of the saddle before the beast hit the ground. It was the third horse that had been shot out from under him in this battle. As he landed, the bodies of men and horses beneath him broke his fall, and he lay motionless, concussion blanking out his mind.

When his senses returned, he knew time had passed, but he did not know how long. Hours? Minutes? It was dark. The din of the cannon had abated somewhat and seemed further off, as if directed at the eastern shore; or perhaps the blood in his ears and eyes was dulling his perception. He was bleeding profusely from his head, but head wounds tended to bleed disproportionately; he worried more about the wounds to his right hand and his thigh. He was in no immediate agony, so he did not think he had broken any bones. His sense of smell was undiminished, and the stench of the slaughterhouse made him retch; in all his years, he had not experienced carnage on such a massive scale.

Then he heard them – the buzzards who circled after any battle, come to pick the corpses clean of booty. If they found him alive, they would kill him. If he played dead, they would cut off his fingers for the rings, slash off his ears, then kill him anyway. He began to crawl on knees and elbows over the corpses, towards the river that was now a blazing lake of fire. Either the French had set light to Murad's river flotilla, or Murad himself had given Papas Oglu the order to burn his ships as they retreated. As Elfi watched, the fire reached the gunpowder magazines and before his eyes the ships exploded like a thousand fireworks, sailors throwing themselves into the river in a bid to escape. Still, he slithered on his belly over the foul, blood-slick matting of human and animal dead and dying, towards the flaming water.

He did not look at the bodies he crawled over. Some of the fallen may have been his khushdash, men he had grown up with, like Tambourji and Bardissi . . . or they may have been his own Mamlukes and kashifs, boys he had raised to manhood, trained, manumitted, married to his slave girls and set up in fine houses. Elfi did not spare them a downward look or a moment's prayer; there would be time for mourning, later – if he survived.

He reached the bank and unbuckled his belt and removed his scabbard and the pistols tucked into his sash; the firearms would be useless once wet. He took off his tunic and his soft leather boots, all his clothing but his shirt and pantaloons. He unwound his turban and ripped off strips of it to bandage the wounds on his head and hand and thigh. He removed his rings, the other jewels on his person, and his dagger, wrapping them carefully in the folds of the remaining length of his turban and tying the ends around his middle. Then, taking a deep breath, he slid into the water as smoothly as a crocodile.

His only chance would be to swim downriver and resurface as far from the scavengers as possible; assuming he could avoid being shot out of the water by snipers on the banks, or being caught in the floating flames. He was less concerned about crocodiles this far down-river. Elfi took another deep breath and filled his lungs. Perhaps, he thought, some alignment of his stars had kept him practising the art of holding his breath underwater for as long as a hawk took to circle seven times. The time had come when he would be tested. He plunged further into the black water.

From the city beyond the flames a terrible wailing rose in the smoky air and rolled across the water like thunder.

Zeinab's fingers trembled so much she couldn't manage to hook the loops around the gold-braid buttons of her tunic. Her wet-nurse was having almost as much trouble trying to dress Zeinab's younger brother, who was whining and snivelling into his nightshirt; he had been asleep when the nurse had come into their room in the middle of the night. Zeinab herself had been wide-eyed, kept wakeful by the sound of the cannons in the distance, and then, even more terri-fying, the wailing as the people of Bulaq and the bank of the Nile surged towards the city.

'God preserve us, God preserve us!' the nurse repeated. 'Sitt Zeinab, hurry! They say the French have set fire to Bulaq and that the vanguard has reached the Iron Gate! They say they are burning and killing and raping women! God only knows. Your father says we must leave, we must leave right away. He is trying to find donkeys for us, but every donkey and horse in the city has already been comman-deered. What will become of us?'

By dawn donkeys had been bought, at an exorbitant price, to carry Zeinab and her mother and youngest brother; the men and the servant girls would have to walk. Shaykh Bakri had stayed behind, heading for the Azhar where the ulema had congregated.

Zeinab looked around her as they tried to thread their way through the thronged streets; it seemed as if all the citizens of Cairo were on the move, most on foot, carrying what they could. As their slow procession approached the outer gates of the city they were met by a terrible sight: people returning, wailing, bloody, half-naked, the women tearing their hair and screaming: 'The Bedouin! The Bedouin!

They fell upon us as soon as we left the city walls. Turn back! Turn back!'

'Bring me my jewellery coffer.'

'Sitt Nafisa?' Fatoum looked up from brushing Nafisa's hair. The maid's consternation was apparent. 'Shouldn't we be hiding the jewellery?'

'No, fetch it as soon as you finish dressing me.' If she was to meet the emissary of the French, she wanted to inspire respect for who she was: Murad's wife and Ali's widow. Human nature being universal, she knew that an appeal to esteem and cupidity would be a more reliable card than appealing to pity. But what cards were left for her to play in the face of this overwhelming defeat? Her mind buzzed like a trapped bee. What would the French exact of her? How did they mean to deal with her and with the wives and children of the amirs? The worst fears of the city had been laid to rest the morning after the battle when it transpired that the French had not burned and pillaged the eastern shore; it was the fire on the ships that had given rise to that rumour.

But where was Murad? She made an effort to concentrate on her dressing. She stepped into the rose pantaloons Fatoum held out for her, then slipped the embroidered violet tunic over her sheer white chemise and let the girl tie a rose-and-gold sash round her waist, cinching it in. Nafisa smoothed her thick braid over one shoulder and fixed a small toque on her head, then let a filmy veil float down over it.

'Sitt Nafisa, the jewellery.'

'Let me see.'

She rifled through the tooled leather casket the maid held before her, selecting two thick ropes of pearls and winding them around her neck. She picked two ruby drop-earrings and threaded the fine gold hoops through her earlobes, then slipped the matching bracelet and ring on one hand, and an emerald-and-diamond bracelet on the other wrist. She hesitated, then carefully took a large yellow diamond ring out of a velvet pouch and slipped it on her middle finger; it was as big as a pigeon's egg and sparkled like the sun reflecting off ice.

She wondered if the looters who had raided Murad's house in Qawsun had found the coffer her eunuch had hidden under the planks of the second-floor loggia. Ibrahim Bey's house in Qawsun had been raided too, and several houses belonging to the other amirs, abandoned in their rout.

She had had no word from Murad, but he was alive, that much she knew. The servants on their estate in Giza had reported that their master had appeared and disappeared like a whirlwind, dismounting barely long enough to snatch up the coffers of treasure hidden for that eventuality – and then he was gone.

For the last time, but not the first, she allowed herself a moment of regret. Regret that Murad had not turned out to be the worthy heir of Ali Bey the Great that she had hoped he would become, with her help, when she married him. Seeing in Murad an energetic, domineering temperament that brooked no rival, she had chosen him for a mate. But his instinct to dominate others was not matched by the ability or the judgment to govern them. In their years together, she had learned to handle him with the finesse of a spider weaving a web, but he was ever conscious of the long shadow of Ali Bey. Sensing that he did not measure up to her first husband, he became bitter and intractable, resentful of her interference.

Shaking off that final moment of regret, Nafisa got to her feet. The emissary of the French was at her door. General Bonaparte had sent his own stepson, Eugène de Beauharnais, as a gesture of goodwill.

With as convincing a show of calm as she could muster, Nafisa waited for him to come up to the second floor reception hall. She had ordered the finest Bukhara carpets laid on the stone floor and the most sumptuous, gold-embroidered silk pillows spread over the wooden banquettes. Within a few moments she heard a springy step on the staircase; her first impression was of a smooth-cheeked boy in skin-tight breeches and a short, close-fitting blue coat. He hesitated for no more than a moment before advancing towards her.

'Madame.' He gave a crisp bow. 'Eugène de Beauharnais, delighted to make your acquaintance.'

She inclined her head in acknowledgement, momentarily disconcerted by the sight of the man who had followed Beauharnais up the stairs: Bartholomew – or Fart Rumman, 'pomegranate seed', as people called him derisively in the street. She was astonished at his appearance: he wore a fur stole, a preposterous plumed red silk hat, and a new air of presumption. A Greek mercenary known for his dishonesty and brutality, he had been a simple artillery man of Elfi's who made money on the side selling glass bottles in the souk. That the French had been ill-advised enough to choose a man of such low standing and unsavoury reputation for translator or agent did not bode well. Behind Bartholomew, her chief eunuch Barquq had taken up his post by the door, arms crossed, his expression unreadable.

Nafisa gestured to the French emissary in the direction of the banquette against the wall. 'You are welcome in my house, sir. Please, take a seat.' She noted that he waited for her to be seated before flipping his coat-tails to sit down, his sword clanging at his side.

She clapped her hands for the eunuchs to bring refreshments, and they appeared promptly, carrying big brass trays that they set up on folding wooden tripods. They offered the Frenchman silver goblets with a choice of syrups: almond milk, pomegranate, carob, tamarind. The emissary picked the pomegranate, lifted the goblet in her direction and sipped; an odd expression went over his face and he set it down hastily.

'Madame, allow me to convey the compliments of Consul Magallon and most particularly of Madame Magallon, who desire to be remembered to you warmly. They speak of you as a lady of great heart and superior intellect, a person of the utmost influence in this city. In the absence of your husband and the other Mamlukes, we count on you to be our first interlocutor and intermediary.'

Though Nafisa understood enough French to follow the gist, she allowed Bartholomew to translate. She gestured to the eunuch to offer the young ambassador plates of sweetmeats: nuts, Turkish delight flavoured with rose-water, dates stuffed with almonds and preserved in syrup. He politely picked a square of the Turkish delight and tasted it, then put it down, discreetly trying to brush the powdered sugar off his fingers, swallowing and licking his dry-looking lips. Barquq immediately went to him with a pitcher of water, a basin and a napkin.

'Ah,' Beauharnais exclaimed in palpable relief, raising his goblet in the direction of the pitcher. The eunuch concealed his surprise at this gesture and impassively kept the basin under the guest's hands till he understood and held his hands out to have the eunuch pour water from the pitcher over his fingers and dry them with the folded napkin.

Beauharnais' attention was drawn to the rose faience clock in the corner and he smiled. 'Madame, I congratulate you on your good taste.'

'A present from Monsieur Magallon.'

'Indeed. But does it not tell the time?'

'Not for a long while now. The dust from the sandstorms here during the khamaseen season must have spoiled the mechanism.'

'I am sure we can find someone in our entourage of savants who would know how to repair it; they are geniuses at everything! I must remember to send you someone.'

At last the emissary came to the purpose of his visit. 'General Bonaparte would like to assure you, madame, that you yourself, and the wives and children of the other Beys, are in no danger for your lives or honour.'

Nafisa inclined her head. 'Forbearance in victory is the mark of the noble. Please assure your general of our eternal gratitude.' She embroidered on these compliments, waiting for the other shoe to drop, which it soon did.

'Naturally, the property of the amirs, whether in houses, gardens, farms, land or goods, must be considered the property of the French State, just as we confiscated the property of our own French émigrés. All of this property will be duly inventoried and evaluated, in due

29

course, and you may redeem part of it for your own use – one of your residences, for instance. In return for a certain sum, of course. We will consider you our privileged interlocutor, madame, in our regrettable but necessary efforts to raise a levy on the citizens of Cairo in general, each according to his station and his means. Beginning, naturally, with yourself and the wives of the Mamlukes.'

At this point Bartholomew, whom she had not invited to sit down, began unrolling what looked like a long list, but Beauharnais raised a hand. 'Not now, my good Bartholomew, not now, surely. There will be time enough for that later. My visit today is only to reassure you, madame, of our good intentions.'

'Thank you, sir. May I ask how I am to proceed in collecting this ransom?'

'We leave that to your discretion, madame. But official tax collectors will be appointed and assisted by worthy gentlemen like Monsieur Bartholomew here, the new chief of police –'

Nafisa caught her breath; Fart Rumman – chief of police! Might as well set the hyena to guarding the henhouse.

Bartholomew cleared his throat. 'Malti the Copt will be at the head of the tax collectors,' he offered.

'In the meantime, madame, we know we can count on you to set an example to calm the spirits of those who do not yet know the forbearance and the generosity of the French Republic. I thank you for your hospitality, madame.' Beauharnais had risen from his seat.

'One moment, sir. If my husband is alive – and I have had no word from him – on what terms may he hope to sue for peace?'

'That, madame, is not within my competence to discuss. But the appropriate emissary will be sent you at the right time, I am sure. I bid you good-day.' He bowed again.

Nafisa rose in her turn, and then on impulse twisted the yellow diamond ring off her finger and handed it to Beauharnais. 'For your general, with my compliments, as a gauge of good faith.'

Beauharnais bowed and took his leave. Nafisa remained standing as he descended the spiral staircase, Bartholomew on his heels.

She stared at the lovely rose faience clock in the corner, making a mental note that it would be the first item she would render as part of the levy the French were imposing. Then she looked at her finger where the pigeon's egg diamond was no more. What was it that Amr, the Arab conqueror of Egypt, had said? 'If there were no more than a thread linking me to a people, it should not break; if they tightened their grip, I would slacken, and if they slackened, I would tighten.' Nafisa would try to keep the thread of civility between her and the French from snapping; but for how long?

And where was Murad? At least he was alive. But Elfi? Of him there had been no word.

Dusk fell for the third night since Elfi had emerged from the river, and he welcomed the respite from the relentless sun over the desert. He was riding in a north-easterly direction, away from the delta, skirting the villages and the cultivated land and sticking to the sand dunes as he headed towards the Red Sea and the Sinai.

Ibrahim Bey and his retinue were heading for Istanbul. Elfi had learned this when he traded his diamond turban pin for a horse at a village in Sharkia, the seat of the eastern provinces that had been his fief only a few days earlier. He had not been recognized in his altered state, but the diamond pin had given him away as a Mamluke, and he had not tarried beyond buying the horse and a pistol and a leather skin of water. He still felt dizzy every now and then, but the wound to his head had stopped bleeding and the cut on his thigh was healing. His right hand continued to worry him, oozing yellow pus and throbbing constantly, yet he could not risk seeking attention at one of the estates he owned, for he could not trust even his own servants.

His plan was to keep moving towards Gaza and on to Syria, and eventually regroup with those of his Mamlukes who had survived. He spurred the horse, and it picked up pace for a desultory mile. Water, he thought, licking his cracked lips; he would have to find water, and soon, for the horse was thirsty, and he had already let it lick the last drops from his water skin. He debated the risk of approaching a village or a Bedouin encampment.

In the desert dusk before him, something was shimmering like a slender column of dust in a sandstorm. Elfi blinked. If he was starting to hallucinate with thirst, it was a bad sign. He shook his head and his vision came into focus: a Bedouin woman, standing upright, quivering like a reed, her sequined veil and her silver necklaces and bangles glittering in the fading light. He spurred his horse but the animal whinnied and held back, teeth bared, as if it had seen a Jinn. The woman, if that was indeed what she was, gave no sign of having heard his approach. There was something eerie about her, as if she were in a sort of trance, her large brown eyes dilated and staring at the empty air.

Then Elfi saw what transfixed her gaze: on a mound not two feet in front of her was a large snake, half-erect, hissing, flicking its tongue, preparing to strike; in its malignant concentration it seemed as mesmerized by the woman as she was by it. If he moved fast enough, Elfi calculated, he might be able to save her; if he did nothing, the snake would strike within seconds.

Transferring the reins to his bandaged right hand, Elfi spurred the horse into a gallop, snatched the woman up with his good arm and carried her that way for a few yards before slowing his horse to a trot and setting her down.

She stood blinking up at him and shuddering as the fear released her from its grip. He could see that she was young, about fifteen, and lithe in the way of desert women.

'What are you, a Jinniya? What are you doing out here alone? Where are your people?' His voice rasped hoarse with thirst. Yet, thirsty as he was, he knew the wisest thing to do would be to head in the opposite direction rather than risk an unpredictable encounter with the Bedouin. Her people were more likely to kill him for his horse than offer him water for saving their daughter. He turned his horse's head and spurred its flanks, then, changing his mind, wheeled around and came to a halt before her. In his life, Elfi thought, he had regretted acts of mercy more than those of cruelty, and he might yet live to regret saving this girl from the terrible death of thirst in the desert.

'Are you lost? You'd better answer, my girl, for I'd just as soon leave you here to die on your own. What tribe are you? Abbadi? Muwaylih?'

The girl hesitated, then pointed east beyond the dunes.

'All right then, come on.' He winced as he transferred the reins to his throbbing right hand, and held out his good hand to her. She hesitated, then reached up, grasped his hand and leaped, barely tapping his foot with hers as he hoisted her into the saddle behind him. Her body settled warm and pliant against his back and he twisted round to look at her. Whatever she thought she read in his eyes made her pupils dilate as they had when she had stared at the snake. Elfi quickly clamped both her hands in a vice with his left hand; Bedouin women were taught to carry daggers, and to use them, as soon as they reached puberty. 'I won't hurt you. I'm thirsty enough to cut your throat just to drink your blood, but I won't rape you.'

With his free hand he fumbled at her waist and found the dagger in her wide belt of embroidered cloth, and took it and tucked it into his sash. Then he pointed the horse towards the dunes. Another night spent under the stars, he thought; would he see the day when he could lie under the roof of his Ezbekiah palace?

THREE

The Savants of the Nasiriya

'Cairo is an immense city. The Saint-Honoré quarter is at one end, the faubourg Saint-Victor is at the opposite end. But in this faubourg there are four Beys' palaces side by side, and four immense gardens. This is the location we were assigned. All the French, as you can imagine, live near the General in the Saint-Honoré quarter, but they are obliged to come visit us to take part in our promenades and our delights. That is where the real Champs Élysées are!'

Geoffroy St-Hilaire, *Lettres écrites d'Égypte par Geoffroy Saint-Hilaire*

Zeinab stood on the terrace of her father's house and looked across the Ezbekiah Lake – still dry in this season – at Elfi Bey's palace on the opposite shore, looming behind its high walls. The French had crossed to the Cairo side of the Nile on Tuesday and their chief general, whom they called Bonaparte, had taken up residence in Elfi's palace, all newly furnished as it was. Her tutor Shaykh Jabarti had remarked grimly, 'Just as if the amir had had it built expressly for the commander of the French. Let that be a lesson for you, Zeinab,' he added. 'Men of understanding should not waste their efforts on the perishable things of this world.'

Jabarti and her father, Shaykh Bakri, along with the chief ulema and other city leaders, were at that very moment at Elfi Bey's palace responding to a summons from the French commandant. Zeinab had watched her father set off in the morning, wearing his grandest turban and his best kaftan. Now she peered through the lattice of the mashrabiyya window overlooking the street side of the house, ostensibly on the lookout for her father's return, but secretly hoping to catch a glimpse of a Frenchman; her curiosity about the Franj was insatiable.

Dada, her wet-nurse, told her that the French walked about the markets without arms and without aggression, smiling at people and offering to buy what they needed at the prices they were used to paying in their own country: one would offer to buy a chicken for a French riyal, another an egg for a silver half-penny, and in that manner they were winning the confidence of the populace.

'The shopkeepers go out to them with stuffed pancakes, roast chicken, fried fish and the like,' Dada reported. 'The markets and the coffee houses have all reopened. Some dishonest bakers have even started to cheat by mixing chaff into the flour for their bread. And the Greeks have begun opening up taverns wherever the French have moved in. The Franj have taken over the houses of the amirs, not only here in the Ezbekiah but also in the Elephant Lake district, where they have seized Ibrahim Bey's house. Today Consul Magallon took up residence in one of Murad Bey's houses – and to think he and his wife used to be such friends of Sitt Nafisa! And if it were only the Franj! Even Bartholomew Fart Rumman has helped himself to Ismail Kashif's house, and what is a hundred times worse, to his wife as well. Poor Sitt Hawa! God only knows what will happen to her if Ismail Kashif ever returns.' The wet-nurse finished braiding Zeinab's long black tresses and rubbed a drop of almond oil between her palms to smooth the fly-away strands.

'Dada, what manner of men are they? Are they reported to be very beautiful?'

'Just listen to the child! Some are, some aren't, like the sons of Adam everywhere. They shave both their beard and moustache; some leave hair on their cheeks. The barber tells me they do not shave their head or pubic hair. They have no modesty about their bodies. They mix their food and drinks. They never take their shoes off and tread with them all over precious carpets and wipe their feet on

35

them. But you will see them soon enough, Sitt Zeinab; more and more of them are entering the city every day.'

The clanking of the gate alerted Zeinab to her father's return and she ran to greet him in the inner courtyard. On the way she snatched the washcloth a servant was dipping in rose-water and proffered it herself to her father to wipe his face and hands. She stood by, shifting from foot to foot in her impatience, while her father took his time to sit on the wooden bench in the shade of a eucalyptus, remove his shoes, cross his legs under him, turn back the voluminous sleeves of his kaftan and perform his ablutions with the perfumed washcloth. Zeinab's mother made her appearance, a little breathless with hurrying; she was a plump woman and easily winded.

'Well, Shaykh Khalil?' She offered her husband a cup of carob juice and took a seat beside him. 'What news, *inshallah*? How did the French receive you?'

'With all proper regards – even if they are a people who come to the point rather more promptly than we would think courteous. After the preliminary compliments conveyed by the translator, their commander in chief addressed us and consulted us concerning the appointment of ten shaykhs to form a diwan, a council that would govern local affairs.'

'A diwan of clerics! God be praised.'

'Indeed. It bodes very well that the French seem disposed to recognize our position among the people. Shaykh Sharkawi was chosen to head the diwan, as the most prominent of the ulema, and after him, I myself was nominated, along with Sadat and Mahruqi, as is proper. Three French commanders were also appointed, including their daftardar who has commandeered my house on the Elephant Lake. But no matter . . . It was when the affair was concluded that the trouble began.' He paused to take a sip of juice.

'What trouble, Father?' Zeinab blurted.

Her father frowned. 'Learn to control your curiosity, child, or you will be sent back to your nurse.' He took a long drink of carob juice. 'It was when we rose to take our leave that the chief general went to Shaykh Sharkawi and kissed him on both cheeks, then with a flourish draped a blue, red and white shawl around his neck. The shaykh immediately removed it and flung it on the ground. "I will not forfeit this world and the next," he exclaimed. Bonaparte flushed with rage and remonstrated with him through the interpreter. "The commander in chief intends to exalt you by bestowing his attire and emblem on you. If you are distinguished by wearing it, the French soldiers and the people will honour and respect you." Sharkawi replied: "But our good standing with God and our fellow Muslims will be lost."'

Her father clapped his hands for his pipe. 'This infuriated Bonaparte. I tried to soothe him and asked exemption from this measure, or at least a delay in its implementation. Bonaparte retorted: "At least you must all wear the rosette on your chest."'

'What is this thing they call a rosette, Father?'

'It is an emblem made of three concentric colours of ribbon – the same blue, white and red as their flag and their shawl. As soon as the shaykhs left the council, they each in turn, starting with Shaykh Sadat – how that man loves to grandstand before the common folk! – removed the rosette and flung it on the ground, in front of the assembled crowd outside. I had no choice but to follow suit. Shaykh Jabarti told me privately that he does not himself hold that wearing such an emblem is against Islam, particularly when it is imposed and harm can result from disobedience; but he knows that the people hold it to be sacrilege. It will remain to be seen how this matter is resolved. As the proverb goes: If you wish to be obeyed, command that which is feasible.'

'Mabruk, Shaykh Khalil, congratulations on your appointment to the diwan.' Zeinab's mother signalled to the servant to light the apple-scented tobacco in the small clay cup at the top of the glass hookah. 'Having the ulema and the French on the same footing in the diwan . . . it's more than the Mamlukes ever did for the clerics. When does the council meet for the first time?'

'Next week. We have our work cut out for us in the first session: we have to appoint officials to replace the Mamlukes and their retainers in all the functions they performed. The one stipulation the French laid down was that no member of the Mamluke caste would be allowed to hold any position, official or otherwise. Jabarti told the French the common folk feared no one but the amirs, so they allowed some descendants of the ancient houses to assume certain posts. Elfi Bey's khatkhuda, Zulfikar, was appointed to be khatkhuda to Bonaparte. But there is another matter of more immediate concern to me . . . an opportunity to advance my position with the French . . .'

'Really, Shaykh Khalil? God be praised!' Zeinab's mother leaned in eagerly.

Shaykh Bakri blew rings of apple-scented smoke in the air. 'The French commandant also announced that Omar Makram, the Naqib, who fled the city, would be replaced as chief of the syndicate of the House of the Prophet. Naturally, they will be nominating a successor . . .'

'Oh! Shaykh Khalil! I see where you are going with this: you yourself are of the lineage of the Prophet. God be praised!'

'Now don't get ahead of yourself, wife. But I am indeed one of the most prominent, and head of the Sufi guild of the Bakris besides, so it is not out of the question.'

'There is no one worthier!'

'But I have many enemies among the ulema who will no doubt undermine my candidacy. If there were a way to consolidate my position with the French . . .' He drew Zeinab towards him and looked at her speculatively. 'A marriageable daughter, now . . . perhaps an alliance?'

Zeinab spared no more than a moment's attention to her father's musings. She twisted the end of her braid in her fingers, waiting for the opening to ask the questions that really piqued her curiosity: Were the commandants handsome? Were there any French ladies in sight? What did they look like? Was it true they walked about unveiled and bare-bosomed?

Nicolas Conté stopped in his tracks momentarily to listen to a street urchin singing his wares. The boy's soprano reminded him so much of his son Pierrot's pure soprano when he still sang in the choir that he was cut to the quick with a pang of longing for his son, for the sweet chant of choir boys, in this city where the only choir he heard was that of the muezzins chanting the call to prayers from dawn to dusk.

The urchin's cry died away in the Cairo air and in two long strides Conté caught up with his companions in the dusty alley. He was brimming with impatience to discover Cairo, finally. Ambassador Magallon had offered to guide him and St-Hilaire to their new accommodations, the mansion commandeered for the Scientific Commission.

'The mansion you will be occupying is in the Nasiriya district – the name means victory in Arabic – to the south-west of town,' Ambassador Magallon was saying. 'You will be taking the house of Hassan Kashif, and the adjoining beys' palaces and their gardens. An excellent location, I should say, but for the disadvantage of being so far from the Ezbekiah where the generals have made Elfi Bey's palace their headquarters.'

'Ah! One wonders if this is entirely by chance?' Geoffroy raised an eyebrow. 'I heard General Bonaparte say once that scientists were much like women for gossip and rivalries and squabbling. A fine opinion our general holds of us!'

But Nicolas was absorbed in the street theatre around him. His senses were disoriented by the assault of the unfamiliar, and his eyes needed an interpreter as much as his ears. His first impression of Cairo was overwhelming. The city seemed immense, sprawling and bewildering, a maze of narrow streets and blind alleys; the houses in general – apart from the palaces and mansions of the amirs and notables – turning blind facades and cold shoulders to the street. Most were one or two storeys high, with the exception of the houses in the market, which were narrow and rose two or three storeys above the shops on the ground floor.

Nicolas had never encountered as cacophonous and mixed a city, a veritable Tower of Babel spoken on the street; the people a mixture of races and religions from all over the Ottoman empire and Europe:

Turks, Circassians, Egyptians, Bedouin, Moroccans, Italians, Muslim, Copt, Greek Orthodox, Syrian Catholic, Jewish. The men seemed generally well-made and fine-figured, with skin so tanned by the sun as to resemble leather. Women were rare, and veiled in robes from head to foot.

'There are several of these large covered markets around the city – wikalas, as they are called,' Magallon explained. 'Each specializes in a particular kind of trade: dates, fabric, camels, slaves . . . and they have done so for centuries. Sitt Nafisa's wikala at Bab Zuweila, for instance, specializes in coffee and spices, since that is where the caravans from Arabia unload their wares.'

'Ah! Speaking of Sitt Nafisa, Citoyen,' Nicolas interjected. 'I had promised my wife to report to her at the earliest opportunity on the interior of the harem, as she is most curious to know how Muslim ladies entertain *chez elles*. I understand Madame Magallon was one of this lady's intimates?'

'It is not a simple matter to arrange an invitation to the harem,' Magallon demurred. 'The Oriental idea of home and privacy is very different to ours.'

'Indeed! Look around you – the houses and doors we pass remain resolutely closed in our faces,' Geoffroy St-Hilaire gestured broadly to both sides of the street.

'Apparently we have been preceded by the reputation of our troops for zeal in making the acquaintance of the fairer sex,' Nicolas suggested dryly. 'But our exemplary behaviour here will soon dispel suspicion and open hearts and hearths to us, I am persuaded.'

At that moment a fleeting motion above made him look up and he caught a glimpse, through a crack in the wooden lattice of a small balcony, of a young girl's enormous dark eyes avid with curiosity in a round, pale face. When her eyes met his she withdrew behind the shutters like a squirrel up a tree. For some reason, Nicolas made no mention of this unique sighting to his companions.

As they headed away from the souk and along another canal, Geoffroy looked around him in despair. 'But this city is bewildering! I will never learn my way around here!'

'To get your bearings,' Magallon suggested, 'it helps to think of the Nile running on a south to north axis, with the city on the eastern bank, and Giza and the pyramids to the west. One point of reference you can see from anywhere in the city is the Citadel up on the Mokkattam hills.' He pointed to a vast walled complex built around an ancient fort overlooking the city from the east. 'The fort dates back to Sultan Yussef Salah al-Din, the Saladdin of the crusades. That is where our garrison is now housed.'

'These streets are too narrow for a carriage, let alone our heavy cannon,' Nicolas observed as they headed down another narrow, winding alley.

'They weren't designed for them. In fact, in some cases two persons on horseback cannot meet and pass each other without some difficulty. It used to be, when one of inferior rank became aware of a Bey or powerful figure approaching, he was obliged, out of respect and regard for his personal safety both, to take shelter in some cross lane or doorway, till the other with his numerous attendants had passed. Before our invasion, no Christian or European traveller was permitted, except by special favour, to mount horses in Cairo – only asses.'

With his military engineer's eye, Nicolas could not help noticing other impediments to the proper circulation of troops: within the city walls, each quarter, indeed each lane and alley, seemed to have fortified gates at the entrance that were locked at night – Magallon estimated their number at seventy. Decorative as some of these gates were, their presence, along with the absence of streetlights, would hinder the circulation of French troops after nightfall, and would complicate quelling any uprising by the citizenry, should one occur. For the moment, though, the glances in their direction seemed more curious than hostile.

In another half-hour they reached the Nasiriya. 'Aha! The Faubourg Saint-Victor! Finally!' Geoffroy exulted. Magallon led them into a spacious mansion.

'This is the palace of Hassan Kashif. I present to you the new location of the Institute of Egypt!'

Nicolas and Geoffroy looked around the mansion with its high ceilings, its graceful colonnaded arches and its intricate decorative woodwork. Geoffroy declared it superior to the finest academic institution in France.

'The main salon will serve as your assembly hall –' Magallon gestured around the arcaded hall. 'I must tell you that it served quite a different purpose originally, as the salon for the ladies of the harem.'

'A titillating detail that, alas, will not suffice to lend piquancy to the predictably tedious deliberations of our august commission!' Geoffroy lamented.

Nicolas was more interested in the house next door, also formerly owned by said Hassan Kashif, that was allocated to him for his balloonist brigade and their workshops. Here he would recreate the École nationale aérostatique de Meudon! His heart rose in his chest with the thrill of anticipation. He and his confreres would form a true elysium of savants here in the Nasiriya. The secretary of the Institute, Fourier, was lodged in the house of Sennari, Murad Bey's Sudanese Mamluke. Nearby would be the naturalists St-Hilaire and Savigny, the architects Balzac and Lepère; the geographers, the pharmacists, the mineralogists; and the painters Rigo and Redouté. Nicolas had already designated the perfect spot for their informal gathering place of an evening: the large garden of an adjoining house, that of Qassim Bey, with its gigantic sycamore tree and fragrant acacias.

His reverie was interrupted by the appearance of Dr Desgenettes.

'Ah, Docteur, welcome! Have you been to inspect the quarters you were allocated for the hospital?'

'I have indeed, on the Elephant Lake. I am also to set up another hospital in the Citadel. We have just been touring the premises with General Bonaparte. You will never guess what our general is writing urgently to request from the Directoire.'

'What could that be?'

'Prostitutes.'

'Did you say prostitutes?'

'Precisely. Bonaparte is writing urgently to Paris to request that the Directoire ship out at least a hundred prostitutes on the next available ship. The shortage of women is beginning to pose a serious problem to the health and morale of our troops. After all, with thousands of Frenchmen here, and only a couple of hundred women – and those not even *filles publiques* but wives – where are our men to seek *le repos du guerrier*? And in this one crucial instance we cannot hope to live on the land, as the general has warned most sternly against offending local sensibilities, and Muslims are most punctilious in these matters.'

'Surely there must be local *filles de joie*?'

'Few, and those are joyless indeed, with figures flabby from childbearing. And as for hygiene . . .' He shrugged. 'No, it is a serious problem, and Bonaparte has written to the Directoire demanding a hundred prostitutes immediately; we shall see what comes of it.'

Through the open window a chant rose like a plume of smoke, and was echoed from first one, then a dozen minarets around the city, till the sultry sunset air swelled with the chants of the muezzins and the twittering of the birds going to roost in the trees. Nicolas stood before the window, enchanted by the purity and light of the achingly graceful minarets soaring into the hazy mauve sky.

'Ah, Docteur, if monuments are windows into the soul of a civilization, then these Mamlukes, whatever they are today, must once have been a race that valued beauty and balance above all.'

Zeinab stared out of the mashrabiyya window at two French soldiers in the street below, fascinated by the long, floppy brown hair that hung to their shoulders and the skin-tight white breeches that moulded their legs and outlined their crotches and loins; she had never seen men walking about looking naked before. But what the soldiers were doing worried her. They were tearing down and breaking up the great wood and leather gates that protected the neighbourhood at night, and loading the dismantled doors on carts.

'My teacher, is it true what Dada says? That the reason the French are tearing down the gates to the neighbourhoods all around the city is so they can murder us all while the men are at Friday prayers?'

'Your wet-nurse repeats whatever rumours she picks up in the marketplace. No, the French are tearing down the gates so that their carriages and troops can enter the neighbourhoods unhindered in case of an uprising against them. They decree that the streets are not wide enough for the passage of their troops and particularly for their general's carriage – which requires six horses to draw it – so they intend to demolish anything that extrudes into the street in front of the houses, including the small steps and benches that shopkeepers sit on.'

'Even the earthenware jars for thirsty passers-by?'

'Even those must go, no matter what hospitality dictates.' Shaykh Jabarti shook his head. 'They do not understand our ways. They tear down the gates, and then they force each householder to keep a lantern lit before his door all night, and fine him if it goes out or if some lout deliberately extinguishes it, as if people had nothing better to do than stay awake all night making sure that their lamps do not go out. Nothing will come of this but ill-feeling.'

It was true, thought Zeinab, a sullen silence reigned in the city. The shops closed early, people kept to their homes. Festivities went uncelebrated, by tacit consent. The heads of the guilds, who would normally be vying at this time to put on the showiest parade for the upcoming festival of the Nile flood – particularly as it coincided this year with the birthday of the Prophet – would have nothing to do with it, in protest at the occupation. And the French would be none the wiser.

FOUR

Aboukir

'The enemy is before you and the sea is behind you. You will fight or die. There is no retreat.'

Tariq bin Ziyad, Moorish Conqueror of Spain.

Nicolas Conté looked up from his code book and blinked at the brilliant sky above him. From the ramparts of the white medieval Mamluke fort the bay of Alexandria stretched out before him, reverberating in the blue glare. The sun had begun to set, streaking the sky glorious mauve and orange, and a sweet breeze blew across the bay. Nicolas was glad his mission – to build the optical telegraph that was to relay messages between the city and the fleet – had brought him to the seashore, away from the stifling heat of Cairo in August. His engineers were supervising the building of the wooden rods, painted black, to be mounted as the arms of the semaphore, and training operators to set them at the proper angles to represent 196 symbols. Nicolas himself was concentrating on combining symbols to yield words and phrases; he had already devised two thousand out of a possible eight thousand plus – when a watchman cried the alarm and he looked out to sea. With the sun low in the sky, they saw a fleet of ships over the horizon, black sails deployed to the fullest, and to a man they leapt to their feet, hoping against hope that it was reinforcements from Spain.

But it was Nelson; this time he would not miss the French fleet trapped in Aboukir Bay to the east of the city. A cry of frustration escaped Nicolas: the semaphore would at least have allowed him to

45

warn Admiral Brueys and the other captains on the ships, but the system was not yet up and running. As Nicolas watched in helpless agony from the top of the fort, and the entire city and garrison watched from rooftops and terraces, the English fleet opened fire with fourteen hundred cannons at once. The blare was indescribable, the superiority of English firepower stunning. As the sun set, the flagship of the French fleet, *L'Orient*, exploded when its gunpowder magazines caught fire. Nicolas knew the terrible sight would be seared in his brain for as long as he lived.

As nightfall turned the bay into a lake of fire, the guns fell mercifully silent. But there was no time to waste; he knew he had to prepare for the eventuality of an attack on the city itself. He set his engineers to work outfitting ovens with reflectors to heat cannonballs and improvising a floating fire pump. All night they laboured at their hellish tasks, dripping sweat, until with the dawn the English resumed firing, to complete the devastation they had started the night before. The pitiable sights that daylight disclosed were unspeakable: the thousands of dead, drowned or burned alive.

Finally the English ships withdrew. The city had been spared; apparently Nelson had decided that the Army of the Orient was no threat to him at the moment, trapped as it was in Egypt.

Two weeks later Nicolas stood in the great hall of Elfi's palace in Cairo listening to the commandant addressing the assembled commanders. Bonaparte had just returned from a skirmish with Ibrahim Bey in Gaza, and learned the terrible news of Aboukir for the first time. He took the blow with a sang-froid that impressed Nicolas.

'We are called upon to do great things, and we shall do them,' Bonaparte reiterated simply at the conclusion of his speech. 'Destiny has called upon us to build an empire, and we shall build it.'

As Nicolas turned to leave, Bonaparte called out to him. 'Citoyen Conté! A moment. Come, take a turn with me in the garden.'

As they strolled in the welcome shade of the gazebo, Bonaparte laid a hand on Nicolas' shoulder. 'I need you for a matter of considerable urgency and some delicacy.'

'At your service, Commandant.'

'How soon can you put on a balloon demonstration?'

Nicolas could not hide his astonishment.

'We must impress the populace,' Bonaparte explained. 'We must put on a very grand show, something to take their breath away, to inspire them with admiration and dread in equal measure, and impress on them indelibly the superiority of French military science. We must try to keep the sinking of the fleet a secret from Cairo for as long as possible, but we cannot hope to do so indefinitely, and when the news comes out we must have something spectacular to divert attention. I feel the mood in the city turning sullen and dangerous, and we must reverse that. Besides, a grand celebration will combat despondency in our own troops; we must guard against that, I have seen disquieting signs of it from the beginning of this campaign. So, I am counting on you and your balloonists! It is a very important mission I am confiding in you. How soon can you be ready?'

'We have not yet unpacked our *matériel*, or ascertained its condition; some of it has been lost or destroyed. Our priority has been to complete the semaphore and extend it from Alexandria to our garrisons in the Delta – and eventually to Cairo. Surely that should be the first order of business? The news of Aboukir took two weeks to reach you, Commandant, because couriers sent overland are routinely assassinated.'

'I know, my dear Conté,' Bonaparte insisted, clapping Nicolas on the shoulder. 'But make the balloon your first priority nonetheless. Believe me, it *is* more important. One hundred days – remember, a campaign is won or lost in the first hundred days. And we must win these people's hearts and spirits. Now that we have lost the fleet, this is one battle we cannot afford to lose. You understand me? How soon can you set up a demonstration?'

'I cannot guarantee success for several weeks – even months. My equipment for producing hydrogen has been lost with the sinking of the fleet, and the alternative – to try to fly a Montgolfière – is far less reliable. I would be very reluctant to essay a hot-air balloon publicly.'

'No matter, fly a Montgolfière then, my dear Conté; it will do very well to impress the Cairenes and raise the morale of our troops. Much is riding on this. I will have it announced for the Prophet's birthday, whenever that is. I have heard, through my spies, that it is normally a very festive occasion, but the citizens of Cairo are not celebrating it this year, in silent protest at our presence. I will command that it be celebrated with all due pomp, whether they like it or not. And to make sure to bring out the crowds for that occasion, I will announce that there will be a great exhibition of a flying ship such as they have never seen. A ship that can transport the French army across the sky and from which they can attack their enemies! That will go far to stamp out the regrettable impression left by the destruction of our fleet.'

With that, Bonaparte turned and strode back to the palace, leaving Nicolas with one thought: to ascertain the extent of the deadline he had been given. He tracked down Magallon in the courtyard.

'The date of the Prophet's birthday?' Magallon looked puzzled. 'Well, it changes from year to year – the Muslims follow a lunar calendar, you know. But at any rate it must be this month. Why?'

Nicolas groaned; that very month! He was not ready, but as Bonaparte would have already put the word about, there was no help for it. His commandant seemed not to have considered the consequences of a fiasco, he thought grimly; but then it would be Nicolas who would bear the brunt of a disaster. He could not allow the balloon demonstration to be a failure.

'What manner of woman is it?'

'I do not know, mistress. She is cloaked from head to toe, and insists on speaking to you herself; she will not uncover her face or so much as her eyes. She will not disclose her business and I do not trust her. There is something threatening about her manner. Should I try to dismiss her?' said Barquq, the head eunuch, looking flustered.

Nafisa hesitated. The fact that the eunuch had not yet dismissed the stranger meant that he had been intimidated or his palm had been greased, and that indicated that the woman was not here for charity. Her curiosity was piqued. 'Send her to me.'

She sat back down on the window seat and let her maid continue to brush her hair. Her eyes were drawn to the corner of the room where the French clock had once taken pride of place; it was empty now.

The eunuch reappeared with a black-cloaked figure close on his heels. The woman was unusually tall, and her coarse style of dress, her bearing, and what could be surmised from her build and the size of her feet under the long robes, suggested that this was not a lady, and probably not a woman from the city at all. The silver coins sewn on to her veil, and the style of the veil itself – opaque, black, and covering the entire face – was characteristic of the Bedouin of the eastern desert, except that Bedouin women tended to be small and thin. Nafisa had never seen a woman of this build, apart from the rare African tribeswomen from the upper reaches of the Nile. The woman inclined her head and stood by the stairs, silent.

'Come, mother,' Nafisa beckoned with some impatience, 'you are among women now and may unveil. What is your business?'

The woman bowed again and made a gesture in the direction of the maids and the eunuch, indicating that she wished to speak with Nafisa alone.

'Now really, you go too far,' Nafisa sighed. She flicked her fingers, dismissing her attendants. 'All right, then, but be brief, I have little time.'

The woman took a step forward, and whispered in a strange, high voice: 'What I have to say is for your ears alone. I bring you news from your husband.'

'You?' Nafisa snorted. 'Who are you?'

'I will tell you, by and by. Have the French approached you with terms for Murad Bey?' The high voice cracked, like a falsetto.

Nafisa stiffened and ice water ran in her veins. 'You will tell me who you are, this minute, or I will call out, and you know my eunuchs are behind the door.'

The woman raised her hand, palm up, in a gesture to stop her, then approached. 'I will uncover, but pray do not cry out. I mean you no harm.' It was no longer the high falsetto voice. The veil and shawl were cast off to reveal a blond beard flecked with grey and hard blue eyes in a sunburned face.

Nafisa's shock and alarm gave way to astonishment as she recognized the man before her. 'Elfi Bey?'

'Hush.' He looked over his shoulder in the direction of the door. 'Forgive my intruding on you this way. If the Franj capture me within the city walls they will kill me outright. This disguise was the only way to go unrecognized.' He seemed more amused than mortified by his ignominious appearance. 'There are only too many people on the street who would have turned me in for the price on my head.'

He turned away discreetly as Nafisa snatched a Damascus silk shawl off the window seat and wound it around her head and shoulders.

'It is good to see that you are alive and well, Elfi Bey,' she said, regaining something of her composure. 'The rumours have been flying around the city that you have taken refuge with the Bedouin, that you have been seen in the western desert, but also that you raid the French convoys in the east, and then again that you were seen in the north near the Syrian border with Ibrahim Bey. Some reports even had you sighted on foot, with a lion on a leash. One cannot know what to credit and what to dismiss.'

'It is all true – even the lion. I have been moving around constantly, never spending two nights in one place. But I have established rear camps with the Abaddi in the eastern desert, and another in Kharja oasis in the Libyan desert.'

'The Bedouin? Surely they are not to be trusted?'

'We shall see. They have their own sense of honour; when they give a stranger safe conduct, the whole tribe, every man, woman and child – will stand behind their pledge to the death. But no outsider can trust them completely.'

'And Murad? What news of him?'

'Murad Bey is headed south, and keeps just a step ahead of the Franj.'

'Magallon came to see me yesterday – with Rossetti. All smiles and compliments, as if nothing had changed.' Rossetti, the ex-consul and long a resident of the Venetian quarter of Cairo, had been a confidant of her husband's and had frequented the house almost as often as Magallon. Before the two men left, she had made a point of handing – with a smile and a regal inclination of her head – the French clock to Magallon as part of the ransom she had been asked to pay. The pained look on his face had been the one fleeting moment of satisfaction she had derived from that humiliating meeting.

'Rossetti said they were authorized to offer Murad the province of Girgeh up to the first cataract in return for acknowledgement of the suzerainty of the Franj and paying them tax on the land. And he is to keep no more than five hundred cavalry. In other words, he would be a tax farmer under the Franj. I replied that I would have to hear from my husband first.'

'They would have not heard the news from Alexandria yet. Bonaparte himself has not heard the news, he is in the north chasing Ibrahim Bey.'

'What news is it you speak of?'

He stopped suddenly and drew the veil across his face, holding up a finger.

She heard her eunuch outside the door. 'Mistress, you called for me?'

'No, not yet. I will call you in a few minutes.'

'I must hurry.' Elfi lowered the veil. 'The French fleet was destroyed last night in the bay of Alexandria; without it they are trapped in Egypt. I was with Ibrahim Bey near the Syrian border and we were able to hold off Bonaparte's cavalry – on horseback they are no match for Mamlukes, so they must rely on their great advantage in infantry and artillery, and that slows them down. Ibrahim Bey was able to escape to Syria with all the booty from the Mecca caravan. He will make for Istanbul and plead with the Sultan for reinforcements. The English are allies of the Porte and if he asks them to come to his aid that will be a sufficient excuse for them to intervene. This is not the time for Murad Bey to accept terms of surrender.

51

That is what I came to warn you. Hold them off any way you can. Make a counter-offer on behalf of Murad Bey, offer monies in exchange for evacuation . . . I must go now.'

'But why put yourself in danger by coming here in person? Why did you not send an emissary?'

'I could have taken that risk on my account, but not on yours. There was no one I could trust not to betray you if he was caught.'

He covered his face and head completely and there stood before Nafisa the veiled Bedouin woman. 'May I see your face in good health, Sitt Nafisa.'

FIVE

The Banquet

'A universal man, with the passion, the knowledge and the genius for
the arts, precious in a far away country, capable of turning his hand
to anything, of creating the arts of France in the desert of Arabia.'

Napoleon Bonaparte on Nicolas-Jacques Conté

Zeinab took the tiniest lick off the arm of her doll, and the sweetness of the spun sugar titillated her tongue. This would be the last
year she would be given a sugar-paste doll for the mulid of the
Prophet, she thought with equal regret and satisfaction: after all, as she
had grumbled to her mother, she was a girl of marriageable age now,
no longer a child. But she had secretly rejoiced in the particularly
gorgeous doll with the bold black eyes painted on the almond-paste
face, and the pleated, pink tissue skirt fanned out around her.

Only a few days ago it had seemed as though there would be no
mulid dolls this year, and no sugar-paste horse for her younger
brother, either. No one was in the mood to celebrate with the Franj
occupying Cairo, and so many families in the city mourning their
dead. But then the Franj had decreed that the mulid would be celebrated as usual, as would the ceremony of the Nile flood; fines would
be levied on merchants who did not keep their shops open and
festoon them with garlands, and on any guilds that did not organize
a parade.

But it was not thoughts of the parades or the musicians, the dervishes
or the dancers that excited Zeinab to the point of sleeplessness: it was

the prospect of witnessing the Franj's flying ship. They had posted signs all over town announcing that after the annual ceremony of the Nile flood, and after the mulid parade, they would demonstrate a special flying ship that could fly over the houses and the trees and the city walls and, who knew, perhaps over the Red Sea itself; a flying ship in which people could ride over the clouds like the magic carpets in the stories of the *Thousand and One Nights*. The French claimed they had used these flying ships in battle to spy on their enemies and defeat them. The soldiers had distributed posters printed on their Arabic press announcing that this great French invention would take off from Ezbekiah Square that Friday.

Zeinab's excitement had been roused to fever pitch by the sight of preparations on the Ezbekiah esplanade not far from her house, where for several days the French engineers had been seen building a platform and setting up their equipment. She had begged to be allowed to attend the great spectacle, and her father had promised, but she fretted that he might forget all about it or change his mind.

All morning Zeinab looked out of her mashrabiyya window at the mulid procession passing in the street below: the drummers and the shrill pipers, the dancing women swaying their hips, the tumblers, the shrieking monkeys and chained bears, the serpent handlers, the puppeteers with their vulgar cries, the singers and the female poetesses. The street sellers hawked their wares: tamarind, carob and liquorice juice, roasted peanuts and ruby-red watermelon, date-and-nut-filled pancakes. Then the guilds, each in turn, parading with their banners: scissors for the tailors; a net for the fishmongers; bracelets for the jewellers; a gun for the barudis, the gunpowder manufacturers. The Sufi orders followed, preceded by the dervishes whirling their capes in rhythm with the chanting and drumming. The float in the shape of Noah's Ark came next, heralded by a resounding fanfare.

Zeinab could hardly bear to wait for word from her father. Shaykh Bakri himself had gone ahead earlier in the morning with other notables accompanying the commandant of the French to the Nilometer for the annual ceremony of the breaching of the dam.

An hour or so later the floodwaters of the Nile had come rushing through the khalig canal, and the firing of cannon and the shouts of rejoicing had carried all the way to the Ezbekiah. By now, Zeinab calculated, there would have been ample time for the commandant and his party to ride back for the demonstration of the great flying machine.

Dada burst into the room, holding Zeinab's younger brother by the hand.

'Yallah, Sitt Zeinab, Shaykh Bakri sent for us. Let us hurry or we will miss the flying of the airship!'

Zeinab jumped up and let her wet-nurse dress her, for the first time, in a long black cloak and a small, transparent white yashmak veiling the lower part of her face. She felt very grown up.

They hurried down to the Ezbekiah esplanade, where the sun had crossed its zenith. A bevy of Frenchmen with their shirtsleeves rolled up were hurrying up and down the steps leading to the great wooden platform. Tall masts had been set up at each of the four corners of the platform, and an enormous sail was stretched out between them. It looked like no other sail Zeinab had ever seen: the fabric was of silk in the dark blue, white and red that everyone had come to associate with the French, and it was encircled by a design featuring a golden crown and an eagle. The ends of the gigantic sail were being drawn in and attached with cords to a large basket that sat in the middle of the platform.

Zeinab never took her eyes off the head engineer who was clearly in charge: a dark, curly-haired man with an eye patch who gave orders right and left and occasionally stood back to mop his brow with the scarf tied round his neck. In the manner of the French, he was clean-shaven and bareheaded, and did not disdain to put his own hands to the task in his impatience. From time to time he sat down and brought out a leather-bound stack of papers and began sketching rapidly.

Her curiosity to see inside the mysterious cane basket at the centre of this bustle was like an unbearable itch. She grabbed her brother's hand and edged as close as she could, despite her nurse's remonstrations. Then she saw Shaykh Jabarti, completely engrossed, standing very close to the platform, and that encouraged her to advance till she could speak to him.

'My esteemed teacher, what is in that basket?'

Shaykh Jabarti turned and looked down at her in astonishment, then recognized her through the transparent yashmak.

'Ah, so they dress you as a woman now, do they, little monkey,' he grumbled. 'Well, perhaps we can obtain permission for you to see.'

Shaykh Jabarti spoke to one of the translators, who spoke to the chief engineer; he nodded, in a harried manner, hardly glancing at them.

With Shaykh Jabarti leading the way, Zeinab and her brother climbed the stairs to the platform and approached the basket. Close up, it was sturdier and larger than it looked, easily accommodating two or three standing men, and high enough to reach the armpit of a man, so what the French had claimed about sending soldiers up in the air could be true. But would there be air to breathe that high?

She could not see all the way inside the basket, but there seemed to be some sort of large lamp or stove with a wick, and straw and other stuff around it. Presently the chief engineer gave the order and fire was set to the wick in the lamp. The crowd exhaled in alarm as the flames shot up, and then went speechless in awe as the sail began to fill up like a balloon, the cords tying it down to the masts taking the strain.

A fanfare announced the arrival of the procession of the commandant and the accompanying notables, and Shaykh Jabarti signalled to Zeinab that it was time to get off the platform and to return to her nurse, who was standing further back.

The great assembly of the French arrived, officers and gentlemen and the laughing ladies in their finery. She had never seen women like them, with their bosom-baring wisps of gowns, and their cascades of curls under high-brimmed, feathered bonnets. Zeinab absorbed every novel detail of their attire: gloves and fans, reticules and parasols, down to the embroidery on the hem of a shawl and the lace trim of a bonnet. One lady in particular stood out with her fluty laugh and her hair of spun gold; the feathers and ribbons on her bonnet, her gloves and slippers were all dyed a shade of delicate mauve that offset the palest pink of her gown. The commandant of the French noticed her and stopped to speak to her for a few minutes, and she tossed her head and laughed till he moved on.

Zeinab watched the commandant approach the platform and greet the chief engineer and his helpers. They seemed to be having an argument, the man with the eye patch shaking his head repeatedly and mopping his brow, the general making encouraging gestures and waving to the assembled crowd.

By now the balloon had formed an egg-like globe, tapering down to the basket, and straining alarmingly against the cords whenever a breeze blew, like a marid struggling against his chains. A cannon was fired to announce the launch, and everyone held his breath. Zeinab was disappointed that no Frenchmen would be climbing into the basket after all. Then the chief engineer gave the sign, the cords holding it down on all four sides were cut simultaneously, and the great sphere rose in the air, greeted by a deafening cheer from the crowd. Zeinab held her breath, her eyes fixed on the airship rising in the sky, lurching slightly as it caught in a breeze.

The French clapped and called 'Bravo!' The Egyptians gasped and exclaimed 'God is great!' The flying ship rose still higher, leaning in the lazy wind, then seemed to stall as the wind died down. For a few minutes nothing happened; the great sphere hung in the air. The spectators began to fidget, while the French officers continued to nod and smile, encouraging the crowd to wait and see.

Then suddenly the basket detached itself from the sphere and came crashing down in flames. The crowd shouted in alarm and dispersed as the great balloon deflated and came floating down, scattering a quantity of printed leaflets.

Zeinab's eyes went to the chief engineer, who was standing with his hands on his hips, shaking his head, circles of perspiration staining his shirt at the armpits. His frustration was unmistakable even at that distance, and for some reason she felt a pang of sympathy for that total stranger.

'Come,' she heard Shaykh Jabarti say, 'this was no flying machine for transporting soldiers great distances. This was no more than a very large kite of the sort knaves at street fairs fly to entertain children.'

Then her maid was calling her and her brother. 'Sitt Zeinab, come quickly, we must return to the house. Shaykh Bakri has invited the commandant of the Franj and his generals to a banquet tonight. And he has ordered that you make yourself ready should he require you to make an appearance.'

'Me? I am to be called into their presence? Why?'

'He must have a purpose in this, and it is not our place to question it. Now hurry!'

Nicolas headed on foot for the Ezbekiah, where he had been invited to attend the banquet given by Shaykh Bakri in honour of the commandant; the generals and the heads of the Scientific Commission were also invited. He was walking in the company of Geoffroy St-Hilaire, Dr Desgenettes and Ambassador Magallon, colleagues whose company he appreciated under ordinary circumstances, but on this occasion he was lost in his own gloomy thoughts, chewing over the disappointing outcome of the Montgolfière demonstration. He had worked like a conscript for the past two weeks – ever since Bonaparte had given him the order – and he had worked his loyal workshop heads nearly as hard, to get the balloon ready for the appointed date, the fateful festival of the Prophet. His heart had risen as the handsome new aérostat had inflated before his eyes, an imposing balloon thirteen metres in diameter, decorated with the inscription *The Battle of Rivoli*, and ringed with a civic crown and laurel wreaths. Ah, but would it fly and would it be stable?

He had not hidden his misgivings when the commandant and the generals returned from the ceremony of the Nile flood; he had told them flatly that he could not vouch for the performance of the hot-air balloon.

'Could we not send up a soldier or two in the basket?' Bonaparte had inquired. 'There will be no lack of volunteers, I am sure of it.'

58

'I refuse to risk the life and limb of any man.'

'My dear Conté! At least let us send up a sheep or other animal, as the Montgolfier brothers did with their first experiments?'

Thank God he had stuck to his guns, Nicolas thought now as he was ushered into the double gates of the Moorish-style house where they had been invited; the much-vaunted airship had come undone and descended ignominiously, much to the alarm of *tout Caire*, all assembled for the spectacle, agog and agape. No one could claim he had not warned Bonaparte, but he expected his reception by the commandant to be rather chilly all the same.

So he was considerably surprised, after he and his party had been greeted in the outer courtyards by a gauntlet of servant boys proffering rose-water, and then had penetrated into an inner courtyard where most of the guests were already assembled, to be hailed from a distance by an unexpectedly good-humoured Bonaparte.

'Conté! Come join us!' Bonaparte beckoned him over to the head table, where he sat with his host, the chief generals and two other clerics. 'This is the man of the hour, Shaykh Bakri. Let me introduce you to our chief engineer. Citoyen Conté, this is our host.' A pale, lean-faced man, black of beard and brow, inclined his head and brought a well-tended hand to the front of his crimson kaftan in a gesture of welcome. Nicolas was struck by the sardonic eyes under the black turban.

'And these are Shaykh Sharkawi, the head of the diwan; Shaykh Jabarti, the eminent historian; and the judge,' Bonaparte continued, presenting the other three clerics at table. 'Sit down, Citoyen.'

Nicolas took a seat between General Menou and Ambassador Magallon. He looked around the banquet hall: the hundred or so guests were seated on low benches lined with carpet cushions, and enormous brass trays were brought in and set up on tripods to serve as low tables for each group of ten or twelve guests. Serving boys came around with pitchers of rose-water and basins in which the guests rinsed their hands.

Bonaparte attempted some badinage with his hosts through the translator, Venture du Paradis, but it was heavy going; the Egyptian clerics sat sober as judges under their enormous Kashmir turbans. That, and the absence of wine, made for a decided lack of ambience. Ambassador Magallon, noting Nicolas' discomfiture, whispered: 'This Ottoman gravity is so antithetical to our French gaiety, is it not, Citoyen? But it is the rule on formal occasions, I am afraid.'

Meanwhile a procession of servants laid the large brass trays with plates of salad vegetables and flat rounds of bread. Before the guests could do more than contemplate sampling these aperitifs, they were pre-empted by the rapid succession of courses brought in by the servers and laid before them: meats in unfamiliar sauces, vegetables, pastries, creams, all generously seasoned with a variety of exotic spices. Conversation was abandoned altogether in the attempt to do justice to this bewildering and disorganized abundance. Some of the Egyptian *convives* dispensed with cutlery, using pieces of bread to scoop up mouthfuls of the various dishes; others, like Shaykh Bakri, attempted to wield spoon and knife in the European manner, no doubt in honour of their guests.

In the pause that followed, as the guests leaned back against the pillows, Bonaparte attempted to engage the notable clerics at table on the marvels of science – somewhat inopportunely, Nicolas felt, given the miracle-manqué of that morning – and exhorted them to revive the study of the sciences as their ancestors had done in the days of the Caliphs.

Shaykh Sharkawi, the head of the diwan, replied – through Venture du Paradis – that the Koran encompassed all knowledge.

'Ah, but does the Koran teach you to cast a cannon?' Bonaparte retorted.

He looked disconcerted by the solemn nods in the affirmative from the shaykh and his confreres. But Nicolas was not at all sure that they were all as gullible as they would appear. Bakri gave the impression of a sharp and worldly man under his pious airs. As for Jabarti, Nicolas had seen his dour face nearly every day at the Institute, peering with ill-concealed avidity at French instruments and poring over the Arabic translations in the library for hours on end. During the preparations for the aérostat exhibition he had been a constant presence, even if he deigned to ask few questions.

'You know so much about Islam and Muslims, Commandant,' Shaykh Bakri remarked, through the translator. 'You should become a Muslim.'

Bonaparte seemed to take this in good spirit. 'My dear Bakri, were you to issue a fatwa dispensing me from circumcision, and allowing me to indulge in alcohol and pork, I would consider it!'

Nicolas shifted in his uncomfortable position on the low bench; he was developing a cramp in his left leg, and hoped the banquet was drawing to a close. But the pièce de resistance was still to come. To each table was brought, on an enormous platter carried by two servers, a whole spit-roast lamb on a mound of rice with nuts and raisins. Then each lamb was carved open to reveal, stuffed inside it, a whole goose, and that in turn was stuffed with a duck, and the duck was stuffed with a whole chicken, and the chicken was stuffed with pigeons, all cooked together. By then Nicolas, and he suspected the other French guests as well, had lost all appetite, but out of politesse they applauded this culinary *tour de force* extravagantly.

The barely touched stuffed lamb was no sooner removed from the table than a succession of sweet pastries was proffered, and that was followed by another ritual of finger rinsing. Throughout, only water had been offered to drink. Nicolas found the local water, drawn from some three hundred public fountains around the city, to be quite acceptable. Finally the excellent Yemeni coffee was served, strong and thick as syrup, along with the long water pipes that were ubiquitous in the country. Nicolas noticed that the Egyptians seemed to take little delight in the pleasures of the table but were addicted to their coffee and tobacco.

Nicolas shifted again in his seat and rubbed his cramped left leg discreetly; Magallon, noticing his discomfort, invited him to take a stroll on the terrace to admire the view over the shallow lake. By now the Nile water that had been released with the breaching of the dam in the morning had come rushing through the khalig, the main canal, and was beginning to fill the Ezbekiah esplanade.

'A pretty sight, is it not,' the Consul smiled.

'Rather like Venice,' Nicolas concurred. 'The Ezbekiah esplanade must be easily three times the size of the Place de la Révolution in Paris, wouldn't you say?' He breathed in the scented air and identified the separate fragrances of carob, eucalyptus, sycamore and lemon. A few slender boats with gay paper lanterns languorously crisscrossed the water, steered by gondoliers. 'It must be a good sign that the locals are in a festive mood.'

'Ah, but exactly – this scene before you is far more subdued than would typically be the case on such an occasion. There are very few Muslim people of quality among the revellers, other than the members of the diwan who are more or less constrained to be here. And it was the same this morning at the ceremony of the breaching of the Nile dam; mostly Ottoman Greeks, Syrian Christians, Copts. Not many Muslims, other than the street mob. And out here on the Ezbekiah; on a summer night, and a major festival, you would have seen many more boats, lights, music playing, and all the *riverains* would be out escaping the summer heat in the cool of the evening. Veiled Muslim ladies as well as men.' Magallon made an expansive gesture that encompassed the view from the terrace as well as the banquet hall behind them. 'All of this has the feel of a staged play to me.'

At that moment, as if marking the end of the first act of a play, General Bonaparte stood up and raised his hands and every head turned to his table. Bakri stood up as well. Nicolas and Magallon hurried back to their seats while the commandant prepared to speak.

'As you know,' he announced, 'the post of chief syndic of the Prophet's descendants is unoccupied.' Given the circumstances under which the late holder of that title had been relieved of his duties, Nicolas was not surprised that Bonaparte made no reference to them. 'I hereby invest an honourable member of that order, Shaykh Bakri, as the new Naqib Ashraf.' Bonaparte beamed, kissed Bakri on both cheeks, draped a sable pelisse around his shoulders and bestowed a diamond ring upon him.

The fact that the interpreter did not feel the need to translate was an indication that the news did not come as a surprise to those in attendance; but not knowing the customs of the country better, Nicolas could not gauge the sober nods of the ulema. He did, however, catch a particularly dour, not to say sarcastic, twist of the lips on the face of Jabarti. Bakri seemed gratified and looked as if he had every intention of keeping the sable-trimmed red velvet pelisse on his shoulders, in spite of the stupefying August heat.

Bonaparte then sat down, somewhat anticlimactically, and Shaykh Bakri followed suit, clapping his hands, at which signal half a dozen young women filed into the hall, eyes downcast, carrying lutes and castanets. The French applauded with unfeigned enthusiasm. The Mamlukas, as white female slaves were called, took turns playing the instruments and dancing: a slow, sinuous, suggestive rolling of the hips and belly, although with none of the practised lasciviousness of the *almées*, the professional dancing girls, whom Nicolas had seen during the parade. Two of the girls who entered the banquet hall balanced four-branched candelabras on their heads as they danced, keeping the posture of their heads and necks absolutely still as their arms and hips swayed and the candles flickered. They were comely enough, Nicolas thought, fair complexioned if somewhat too generous in form, the chief attributes of beauty in the eyes of the Oriental, he had heard.

'Rather opulent, don't you think?' he murmured to Magallon, under cover of the music.

'Indeed. But you must know that some of our countrymen have developed a taste for these Mamlukas, *faute de mieux*. Lepère' – he referred to the Director of Bridges and Pavements – 'yesterday bought a Caucasian just arrived from Constantinople for three thousand six hundred pounds.'

Nicolas grimaced at the thought of a French Republican – and an engineer, at that! – purchasing a concubine in the slave market. But he had heard that although the troops frequented the *filles publiques*, officers and civilians of any rank spared themselves that unappetizing and insalubrious recourse and had been known either to buy Mamlukas in the open market or more often procure them during raids on the houses of the Mamlukes. Nicolas found such proceedings distasteful, but at least, he thought, it was some consolation that the women would surely be treated better by a Frenchman than they had been by their former masters.

'General Dugua,' Magallon whispered, 'has taken a Mamluka from Murad Bey's household, Fatoum by name, a lithesome beauty, apparently. But I will wager our Bonaparte is at no risk of succumbing to the charms of an odalisque. Did you not notice that little encounter that took place under your nose this morning?'

'This morning I noticed nothing, I confess, but the rips in my balloon and the direction of the wind.'

'No, of course. But everyone else noted that the general was quite taken with the delicious blonde Pauline Fourès. A milliner's apprentice from Carcassonne by trade, and the wife of a lieutenant of the 22nd Chasseurs. But since she has a reputation *pour avoir la cuisse légère*, and we know how urgent our general is in matters of the heart, it would not surprise me if a first assignation had been planned for this very night.'

This casual gossip on the part of a diplomat like Magallon surprised Nicolas, but the ambassador's indiscretions, regarding matters that were more or less public knowledge, seemed to be the tactic of an astute man seeking to gain the confidence of his interlocutor. Magallon's comment explained the unexpected good humour of the commandant that evening. It was rather amusing to imagine Bonaparte dying of ennui as he reclined by Bakri's side, his thoughts on an entirely more pleasant prospect awaiting him in his chamber in Elfi's palace.

Shaykh Bakri clapped his hands and the dancers filed out. Bonaparte stretched his legs and showed signs of bringing the evening to a close. But then the third act, as Nicolas thought of it, came to a startling conclusion. A last cup was to be served, apparently, at a signal from the host. A young girl of about twelve or thirteen entered, carrying a tray with cups of the honeyed concoction called almond milk, and Shaykh Bakri introduced her as his youngest daughter.

A little chubby in the cheeks and under the chin, in the manner of children, she had enormous liquid eyes, with eyebrows like a bird in flight. She gave off a strong perfume of gardenia, and no doubt had been sprinkled liberally with the essence before being sent before the guests. Intimidating as the occasion must have been for the child, she nevertheless could not resist darting curious glances at the French from under the impossibly long, thick lashes some Egyptians had. Nicolas found himself reminded of one of his own children – not his blonde and languid Madelon, not in the least, but rather irrepressible little Cola with his bold black eyes.

Bonaparte seemed aware of the compliment the shaykh paid him by bringing a member of his family out of the seclusion of the harem to greet him, and showed his pleasure accordingly. 'What a sweet child! And I am delighted to hear she is receiving an education with Shaykh Jabarti. You are the rare enlightened man among your peers, my good Bakri, and must set a fine example, particularly when it comes to the emancipation of women. I congratulate myself on my choice of Naqib of the Prophet's House.'

After that the confusion started. Shaykh Bakri said something to Venture du Paradis, the gist of which seemed to be that he would be honoured to have Bonaparte ally himself by marriage to the house of the Prophet, through his daughter Zeinab. He was referring, improbably as it seemed, to the bright-eyed little person who had just served them nectar and had by then returned, Nicolas presumed, to her mother.

There was some consternation among the French at table. Bonaparte protested: 'I am sensible of the honour, my dear Bakri, very sensible, but I cannot consider it. To begin with, I am married!'

That argument, Nicolas thought, would carry no weight at all with the shaykh, who undoubtedly had more than one wife and any number of concubines, as Bonaparte must know.

'Besides, your daughter is too young, surely?' the commandant added.

The rather involved answer was that the girl was of marriageable age, according to her mother, but, if he wished, Bonaparte could contract the alliance now, take her into his household and only consummate the marriage when he felt the time was right, as custom allowed.

Shaykh Bakri's expectant expression was beginning to take a grim turn, and conversation had died down at the tables all around. Magallon and Venture du Paradis wordlessly communicated their concern to the commandant. Bonaparte immediately grasped the full sensitivity of rejecting an offer of political alliance with his single most reliable collaborator in a hostile city, and, what was more, with the house of the Prophet among a people of a different faith.

'In that case, my dear Bakri, in that case, why, it would be an honour, of course, to be allied to the house of the Prophet!'

A collective sigh of relief rose from the hall, like a hiss of steam escaping from a kettle. Everyone rose – the French bowed, the Egyptians followed suit. Nicolas headed for the door along with the other guests, attended by a host of serving boys sprinkling them with attar of roses and showering them with petals till they had crossed the courtyard and exited out of the double gates to the street.

'What a remarkable evening!' Nicolas exclaimed to Magallon as they erupted into the tepid night air. But no sooner had they taken a few steps towards headquarters than Bonaparte was waylaid by a grim General Dugua.

'Bad news, Commandant. The Ottoman Sultan has just declared war on France, and declared it the duty of every Muslim to resist what he calls "the sudden and unjust attack" of the French in Egypt.'

Bonaparte took the setback in stride. 'It was to be expected, sooner or later. We couldn't maintain the fiction that we were in Egypt with the Grand Seigneur's blessing for much longer. But we must be prepared to deal with the population on a hostile footing from now on; sedition must be avoided by any means necessary.'

'It has started already, Commandant.' Dugua handed Bonaparte a scrolled letter. 'We have intercepted two couriers with a letter from Ibrahim Bey in Gaza addressed to the ulema – the very shaykhs we have just dined with.'

Bonaparte handed the scroll to Venture du Paradis, who scanned it and translated. 'This is the gist of it: "Stay calm, take care of yourselves and the people. His Majesty the Sultan in Istanbul has dispatched troops to come to our aid. God willing, they will arrive soon."'

The commandant nodded. 'Have the two couriers beheaded, and announce that this is the punishment awaiting anyone who carries letters from the Mamlukes or to them. I mean to have five or six heads cut off in the streets of Cairo every day. So far we have dealt with them gently to counteract the terrifying reputation that preceded us. Today, on the contrary, we must take the proper tone with them to make these people obey; and for them, to obey is to fear.'

As he watched Bonaparte and the generals depart for headquarters, Nicolas could see that events had driven the incident at Shaykh Bakri's out of the commandant's mind entirely; whether it would have any consequences for the young girl in question, he knew too little of the culture to so much as hazard a guess.

SIX

The First Insurrection

'We governed blindly a country unfamiliar to us in its customs and language.'

> G. Rigault, *Le Général Abdullah Menou et la dernière phase de l'expédition d'Égypte*

'Sitt Zeinab, come speak to your father, he has asked for you.'

Normally Zeinab would have obeyed such a rare summons with alacrity, but she was glued with horror to the mashrabiyya window that overlooked the street. The cortège of the new police chief wound its way along the street in the direction of French headquarters, carrying something on the ends of pikes. As they approached she was able to make it out: human heads. She spun away from the window and hid her eyes in her shawl.

'Sitt Zeinab, did you not hear me?' the nurse repeated, arms akimbo. 'Shaykh Bakri himself is asking for you!'

'Dada, I can't bear to look! Who are they?'

'Who are who?' The nurse came to the window. 'What are you watching? Oh, it is that God-forsaken Fart Rumman. God preserve us! Those poor heads! Why are you watching these horrors?'

Zeinab brought her head out from under her shawl but kept her back to the window. 'Were they spies for the Mamlukes, Dada? Or Bedouin raiders?'

'They don't look like any Bedouin I've ever seen; nor Mamlukes either, they don't have moustaches. They're poor fellahin, most like.

68

Whenever Fart Rumman is sent out on patrol to catch spies and marauders, he rounds up anyone he can find and beheads them and brings the heads back to please his French masters, and they are none the wiser. Come down now or your father will have *my* head if you keep him waiting.'

Zeinab found her father sitting on the bench in the inner courtyard, his hookah bubbling beside him, quill in hand, drafting a document. Her mother, reclining alongside, brought a finger to her lips in warning to Zeinab. 'It's a very important letter that the French have entrusted your father to write on behalf of the diwan and all the ulema of Cairo,' she whispered. 'It will be addressed to the Sultan in Istanbul himself, and the Sharif of Mecca! Many copies will be made of it and it will be posted all over the city.'

Zeinab tiptoed to her father and peeked over his shoulder. *The French are the friends of the Ottoman Sultan and the enemies of his enemies. Coinage and Friday prayers are in his name and the rites of Islam are kept as they should be.* She had time to read no more before her father leaned forward to write and the wide sleeve of his kaftan obscured her view. When he straightened up again, she read: *They are Muslims respecting the Koran and the Prophet, and they have provided for the celebration of the Prophet's birthday with such worthiness and splendour as would bring joy to believers.*

Shaykh Bakri leaned back, shaking his head. 'The French think words are enough to dampen down sedition . . . but I can feel it running through the streets like the precursor to the plague.'

'I am sure your wording is inspired, Shaykh Khalil,' his wife soothed him.

'The drafting of it is not so difficult. Getting it signed by the other ulema will be the hardest part, and without them the letter has no credibility.' He put down his quill. 'But never mind that now. Come here, Zeinab, sit before me. I have great news for you, child.'

'Yes, Father?'

'You are to be married this month.'

'Married, Father? Who –?'

'It is a great honour, a very great honour. You are betrothed to the commandant of the French – Bonaparte himself.'

Zeinab felt the world spin around her, and then her mother sprinkling her face with rose-water and laughing. 'The child is overwhelmed. Praise be to God, Zeinab! Thank your father! You are the luckiest girl in Cairo today.'

Zeinab nodded, still speechless. She was indeed the luckiest girl in Egypt. The commander of all the French! And an avowed Muslim! Even if he had been old and ugly, it would have been a great honour, but he was young and beautiful as an angel: she had peeked at him through her lashes at the banquet.

Her mother put one hand to the side of her mouth and threw back her head to ululate with rejoicing, but Shaykh Bakri stopped her with an upraised hand. 'Not now, woman! It is not the proper time. Wait until I get this letter signed! Can you imagine if the news gets about! I have too many enemies in the diwan as it is.'

What did the happy news of her betrothal have to do with her father's enemies in the diwan? Zeinab wondered. But only for a moment.

'Please take a seat, Sitt Nafisa,' Ambassador Magallon offered. 'We are listening.'

Sitt Nafisa inclined her head and sat down, tucking her sheer yashmak more securely behind her ear. She took a deep breath as she faced the three men on the bench before her in the west court-yard of Elfi's palace: Magallon, and the two other Frenchmen who had been appointed directors of the newly created Registry of Civil and Commercial Affairs. Malti the Copt sat beside them as legal expert, which was surprising enough in itself, for he was a tax collector by profession and entirely ignorant of Islamic law.

'Thank you.' She cleared her throat. She reminded herself of her vow: to maintain the ties of civility with the French at all costs. She was reluctant to put those fragile ties to the test so soon, but the suits she had come to plead could not be postponed. She began with the obligatory compliment: 'May my request fall on the ears of justice and magnanimity. I have come today with three suits, one of which is my own, and two more on behalf of others.' She looked at the translator, Venture du Paradis, who conveyed her meaning.

'Proceed, madame,' Magallon nodded.

'As you may know – at least Ambassador Magallon knows – my sabil on Sugar Street –'

'A charitable waterworks, with a public fountain and baths for the poor,' Magallon explained to his colleagues.

'Thank you, sir. Concerning my sabil, then; taxes have been imposed on the religious endowment that supports it, although all such purely charitable works – sabils, mosques, hospices, almshouses, orphanages and the like, have from time immemorial been exempt from taxes – as Ambassador Magallon, who knows our ways, can attest.'

'Indeed, madame,' Magallon concurred. 'But that is not the way of the Republic.'

'Sir, you know the poor depend on these charities, and it would mean great hardship for them if they were cut off. Not to mention the ill will that will accrue to the French as a result of these measures.'

'Surely, madame, the revenue from your caravanserai at Bab Zuweila – the commissions the merchants pay you to use the trading floor and the store rooms, the workshops, the lodgings and baths – those revenues alone must come to a considerable sum.'

'They did, sir, and every piaster was dedicated to support the sabil. But the income from my wikala at Bab Zuweila has plummeted since the invasion. As you know, the caravans from Mecca are disrupted, trade and pilgrimage are down to a trickle, and what little revenue there is, is entirely consumed in paying the taxes you impose.'

'You are a very wealthy woman, madame, and I am sure you will find the means to continue to fund your charity.' It was one of the other two Frenchmen – Tallien – who spoke. He made as if to rise.

'Sir, you have confiscated my estates!'

'That, madame, is the fault of your husband, Murad Bey, and of his amirs, who continue to wage war against us and lead the insurgency in the south.' Tallien's tone was acrimonious. 'Will that be all?'

Nafisa took a deep breath. Clearly, she would get no sympathy for the plight of her sabil. Mindful of her pledge to herself, she knew that the wiser course would be to withdraw. But she had promised to bring two other suits, and she could not disappoint those who relied on her. She forced herself to continue with her supplication.

'I will not trouble you much longer, sir. But I promised to speak on behalf of Sitt Adila, Ibrahim Bey's daughter.' She paused, looking directly at Magallon and Malti the Copt, hoping to remind them that Adila had taken the Franj and the Christians into her home for protection before the French entered Cairo. 'Sitt Adila's husband was killed in the Battle of Imbaba, and she is now trying to recover some of his property. But she is being told that she should have declared this inheritance within twenty-four hours of his death, and that it is too late now, the property is impounded for the benefit of the French Republic. Surely it was not possible for her to know for a certainty when her husband died in battle?'

'We cannot take all these circumstances into consideration, and in any case the property of the renegade Mamlukes is considered forfeit, as you know. Is there anything else, madame?' Magallon made as if to rise.

'One last suit, sir, I beg of you. Believe me, I would not stand here before you,' she added, trying to keep the bitterness out of her voice, 'if it were not on behalf of someone even more helpless than I. It concerns my Mamluka, Fatoum, whom I have raised since child-hood. I had sent her with my chief eunuch, Barquq, to run an errand for me at my Giza estate – unwisely, I realize, in these lawless times.' Nafisa had sent Fatoum to recover a coffer of jewellery buried under the planks of the hall at the Giza house; there had been no one but Fatoum and Barquq whom she could trust with such a task. There was no need to go into these details, however. 'As I said, sir, on the route to Giza they were attacked by a band of soldiers and the girl was abducted. My eunuch, who was severely injured by a blow to the head but managed to return home, says the soldiers were French or belonged to a French militia. Since then I have had no news. What has become of Fatoum? I would be most grateful if you would make inquiries.'

'We will make inquiries, madame. If the girl was injured or killed, the perpetrators will be hanged, even if they turn out to be French.'

'Thank you, sir! I knew I would not appeal in vain to French justice. And thank you for your patience in listening to me.' She rose, gathered her abaya about her, bowed, and exited the hall.

Did the French even realize how unpopular the measures they were taking would make them, imposing taxes on the very charities the poor relied on for shelter and water, schooling and hospice care? They should not be surprised if there were an uprising of the people.

As she rode back towards her house in the Red Quarter, her chief eunuch on the mule before her and a maid on the donkey behind her, people in the street recognized Nafisa in her white veils and greeted her with cries of, 'God bless you, Sitt Nafisa the White.' She nodded to Barquq to hand them a coin or two, discreetly; it pained her not to be able to give more.

The poor and the weary travellers who came to fill their jars at her fountains; how could she let these people down? But the dream that was closest to her heart was to build a school, a kuttab for orphans. God had not seen fit to give her children, so the young of the poor and abandoned would be her consolation.

Closing her eyes, Nafisa made a vow: somehow she would find a way to fund her sabil on Sugar Street, even if she had to sell every last piece of her jewellery; and the day that peace returned – if God saw fit to spare her so much as a piastre – she would expand the sabil and build a school for orphans above it. When she opened her eyes again, her heart felt lighter. And yet, as she rode on, she could not dispel a miasma of unease, a sense of the simmering discontent among the people, like a low-grade fever, that had been in the air for days now.

As she headed around to the east bank of the Ezbekiah, she saw a stream of people coming down from the Citadel, their household goods piled on ox-carts or in bundles on their heads; the French had ordered the inhabitants of the Citadel to evacuate their dwellings and go down to the city to live. A procession of French soldiers marched in the opposite direction, dragging artillery uphill. The Citadel was being fortified, many of the walls and houses destroyed, including the palace of Sultan Yussef Salah Eldin.

Her malaise grew as she noted small anomalous signs: sullen expressions on faces; streets where no children played; a diffuse murmur in the distance. A watchfulness. The city was watching.

As she rounded the far end of the Ezbekiah Pond, she heard shouts and jeers. Barquq looked back at her, shaking his head to indicate that they should turn around. But she pressed on, as if driven by a premonition, and as they turned the corner she saw a mob of some forty men and women buzzing like angry bees around the gate of Shaykh Bakri's house. Then she heard a young girl scream: 'Mother!'

It was the third night of Zeinab's wedding, and she was still waiting for the groom to send for her. The quick glimpse she had stolen from under her lashes, the night of the banquet when her father had sent for her to come in with the little cups of almond milk, had been their last encounter. She had not been present, of course, at the actual signing of the marriage contract; that, she vaguely assumed, had taken place by proxy. There had been no lavish banquet or wedding celebration, as there had been when her older sisters had married; no winding wedding procession from the bride's house to the groom's, with pipers and drummers and fanfare; no women ululating and singing. Instead she had been quietly, almost secretively, conveyed to the French general's headquarters in a covered palanquin, with only her nurse for company. Zeinab was keenly disappointed but consoled herself with the thought that, in these times of war and unrest, celebration was not in order.

She had submitted without demur to the ordeal of preparing for her bridal night: the hot honey wax to remove every stray hair on her body; the scrubbing of elbows and feet with pumice stone; the washing and brushing and oiling of her long black locks; the rubbing of ointments and perfume into her skin till it was as flushed and smooth as a baby's. Then she had been dressed in the finest silks and hung with rubies and diamonds till she sparkled like the French chandelier in the salon downstairs.

Overwhelmed by the great honour bestowed upon her, she had trembled with anticipation of the moment when she would be called to the commandant's apartment on the other side of the courtyard. But there had been no word from her husband that first night, nor thenext. Telling herself that he might appear at any moment, she had bathed in rose-water and changed into a fresh chemise several times a day. She cleaned her teeth with the wood toothpick every time she had anything to eat, and drank mint tea to keep her breath perfumed. She sprinkled herself with attar of gardenia, and had her nurse comb and braid her hair whenever she dozed off and got dishevelled.

But three days had passed and she was still alone. With nothing to do and no one to talk to, she dozed a good deal. As the edge of her excitement dulled, she was beginning to miss her mother and sisters, and even her pesky little brother. Whenever she heard any commotion in the great courtyard she would slip out of her chamber to the gallery and peer through the mashrabiyya, watching the French officers come and go, calling to each other in their language, and Zeinab would try to fathom the meaning of their words. Once or twice she caught a glimpse of Napoleon himself, but her husband kept strange hours and was always in a hurry, so she often missed his passage.

'Go to sleep,' her nurse told her. 'I will wake you if I hear anything.'

'But what if he sends for me and I am all dishevelled with sleep?'

'I will wake you if I hear anything. Now go to sleep, and let me get some rest also, for pity's sake.'

'I won't,' Zeinab insisted, reclining carefully back against the pillows. 'I'll wait up; I'm sure he will send for me tonight.'

When she woke up the room was filled with daylight and French voices, and a strange face was looking down at her.

Zeinab sat up, trying to shake off the heavy tentacles of sleep. A French lady with glossy dark curls and a kind smile was standing at her bedside, looking very grand in a wide blue hat with long red plumes. The Franj lady tipped up Zeinab's chin and smoothed a strand of hair off her damp forehead, all the while keeping up a running commentary that Zeinab could not understand but that seemed to be directed at the other Franj woman in the room, apparently the grand lady's attendant.

In the next hour Zeinab submitted to a blur of bustle and unintelligible chatter as the maid dressed and coiffed her under instructions from the lady in the blue hat. Zeinab's own nurse, whose position had been so unceremoniously usurped, watched, open-mouthed, while her charge was dressed in a pair of white pantaloons and white stockings; over that went a narrow silk shift of pale green, and over that a high-waisted, short-sleeved dress of the sheerest white muslin embroidered with delicate sprigs of violet pansies. Zeinab held her breath with enchantment; she had only dreamed of wearing anything as pretty as the fantastically fanciful costumes of the French ladies. The dress dragged at her feet and she was made to stand on a stool while the maid pinned up the hem till it hovered at her ankles.

Meantime the grand lady in the blue hat sat on the edge of the window seat, swinging her elegantly boot-shod foot and slicing pieces of fresh apricot. She alternated between eating the fruit and feeding it to Zeinab, laughing as she wiped a trickle of juice off the corner of the girl's mouth.

The maid piled Zeinab's heavy hair up on the back of her head and tied it with pale green ribbons, then loosened some strands over her forehead and curled them into tight curls with red-hot iron tongs; finally, she wound the long locks dangling at the back round the steaming iron till they spiralled in bouncy ringlets.

Then it was time for the finishing touches. Zeinab, who had never worn gloves before, giggled as the maid struggled to pull a pair of elbow-length pale green gloves on to her hands. The tips of the fingers on the gloves were too long and stuck out; the grand lady pinched the empty tips and then Zeinab's cheek, laughing.

The flat, pale green slippers went on much more easily, but when the maid had finished criss-crossing the long ribbons around her ankles and tying them in a bow, the slippers felt odd on Zeinab's feet. They were so thin and delicate, not at all like the high-platformed wooden clogs Egyptian women wore in the street to keep their feet out of dirt or refuse.

Zeinab watched in fascination as the maid picked up a straw bonnet, ripped off its yellow trim, and began sewing on pale green ribbons and silk violet pansies. But the grand lady, apparently bored, showed Zeinab how to crook her arms and loop a thin white shawl over her elbows, and demonstrated how to wield a bone-and-paper fan. At last she stood back, looked Zeinab up and down, nodded in satisfaction, and beckoned her to follow, not waiting for the miracle of the bonnet to be completed, much to Zeinab's disappointment.

As they wound their way down the stairs Zeinab, realizing that they would be emerging into the courtyard that was always full of soldiers and strange men suddenly became aware of her naked neck; her bosom, exposed nearly to the nipple; her bare arms under the short puff sleeves. She held back for a moment, grabbing her shawl and winding it over her head and bosom, then held the fan up so it covered her face. The lady in the blue bonnet looked back over her shoulder and laughed, shrugging her shoulders in resignation.

As they crossed the courtyard and came out into the street, the soldiers and officers all saluted; the lady in the blue hat must be very grand indeed, at least a general's wife, Zeinab concluded. This was confirmed when she heard the soldiers address the lady 'Madame la général' – a lady general!

A horse was brought for the grand lady, and she hooked up her skirt and took hold of a whip. One of the soldiers gave her a leg up into the saddle, where she sat sideways and towered over Zeinab and the maid, who were mounted on mules. Zeinab had ridden mules and donkeys before, but never in this strange attire, and never in such grand company. They were heading south, towards the Nasiriya neighbourhood. Zeinab wondered briefly about their destination, but she would have followed that lovely, kind lady anywhere.

Zeinab looked around as they rode by, observing the French soldiers and civilians lounging spread-legged, cups in hand, in front of the taverns that had sprung up overnight. They passed a group of Frenchwomen riding astride donkeys, kicking their heels up in the air and exchanging pleasantries with their grinning grooms, laughing so loud they could be heard long after they had turned the corner.

She saw the police chief and a dozen of his militia on horseback, gaudily dressed in silks and velvets and even fur-trimmed pelisses in the warm autumn air. Some bystanders jeered at them, shouting some kind of taunt about a massacre in the villages around Lake Manzala. The police beat them back with sticks and threatened to arrest anyone who mentioned such affairs or who jeered at French troops.

As Zeinab trotted along behind the lady general, they passed a group of Azhar University students walking by with their books under their arms. One of them looked Zeinab straight in the eye and spat on the ground. She was shocked. Did he take her for a Frenchwoman in her borrowed clothes? But then she realized it was worse: the insult had been aimed at her, quite specifically, not the Frenchwomen. She drew the scanty shawl more tightly around her head and shoulders.

But within minutes the unpleasant incident was banished from her mind when they drew up at Hassan Kashif's house, where the French had set up their university and workshops. There they dismounted and were met in the inner courtyard by several French ulema, including the dark man with the eye patch whom she recognized as the chief engineer from the flying-machine display.

He looked amused when he saw her, and said something to the lady general, who laughed. Zeinab bristled. He smiled at her absently and patted her cheek, then turned his attention to the lady general and pointed out the enormous sun clock that had been mounted high on one wall of the inner courtyard.

Zeinab followed them as they went into the busy hall, where men in shirtsleeves were bustling about and bending over various marvellous instruments. There were compasses and clocks and long brass-plated instruments aimed at the heavens; there were kilns and ovens, and distilling vats full of bubbling liquid, there were smoking kettles and bottles filled with all kinds of concoctions. It was like the magic cave of Ali Baba and the Forty Thieves. She wished she could ask questions or at least understand the exchanges between the chief engineer and the lady general as she followed them from room to room around the courtyard.

The chief engineer, noting her curiosity, beckoned her over to one corner. He placed a small amount of an ordinary-looking powder on a mortar and then gestured for her to put her fingers in her ears. When he picked up a hammer and gave the powder a sharp tap, a huge bang resounded through the hall. Zeinab jumped. The engineer smiled at her, chucked her under the chin, and strolled off with the lady general, talking all the while in their language.

Just then she recognized a familiar figure in a grey turban absorbed in poring over an instrument that resembled a long funnel mounted on a wooden stand. Never had she imagined it could give her such comfort to see the dour face of Shaykh Jabarti. She hurried over.

'My esteemed teacher!'

The shaykh started and stared at her. One cloud after another passed over his face so quickly she could not catch his expression. But when he spoke he did not comment about her appearance, and she was not sure whether to feel deflated or relieved by this.

'Well, well, what are you doing here?'

'The lady general over there brought me to visit the French Institute. Is it not amazing? Like a sorcerer's den!'

'These people have vast knowledge of many things and many combinations of things; they obtain unimaginable results. They have invented machines that can see what is invisible to the eye.' Shaykh Jabarti shook his head in wonderment. 'But the most magnificent yet is their library. Come, I will show you.'

But as she moved to follow him, Shaykh Jabarti raised his hand for silence, straining to listen. There was a moment's distant confusion of noise; then it died down. 'There has been some disturbance in the Azhar quarter this morning,' he explained. 'A crowd made up of the blind, of children from the Koranic schools, muezzins and the sick from Mansuriya hospital, all gathered at your father's house, complaining of the cutting of their pensions and bread rations because the proceeds of the religious endowments have been suspended. This may or may not be related. Not to worry. Let us visit the library. It is on the second floor.'

'Will we be allowed to go in?'

'That is the amazing thing about it. Not only their ulema but ordinary people, the lowliest soldiers, come to consult the books here. Should a Muslim come here – just out of curiosity, you understand – the French would not restrict his access but allow him to penetrate even to reserved areas; they greet him with kind words and smiles, particularly if they find in him competence, knowledge and curiosity for the study of the sciences. It is properly amazing!'

Zeinab stifled a smile; the shaykh was no doubt referring to himself. They had reached the mezzanine, and Shaykh Jabarti stopped to catch his breath, but she suspected he was stopping also to listen for more sounds of tumult. She looked around the hall, which was lined with shelves stacked with leather-bound books of all sizes; they were in the languages of the Franj, so she could not make out the titles.

Just then Zeinab heard the muted din again, and by the way he frowned and raised his nose in the air as if the better to hear, so did Shaykh Jabarti. A moment later he resumed their tour, but with a distracted air.

'Come this way –' He led her to a table where a large book was laid open on a bookstand. The book was brilliantly illustrated in colour and gold leaf, with an image of the Prophet Muhammad – she recognized him right away by his turban and his horse Baraq – as he rode from the Rock of Jerusalem. In another picture he stood looking towards the heavens, in his right hand a sword, and in his left the Koran, as if menacing all of creation; his companions stood around him, also holding swords.

'Did he really look like that, my teacher?'

'It is portrayed according to their knowledge and judgment. But look here: there are pictures of the Holy cities of Mecca and Medina, and Istanbul with its great mosques. This book has been translated from Arabic into their tongue,' Jabarti explained. 'These French make a great effort to learn the languages of others. I have heard some of them practise Arabic, and even recite verses from the Koran as an exercise in diction. Their printing press is also housed in this place, and it prints in Arabic characters; that is where the French produce all those leaflets and proclamations that they distribute around the city. Perhaps we can get permission for you to see it.'

Suddenly they heard a loud report, as of gunfire, followed by shouts, nearer and more distinct than before, and this time Shaykh Jabarti stiffened.

'Come, child, we must get you back to the Ezbekiah. Let us go down to the courtyard. Who brought you here?'

'The lady general. What is wrong?'

'There were demonstrations this morning at the Azhar University and in the slaughterhouse quarter of the Husayniya. The shopkeepers have shut down. Now it sounds like a mob is agitating outside the judge's house. It could turn into a full-scale insurrection, and you will be in grave danger if they catch you on the street dressed like this.'

They hurried down to the courtyard. The sounds of shouts and sporadic gunfire had drawn closer, and there was confusion among the French, with people running back and forth and calling to each other. Soldiers were barring the gates and carrying guns to the rooftops. The chief engineer seemed to be giving orders to carry away the more portable of the magical instruments. The lady general was nowhere to be seen.

Zeinab followed Shaykh Jabarti to the gate. He signalled to her to hold back while he stepped out and looked up and down the street. He ducked back in, looking grim. Then he slipped his long black abaya robe off his shoulders and handed it to Zeinab. 'Here, cover yourself with that – all of you, from head to toe. And use your scarf to hide your hair and as much of your face as you can. If the mob catch Shaykh Bakri's daughter looking like a Frenchman's whore . . .'

The noise of the rioters was growing alarmingly close by the minute, and it seemed to be coming from several quarters at once, from the Gate of Victory to the Gate of Zuwaila. Out in the street, Jabarti urged her on, and she clutched the ends of the long abaya robe and tripped along as fast as she could, casting glances behind her. Around the corner of the street came the vanguard of the mob, brandishing torches and guns and axes and butchers' knives.

Suddenly a wailing cry rose from the minaret of one of the mosques, but it was not a chant for prayers. 'Victory to Islam! Long live the Sultan!' The battle cry was picked up by another, stronger voice from another minaret and relayed from minaret to minaret across the city, a staccato counterpoint to the constant growl of the mob as it approached the Institute.

Zeinab was too out of breath and too terrified to ask questions as she trotted beside Shaykh Jabarti, heading north along the canal in the direction of Ezbekiah.

They could hear the rioters only steps behind, and Shaykh Jabarti exhorted her not to look back. Along the way, angry people were throwing up barricades of stone and wood ripped from benches, in anticipation of the French troops who would surely turn out in retaliation. Once or twice they were challenged, but Shaykh Jabarti pushed on while Zeinab kept her head down and clutched the abaya about her.

Finally Jabarti stopped, panting hoarsely and pressing his hand against his chest over the sash of his kaftan. 'Can you find your way back to your father's house from here? Go on, then, hurry. I cannot keep up this pace and you will not be safe until you reach the Ezbekiah. The French garrison will protect the Franj quarter from the mob. Go on now, don't argue.'

Zeinab hurried on, looking back at Shaykh Jabarti till she rounded the corner. A man darted out of the shadows and grabbed her arm, pulling at her abaya. She screamed and a woman at a window shouted at him to let the girl go. Zeinab set off again, almost at a run. She was out of breath when she saw the wall of her father's house.

She stumbled up to the gate, gasping, only to stop in her tracks in shock. Her father was being dragged out into the street by an angry crowd shouting insults. One man yanked the turban off Shaykh

Bakri's bare head and Zeinab turned away in shame at the terrible indignity. Then she saw her mother, one of her older sisters and two of their Mamlukas being dragged out in the street, the rioters tearing at their clothes and yanking the bracelets off their arms. Unable to stop herself, Zeinab screamed: 'Mother!'

The crowd turned, and one husky woman ripped off Zeinab's borrowed abaya, baring her scanty dress beneath. 'Here's the French general's whore!' she shouted.

At that moment a voice rang out like a bell. Zeinab could not make out the words, only the calm authority behind them. The mob froze, and turned to the speaker, a veiled lady riding on a mule. Someone recognized her and cried: 'It's Sitt Nafisa!' The furious shouts died down to angry lowing, then to shamefaced muttering. Zeinab's mother and father were released.

Then Sitt Nafisa's eunuch was wrapping the abaya over Zeinab's shoulders and hoisting her up behind him on the mule and they turned and headed towards the Ezbekiah headquarters. Zeinab was too paralysed by shock to ask questions until she was jolted out of her stupor by the sight of the French guards waving her through the gate of Elfi's palace and realized that Sitt Nafisa meant to leave her there.

'But I want to go back to my mother and father,' Zeinab blubbered.

'Listen to me, child. The only safe place for you now is under the protection of the French. Perhaps by and by,' Nafisa tried to console her, 'perhaps by and by you can go back to your family, when passions have cooled. But if you go back to them now you would be putting them at risk as well as yourself, and you don't want to do that, do you?'

'Please don't leave me alone here!'

'Be brave, Zeinab. I am so sorry for you, my poor child!'

PART II

The Reversal of Fortune

In an expedition to Egypt you would face three enemies:
the English, the Ottomans, and Islam; the last is likely to be
the most redoubtable.

Volney, *Voyage en Syrie et en Égypte 1783–1785*

SEVEN

The Plague

Nicolas Conté rode along the narrow streets of the city, accompanying Bonaparte as he assessed the damage to the Institute and the hospital and other French installations around Cairo. Only a week ago, Nicolas thought bitterly, he had looked forward to showing Bonaparte the new windmills he'd built on Rawda Island, finally up and running. The Egyptians could buy their flour there just as the French did, and Nicolas had had high hopes that such measures would go a long way to winning their hearts, and to reconcile them with the French occupation. But today he could no longer entertain any such illusions. The honeymoon was over; the bridegroom, seeking to seduce, had found himself a ravager in the eyes of his bride.

The insurrection had been put down swiftly and with overwhelming force. The heavy artillery brought up to the Citadel had fired down at the city until entire quarters were destroyed: people, houses, mosques, caravanserais – everything razed to the ground. They had targetted the Azhar in particular, for it was there the uprising had started, with the Shaykh of the Blind leading a mob to the judge's house to protest the cutting off of alms. When General Dupuy had arrived to investigate, the mob had rushed him, killing the general and his men. It was then the French began their bombardment, and didn't stop until the city surrendered.

But at what cost, thought Nicolas bitterly. They had lost General Dupuy and two hundred good men; the Egyptians, ten times that number. And as he watched the sullen faces turning away at their approach, Nicolas knew that the severity of the repression had bred hatred and dread in equal measure, and that it would not be long before the balance tipped in favour of the former.

When the cortège reached the Red quarter they stopped and dismounted to enter Cafarelli du Falga's house. The doors and windows had been forced and it had been looted.

'It's all gone, Commandant,' General Cafarelli announced grimly as he hopped from room to room on his peg leg. 'All the priceless instruments, everything. When I think that every day, since I took up quarters here, the children would gather before my door to watch me – with my wooden leg – mount my horse unassisted, as if they never tired of this daily miracle!'

'My hospital on the Elephant Lake has been looted as well,' said Dr Desgenettes. 'I lost two young surgeons in the mêlée, and all my equipment.'

Bonaparte looked from one to the other of them. 'What do we do now? We don't even have instruments or tools.'

Nicolas took a step forward. 'Well, then, we shall make the tools.' Almost as soon as he said it, he realized the enormity of the undertaking. 'There is no help for it, we shall have to make do with what we have, and to invent and improvise what we need to replace.'

For a moment they all stared at him. Then Desgenettes was the first to press his request. 'My surgeons need scalpels urgently!'

'My naturalists need magnifying glasses, the astronomers need lenses, the artists need pencils,' clamoured Geoffroy St-Hilaire.

'That may be, but they will have to wait till my generals get their gunpowder and their steel for sabres,' Cafarelli cut in.

'Truly, Conté, you are the indispensable man, precious in a far country!' Bonaparte clapped Nicolas on the shoulder. 'How soon can you set up gunpowder factories? And do you wish to relocate the Institute to the Ezbekiah? I will relocate all our people there, I believe we will be safer in one fortified zone. The locals are being evacuated out of the Ezbekiah as well as the Citadel.'

Nicolas shook his head. 'Speaking for myself and my engineers, Commandant, we would prefer to stay where we are, in the house of Hassan Kashif and the Nasiriya.'

'I think most of us in the Scientific Commission are agreed on that score,' Geoffroy concurred.

Bonaparte nodded. 'Then I will make dispositions to make you safer. A fort and garrison will be set up on Scorpion Hill to guard the Institute.'

On the ride back, Bonaparte signalled to Nicolas to bring his horse abreast. 'I have an even more pressing task for you, Citoyen Conté. Now that the Porte has openly declared war and Ottoman ships have joined the English blockade, the embargo against us is complete. We are trapped in Egypt. The only way out is to prepare a campaign for Syria.'

Nicolas was taken aback. 'Syria?'

Bonaparte nodded. 'In this operation I have three aims: firstly, to assure the conquest of Egypt by constructing a stronghold beyond the desert; secondly, to oblige the Porte to justify itself; thirdly, to deprive the English fleet of the supplies that it draws from Syria.'

'I see. A campaign against Syria. When, Commandant?'

'Soon. It is imminent. I have a challenging task for you, Citoyen Conté, on which the entire campaign may well hang. Transporting our siege artillery by ship to Syria runs the almost certain risk of interception by the English blockade; Commodore Sidney Smith watches our every move. The alternative, transporting our heaviest cannon overland, risks having it bog down in the sand dunes. Can you think of a solution?' Bonaparte fixed Nicolas with his keen eyes.

Nicolas took a moment. 'If I can invent an axle that will enable us to transport the heavy cannon over the sand . . .'

'Exactly, exactly, my dear Conté! I leave it to you then, to make this your priority. The campaign is imminent!'

Nicolas groaned inwardly. Given enough time, he was confident that he and his engineers could come up with the proper design for the axle, but it seemed as if this was one more challenge that Bonaparte would give him inadequate time to meet.

As he accompanied the generals back to the Ezbekiah and passed through the courtyard of Elfi's palace, Nicolas caught a glimpse of the tail of a scarf floating from the window above him, and looked up to see a flash of eyes like dark pools under winged eyebrows. The girl, of course, the naqib's daughter, Bonaparte's little bride. So she was safe. He had thought of her, once, the night the Institute was besieged by the mob, wondering what had happened to the child. But the events of the past two days had driven the thought to the back of his mind.

It was the second day after the uprising, the second day for Zeinab alone in a room in the palace echoing with running footsteps of soldiers and hectic exchanges in French of which she understood nothing. In the commotion, no one had given a thought to her beyond leaving a pitcher of water for her to drink and a handful of dried dates. It was on the second day, at nightfall, that the sound of cannon-fire ceased, and she cried herself to sleep. She woke to the sound of her nurse coming into the room.

'Dada!' Zeinab flung herself at her neck. 'Dada!'

'Now, now, Sitt Zeinab, let me look at you. What have you done to yourself with your weeping? Your eyes are so swollen and red I wonder you can see at all.'

'Dada, how are my mother and father? My little brother?'

'They are safe, praise be to God who sent Sitt Nafisa to intervene. The mob had dragged them up and down the streets – but never mind that now, they are safe, hiding in one of the judge's houses. Sitt Zeinab, have you had anything to eat at all? No, I thought not. Here, your mother sent you the few things she could scrape together.' The nurse unwrapped a cloth parcel. 'I had the Devil's own time getting here; there is a curfew and Egyptians are not allowed out of their neighbourhoods or on the streets from sundown to sunrise. Such devastation, such mourning. Such a wailing, Sitt Zeinab, such a wailing!' The woman slapped her cheeks. 'But there is worse!'

'What, Dada?'

'Last night the French swept through the streets of the city like a torrent, like Satan's own troops. They desecrated the Azhar, riding into the mosque with their horses, and spitting and pissing on the carpets. They smashed the lamps and broke the coffers and threw the Korans on the ground and trampled them underfoot and defecated on them.'

'God preserve us!'

'I tell you, Sitt Zeinab, it is a good thing your father is in hiding, the way the people feel right now about anyone who was a friend to the French . . . Even I am afraid for my safety when I leave the house. God knows I wouldn't have come here if I hadn't nursed you with these very teats!'

'But, Dada, I want to go home. No one cares whether I live or die here.'

'What about your husband?'

'My husband? You mean the commandant? He doesn't know I exist!'

The nurse shook her head. 'At any rate, you mustn't think of trying to leave here. The ugly mood this mob is in, you would be torn to pieces if you were recognized. Not to mention the calamity you would bring on the heads of your family. No, Sitt Zeinab, there is no helping it; you must stay where you are. I'll try to come back when I can.'

'Dada, you won't leave me!'

'No, not right now, but I have to go back before the curfew. Don't fret now, and try to eat something. Then we'll try to find some water and wash you up.'

The next morning, Zeinab watched by the window overlooking the outer courtyard of the palace till the sun was high in the sky, but there was no sign of Dada. She watched the French soldiers come and go through the gates. At one point the police chief, Bartholomew, passed through on his horse, dragging prisoners in chains behind him. She turned away and put her hands over her ears to block out their screams and curses.

The hours passed, the sun rose in the sky, and she tried to calculate how many hours were left before the sun would set and curfew came into force and she would have to give up on seeing a familiar face. Then a commotion before the gates made her rush back to the window in time to see a procession of ulema on mules filing solemnly through the courtyard and dismounting at the other end.

A delegation of ulema! Was her father among them? But as they passed under the arched portico all she could see was the tops of their black or grey turbans. Zeinab snatched her scarf, wrapped it around her head and shoulders, and ran out of the room. The French guards she crossed on the way spared her no more than a glance as she followed the sounds of voices to the gallery overlooking the inner courtyard.

Below her in the inner courtyard she saw several of the French generals standing on one side, and the ulema facing them on the other. Her heart pounded and she clamped her scarf over her mouth when she recognized the commandant, Bonaparte – her husband, who had forgotten her very existence! He was pacing up and down, fury apparent in his voice and his demeanour.

Then one of the ulema stepped forward; she recognized Shaykh Jabarti by his voice, and strained to hear. He was asking for a general amnesty and a withdrawal of French troops from the Azhar. The commandant replied in angry tones, while the translator struggled to keep up. Then Bonaparte stopped pacing and barked out an accusing question. 'Who among you was in collusion with the insurrectionists?'

There was a stricken silence from the clerics. He repeated the question, growing angrier. Still silence. Then he shouted: 'I know! I know each and every one of you!' He pointed at this cleric or that, and the guards converged on them and arrested them and dragged them away. Zeinab recognized the Shaykh of the Blind, with his rag over his eyes, and Shaykh Mahruqi, but not the other men arrested. Her father and Shaykh Jabarti were not among them.

Sitt Nafisa the White looked around her as she rode towards the Ezbekiah as though she were seeing Cairo for the first time. As far as the eye could see, roads were being cleared, houses demolished and mosques turned into fortifications. Pounding resonated from dawn to dusk, and the dust barely settled overnight as the French threw up a ring of garrisons around Cairo, from Al-Zaher Mosque, renamed Fort Sulkowski, in the north, to the new fort of the Institute in the south.

That day the diwan was convened for the first time since the insurrection, without the shaykhs who had been accused of abetting the uprising. In the aftermath of the revolt Nafisa came to see her presence in the Ezbekiah that day as providential: she had been in time to see the mob roiling in front of Bakri's house, dragging the shaykh and his wife and children out into the street. She had been in time to intervene. It had taken all her credit with the people, all her authority, to command the mob to release them and let them return to their home. The youngest girl in particular, tricked up in a scanty French frock, might have been torn to pieces had Nafisa not intervened.

Her heart went out to the child. Poor thing, what fault was it of hers if her father used her as a pawn of his ambitions? She was a mere lightning rod for the people's rage at the occupation and collaborators like Shaykh Bakri who sought to profit from it. That the naqib's daughter should have been sent to live with the French general was an unforgivable outrage. Nafisa wondered how the poor child was faring, alone and unwelcome among strangers. She had heard nothing of her since the day of the uprising.

Sitt Nafisa continued on her way, passing Shaykh Jabarti on the road, no doubt on his way to the diwan. He bowed, as was his wont when he recognized her, and she inclined her head very slightly in acknowledgement.

Bartholomew rode by in a great cloud of dust at the head of a contingent of janissaries. The newly minted militias of the French had multiplied since the insurrection: Moroccans, Syrian Orthodox, Copts, Africans, renegade Mamlukes. Heavily armed and barely trained by the French, they would be replacing the army Bonaparte was taking with him on the Syrian campaign. The thought of un-disciplined irregulars let loose on the populace under the command of men like Bartholomew made Nafisa's blood run cold.

Bonaparte was leaving General Dugua in command of Cairo. Nafisa wondered how poor Fatoum was faring; she had heard that Dugua had made her abducted Mamluka his concubine.

Nafisa saw two French soldiers putting up posters – another of their interminable proclamations, no doubt – and gestured to Barquq to obtain one on her behalf. She read it with growing astonishment.

From the commander of the French Armies, Bonaparte, to the people of Egypt, high and low . . . Anyone who shows enmity towards me or quarrels with me acts with a deluded mind and perverse thinking; he shall find no saviour from me in this world nor from the hands of God in the next. The sensible person knows that our acts were ordained by God. He has decreed in eternity that I come from the West to Egypt to destroy its tyrants and to carry out the order I was charged with . . . The time and day will come when it will be evident to you that all my acts and rulings were by irrevocable divine decree.

Nafisa studied the proclamation, bemused at the marked change in tone. No longer was it issued, at least ostensibly, under the cover of the ulema or the diwan, nor did it make any loyal references to the Ottoman Sultan, a position no longer tenable now that the Porte had officially declared war on the French. This latest proclamation seemed to claim for Bonaparte himself the mantle of the Caliphate; indeed, it went further, seeming to appropriate the divine attributes of Mercy and Omniscience. Nafisa looked around her and studied the expressions of the people in the street who stopped to read the posters; she wondered if the supreme commander of the French realized to what extent he had overshot his mark.

A cavalcade of troops trotted by, drums beating, dust swirling in their wake like a sandstorm. How would all this madness of war end?

Camp outside Acre
13 May 1799

My dear Geoffroy,
At last the order has been given to strike camp and head back to Cairo and I have a moment to answer your letter. You write: 'The work of the Commission of Arts and Sciences will excuse in the eyes of posterity the levity with which our nation flung itself, so to speak, into the Orient.' Your words come as comfort at a time of greater trial than you can imagine. The avant-garde that heralds our arrival and brings you this letter will trumpet the great victory of the Syrian campaign. The truth is otherwise. These past three months have left me sick at heart.
All went according to plan at first. As we advanced into Palestine, first El-Arish, then Gaza, then Ramla, fell within days,

and our optimism seemed rewarded. The challenge of the Syrian campaign, for me, was to facilitate the transport of our heaviest cannon across the desert without bogging down in the sand dunes. I was able to create an axle adapted to the sand that would indeed make that possible, and proposed it to Bonaparte; after some hesitation, he chose to send most of our artillery by sea instead. In the event, Sir Sidney Smith and two English ships intercepted our flotilla and captured a crucial part of our siege artillery, which was eventually to prove fatal. Our own heavy ordnance was used against us to defend Acre.

Historians will write that our destiny was thwarted before the walls of Acre, at the hands of Jazzar Pasha – the Butcher, as he is called. But I will confide in you that it was earlier, at Jaffa, that the poison entered the blood in this campaign.

Jaffa resisted to the tune of two thousand dead before it surrendered, and we took an even greater number of prisoners. Bonaparte sent the Egyptians among them home. Then, three days after the fall of Jaffa, the general ordered the remaining prisoners executed; and when we ran short of ammunition, he had them put to death by sword and axe – all two thousand five hundred men. The general's justification was that a few hundred of the garrison of El-Arish had violated the terms of their pardon and were caught when Jaffa fell. In truth, we had no means to feed that many prisoners nor troops to guard them.

War is barbaric of necessity, I know; I have studied history: Alexander, Caesar, all the great conquerors were ruthless. But I feel a bruise on my soul. The prisoners met their fate with that maddening Oriental resignation, performing their last prayers and then kneeling and bowing their heads for the executioner's sword. And as if these ghosts were exacting their revenge posthumously, it was at Jaffa that the plague reared its head and gave us no quarter thereafter. And if the troops defending Acre never considered surrender for one moment, was it not the fate of the garrison of Jaffa that served as an example to strengthen their resolve?

The conduct of Desgenettes and the physicians under him when the pestilence declared itself compelled the admiration of everyone who witnessed it, even if he refused to utter the word plague in front of the troops and spoke only of an 'epidemic'. He kept his sang-froid at all times and his devotion in attending to our soldiers went a long way to quelling panic. Desgenettes even went to the potentially suicidal extreme of inoculating himself publicly.

Bonaparte himself was fearless, visiting the sick and touching their sores as if he knew himself to be immortal. But as we retreated from Acre, the terrible problem arose of how to evacuate our plague-stricken soldiers left behind in the camp hospitals at Jaffa and elsewhere. Bonaparte asked Desgenettes to administer opium to the sick in the hospital at Jaffa in order to put them out of their misery, and to reduce their chances of infecting other troops. He argued that it would not be practical, or even feasible, to transport them with us.

Desgenettes flatly refused to follow his orders; he answered simply that his duty was to save life, not end it. In the end it was Royer the pharmacist who administered the opium in Desgenettes' place.

So it is with heavy heart that we retrace the path we took in February with such gallant hopes. So many comrades fallen: Cafarelli du Falga, our inestimable Peg-leg; the irreplaceable Venture du Paradis, with his astonishing talent for languages. Ah, Geoffroy, how their absence will be felt at the meetings of our Institute!

But we will return in triumph, never fear. Bonaparte has taken every precaution to invest our arrival with the grandest pomp in the hope of keeping the population of Cairo in the dark. He has already sent ahead the banners captured from El-Arish and Jaffa and ordered them to be flown from the minarets of the mosques, and we shall enter Cairo from the Gate of Victory with such honours and laurels as to rival Caesar's triumphant return to Rome with Cleopatra in chains.

*One consolation is that I can look forward before long to
reuniting with you and all our good friends under the sycamore
tree in Qassim Bey's garden. Ironic, is it not, that what once
seemed like exile, seen from an even greater exile, has all the
allure of home? Do you still gather there of an evening? Or
have you in Cairo not been spared the pestilence any more
than we have in Syria?*

> *Your devoted*
> *Nicolas-Jacques Conté*

Sitt Nafisa was unsealing a letter she had just received from Elfi Bey on the Syrian front, wiping it down with vinegar as a precaution against the pestilence, when she was interrupted by her eunuch Barquq coming up the stairs.

'Sitt, Ambassador Magallon and the French doctor are at the door asking to speak with you.'

She stowed away the letter. 'Show them into the inner courtyard and offer them something to drink. Coffee – the French won't drink anything that has not been boiled, for fear of the plague. I will be down as soon as I have veiled.'

She had no doubt the doctor's visit was related to the plague. Commandant Dugua had ordered proclamations plastered all over Cairo warning people that they must report on any family member or neighbour who came down with the appearance of symptoms. Women of ill repute, if caught within the city walls, were to be put to death. Moreover, the presence of any stranger who came to town, Mamluke or other, must immediately be signalled to the authorities; failure to comply would result in severe punishment for anyone caught hosting an unreported visitor. That last paragraph had given Nafisa pause: the danger of the plague was real enough, but were the French also using the pretext to monitor the entrance and exit of anyone passing the city gates, in order to catch Mamlukes and spies?

In minutes she was ready and went down to greet Ambassador Magallon, and a man in his forties who bowed to her rather stiffly: the doctor.

'Madame, you will allow me to dispense with courtesies, the urgency of the situation dictates it. We have come to ask your help in preventing the spread of the plague.'

Nafisa nodded and he continued.

'I believe we have the proper measures in place to contain the disease where French troops are concerned, but we cannot do much for the Egyptian population. We simply do not have enough medicine, or beds in the hospitals, or physicians. I have had to give orders that only Europeans and Syrian Christians may be treated at the hospitals, or have medicine dispensed to them by our pharmacists, except by order of a European physician. Believe me, madame, if I had the means to treat everyone, I would.'

He looked directly at her and Nafisa surprised herself by saying, 'I believe you would, Docteur.'

'Thank you for that, madame. All I can do for the general population of Cairo is disseminate information on hygiene and quarantine. There are so many measures that will make a difference. Bedding must be aired in the sun every day, and all raw food must be macerated in vinegar. The household must report to the police immediately if there is a case of contagion, and if there has been a death all bedding and clothing that has come in contact with the diseased must be burned.'

Desgenettes waited for Magallon to finish translating, then continued:

'The sick person must be isolated for a month and ten days. The bodies must be disposed of properly, and there must be no funeral cortege or prayer service.'

Nafisa shook her head. 'It will be difficult to convince the people of that. It is not our way to isolate a sick person from his family. And it's against our religion not to pray over the dead.'

'But during the pestilence, exceptions must be made,' Magallon interjected. 'That is where your help will be invaluable, madame. There is no one in this city with your influence, not even the ulema.'

Sitt Nafisa hesitated, but not for long. If collaborating with the French would diminish the terrible toll of the pestilence on her city, she would do whatever it took. She nodded to the doctor. 'What needs to be done?'

'French soldiers will do the rounds of every house in the city, house by house, room by room, to ascertain that there are no fresh victims of the epidemic; and then start over again.'

'There will be great resistance to having men, French or otherwise, enter houses to inspect the upper floors and the harems,' she pointed out. 'You must have local women to accompany the soldiers – a woman for every neighbourhood, and a man to transmit the instructions in Arabic. Only the women will go upstairs into the harems. You must tell them you will be paying them for the risks they are taking.'

'I knew your help would be invaluable, madame!' Desgenettes exclaimed. 'It is an excellent idea. We will train these women in recognizing the symptoms, explaining the measures of hygiene . . . indeed, madame, it is one of my dreams to establish a school for midwives here in Egypt, as soon as circumstances allow.'

'That would be a great good work, Docteur,' she responded noncommittally. Collaborating in containing the epidemic was one thing; she was not sure she wished to see the French masters of Egypt long enough to found a school of midwifery.

'Moreover,' Magallon interposed, 'the diwan has been ordered to suspend the pilgrimage to Mecca this year. The Feast of the Sacrifice has also been cancelled – the flocks of sheep will be put in quarantine. The people might not understand . . .'

'I will do my best, sir, to use what little influence I might have to convince them of the necessity.'

As they made to depart, Nafisa detained Magallon. 'Might you have heard what became of the young girl, Zeinab – the daughter of the naqib, Shaykh Bakri, whom I remitted to the care of French headquarters the day of the uprising?'

'The girl who was betrothed to General Bonaparte?'

'The same.'

'I will make inquiries, madame. Madame la Générale Verdier might have some idea.' Magallon bowed and followed Desgenettes out of the hall.

EIGHT

The Tivoli

'The poor scientists of Cairo were brought to Egypt to add a line of glory to the history of Bonaparte and were kept there so no one would find a line of reproach in that of Kléber.'

Geoffroy St-Hilaire, in a letter to Cuvier, Cairo,

27 November 1799

Nicolas leaned back on the rug-upholstered cushions laid out under the sycamore tree in Qassim Bey's garden and surveyed the coterie of savants gathered for their ritual of catching the breeze on a hot August evening. The bitterness of the retreat from Acre was somewhat forgotten in the recent victory over Turkish troops at Aboukir; Parseval was reading an ode he had written in honour of Bonaparte for the occasion. But Geoffroy seemed restless. He leaned in towards Nicolas.

'Where is everyone? Beginning with our good director? There is something going on, I can sense it.'

Nicolas looked around. Director Monge was missing, true, and also Vivant Denon the archaeologist . . . who else was absent?

Nicolas was distracted that evening by thoughts of his family back home. He had not received a single letter from his wife Lise since he had set sail from France over a year ago. The cursed English blockade played favourites with mail as arbitrarily as chance at cards, and for all he knew – for all he hoped and believed – his wife might have been writing to him faithfully. Victory over the

Turks at Aboukir, sweet as it was, had done nothing to improve the situation of the French in Egypt. Since Nelson destroyed their fleet, they had been and would remain at the mercy of the English blockade. And what little mail did get through was liable to be lost in Bedouin raids or held up by the quarantine and other measures to prevent the spread of the plague. But Nicolas could not help the doubts that flitted through his mind: what if the absence of letters from home had nothing to do with the blockade? Had his long absence led to an estrangement on his wife's part? Had Lise found consolation elsewhere?

Ah, there was Dr Desgenettes coming through the portico. He looked exhausted, and no wonder, as he literally divided himself in quarters, overseeing at the same time the quarantine at the port of Bulaq on the Nile and the three hospitals: at the Elephant Lake, at Ibrahim Bey's Eini Palace, and at the Citadel.

'Come, Docteur, have a glass of carob juice with us.' Nicolas made room for the physician beside him. 'How goes the epidemic?'

'I think we have turned the corner.' Too tired to join them sitting on the ground, Desgenettes leaned against the tree trunk.

Geoffroy, observing the doctor's *ancien regime* stiffness, smiled and twirled his Mamluke-style moustache; he himself had mastered the art of sitting cross-legged with as much ease as a native.

'It is thanks to your efforts that the pestilence is contained, Docteur.'

'Or to General Dugua's ruthlessness. He has just had the chief of police – Bartholomew, is it? – drown thirty prostitutes caught soliciting the troops. But we have the epidemic under control, I believe, where our own people are concerned. I only wish I could do more for the natives.'

'You do what you can, Docteur,' Nicolas soothed him.

'What's this?' cried Geoffroy, suddenly jumping up to peer through the arcades of the loggia. 'Something is decidedly amiss here.'

Nicolas and Desgenettes looked up, startled. There was a sudden flurry of activity from the direction of the loggia: servants were bringing trunks down from the house and Monge, Vivant Denon and Berthollet emerged behind their luggage with a harried and secretive air.

Geoffroy intercepted them, followed closely by Nicolas, Desgenettes, and the other savants assembled in Qassim Bey's garden. They surrounded the director and his companions and bombarded them with questions.

'Where are you off to, may I ask, Directeur Monge?' Geoffroy demanded.

'Why, my friends, we thought we would take a few days to visit the oasis of Fayoum. The air is most salutary, apparently.'

'Fayoum? Is there not a Bedouin uprising there?'

'In fact Citoyen Monge means Rosetta. General Menou there vaunts a veritable Eden,' Berthollet amended hastily. 'Besides, the discovery of the Rosetta Stone is so thrilling, we wished to see its inscriptions for ourselves.'

'At this time of the evening? What could make your departure so urgent?' Desgenettes queried with his air of quiet irony.

Monge threw his hands up in the air. 'Well, if you must know, friends, we are leaving this evening for the coast. We are sailing to France with General Bonaparte.'

Nicolas was thunderstruck. Bonaparte was abandoning them in Egypt! In the moment of shocked silence that ensued, Monge pleaded: 'Friends, forgive us, we have been sworn to secrecy! You can imagine, General Bonaparte is taking all precautions to prevent the news of his imminent departure from leaking to the British! It is dangerous enough as it is to run the English blockade. Dear friends, we ourselves did not know of it till this very afternoon!'

'Who else is going with Bonaparte?' spat Fourier the mathematician, the first to regain the use of his tongue.

'A handful of generals, and the three of us scientists.'

'How could you abandon your fellow savants? And the Institute?' Geoffroy berated them.

Vivant Denon collected his porte-manteau. 'Come, Citoyen Monge, we must hurry. Dear confreres, we will miss you and our delightful evenings in Qassim Bey's garden! I was very comfortable in Cairo, but it was not to find myself comfortable in Cairo that I left Paris.'

With that parting shot the three chosen ones hastily left the premises.

'That miserable *ambitieux*!' Geoffroy fumed. 'He will be publishing his discoveries in France and covering himself in glory while we mark time here in Egypt!'

'The question, at the moment,' Nicolas interjected, 'is who will replace Bonaparte as commander in chief of the Army of the Orient. Let us go to headquarters immediately and find out.'

At the Ezbekiah, they found Bonaparte gone and Elfi Bey's palace in uproar as news of his sudden departure spread. General Poussielgue greeted them with a bitter injunction: 'Let us suppose that a cannon ball had blown him away, and let us carry on.'

'He had dinner with Bonaparte earlier this afternoon and was kept in the dark,' Desgenettes confided in an aside to Nicolas. 'You can imagine how humiliated and resentful he and the other generals are. For myself, I cannot say I am inconsolable at Bonaparte's departure.'

Nicolas was not surprised: Desgenettes had locked swords with the general during the Syrian campaign. The great question on every man's mind was the choice of successor as commander in chief. Speculation ran rife.

'Bonaparte will have named Kléber,' Geoffroy affirmed. 'The men admire him, Teutonic god that he is. I am sure a courier is on the way to him in Alexandria right now.'

Nicolas had his doubts; he remembered Bonaparte calling the tall, blond Strasbourg native '*cet Allemand*'. For his part, Kléber was reported to have ranted at 'the outsize ambition of that miserable charlatan'. There was no love lost between the two men.

'Might he name General Menou instead?' Nicolas suggested.

Desgenettes shook his head. 'Menou is not popular with the troops, and his misalliance with an Egyptian will count against him.'

To the derision of his countrymen, Jacques-François, ci-devant

Comte de Menou, had recently taken to calling himself Abdullah-Jacques Menou, after his marriage to a prosperous merchant's daughter, who was expecting their first child. His 'misalliance', however, was far from unique; many of the French, overlooking the fact they already had a wife back in France, had taken an Egyptian bride – Geoffroy included.

As if reading Nicolas' mind, Geoffroy added: 'I have my little dark family myself, of course, on whom I lavish temporarily the tenderness I cannot give my family in France – but then, I am not a general. No, my money is on Kléber. Anyone who knows Kléber knows his mind; as soon as he can negotiate an honourable truce and repatriation with the English, he will put an end to this campaign. His priority is to save what remains of the Army of the Orient; he is not in favour of colonizing Egypt, thank God – unlike Menou.'

Nicolas found an echo of 'Amen' rising from his heart. This enterprise, begun with such conviction and idealism, had turned into something none of them, he suspected, could have envisaged or desired. Ever since the Syrian campaign, his heart was not in it; he was beginning to see that he himself had been more naïve than most in his belief in the universality of the republican principles they had come to disseminate. Tonight's news was the last straw: Bonaparte's abandonment of the stranded Army of the Orient in Egypt smacked of pragmatism and ambition that had nothing to do with any 'civilizing mission'. No, thought Nicolas, it was time to leave Egypt and its infinitely bewildering complexities, before the mission deteriorated further. Already the energies of the French were entirely concentrated on the survival of the Army of the Orient, at any cost. But he did not voice his disloyal thoughts; he left it to the irate Geoffroy to rant on.

'As for the work of the Scientific Commission, I believe it is done,' Geoffroy was repeating. 'I for one intend at the earliest opportunity to demand to be repatriated. I have collected all the natural specimens I can hope to collect, and they are deteriorating rapidly in their preserving solutions. Meanwhile, my peers in France are publishing their discoveries and covering themselves in glory!'

'General Kléber is likely to remain insensible to these arguments,' Desgenettes remarked dryly.

Seeing the lack of sympathy in the eyes of his companions, Geoffroy burst out bitterly: 'It is different for you, Conté, and for you, Docteur! As long as there is an army in Egypt you are indispensable! But we poor scientists, having been brought to Egypt to add a line of glory to the history of Bonaparte, find ourselves kept here so no one may find a line of reproach in that of Kléber!'

Nicolas, distracted by a movement behind the mashrabiyya of the second-floor loggia overlooking the inner courtyard where they were assembled, looked up. Framed in the window was the pale face of a young girl, an expression of desolation and bewilderment in her wide eyes such as he had never seen. Bonaparte's little bride! Of all the people the general had abandoned in Egypt, had he given any of them less thought than the naqib's little daughter? Nicolas' heart went out to the child. What would become of her now?

Gone in the night. The chief general was gone, without a word on her fate. What was to become of her now that she had been repudiated before she was ever a wife? Zeinab turned her face to the wall and wept. It seemed to her she had not stopped weeping since the day Sitt Nafisa had dropped her off at Elfi's palace. The chief general had not acknowledged her by so much as a word or a glance. She had been left entirely on her own, save for her nurse. When Bonaparte returned from the Syrian campaign, she had cherished a hope, faint as it was, that he might remember her existence, either to make her his wife or to send her back to her people. But now he was gone, gone for good, and she was left in limbo. What was to become of her? She moaned into her pillow.

Dada came to her bedside and smoothed her hair back from her forehead.

'Sitt Zeinab, it may be for the best. At least now perhaps we can go back to your father's house. Do you not miss your mother and your little brother?'

Zeinab shrugged her away and turned her face to the wall. Go back? She missed her family desperately, but how could she go back? She was not even divorced. She would bring disgrace upon her father's head. Yet how could she continue to stay here with the French, without a husband? What was to become of her?

In a few moments she heard a quick, light step approaching and looked up. It was the lady general. Like an angel of mercy, Zeinab thought, appearing in her moments of despair.

'Come, *ma petite* Zeinab, let us go to the Tivoli this evening. You don't know what that is? Of course not, but you will see, it is delightful, there will be all sorts of entertainment: music and dancing and cards and theatre – not the Guignol you have here, real theatre!' She spoke as naturally and gaily as if she had not noticed Zeinab's reddened eyes. Zeinab found that she could follow the gist of her remarks quite easily, she had picked up the language of the French over the past five months of living among them.

'Hurry up and dress, *ma petite*,' the lady urged. 'Why don't you wear that pretty muslin frock with the pansies, the one I gave you? Let's see if it still fits you, I have the impression you've grown inches taller these past few months.'

'Ah, just as I thought.' Madame Verdier sized Zeinab up and down when she had dressed and stood before her. 'The dress is a good hand-span too short, and needs to be let out in the bosom and nipped in considerably at the waist. I'll send you my maid to let down the hem and pin and tuck and do alterations. She can dress your hair as well.'

Madame Verdier lifted Zeinab's chin in her hand. 'But what a little beauty you have turned into, *ma petite*. Who would have thought you hid such fine bones under those chubby cheeks? Now, hold your head up and your shoulders back, and show off that long swan's neck.'

Zeinab blushed and looked down till Madame Verdier had left, but then she examined herself in the mirror as she waited for the maid to come. She didn't think she looked pretty; her mother would have said she looked thin and drawn, and tried to stuff her with sweetmeats. She no longer had the round moon face of the princesses of fairy tales; the planes of her cheekbones and the line of her jaw caught the light. Her dark pools of eyes, the birds on the wing that were her eyebrows, finally looked as if they belonged on the pale, chiselled landscape of her face.

As soon as the maid had fitted the dress to her newly configured form, Zeinab hurried down to Madame Verdier. It was a warm summer evening, but not oppressively so, and the lady suggested they walk to the mansion the French had renamed the Tivoli after a famous pleasure dome in their capital city. A few minutes later they entered a lovely palace built around a large intramural garden of orange and lemon trees. Inside the Tivoli it was bright with light and lively with chatter and music. There were French officers and civilians, and a few prosperous-looking merchants who seemed to be from the local Venetian, Greek and Syrian communities.

'But really, it is open to Muslims and Jews as well; anyone in the local community who pays the monthly membership fee – not a negligible sum, admittedly. We hope, you see, that your compatriots will come to know and adopt our customs,' Madame Verdier explained.

Zeinab looked more closely at the women in the company; she thought she could tell the Frenchwomen from local foreigners or Mamlukas attached to the French, mostly by their manner; everyone was dressed in the French style, as she was. Some of the Frenchwomen's thin dresses looked wet and were plastered against their breasts and thighs. Madame Verdier noticed Zeinab's shocked expression and smiled.

'It's the latest fashion in Paris, apparently, to spray one's dress with water in order to achieve that nearly transparent look. I can't be bothered myself. Let me see if I can order some ratafia for us.' Madame Verdier moved in the direction of the terrace where a table was set up with bottles and glasses, but she was waylaid every step of the way by acquaintances claiming her attention. Zeinab waited in a corner, studying the room. At one of the gaming tables she recognized General Dugua; standing behind his chair was a slender young woman, Fatoum, who had been one of Sitt Nafisa's Mamlukas. At the far end was Bartholomew, the chief of police, throwing his head back to gulp the drink in his hand; beside him, holding her fan up to her face, was a sad-eyed woman who must be Ismail Kashif's abducted wife.

Madame Verdier returned, trailing in her wake a jaunty young Frenchman with pointy moustaches in the Mamluke style. He smiled as he handed Zeinab a drink, and nodded to Madame Verdier. 'Excuse me, madame, the galvanism experiment will start in a few moments.' He turned and left.

'Would you like to watch the Comédie?' Madame Verdier suggested. 'The *Courier de l'Égypte* announced a new play for tonight's programme: *Les Deux Billets.* But you may not be able to follow it. Perhaps dancing? I hear the orchestra striking up in the garden.'

'But I don't know how to dance, madame, and truly, I don't want to. Oh, is that the chief engineer?' She had caught a glimpse of the dark man with the eye patch passing through the loggia.

'It is indeed Nicolas Conté, our man of genius. Have you met him?'

'No, but I remember him from the balloon . . .' she searched for the word 'exhibition' in French.

'Ah yes, the Montgolfière. He is the chief of the balloonist brigade, indeed, but he is actually even more famous in France for the invention of the pencil.'

'Pencil?'

'Pencil. When the English monopoly deprived the Republic of its source of graphite for writing, it took Conté only a matter of days to come up with a substitute, a mixture of powdered graphite and clay that can be moulded and wrapped in wood: a pencil. Gaspard Monge says of him that he has all the sciences in his head and all the arts in his hand. A true Renaissance man. Would you like to meet him?'

Zeinab shook her head, suddenly shy.

'Come, he doesn't bite. I think I know where to find him – in the library.'

Zeinab followed her to the reading room where they found the chief engineer sitting at a table, immersed in scribbling strange symbols on a small pad. Zeinab was fascinated: in his hand he held one of the very pencils he had apparently invented.

'Still working on symbols for the semaphore, *mon cher* Conté?'

He looked up, saw them, and stood up gallantly, as Frenchmen did for ladies.

'Madame Verdier, what a pleasure.'

'It is an unexpected pleasure to see you here, Citoyen, you honour us so rarely with your presence at these frivolous occasions! What do you think of our friend Wolmar's experiment with local ratafia?'

'More than acceptable, madame. The Egyptians make spirits from figs, raisins, dates even . . . but Wolmar has succeeded in making a truly fine local ratafia.' He was appraising Zeinab out of the corner of his eye as Madame Verdier tapped him on the arm with her fan.

'But let me introduce an admirer of yours. This is Zeinab, Shaykh Bakri's daughter.'

'Can it be the little girl who –?'

'It is indeed. What a swan the little duckling turned out to be, *n'est-ce pas*? And she is learning to speak French at such a rate! I was just telling her that you are our man of genius.'

Zeinab curtsied, the way she had seen French ladies do. He smiled and bowed. There was a kindness in the way he looked at her that she remembered from their previous meeting at the Institute the day of the insurrection – a lifetime ago, it seemed to her now. She lowered her lashes, at a loss for something to say. Madame Verdier slipped smoothly into the conversational gap.

'Citoyen Conté, I must tell you we are pinning our hopes on you in a matter of the highest importance! When can we expect the manufacture of decent beer? All the French in Egypt are ill from drinking water! Surely you can make this your priority over the semaphore?'

'We need an optical telegraph urgently; the mail is so unreliable,

whether down the Nile or overland. Couriers are routinely assassinated or waylaid by the Bedouin.'

'Pigeons,' Zeinab blurted out and blushed.

'Pigeons?' He raised his eyebrows.

'In Egypt, we use pigeons. They are fast, and hard to spot.'

'But that's medieval!' The chief engineer laughed, and Zeinab
blushed. 'Still,' he rubbed his chin thoughtfully, 'I can see the prac-
ticality. Not reliable, but practical. Sometimes the simplest methods
are the most efficient; one should never discount local practices.
I plan to make a study of artisanal industries in Egypt. Some of
my colleagues dismiss the locals as a work force, but I have found
the Egyptians to have a genius for imitation, and I have been able
to employ them profitably both in the Mint and the gunpowder
factories.'

'If you ever need an assistant or an interpreter . . . ?' Madame
Verdier suggested. '*La pauvre petite, on ne sait pas quoi en faire depuis
que . . .*' She paused significantly.

'As it so happens, I do,' the man with the eye patch sized up Zeinab.
'Tomorrow I will send out a team of engineers to tour the city
observing local practices, particularly in industry and architecture.
Partly for the documentation of our Institute, but also to note useful
techniques, that sort of thing. I will certainly need an interpreter and
guide. Would you be willing to assist me?'

Zeinab had understood only the general tenure of what he was
saying, but enough to nod her head vigorously.

'Well then, young lady, your services are officially engaged as assistant and interpreter to the Institute of Egypt. I will send for you early
tomorrow, so do not stay up too late this evening.'

'An excellent idea,' Madame Verdier applauded. 'But meantime,
the child must sample the distractions! There is a galvanism experiment about to start in the next room, let us not miss it.'

Zeinab had no idea what that was, but she followed the lady general
and the chief engineer into the next room, where a dozen people
were chattering excitedly around a table on which was set up some
form of machine with what looked like two revolving glass globes

and a belt from which sparks flew. Several people held hands – the young man who had brought the ratafia among them – and then one of them touched the belt with a wire and they all shook and twitched wildly till he let go. They fell back, gasping and laughing. Zeinab was shocked, she had never seen anything like it.

Then the young man named Geoffroy called out: 'Who's next?' And gestured to Zeinab. 'Come on, it's quite safe, truly.'

Zeinab shook her head.

'Come, don't be a baby,' he cajoled. Half a dozen people were holding hands and looking at her expectantly. Zeinab hesitated. Then the chief engineer gave her a look out of his one good eye, and walked over to the table and grasped the hand of the last person in line. He held out his free hand to Zeinab, with a quiet nod.

She knew then that it would be all right. She stepped into the circle and placed her palm against his and closed her eyes, and even as the shockwave travelled through her and shook the bones of her shoulder hard enough to dislocate her arm, she knew it would be all right. The chief engineer had given her that little nod, and she trusted him completely.

'But what is that cane for?' Zeinab asked the chief engineer doubtfully as they prepared to enter the yard of the chick hatchery that he had chosen to visit that day. She picked up the hem of her skirt to keep it out of the dirt and the scattered pieces of watermelon rind. She hadn't known quite what to expect when she had agreed to be the chief engineer's assistant, but she was a little taken aback at the kind of mean cottage industry they were about to enter. What did he expect to learn? And why was he carrying that cane?

'I use it as a discreet measuring rod. I have notched it for measuring, and I can stand it up against a door, or a wheel, for instance, and measure the distance from the floor or wall, without making a fuss. Let's go in.'

They entered the long, low building, and Zeinab was struck immediately by the warm, close air; the interior was considerably warmer than the street outside, and there was a distinct, if not overpowering, smell of dried dung, used as fuel. The man who ran the hatchery came up to greet them, but Conté held up a finger while he paced off the room.

'Fifty feet long and twenty-five feet wide,' he remarked as he made a note in his ever-present notebook, 'and ambient temperature about thirty-one degrees.' He put away his thermometer and greeted the man, who led them down the passage in the middle of the building.

'As you can see,' the hatchery owner pointed right and left, 'there are two tiers of ovens on either side, in each of which about a thousand eggs are placed at a time, resting in straw over the embers of the fuel.'

Zeinab translated, and the engineer nodded.

'Ah! Interesting. Pray continue.'

'The eggs remain in the lower tier of ovens the first eight days, then they are removed into the upper one for the next fourteen. In the course of the final twenty-four hours the chick breaks the shell, and a few hours later it is taken out and placed before a fire for a little while, after which it runs out into the courtyard and pecks at rice all on its own.'

Conté measured the distance between the two tiers of ovens with his cane, all the while asking rapid questions about the management of the fires, the exclusion of the outer air, the mode of turning the eggs every day, the degree to which the heat was increased or diminished in proportion to the weather, the number of batches that could be hatched in the winter months. He ignored Zeinab's repeated pleas to ask these questions outside, where the atmosphere was less oppressive. Finally he appeared satisfied and led the way out of the hatchery.

'Remarkable! I wonder why nothing like this has been attempted in Europe. It would allow for the multiplication of batches of chicks by dispensing with the brood hen, thus resulting in a great reduction in the price of chicken.'

As they stepped out into the courtyard, they were approached by a stocky, dark-skinned woman in a milaya, presumably the hatchery owner's wife. Zeinab herself was wearing European dress but with a shawl draped over her head and shoulders.

112

'*Ahla*,' the woman smiled. 'That's the chief engineer, isn't it? I recognized him by his eye patch. My sister's son is a barudi, he works in the gunpowder factory the French set up on Rawda Island. This Franj is a good man, he hires Egyptian workers; the others think we're good for nothing. You must stop and have some coffee.'

A few minutes later, as they took their leave of the woman, she whispered to Zeinab: 'Ask him if there are any more jobs for barudis; my son also is looking for work. He worked in the spice trade, but with the English blockade the trade has fallen off, and he is out of work. So many people are out of work these days.'

Conté was carefully adding the sketches he had made to the stack in a leather folio. He smiled when he noticed Zeinab looking over his shoulder, and handed her the drawings one by one to look at before putting them away. There were rough sketches of the chick hatchery; a detailed sketch of the large gunpowder factory set up in the Qayt Bey Mosque; and one of a small olive press powered by a donkey. But there were also drawings he seemed to have made just because someone caught his eye, like an old, bowed water-carrier, a woman in a yashmak and black cloak, and a barber in a kaftan and turban shaving the head of an elderly customer sitting in a chair before him.

'Oh, I like this one.' Zeinab lingered over the one of the barber-shop. 'They look so real. You can tell how tired the customer is from the way he sits slumped like that.'

'If you like it, I will colour it for you with watercolours, and you can keep it.'

'Would you? For me?' The novelty of the idea of owning a painting left her round-eyed. Her father, along with the other members of the diwan, had had his portrait painted by the official French painter, Rigo, on orders from Bonaparte, and the portraits had been hung in the assembly hall of Elfi's palace. It had been explained to her that it was the custom with the Franj to paint the portraits of important people and display them in official places. Shaykh Bakri had been very sensible of the honour and had posed in his black turban and red, fur-lined pelisse, holding a long pipe in his hand. The resemblance was so good that, whenever she passed that particular picture in the hall, she walked sideways, drawing her shawl over her bosom.

'You paint better than Monsieur Rigo. But why a barber? He's not an important person.'

Conté laughed. 'Come, child, I have no pretensions to rival Rigo! Although I did once earn my living as a painter, a long time ago. Why the barber? Hmm, let me see. There are people you paint because they are important, and others you paint because they are beautiful, and still others you paint because they are interesting. *Exotique* – do you know what that word means?'

'Will you ever paint me?' As soon as the words left her mouth she blushed and pulled her shawl over the lower part of her face.

'We shall see, *ma petite* Zeinab, we shall see,' he smiled. 'Let us go, I have much work to do today. I need to supervise the lifting of that gigantic fist of Ramses from Memphis – what do you call the village? Mit Rahim – we're using a balloon to lift it and carry it to the Institute.'

She followed him, too embarrassed to ask: if indeed he did paint her one day, would it be because she was important, or beautiful, or *exotique*?

That night, for the first time since the insurrection, Zeinab did not cry herself to sleep. Her mind had at last found some relief from the anguished question: 'What will become of me?' She was no nearer an answer, but since the chief engineer had taken her under his wing, her worry and sorrow were lighter to bear. There was an air of quiet confidence about him, an unspoken kindness, that inspired trust. When she woke in the morning her thoughts turned to him as a flower starved of light turns to the sun.

NINE

The Second Insurrection

'For me, who have no wish to see assassinated one by one the rest of this army, to no real advantage for the homeland; for me who has seen this expedition as a complete failure . . . I will continue in my resolve without worrying whether blame or praise await me.'

Kléber to Desaix, on his decision to negotiate a retreat

'Kléber and his army can annoy us much less where they are than in almost any other possible situation.'

Lord Grenville to Prime Minister Pitt,

2 June 1800

Nicolas looked up as a visibly excited Geoffroy entered the loggia of the Institute, newspapers and letters in hand. 'Ah, Geoffroy! Any post for me?' Nicolas had still not received a single letter from his wife.

'No, I regret, *mon ami*. But I wouldn't worry; you know it's this cursed English blockade. But listen, Nicolas. Did you hear the latest? Headquarters is in great embarrassment. A letter from General Kléber to the Directoire has been intercepted and published by the English! It could not have come at a more delicate moment, with Poussielgue and Desaix in negotiations with the Grand Vizir at El-Arish. It seems Kléber's report painted a particularly dismal picture of our situation for the benefit of the Directoire: El-Arish fallen to the Turks after part of our garrison refused to fight; the army of the Grand Vizir massing in Syria; Jazzar of Acre undefeated; the indefatigable Beys

115

conducting a hit-and-run war of attrition. Murad in the south, with Wahabbi zealots from Arabia rallying to him in response to the Sultan's call for jihad; Ibrahim in Gaza; Elfi in the eastern provinces. The British fleet besieging us by sea. Our troops, reduced to half their original number, and short of everything from gunpowder to uniforms. The country unstable, the hearts of the people alienated. Cairo hostile, Alexandria indefensible. In brief, Kléber proposes to negotiate the return of Egypt to the authority of the Sultan, in exchange for the evacuation of our army at the expense of the Turkish fleet.'

'And the letter fell into the hands of the English? Good God! No doubt Commodore Sidney Smith will exploit it to the fullest in the negotiations at El-Arish. And one can only imagine the demoralizing effect its publication will have on our troops.'

'I for one am glad of anything that will persuade the Directoire to evacuate us back to France, and I know you feel the same in your heart, Nicolas. Is there a Frenchman in Egypt who is not weary of this enterprise and ready to go home? Besides, the situation in Europe is so grim, would the Army of the Orient not be better employed defending the Fatherland?' Geoffroy spread out fairly recent editions of the French and English papers on the table before Nicolas. 'Look at this.'

'Where did you get these, Geoffroy?'

'Sir Sidney Smith obligingly brings them to our attention.'

The newspapers painted a grim picture indeed. All hopes of reinforcements to Egypt were lost; Bonaparte seemed to have all but forgotten the stranded Army of the Orient while he staged *le coup d'état du 18 Brumaire* and seized for himself the great role of First Consul. The general was following in the footsteps of Caesar, and Nicolas suspected that Kléber was not the only man who resented his boundless ambition.

If there was to be an evacuation, thought Nicolas as he leafed through the papers, so be it. He had believed in this mission more than most, but even he must bow to the evidence. The entire enterprise was beginning to look foolish, even wicked. He wished to be done with it and return to his own country. Somehow, the home-sickness that had been tolerable when there was no end in sight was more acute now that he could see the day approaching. Impatience grew with hope, he found, contrary to popular wisdom.

But what of those they would leave behind, those who had lived with the French or served their interests, like the young Zeinab? His thoughts were interrupted by Geoffroy.

'As for me,' Geoffroy was saying, 'I have my bags packed, so to speak. I need only one more specimen, the Holy Grail that will immortalize my name and lend credence to the theory that the organ-ization of all vertebrates can be referred to a single archetype! I will employ what time is left to us here to complete my survey of the lizards of the Sinai and the fishes of the Red Sea. *N'en déplaise* Shaykh Jabarti, who rather cuttingly commented, when he attended my lecture on the Tétrodon at the Institute, that so many words expended on any one fish were wasted when God had created hundreds upon thousands. These people truly have no appreciation of the spirit of scientific inquiry!'

'A risky undertaking, is it not, an expedition into the Sinai, with the Bedouin on the warpath and the Mamlukes at large?'

'True! But we will evacuate Egypt any day now, and will regret not taking the opportunity to see more of the country while we could.' Geoffroy put an impulsive hand on Nicolas' shoulder. 'Why don't you come with me, *mon ami*?'

Nicolas hesitated. At that moment a change of air from Cairo was tempting. He smiled at Geoffroy. 'Why not!'

Three days into their expedition, Nicolas was beginning to suspect that their little party – the dragoman, the two Egyptian servants, the Bedouin guide, the camels – had drifted further north and east than anyone had intended, when suddenly they caught sight of a rapidly moving cloud of dust on the horizon. From the terror with which the guide cried out, 'Abbadi!' Nicolas assumed they were in grave danger. Geoffroy had come to the same conclusion: 'Bedouin marauders!'

In an instant the cloud of dust encircled them, but the cut-throats did not fall upon them immediately; instead they indicated that the French party should ride with them in a north-easterly direction. Geoffroy and Nicolas complied, encircled by the dust cloud as if they were travelling in the eye of a storm.

Riding in this trance-like state, Nicolas lost track of the time, until at length they passed a bank of russet cliffs, on the other side of which they saw rising in the shimmering haze of the desert a large pavilion, hung with colourful draperies and surmounted with a pennant, rather like the arbours scattered throughout French parks. In the background there was an encampment with tents and a bustle of horses and men. Nicolas and Geoffroy looked at each other in utter bemusement at this incongruous apparition in the middle of the desert.

'This is surely a hallucination brought on by heatstroke,' Geoffroy ventured, half seriously.

They were ordered to dismount and ushered forward unceremoniously by their escort. As they approached, Nicolas noted that the pavilion was indeed quite large, made of solid wood, and mounted on a dais, with several drapery-hung windows. A fine Turkish carpet led up the four or five steps to the entrance. Half-reclining on a cushioned divan facing the entrance was a blond-bearded man in an azure turban, holding a pipe in one hand and a mountain lion on a chain in the other.

They stumbled up the steps and proffered the salam greeting to the man in the azure turban, while the crouching lion raised its head and snuffled with an alarmingly inquisitive air. Silently the man inclined his head; close up, he looked so little like a Bedouin in every respect – dress, colouring and bearing – that Nicolas was lost in surmise.

The blue-eyed man questioned Geoffroy's dragoman curtly and, apparently satisfied with the answer, nodded in the direction of the cushioned divan next to him. Nicolas and Geoffroy took this for an invitation to be seated. It seemed a promising beginning, but until libation or collation had been offered, there was no assurance of safe conduct, as far as Nicolas understood the customs of the desert, so he remained on his guard.

There then followed the strangest interlude Nicolas had ever experienced. Along with Geoffroy, he attempted to satisfy his host's apparently insatiable curiosity as to their work and that of the Institute, with the dragoman interpreting. Their discourse ranged far and wide; their host seemed curious, not just about French military arts, which Nicolas expected, but also about European laws, systems of government, taxation – most memorably to Nicolas, he asked what the interest rate was in France, and seemed disappointed by the answer.

A lithe young Bedouin woman with bold brown eyes above her sequined veil slipped in and out of the pavilion, serving them dates and sheep's milk. When she had served their seated host, he reached out an arm and the girl slipped into its embrace and pressed her flank against his shoulder with a passionate abandon and a naturalness of manner that moved Nicolas. The man in the azure turban held the girl in the circle of his arm for a moment, caressing her haunches, and then released her with a sharp dismissive tap. She picked up the tray and exited.

The evening wore on in this manner, and eventually they were served lamb, baked entire in an earthenware casing buried in a sort of kiln in the sand; when it was ready, the pot was extracted and then broken to serve the tender meat.

'Quite a successful method of preparation,' Geoffroy hazarded in an aside to Nicolas, 'even if my appetite is somewhat spoilt by the assiduous attention of that lion.' After they had been served, the dish was removed and shared by the retainers outside the pavilion.

By the time the stars had filled the desert sky a mellow feeling of fatalism and the heavy lethargy of the replete began to engulf Nicolas and Geoffroy, and they dozed on and off to the melancholy air of a reedy flute playing somewhere outside the pavilion. Their host seemed engrossed in studying a book of astrology illustrated with constellations and zodiacs.

Without warning, the man in the blue turban clapped his hands and stood, as did the lion, and Nicolas and Geoffroy stumbled to their feet. All around them there was a bustle to pull up stakes and mount horse and camel. The pavilion was dismantled with greater speed and ingenuity than Nicolas would have believed possible, and the various components loaded on three or four camels. The kiln was covered up with sand. Within an hour everything was packed and the camp was on the move, and with it the French party.

Despite the fact that it was the middle of the night, their host seemed to be able to navigate perfectly by the stars; he knew the names of all the constellations and the major planets, by observation, apparently, in the untutored manner of the Bedouin. But by then Nicolas had no doubt that he was not one of them; he thought he recognized a Mamluke in him, and in a dozen of his horsemen, among the undifferentiated horde of the Abbadi.

'Where do you think we are being taken?' Geoffroy wondered as they rode side by side.

'Be patient. To inquire is useless at best, impolitic at worst. We shall find out sooner or later.'

They rode along for at least two hours and, as the day was breaking, a vast encampment loomed in the distance, flying the colours of the Grand Vizir.

'The Turks!' Geoffroy cried out in alarm. 'Our Mamluke host intends to hand us over in chains as prize prisoners to the Ottomans!'

'Wait –' Nicolas peered into the distance as they approached '– there are English flags as well. And look, our own Tricolour! This must be El-Arish!' He breathed a sigh of relief at identifying the camp where the truce negotiations were taking place.

At this point the Abbadi Bedouin fell back, leaving the Mamlukes to escort Nicolas and Geoffroy to the outskirts of the French camp. Having delivered them, the man in the azure turban and his followers departed.

Later, safe in the French camp, they recounted their adventure to General Desaix. 'Ah,' he nodded, 'that would be Elfi Bey. He has been an unofficial party to the negotiations. Naturally, the Beys have a great interest in the outcome and terms of any truce. He no doubt escorted you here for your own safety, in order to forestall an unfortunate incident that might compromise negotiations at this delicate stage. He is a grand original, according to Commodore Smith; quite unpredictable, keeps his own counsel and never lets his guard down. He is too suspicious to spend the night in the camp of any party to the talks, preferring to retreat to the desert. He has somehow managed to subjugate the Bedouin or reach an understanding with them, fractious as they are known to be, and moves about the desert as freely as a hawk on the mountaintop.'

'I am truly glad you decided to accompany me, *mon ami*,' said Geoffroy, clapping Nicolas on the shoulder. 'Without your testimony I fear our colleagues back in Cairo would accuse me of embellishing my report of this adventure, when we are next reunited under the eucalyptus tree in Qassim Bey's garden.'

'There won't be many more of those reunions in the garden, I imagine, if the negotiations here at El-Arish are advancing. We shall soon be leaving Egypt, is that not right, *mon général*?' Nicolas looked to Desaix, who nodded.

'Amen to that with all my heart!' Geoffroy exclaimed.

'Sitt Nafisa, Consul Magallon has arrived.'

Nafisa rearranged herself so that she was sitting up, with her back to the window, and waited for the ambassador to enter the reception hall. Briefly she wondered what had brought him here; the days when Charles Magallon might have paid her a courtesy call were long gone. No doubt it would have something to do with the imminent departure of the French; Elfi Bey had kept her appraised of the negotiations at El-Arish, and according to his last bulletin the terms of the evacuation were now on the table.

'Madame.' Magallon bowed in his courtly manner, and Nafisa responded in kind, gesturing to one of the eunuchs to bring refreshments.

'I apologize for the quality of the coffee, monsieur. The beans have been stored so long they have lost their flavour, but I have no other; the caravans from Yemen have been interrupted. No mastic or cardamom seed to flavour the coffee either, for the same reason. I am truly mortified to receive you so poorly in my house.'

'It's this cursed English blockade. They have their ships in the Red Sea now as well as the Mediterranean.'

'Of course; but the embargo is so drastic that everyone feels the pinch in Egypt, the poor more than the rest, and the suffering and discontent are laid at the door of the French occupation. My own wikala at Bab Zuweila is all but shut down. But how is Madame Magallon?'

The ambassador, long used to the ways of the East, understood the necessity for the ritual exchange of courtesies and responded in kind. Eventually he came to the purpose of his visit.

'What do you hear from Murad Bey, madame? He has surely grown weary of this long exile from his home and his family, and I imagine you, too, feel the separation sorely. It cannot be easy for your husband, living with a price on his head, knowing that even if he manages to elude General Desaix there is no guarantee that he will elude the plague – as I am sure you have heard, it has been even more devastating in Upper Egypt than in Cairo or the Delta.'

'Life and death are in the hands of the Almighty alone. No man postpones his fate, or advances it, by the merest moment of time.'

'Of course, of course.'

Nafisa smiled inwardly at Magallon's gesture of repressed impatience; she found the French invariably irritated by what they considered 'fatalism'. But, pious sentiments apart, what rational person could doubt that his fate was not in his hands? Could Magallon, or even Kléber answer for his life beyond tomorrow?

'Madame, General Kléber has sent me, in the spirit of the long friendship between us, to ask you to use your influence with Murad Bey and urge him to rally to the French side and accept the generous terms we would offer in exchange for a truce.'

'You overestimate my influence with my husband, sir.'

'Hardly, madame. In the event of conflict, Murad Bey might be considering rallying to the Ottoman cause, or even sitting on the fence, believing that victory for either side would not be entirely in his interest. But when it comes to a choice between two evils, one is clearly far greater than the other. I will confide in you something a person of your intelligence cannot but know already: the French are ready to leave Egypt to the Egyptians. The Turks, on the other hand, have every intention of seizing the opportunity to re-establish their full sovereignty over the country that was once their province. Egypt will lose the independence that your late husband Ali Bey fought so hard to establish thirty years ago. You will see the Ottoman Pasha ensconced in the Citadel again as master of Egypt, and a Turkish army will occupy your beloved Cairo once more. Make no mistake, madame, there will be no truce offered to any of the Beys – not Murad nor Ibrahim nor Elfi. You know better than anyone the treachery of the Porte.'

Why, Nafisa wondered, was Magallon pushing for a truce with Murad now, if the French were preparing to leave? Were they trying to ensure against some rearguard action, or treachery by the Turks? She couched her response in cautious terms.

'I cannot speak for my husband, sir, but Murad might be inclined to remain neutral in any fight with the Ottomans.' God willing, she thought, the day was fast approaching when she would have the satisfaction of knowing she had not broken the ties of civility with the French, right to the last moment.

A month later, the shrill notes of pipes and the ululations of rejoicing outside Sitt Nafisa's window announced the conclusion of a treaty between the French and the Turkish camps at El Arish. The rabble in the street outside had already lost all dread of the French, and insulted, cursed and mocked the troops. Schoolmasters collected the children to march in bands around the city, reciting insolent rhymes against the Franj and their supporters, chanting: 'Victory to the Sultan and death to Fart Rumman!'

The French had translated the truce agreement into Arabic and printed many copies, distributing them in the streets and markets. Nafisa had read all twenty-two stipulations carefully. The French would withdraw from Cairo to three ports: Rosetta, Aboukir and Alexandria, from whence they would be repatriated on Turkish ships. They would evacuate Cairo in forty days. Forty days! After a year and a half of French rule, it seemed hard to believe that it would be over within weeks.

There were two developments that affected her most directly. One was the stipulation restituting all money and property seized from Cairenes; she would be able to fund her sabil again, and fulfil her vow to build a school for the children of the poor. The other was that the amirs were invited to return to Cairo, to their homes and their families. She would finally be reunited with Murad after a separation that had lasted, unbroken, since he'd left to fight the French at Imbaba. And Elfi? The thought barely crossed her mind before she dismissed it with an inexplicable twinge of guilt.

She wondered about the fate of collaborators like Shaykh Bakri. And what of his blameless young daughter? Nafisa had taken an interest in the child ever since the day of the insurrection when she had saved her from the mob. What would become of her after the evacuation? The French had made provisions in the treaty to protect those who had collaborated with them, but would such provisions prove enforceable? She prayed it was not too late for amnesty, and a general reconciliation among the various communities that had been torn by their divided loyalties under the French. 'May God bring this matter to a peaceful end,' she murmured, her relief at the announcement of the end of the occupation tempered by an undercurrent of anxiety when she considered all the eventualities that might intervene between the moment of the announcement and the day of the departure of the last French soldier from the soil of Egypt. And what of the day after? Fervently as she wished to see the French gone, she harboured deep misgivings about the role the Turks would play in the aftermath. Already, unit after unit of Ottoman troops was filing into Cairo, and they had immediately lapsed into their abusive ways.

Nafisa's thoughts were interrupted by the entrance of her eunuch, carrying a letter. Barquq had that air of secrecy he adopted to deliver forbidden correspondence from the amirs. Could this be the letter announcing Murad's imminent arrival? Or would it be Elfi's?

Nicolas Conté headed towards the Ezbekiah headquarters, looking around him with the eyes of a man who would soon be seeing Cairo for the last time. He was surprised to find that his emotions were mixed. His joy at the prospect of seeing the coastline of France and being reunited with his family should have been as cloudless as a clear summer sky. Yet he could not help a nagging feeling of doubt and dissatisfaction.

How could he not spare a care for those they were leaving behind who had thrown their lot in with the French so irrevocably and compromised themselves in their service so thoroughly? Provisions had been made to try to ensure they need fear no reprisals, but their safety could not be guaranteed. Many of the locals appointed to high office under the occupation – Yacub, who had loyally served General Desaix as quartermaster during the Upper Egypt campaign against his former patron, Murad Bey; Malti, chief tax collector; Papas Oglu, head of the Greek militia; not to mention Bartholomew, the much reviled chief of police – belonged to Copt, Greek or other minority communities, and Nicolas feared for them in the case of a reversal of fortune.

He feared, too, for those members of the diwan who had been close collaborators, none more so than Shaykh Bakri. Here Nicolas felt a disquieting tightness in his chest: it was the fate of the daughter, Zeinab, that troubled him most acutely. Over the past few months that she had been a helpmeet to him, he had developed an attachment, a certain sense of responsibility, towards the girl. He worried that, when the French departed, she would be forced to depend on the precarious protection of her father. He wished he were more certain that Shaykh Bakri's influence could be counted on to shield his daughter from reprisals.

Nicolas was jolted out of his disquieting reflections when he reached Elfi's palace to find headquarters in a state of crisis. In the inner courtyard Kléber could be heard roaring like a wounded bull.

125

Nicolas grabbed General Poussielgue by the arm as he passed. 'General, what has occurred?'

'Kléber just received the news that Admiral Lord Keith has refused to ratify the El-Arish Convention, on the grounds that the terms are too favourable to the French. Apparently he insists that the Army of the Orient constitute itself prisoner before the English will agree to the evacuation. The letter Lord Keith has sent is dated anterior to the signing of the convention, but it only reached us today.'

Nicolas was outraged. 'We were tricked by Commodore Smith!'

'I don't believe so. Sir Sidney Smith is so genuinely mortified that one must believe he has no hand in this perfidy. Any blame that may be attached to him is rather of the nature of overstepping the bounds of his mandate in negotiating the truce. He has asked General Kléber to allow him time to seek clarification from London. But Kléber feels tricked and betrayed. He has called off the truce and is determined to stay and fight. Citoyen, I needn't tell you that the news must be kept from the population of Cairo for as long as possible.'

'Of course.' Nicolas grasped the direness of the situation instantly. With the Turkish army outside the city walls, and Turkish troops and Mamlukes within, once word got out that the truce had been broken, all hell would break loose.

'*Hamdillah al-salama*, Elfi Bey, Cairo is illuminated by your presence,' Nafisa offered the conventional greeting to someone returning from a long voyage.

'It is illuminated by the light of its people, I thank you,' Elfi returned.

Nafisa found his appearance a great contrast to the last time she had laid eyes on him, when he had been disguised as a beggar woman. Now he stood before her dressed in his finery: an azure turban, a white coat trimmed with gold braid, and high boots in the style of the Franj. But the two years of harsh desert life had left their mark in the deep tan of his lean face, the crinkles at the corners of his hard blue eyes, the deep creases where the tan had not penetrated.

The tip of the third finger of his right hand was cut off below the knuckle, an injury sustained at the battle of Imbaba.

He had announced his visit in true Mamluke-style, preceded by servants bearing gifts. Her eunuchs in the downstairs hall were unloading the presents he had brought from Syria: bolts of finest damascene silk, caskets of wood inlaid with ivory and mother-of-pearl, and perhaps most precious of all, sacks of pine nuts, pistachios, dried figs, spices, and sahlep, the powdered root of mountain orchids – all in short supply since the blockade.

'You are too kind, Elfi Bey. Your safety alone is present enough.'

'It is less than a token, Sitt Nafisa.'

'How do you find Cairo after this long absence?'

'Much changed. Familiar landmarks gone. New thoroughfares cutting across the city. Buildings razed and others elevated, just as among the citizenry, the high are brought low, and the low high. I have not been to visit my Ezbekiah house yet, but I am prepared to find it much changed. I hear General Kléber has had it remodelled to suit Franj custom: walls removed between apartments, steps between the public and private spaces levelled. But no matter; at least it is still standing.'

The head eunuch came in bearing a tray with cups of creamy milk thickened with sahlep, the top dusted with cinnamon and a sprinkling of chopped pistachios.

'Ah,' Elfi took an appreciative sip. 'How goes the world, Sitt Nafisa?'

'It is a white day, Elfi Bey, when we can see the end of our troubles! I will finally be able to honour my vow to complete the sabil. It will be a proper refuge, with a hostel for lodging and food and baths. I have even thought of an innovation: the furnaces that will be used to heat the water for the baths can also provide free cooking facilities for the poor in the neighbourhood; they can bring their pots of beans to cook.'

Elfi smiled, and she was a little embarrassed at her own enthusiasm over such mundane details, but he nodded encouragingly and she continued: '*Inshallah*, I will build a school for children of the poor, on the second floor of the sabil.' She thought of the little ones sitting scrubbed and bright-eyed at their books, bellies replete with the hot meal they had been served at noonday.

'You have cherished your dream through these years when all the world turned upside down?'

'It is a vow I made on my pilgrimage to Mecca, Elfi Bey, not a dream, and such vows cannot be broken without the gravest consequences.'

He nodded but offered no comment. He was irreligious, Nafisa knew, and not only because he had been raised without religious instruction; if he believed in anything, it was the signs of the stars.

Two of the maids came in with trays of fritters in honey syrup and a selection of sweetmeats. He waved them away and turned to Nafisa. 'And you, lady? Have you been well?'

Her hand went to her cheek; she knew she looked pale. His solicitude, catching her off guard, troubled her on a deeper level than she was willing to acknowledge.

'These two years have taken their toll on all of us, Elfi Bey. The plague as well, although my own household has largely been spared. The measures the French imposed, severe as they were, no doubt helped to curtail the spread of the epidemic.'

Elfi nodded. 'We must adopt the quarantine and other measures even after the French are gone. There's much that we can learn from them.'

'But will it not be up to the Turks? It seems to me they are positioning themselves to establish the Sultan's full sovereignty as soon as the last Frenchman has embarked.'

'That's their plan, clearly, but when the time comes we can deal with the Turks on our own terms, as we have before. I was there at the negotiations at El-Arish. The Porte is weak, and propped up only by the English; they are the true masters of the sea. Their military arts and their science rival those of the French, and we must take from them all we can to rebuild Egypt. Not just the military arts – the laws, the administration. Everything must change, or this country will fall prey again, to the French or the English or another power. The Ottomans can no longer protect us.'

Nafisa pressed her fingertips against her temples; he was right, and she knew that her world would never again turn on its axis in the way it had before the French occupation. Everything must change. Yet there had been the comfort of familiarity in the ways of old; the challenge of the days ahead seemed suddenly overwhelming. She was overcome by a wave of physical weariness. Elfi's eyes narrowed.

'Have you heard from Murad Bey when he will come to the city, Sitt Nafisa?'

'He has sent no word. Perhaps he fears some treachery on the part of the French, or more likely the Ottomans.'

A faint flicker of disdain crossed Elfi's face. 'In his place, I would have run the risk.'

He said nothing more, but she understood him and flushed, partly at the mortification of having to acknowledge that her husband had not missed her sufficiently in two years to brave coming to see her, and partly at the homage implicit in Elfi's elliptical remark. Like a sudden torrential rain after a long, dry spell, she found herself awash with emotions she thought she had put behind her: the aching hunger of the skin, and a deeper longing, for comfort and support. This sudden surge blindsided her and she was as shocked as if it had started to snow in the middle of the Sahara desert.

She turned to the window till she had regained her composure, and when she looked back she saw that Elfi had turned away himself, to spare her or to hide his own discomfiture, she could not tell. They stood, as if shackled to the floor, a few feet from each other. It was ironic, she thought, that they were both iron-bound by loyalty to a man who had long lost his claim to their love or admiration.

She cleared her throat. 'You know Murad signed a truce with the French in return for governorship of Upper Egypt?' She spoke in order to re-establish a normal tone, as much as anything. 'He does not trust the Turks; he feels they will turn against him for his past insults and injuries. He wrote to me: "The arrow that struck the eagle was an arrow made of an eagle's feather."'

'Yes.' Elfi's response was brusque. 'He is right not to trust the Ottomans, but what the French have offered him is worth no more than the paper on which it is written; they are leaving, and the Ottomans might choose not to honour the agreement. On this matter I part ways with Murad Bey; he knows my mind. But he needs fear no betrayal from me. I will always bear a debt to him – and to his house.'

Nafisa understood his allusion. Elfi took a step towards her.

'Know that you can always count on me. You have carried a heavy burden alone, but the worst is behind us. And if ever there is any way I can lighten your load in the days to come –'

A cannon roared in the distance, and Elfi stopped short. 'That's coming from the east, from Heliopolis. Kléber rode out at dawn this morning at the head of his troops and cannon; they put it about that it was part of their plan to evacuate their artillery. But these guns – there's some treachery afoot.'

A clamour in the street was swiftly followed by pounding on the door. Nafisa's eunuch appeared, his impassivity shaken for the first time she could remember. 'There is a messenger for Elfi Bey from his scouts outside the city. The commander of the French is attacking the Vizir's encampment at Heliopolis!'

'That can't be!' Nafisa was astounded.

Elfi was already at the door. 'Send to Murad Bey; tell him Kléber broke the armistice, we must defend Cairo.' Then he turned on his heel and was gone.

TEN

The Assassination

'At the moment, my dear General, we must squeeze Egypt as the
lemonade seller squeezes a lemon, and when we have extracted the last
drop, both in monies and in kind, we will have barely enough for our
needs under the circumstances.'

Kléber writing to Dugua, 22 January 1800

Nafisa tensed, listening for the sound of hoof beats, in the sudden
silence of the French guns. Looking at the devastation around her,
she could hardly recognize her own city. After six weeks of constant
bombardment from the French forts, day and night, the Ezbekiah
and Bulaq were reduced to piles of rubble where the very streets
were no longer distinguishable. Kléber, with the element of surprise
in his favour, had swiftly dispatched the Turkish forces at Heliopolis,
but Cairo erupted in a general insurgency that had held out week
after bloody week. With Elfi, Ibrahim and other Mamlukes within
the walls, the resistance this time was organized, determined, and
armed with ammunition: the barudis took over the gunpowder
factories the French had built on Rawda Island.

By mid-March, with Cairo in ruins, Kléber offered the Egyptians
terms of surrender. Shaykh Jabarti had come to tell Nafisa that the
notables of the diwan were ready to accept, but the popular uprising
had spun out of their control and they had no influence. The amirs
stood their ground and fighting raged on in Cairo and Bulaq.

131

Only Murad had stayed out of the city and out of the fighting, observing his truce with the French.

Now it was near the end of April, and the Khamaseen winds blew over the dismal ruins of the city. Ibrahim and Elfi were at this very moment in negotiation with the French generals, and Nafisa held her breath, waiting for the arrival of a courier with news of the outcome. But when she heard riders approaching her door, it was Elfi Bey himself that Barquq came up to announce.

Elfi looked battered and bitter. 'It is over, Sitt Nafisa. We will not hold Cairo this day.' His shoulders sagged. 'Kléber has given us three days to vacate the city: Ibrahim Bey and I, the other amirs, all our Mamlukes. But we will live to fight another day, mark my words. The French know that they will leave, sooner or later.' He made no reproach, nor even a mention, of Murad's abandonment of his brethren and his city in their time of greatest trouble, and for this Nafisa was grateful.

'May I next see your face in good health, Sitt Nafisa.' He brought his hand to his brow and his heart.

'May you go and return in peace, Elfi Bey.'

'Sitt Zeinab, it is over, the insurrection is over, the French are back in possession of Cairo!'

Dada's considerable bulk blocked the doorway as she paused to catch her breath, one hand leaning on the doorjamb and the other on her vast chest. It was the first time Zeinab had seen her nurse since the day the truce was broken. That day, when the fighting and the uprising broke out, a harried-looking Nicolas Conté had come to take her to the house in Nasiriya. 'You must not think of going back to your father's house now,' he warned her. 'You will be safe here at the Institute, it is under heavy guard, but don't show your face outside till we have the city under control again.' In the six weeks since then, Zeinab had the time to wonder at his solicitude for her safety at a moment of crisis when he was needed so acutely elsewhere. He made the effort to check on her every few days, hurried visits that were her sole contact with the roiling world outside the French Institute.

She had been without news of her family since the uprising, until the welcome reappearance of Dada. She threw her arms around her nurse's neck.

'Dada, Dada, what news of my parents? How is my little brother? Did you just come from them?'

'Oh, Sitt Zeinab, you will never believe the indignities we have suffered! A rampaging mob from the Moroccan quarter attacked your father's house in Ezbekiah the day the insurrection broke out. They seized Shaykh Bakri and stripped him and dragged him bareheaded in the streets to be jeered at and pelted with rotten vegetables! The house has been pillaged by the mob, and some of the women servants raped, God save us!' The nurse slapped her cheeks in despair.

Zeinab went pale with horror and the nurse changed her tune and tried to comfort her. 'But never you mind, Sitt Zeinab, the world has turned again, and now with the French back in power your father is complaining to them of the abuse that landed on his head on account of his befriending them, and he is asking to be compensated for his losses. He is the only Muslim exempt from the punitive levy the French are imposing on Muslims, regardless whether or not they were involved in the uprising. The Christians and the Greeks are exempt, as they took no part, and many were victims themselves – but your father is the only Muslim.'

The nurse shook her head. 'There is such bad blood now between Muslim and Christian, it will never be the same between them again. Even the members of the diwan were locked up in a room at French headquarters for hours till they urinated on themselves or through the window. Then they were paraded through the streets behind Kléber's carriage to the jeers and insults of some of the Copts and the Syrian Orthodox. Mark my words, Sitt Zeinab, the abuses on both sides will not be forgotten. People have long memories. We will see worse days to come.'

The nurse's tone turned bitter again. 'I hide my face when I go out of your father's house into the street, Sitt Zeinab, but still people spit at me and revile Shaykh Bakri. If it were not that I had nursed you with these very teats, I wouldn't stay with your family another hour. God help us the day the French leave for real! And now I must go before curfew, I only promised your mother I would see if you were safe, I'll try to come back later. Now don't hang onto my skirts, for pity's sake!'

Zeinab let her go and buried her head in her pillow again. Cairo was a city divided, and there was no place for her on either side.

A peremptory knocking on the door startled her and she jumped up and wiped her face hastily with her shawl. Nicolas Conté was at the door.

'What's this? You've been crying? This won't do at all, you'll cry yourself half blind at this rate, and then you won't be any use to me or to the Institute. Go wash your face and put on something pretty, I'll take you to the Ezbekiah gardens for a walk this afternoon. I have some business with General Kléber. I'll come to fetch you at two o'clock, so don't keep me waiting.'

There was such a calm authority about the chief engineer that Zeinab's worst fears abated and she found herself obeying him. She bathed her face over and over till the redness and swelling subsided, and squeezed herself into her one French frock, the violet-embroidered white muslin the lady general had given her the day of the first insurrection. She did her best to comb her long hair and twist it into a semblance of the knots the French ladies favoured.

That afternoon, as they dismounted from their hired donkeys and entered French headquarters at the Ezbekiah, the guards saluted when they recognized the chief engineer and opened the gates to Elfi's palace; they relaxed their alert stance long enough to follow Zeinab with curious but appreciative glances.

Nicolas noticed and raised an approving eyebrow at her. 'That's a fetching bonnet.'

'Merci,' Zeinab blushed. 'Madame Verdier's maid sewed it up for me, to match the dress she gave me two years ago.'

'That dress does look rather too small for you,' Nicolas frowned appraisingly. 'Surely the Republic owes you a new frock. Indeed, you should officially be on the payroll for your services to the Institute.

134

Perhaps a silk dress, hmm? What colour? None of those pale pinks or pastel blues, they wouldn't suit your colouring. Let me think . . .'

Zeinab blushed with pleasure and reflexively drew the edge of her shawl across her face, then remembered that Madame Verdier frowned on the gesture – 'a harem reflex', she called it – and dropped the shawl, raised her chin and straightened her shoulders.

It was still early in the afternoon, and they strolled at a leisurely pace in the courtyard of Elfi's palace, waiting for General Kléber to make an appearance. The commandant's headquarters was one of the few houses in Ezbekiah that had escaped the recent bombardment.

Nicolas stopped under the shade of the covered walkway and leaned against the trunk of a large carob tree, propping his sketchpad on his knee. Zeinab spread her shawl on the grass and sat down, tucking her feet to one side of her hips. She was used to the chief engineer suddenly taking it into his head to start sketching, and she knew it could take a while, so she might as well make herself comfortable.

In a minute he called to her: 'Take off the bonnet.'

'Why? Isn't it pretty?'

'It is very becoming, but take it off anyway. You're sitting in the shade, you don't need it.'

Zeinab untied the pale green ribbons and carefully took off the bonnet and set it in her lap, admiring the violet pansies that matched the bouquets embroidered on the faded muslin dress. She watched the soldiers crossing the courtyard; some Frenchmen in civilian clothing were walking in pairs or chatting in corners, waiting for the commandant.

She wondered if her parents would recognize her if they saw her. Once when Conté had sighed, as he paused in the middle of writing a letter, and complained that he had not seen his family in two years, she had answered that she had not seen her own people in nearly as long, and he had run his finger down her cheek and nodded. 'It is true, *ma petite*, I know. You must miss them. But you will be going back to them soon.' It had seemed to her that there was an undercurrent of regret in his voice when he said it, or had she imagined it?

That had been when the French were in the process of evacuating. How the world had changed since then! Now she could not go back to her family. There was no place for her; no place, except her precarious perch at the side of this kind man who was looking at her now, with his painter's eye that saw her and yet did not see her. She sat up.

'Have you been drawing me?'

'Yes.'

'Let me see!'

'Not yet. No, I said, sit back down.'

'But why are you drawing me? Is it because I am *exotique*?'

'You are, but that's not the reason.'

Her eyes widened and her voice dropped to a whisper. 'Then because I am beautiful?'

'You are, but that's not it.'

'But it can't be because I am important? I'm not important at all.'

'You are. To me, you are.'

This time Zeinab did not reach for her shawl to cover her face; she forgot to feel shy. His words suffused her with warmth and confusion; she was not sure how she was supposed to take them. But a bustle by the gate distracted her: General Kléber was making his entrance, with one of the engineers by his side, talking energetically. How tall and ruddy and imposing the general was, with his flaxen curls and big strides! Nicolas was tanned dark as a Bedouin from the sun, and his eye patch made the children in the street call him the One-eyed. Zeinab looked from one to the other, and knew that it was unreasonable of her to find the chief engineer handsomer than General Kléber, but there it was; she couldn't help it.

'Ah, there's the general, and Protain, bending his ear already.' Nicolas began collecting his papers in the leather-bound folio. 'Let me put this sketch away, I'll finish it later. They will come in our direction in a minute.'

A man in Arab dress was following the general through the gate, and Kléber dismissed the beggar, saying, '*Ma feesh*' – I have nothing. But the man persisted, following him with his left hand extended as if reaching to kiss the general's hand. Kléber proffered his hand and the man closed in on him, then suddenly whipped out a dagger and stabbed him repeatedly. Kléber screamed and fell, and Protain shouted for help. The man turned on the engineer and stabbed him and then fled through the gate.

It all happened in seconds. By the time the soldiers outside the gates rushed in, by the time Conté dropped his folder and ran across the garden, the man had disappeared and Kléber was dead.

A black day, Nafisa lamented as she waited impatiently for Shaykh Jabarti. A black day, and God save them from the evil consequences! As soon as the shaykh arrived, she hurried to meet him in the upper hall.

'Well, Shaykh Jabarti, what news?'

'They found the assassin, Sitt Nafisa. He is a Syrian, from Aleppo, named Sulayman, twenty-four years of age, a scribe by occupation, who arrived in Cairo five months ago, and took lodging at the Azhar Mosque.'

'Is he definitely the culprit?'

'There is no doubt of it. He was found with the murder weapon on him, and the engineer who was with Kléber at the time recognized him. But the question now is who instigated this plot. The French asked him if he knew the Grand Vizir of Turkey, and he replied that an Arab like him would not know the Grand Vizir. He was repeatedly asked whether anyone had conspired in his plot, and he denied it. Finally, under torture, he confessed. Apparently there is a link between him and the Grand Vizir through a low-level Ottoman officer named Ahmed Agha he met in a mosque in Jerusalem. But he acted alone, although he had told three ulema at the mosque of his intention the morning of the murder, and they did not denounce him to the French.' Shaykh Jabarti exhaled with relief. 'Thank God, a great calamity has been averted. The French realize the people of Cairo are innocent of the crime.' In the confusion following the assassination the French had trained their guns on the city as if they would obliterate it from the face of the earth.

Nafisa nodded. '*Hamdillah*, thank God Cairo will be spared.'

'The diwan has asked the French to lock the gates of the Azhar Mosque and university; we fear some treachery could lead to a repeat of the terrible desecration that took place after the first insurrection of Cairo. Better to have the Azhar locked up, till God knows when, than to see the horses of the French defile it with their manure.'

'Indeed. But what of the three ulema named by the assassin?'

'Bartholomew was sent to arrest them, and they are being interrogated separately and collectively and under duress. But you will wonder at French justice, Sitt Nafisa,' Jabarti continued, with grudging admiration. 'Rather than summarily executing the assassin based on his confession alone, they instituted a lengthy court proceeding, with judges, and prosecutors, and juries, from among the French generals and scholars. They heard witnesses, and recorded their accounts, and the results of the interrogations and the confessions. All of these details they will publish in long pamphlets in French, Arabic and Turkish, many copies of which they will distribute among the people, that all might see the quality of French justice.'

Jabarti rose, gathering the sleeves of his turban. 'By your leave, Sitt Nafisa, I will head for Scorpion Hill, where the sentence will be executed immediately after the funeral procession for General Kléber. I can hear the pipes and drums, they are returning.'

Nicolas hurried in the direction of the Fort of the Institute on Scorpion Hill. He had not had time to catch his breath since the fateful moment in Elfi's garden when he had heard Kléber cry out and seen him fall. He had been drafted to sit on the commission investigating the assassination, although, as he pointed out, he was no *jurisconsulte*. But then, neither was General Reynier, who chaired the commission, nor Le Père, director of *Ponts et Chaussées*, who acted as public prosecutor. Nicolas had done the best he could, his only guides his conscience and the lights of reason and judgment. Immediately after sentence was passed, he was entrusted with organizing the funeral rites for General Kléber. He had directed the procession with all the pomp and ceremonial honours possible under the circumstances. The execution was scheduled to take place immediately after.

On Scorpion Hill he found a place next to Dr Desgenettes, who was watching the gallows being raised. 'A bad business, if we are now to contend with religious fanaticism.' The doctor shook his head, as the four culprits were dragged in chains to the gallows by Bartholomew.

Nicolas nodded. 'Bonaparte once told me that Ambassador Volney had warned him that in Egypt he would wage battle against three enemies: the English, the Ottomans, and Islam, and that the last would be the most intractable. Volney might yet prove prescient.'

Geoffroy St-Hilaire joined them. 'Have you heard the latest? Bartholomew has expressly asked for the honour of acting as executioner.'

At a distance of a few feet away from the gallows and the French, a vast crowd of Egyptians watched, silent, and sullen. A drum roll announced the first execution. First the three accomplices had their heads cut off, under the attentive but calm eyes of Sulayman the Aleppin. Then followed the burning of Sulayman's wrist, during which he uttered no complaint.

'That must be an excruciating operation,' Desgenettes remarked with a physician's detachment, 'I wonder he can bear it without so much as a change of expression.'

Then suddenly a piece of wood flew off the fire and landed on the assassin's elbow. He uttered a cry and demanded something of Bartholomew. Geoffroy went over to one of the Greek interpreters standing nearby and asked him what the exchange was about. A moment later he returned and repeated the translation, with some relish, for the benefit of Nicolas and Desgenettes. 'Apparently the assassin asked that this additional pain be removed, and Bartholomew mocked him: "What, a man as brave as you, afraid of a slight pain? What is that, compared to the pain you have been suffering for a quarter of an hour with such courage?" Sulayman responded: "Infidel dog, know that you are not worth talking to me; do your duty in silence; the pain I was complaining of was not included in the sentence of my judges."'

After the burning of the wrist, Sulayman of Aleppo was impaled. 'How long will his agony be prolonged?' Geoffroy asked the doctor. 'Four or five hours.'

'Under the circumstances, one cannot help but think that the guillotine is indeed a merciful instrument.'

'Come, Docteur, Geoffroy, I have neither the time nor the stomach to watch that long,' said Nicolas, turning away. 'Will you walk back with me?'

'Willingly.' Both men joined him.

'No one can say justice was not done,' Nicolas remarked, as they headed downhill. Yet he knew the mood of the generals and the troops was turning ugly and that General Menou, who had been appointed commander-in-chief in the interim was bearing the brunt. Damas and Reynier were leading the *fronde*. 'But General Menou finds himself in an unenviable position.'

Desgenettes seemed to read his mind. 'Indeed. He is not forgiven for having professed his adherence to Islam, or for having married a Muslim woman. He is not forgiven for being elderly and corpulent and *vieille* noblesse – in short, everything Kléber was not and nothing of what he was.'

'Exactly! The troops throw his aristocratic origins in his face, muttering about the "*ci-devant* Comte de Menou", and even try to make something of the fact that the crest on his family's arms bears the head of a Moor – no doubt an innocuous reference to some loyal service in the Crusades.'

'It is entirely unreasonable,' Geoffroy concurred. 'He is even accused of treason for having named his son Sulayman.'

'I have it from my young assistant, Zeinab, that it is as common a name among Muslims as it is among Jews, being the name of the prophet Solomon, so that it is no more significant than Jacques among us,' Nicolas pointed out.

He had mentioned Zeinab naturally enough, but Desgenettes gave him a sharp look. Nicolas continued, oblivious: 'And he is no more popular with the natives than with our own countrymen. The tax reforms he has been trying to institute are causing nothing but resentment. Apparently the Egyptians prefer the arbitrary exactions of the Mamlukes!'

'It is the Coptic tax collectors who abuse their power and bring odium on Menou's head, not to mention on their own,' Geoffroy pointed out.

'But the Copts had a monopoly on the profession under the Mamlukes! At least from what Zeinab tells me.'

'They did, but their worst abuses were checked by their fear of their masters. Under French rule, however, they conduct themselves with impunity, insolence and often outright extortion, all of which are laid at the door of Menou's administration. Did you hear what Chevalier Lascaris suggested to Menou?'

Nicolas and Desgenettes were intrigued. 'What?'

'Lascaris proposes to turn this simmering hostility between the sects to our advantage by fanning the flames of sectarian strife rather than stamping them out. He suggested that Menou take the title "protector of religions" and, by posing as arbiter, rule through "the equilibrium of opposing fanaticisms."'

'And what was Menou's response?'

'The general opted to disregard this proposal.'

'Perhaps only a renegade Knight of Malta can hatch such machinations,' Desgenettes remarked. 'But one must avow it was ingenious.'

Nicolas tried to muster an amused smile, but the doctor looked at him thoughtfully. 'It is somewhat surprising to find you so incensed by the hostility towards Menou, *mon cher* Conté. I thought you had little sympathy for him?'

Nicolas was speechless, suddenly understanding why Menou's plight troubled him so. The general was paying the painful price for the transgression of loving and marrying outside his own race and religion. Conté's empathy for the man was born of his own feelings for Zeinab.

For the first time, he was constrained to examine the real nature of his feelings for the girl. His attachment to her had grown insensibly until he found himself enchanted by her presence, enervated by her absence, and solicitous for her happiness. She might be younger than his own daughter, but he could no longer delude himself that this was displaced paternal affection on his part. Nor could he lay his sentiments at the door of mere lust or ennui, although he had suffered, as much as any man, from the long celibacy imposed by this ill-fated expedition. It was not an ephemeral liaison that he sought, *faute de mieux.*

It would have been infinitely simpler if she had been a Mamluka, not a well-born young woman from a prominent family. Simply taking her as a mistress would be to do her a wrong.

And what a grotesque, ill-matched couple they would make! If only he thought his feelings for the girl were unreciprocated, he would have found it easier to ignore them. But untutored as this girl was in the coquetry of Frenchwomen, she betrayed her attachment by unmistakable signs and gestures every time they met. And yet, might this not be the natural reflex of a child cut off from her parents and her own kind, turning to the person she perceived as her guardian? Her father was so reviled by his compatriots that she was hissed whenever she made an appearance in the street. She was really only safe within the walls of the French zones in Ezbekiah or Nasiriya, although she had no real place there either, and was regarded by his countrymen at best with condescension and at worst with bigotry.

By offering her protection in the short term, might he not be placing her at even greater risk in the long term, when the French evacuated?

And when that day came, what of his family in France? Would his wise, sweet wife forgive him a liaison of circumstance, as he would forgive her anything – indeed, would not even wish to know – if she had sought temporary solace in someone else's arms?

The irony of his situation struck him. He had the undeserved reputation of being a man who had the answers to all problems, and here he was tormented by his feelings for a young girl. But he was so little used, and so little suited, to debating matters of the heart, particularly when complicated by matters of conscience. The girl was so young and so friendless, he felt morally responsible for his behaviour towards her.

'You seem sadly preoccupied, *mon ami*,' Desgenettes interrupted his soul-searching when they reached the gate of the Institute in Nasiriya. 'What problem can be troubling you so?'

Nicolas started, realizing that he had been lost in his thoughts for a quarter of an hour and that his two companions were eyeing him with a mixture of curiosity and concern. 'Right now, *mes amis*,' he tried to make light of his distraction, 'I would gladly exchange this particular preoccupation for the most tortuous problems of engineering, for weights and measurements and angles and the predictable laws of Physics!'

ELEVEN

The Dangerous Liaison

'Soldiers, know how to be generous towards the Egyptians. But what
am I saying! The Egyptians are French today; they are your brothers.'
General Menou, Commander in Chief of the French army in Egypt,
ordre du jour of 18 Fructidor, year 8

'So, *ma petite*, what do you think of our Republican New Year festival?'

Zeinab contemplated the gigantic fake pyramid the chief engineer
had ordered erected in the middle of the square. It was surmounted
by strange objects and covered with inscriptions. 'It is very fine
but . . . but what does it all mean?' she asked Nicolas timidly.

'Ah! Exactly as I told General Menou. All this symbolism is likely
to be entirely lost on the native population of Cairo and, as far as
our own troops, I doubt it will do much to raise their morale. He
asked me to organize a New Year festival around the theme of a
marriage of symbols – or a symbolic marriage, if you wish – between
the Revolution and Islam: the Rights of Man paired with the Koran,
the Phrygian bonnet with the Crescent, the Tricolore with the
Pyramid, and so forth. I deem that I am better employed devoting
my energies to setting up wool factories to clothe our threadbare
troops this winter.'

Zeinab hesitated but then spoke up. 'I overheard some of the
comments people were making. They couldn't understand all
the speeches, and they think the pyramid symbolizes the victory of the
French over the Egyptians.'

Nicolas threw his hands up in the air. 'I told Menou I feared that this latest ill-conceived scheme to raise public morale would fall in the water, so to speak, as the Montgolfière did! And still the general insisted.'

'But the illuminations were a great success,' Zeinab tried to console him.

'The illuminations I left to your compatriots, they are experts in the matter.'

He took Zeinab by the hand to walk her around the fake pyramid, but she caught the contemptuous glances of some of the Cairenes milling around, and withdrew her hand, pulling her shawl about her hair. 'Can we go back to the Institute now, please?'

Nicolas looked at her, the shadow of a puzzled frown falling across his face. 'Of course, *ma petite*. I only thought the outing might entertain you.'

She was preoccupied as they made their way back to the Institute and strolled through Qassim Bey's garden in the fading light. 'You seem quiet, *ma petite*. Would it please you to go to the Tivoli this evening for a cup of Wolmar's excellent ratafia, and a little dancing? I read in the *Courier* that there will be a ball.'

'But I don't dance.'

'Then I will undertake to teach you. You may not think it to look at me, but I was quite lively on the dance floor in my day.'

'Another time, perhaps.' Zeinab didn't tell him that it upset her, the way some of the Egyptians in the crowd had stared at her and then turned away and spat on the ground. And at the Comédie or the Tivoli, the French looked at her as if they did not know what to make of her, tagging along behind Nicolas like the Mamluka concubines of the generals.

Nicolas stopped under the sycamore tree and took her chin in his hand.

'What is going on behind those extraordinary eyes of yours? Are you homesick? Is that it? Do you want to return to your family?'

Her head spun in miserable confusion. She was homesick, but how could she go back to her family? Did she even want to return

145

to her family, if it meant being taken from the side of this man who had become her whole world? And why would he ask, unless he wanted to get rid of her? Her heart constricted at the thought.

'It is time we spoke of your future, Zeinab,' he insisted. 'If you were to go back, what would be your situation? Would you be able to remarry among your people?'

She shrugged, her misery turning sullen. 'I don't know.'

'I know there is divorce among Muslims, but of course General Bonaparte left in a hurry, and that matter was never resolved. I wonder if you are still legally bound in some way?'

'I don't know.'

'No, of course. But we should make it our business to find out. Now, let me think, who could give us a definitive answer?'

Zeinab looked at him and burst into tears. She ran down the path and up the steps of the loggia. He caught up with her inside the house.

'What is it? Are you unwell? Was it something I said?' He caught her by the shoulders and she turned to face him.

'Do you want me to go away? Do you want to get rid of me?'

He looked at her, and his whole face softened. 'No, no, no, that is the last thing I want. But I don't know what is best for you.'

'Then keep me.'

He took her face in his hands and blew the wisps of soft dark hair off her brow. Then he kissed her eyebrows, and when she closed her eyes, her eyelids, then the tip of her nose and the point of her chin, and finally her lips, lightly, and drew back. Zeinab opened her eyes; he was looking at her quizzically, expectantly. With some hesitation she tried to reciprocate his caresses: she touched his hair, as he had touched hers, and then stretched up to kiss his eyelids, as he had done hers. He drew back sharply.

'What did I do?'

'Nothing, it's just – I remembered I have this eye patch.'

'I don't mind it.'

'Does nothing about me bother you? Not that I'm so much older, or even my bad eye?'

146

'No! Take off the eye patch if you want.'

'Not yet. One day perhaps, but not yet.'

'Do you take it off in front of your wife?'

He looked taken aback for a moment, then laughed, as if she had brought up something outrageous. But what could be more natural than to mention his first wife in France?

'Yes, Zeinab, I do take it off, but that's different.'

'How?'

'She knew me before. We've known each other since we were not much older than you are today. But you talk too much, Zeinab, did no one ever tell you that?'

'Shaykh Jabarti always said that I talked too –'

He kissed her on the lips again, this time very long, and very deep, and when he released her it took her a moment to catch her breath.

He smiled. 'I suggest you not hold your breath when you are being kissed, it makes for a more satisfactory experience.' He leaned towards her again.

Just then the thought came to her. 'Oh! Shaykh Jabarti.'

'Him again! What of him?' Nicolas looked annoyed.

'You asked who would know if I was still legally bound by my marriage. Shaykh Jabarti – he's a jurist, he would know about these things.'

'Ah. So he would.' Conté leaned back, looking troubled. 'It's important to you that we be married, is it, my Zeinab?' Finally he nodded, and drew her head on to his shoulder. 'We shall see about consulting Jabarti first thing in the morning. Well, not the *very* first thing in the morning, I need to go to Giza first to hire some workers for the new looms at the wool factory. But right after that. Now, *voyons*, let's try that again . . .' He tipped her head back, and parted her lips with his finger. 'Remember to breathe.'

'It depends,' Shaykh Jabarti stroked his beard. 'It depends.'

Zeinab waited, and motioned to Nicolas to be patient; she remembered the ways of her former teacher well enough to know he was taking the time to think. She had worn a cloak and yashmak

147

over her plainest European dress for the occasion, and only removed the outer garments when they were inside Jabarti's house. She looked around the familiar room where she had spent so many hours being tutored and taking dictation in front of the east-facing window, while her brother spun a wheel around a stick in the garden outside. How she had changed since then, and how the world had changed!

Finally Jabarti cleared his throat. 'Let us assume the marriage you contracted with Commander Bonaparte was valid, for argument's sake. Since there has been no divorce, you are still legally married. However, when the husband has abandoned the conjugal bed for over a year, that constitutes valid grounds for divorce.'

Zeinab translated, relieved.

'On the other hand,' Jabarti paused. 'On the other hand, if the husband never "entered" to the wife in the first place, then annulment is an option.'

Zeinab blushed. She thought she understood what the shaykh meant. The general had never come to her at all since she was married.

'What is he saying?' Nicolas asked.

Zeinab shook her head, embarrassed, and not sure how to translate.

'Thank you, Shaykh Jabarti, very kind of you.' Nicolas took her by the hand and drew her towards the window. 'If you will allow us a moment.'

'By your leave, my teacher.' Zeinab followed Nicolas to the window.

'Well, if you are free to remarry, then ask him if he can officiate himself.'

'Now?'

'If we are to do it at all, then the sooner the better, I think, for your sake. Isn't that what you want? I'm willing to recite the profession of the Muslim faith, or whatever it is I need to do. But it will only be a marriage valid here in Egypt, you realize? I've told you I am married in France.'

'I know, of course, I would only be your second wife.'

Nicolas threw up his hands in a gesture of despair. 'You don't

148

understand at all, my little Zeinab. Never mind. Ask him about officiating.'

They turned back to Shaykh Jabarti, who had been sitting impassively cross-legged on the cushioned divan, reading from a book open on his knees. Zeinab shyly brought up the question.

'It depends,' he said, stroking his beard again. 'There are two kinds of marriage: conventional marriage and common law marriage. The essential difference between the two is public announcement or the lack of it. In official marriage, the contract is written, signed and witnessed by two witnesses, and the marriage is publicly announced. In common law marriage, whether or not it involves a written contract, the union is kept a secret between the parties involved. Some Sunni schools of jurisprudence do not recognize common law marriage . . .' Jabarti then launched into a convoluted discussion of the different schools of jurisprudence, of which Zeinab retained only the final sentence: 'The Hanbali school may be more strict, but in Egypt we go largely by the Malki.'

Zeinab translated to Nicolas as best she could.

'Well then, ask him to marry us, and we shall decide later about announcing it.'

Zeinab looked at him.

'I will be honest with you, *ma petite*. I won't deny that I am concerned about echoes reaching my wife in France, but will you believe me when I assure you that it is not my only thought? My first concern is for you, and the possible consequences for you if I were to leave you behind when we evacuate – as we must, one day, I fear.'

At his words Zeinab felt a lump form like a stone in her chest. 'Could you not stay even if the army left? Or could you take me with you? I would respect and obey your first wife as if she were my own mother.'

Nicolas shook his head again, as if she failed to understand. 'Never mind. My sweet girl, ask the shaykh to marry us. I must take you back to the Institute and go to the Citadel directly; the Mint is striking para coins today for the first time on my new machine, I must be there to inaugurate the proceedings. But we will have time to talk this evening.'

Zeinab sat by the window open to the loggia, wondering why Nicolas was so late; could he still be at the metalworks on Rawda Island? She reminded herself that he was a very important person, after all: president of the Institute of Egypt and director of the Mint in addition to all his other responsibilities as chief engineer and commander of the balloonists brigade and who knew what else. Everywhere he went, people recognized him; even the children in the streets recognized him by his eye patch, and their mothers would murmur, 'Allah bless you,' as he passed. It was her fate, Zeinab thought, to be married to very important men and to wait for them. If only he would come in the end, not like the general, who never did.

She had worried about what to wear on this first evening alone with Nicolas. Her mother sent her some new clothes at the beginning of every season, tunics and pantaloons and scarves, but they were all in the Turkish fashion and Zeinab thought he would prefer her dressed in the style of his own country. She looked over her three French dresses and decided on the muslin with the violet pansies; it was the prettiest one she owned, even if it was a little too small, and it was the one he had sketched her in. She wondered what had happened to the drawing; she had never had a chance to see it, what with the terrible event that followed, the assassination of General Kléber. She had forgotten all about it. Did Nicolas still have it?

She opened the small coffer where she kept the jewellery her father had given her when she had been wed to the general. She had not worn it since, but tonight she wanted to look her best for Nicolas. She picked out a pair of dangling pink amethyst earrings and threaded them carefully through her earlobes.

It worried her that she had not had a proper bridal bath, with honey wax to depilate every hair on the body till it was as smooth as a pre-pubescent girl's. She had the impression the grooming rituals of Frenchwomen were different, but she had no idea what Nicolas would expect and there was no one she could ask for advice or assistance;

150

even her maid had gone home for the night. Zeinab yawned, suddenly sleepy. Where was Nicolas? Was he in Qassim Bey's garden, conversing with the other savants? Or had he not come back to Nasiriya? She got up and walked over to the couch at the far end of the room, lay down on her side and closed her eyes.

She woke up to the troubling but delicious sensation of a firm hand caressing her flank over and over, and a warm breath blowing the wisps of hair off her forehead. 'It's time to wake up, *ma belle au bois dormant*,' Nicolas murmured. Zeinab turned to him, still slack-limbed from sleep. He kissed her, feeling the pulse in the hollow of her neck.

'How rapidly your heart beats! Now we need to get this gown off. What a great many buttons, and so tight . . .'

'Wait!' Zeinab whispered in embarrassment. 'I haven't – I mean I didn't know if I should –' She indicated with gestures what she had no words for.

'What? Oh.' He understood. 'No, I assure you I much prefer my women *au naturel*. You are perfect just as you are.'

She reached up and tentatively touched his temple. 'Will you take this eye patch off?'

He winced. 'Not yet, *ma petite*, not yet. Now, *voyons* . . .'

TWELVE

The Beginning of the End

'The religion, the morals and the customs of the local citizenry must be particularly protected; the question of women is the most vital, it is the one Muslims value most; we should be careful to suppress the infractions perpetrated by French soldiers.'

Commander in Chief Menou

Nafisa stood at her window, trying to take deep breaths to relieve the oppression she felt in her chest. In this third year of the French occupation, with the afflictions visited upon the country following one hard on the heels of the other, she felt her courage falter for the first time. It was a physical feeling, like a skipped heartbeat. The destruction of her city, day after day, afflicted her like blows to her own body. Every day the French razed houses, bridges, wikalas and mosques, to build roads and fortifications in their place. The mansions of the amirs around the Elephant Lake were destroyed and their wood and stone carried away to build forts, or used as fuel. From the Gate of Victory to the Iron Gate, Cairo was one continuous scene of devastation, the bones of the city were laid bare, and even the bones of the dead in their coffins were exhumed when the city of the dead was razed. The Ezbekiah Lake was being dammed, it would never flood again. Trees from the gardens and orchards were being cut down to make wagons and barricades, and even the skiffs and boats on the ponds were smashed for fuel. When would this senseless destruction come to an end?

'Sitt Nafisa,' her eunuch had to call twice before she half-turned her head to him. 'Sitt Nafisa, it is Shaykh Jabarti asking for an audience with you.'

For a moment she considered pleading indisposition; she did not feel she could face anyone in this state of despair. Then she took a deep breath and straightened her back. Shaykh Jabarti was one of her surest fingers on the pulse of the city. 'Show the shaykh to the mezzanine while I veil. Offer him rose-water to refresh him.'

In a few minutes she was ready. 'Shaykh Jabarti, welcome. What news?'

'Ah, Sitt Nafisa, how could it be any but black news, in this year of affliction upon affliction!' The shaykh brushed the dust of the street from his kaftan. 'But even the destruction of the city is but a trifle compared to the dissolution of public morals! Palaces and mosques can be rebuilt, but when the foundations of society itself have crumbled . . . The licentiousness of women is such that they have abandoned all pretence at modesty. You can no longer tell a decent woman from a woman of ill repute!'

Nafisa wondered what particular outrage the shaykh had in mind; she had no doubt that there was a specific case he wanted to bring to her attention. At the beginning of the French occupation, it had been the debauched and low-class women who had mingled with the Franj, attracted by their open-handedness and their gallantry towards women. But during the latest insurrection, the French had seized many of the women and girls as booty, and dressed them in French garb, and made them behave like Frenchwomen in every respect, so that it was impossible to tell the victims of abduction from the dissolute women who had gone to the French of their own accord.

Shaykh Jabarti was fuming. 'When the native people of the land are visited with humiliation, degradation and dispossession, and all wealth is concentrated in the hands of the French and their supporters, then corruption spreads,' he spat, as if he had just chewed on bitter cardamom seed. 'Many a Frenchman has taken for his wife the daughter of a local dignitary, while the father gives his daughter away in his lust for power and favour. At the wedding, the Frenchman pretends to embrace Islam and utters the two formulas of belief, for he has no faith of his own he might betray.' The shaykh dusted his palms one against the other in a gesture of despair and disgust.

Nafisa waited for the revelation that would inevitably follow this preamble. A moment later, the shaykh obliged.

'Even the Naqib's own daughter! For shame! With the Prophet's blood in her veins!'

'Zeinab Bakri? Who –?'

'The chief engineer has taken her for a common law wife.'

'Oh! Poor child!' Nafisa shook her head. 'But, Shaykh Jabarti, think – in her situation, so friendless, discarded by Bonaparte, and her father so reviled – what else could she do? They say he is a good man, Nicolas Conté. Perhaps he will be good to the girl.'

'He is a Frenchman. When they leave, what will happen to her?'

'God only knows, Shaykh Jabarti, God only knows. Poor child!'

When the muezzin's chant for dawn prayers ascended and hung in the air like a plume of smoke, Zeinab stirred. Nicolas propped his back against the pillows and drew her head onto his chest. 'But why didn't you tell me, *ma petite*? The general, he never came to you at all?'

'Never.' She played with the greying hairs on his chest, twisting them around her finger.

'But in that case your marriage could have been annulled, and you could have returned to your father and made a suitable match, surely?'

'I don't know. Anyway I don't care, I want to be with you.'

'My sweet.' But he furrowed his brow as if he were troubled, or distracted. 'Where is my shirt? Ah, here it is – no, that's your dress. Irreparably ripped, I'm afraid, in my haste to get those buttons off. But it was much too small for you anyhow, I must remember to get you a new one. Which reminds me – I should go. I need to get ready for a meeting with General Menou and representatives of the textile industry from France.'

'Must you go?' She tugged at his chest hairs to hold him back.

'Aii! Stop that. Yes, I truly must go, much against my will, believe me. You lie here and go back to sleep, *ma petite*. Look at those dark circles around your dear eyes; I feel guilty for not letting you get any rest last night.'

'Let me help you dress.' Zeinab slipped to the floor, and helped him to pull on his boots. 'Will you promise to think of me while you go about your business today?'

He smiled. 'I promise. I will give particular thought to a certain part of you that I have almost decided is my favourite among all your many delicious charms.'

'Where?'

'As I have not quite decided yet, I wish to wait till tonight, when I will have another opportunity to compare and confirm. So you will have to be patient, *ma jolie*. Now go to sleep.'

She stumbled back into bed and let him tuck her in and cover her with a shawl, and blow on her eyelids until she had closed them again. She drifted off to sleep before he had left the room.

When she woke the sun was high in the sky and she blinked at the brightness of the light streaming through the window into the chamber. The sheer draperies billowed up with the breeze then floated down, billowed up and floated down, as if her bed were a sailing ship or a flying carpet. She stretched her arms and then, tentatively, her legs, wincing at the soreness. She felt a little sad and tearful, not because she was sore – last night had hurt less than she had been led to expect from remarks by her older married sisters – but because she was lying there all alone on the morning after her wedding.

When her older sisters had wed, and she had accompanied her mother to visit the new bride the morning after, they would find her sitting up in bed, flushed with bashful smiles, surrounded by her servants, showing off her 'unveiling' present: the jewellery the bride-groom gave the bride the morning after their first night together, as a token of his love. Zeinab's oldest sister had received a bracelet of fine rubies, her middle sister a delicately filigreed gold and pearl necklace. Their mother had been eager to hear the details of the wedding night, all the while looking around approvingly at her daughter's new establishment and her servants.

For Zeinab, there was no one to share the morning, no mother or sisters or servants, and no 'unveiling' present; only the soreness between her legs, and a husband who left their bed at dawn. But it didn't matter, she told herself, Nicolas was a very important man, and it was an honour to be his second wife, and she must be the best wife any man could have. He liked pomegranate juice; she must remember to ask for pomegranates for his dinner, whenever he did come home. But first, as soon as her maid returned, she would take a long bath with pure olive oil soap from Tripoli, and pat attar of gardenia in the parting of her hair, where Nicolas buried his nose, and under her arms, and between her breasts . . . and then she sank in a reverie as she thought of all the different places where Nicolas might bury his nose.

'Sitt Nafisa, Shaykh Jabarti is at the door with urgent tidings.'

'I will be down directly.' Nafisa veiled with all the haste she could muster and descended to the lower hall. 'What news, God willing, Shaykh Jabarti?' She had never seen the scholar so perturbed, his face nearly as grey as his turban. 'Take a seat, please, and tell me what has happened.'

'Sitt Nafisa, half the diwan has been taken hostage!'

'Hostage! The diwan? Why?'

'This morning Menou convened the diwan and announced he was leaving for the coast at the head of an army, and warned against any sedition; at first his threats were veiled. He said, "Sensible people like you should advise the troublemakers. For retaliation strikes not only the troublemakers but others as well."' Jabarti seemed too agitated to take a seat. 'I replied that punishment should be meted out to the guilty only. For did not the Almighty say that every soul shall be pledged for what it has earned. To this, Menou replied: "Guns and bombs have no mind to distinguish between evildoer and good man. Nor do they read the Koran."' Jabarti threw his hands up. 'And he calls himself Abdullah-Jacques Menou!'

156

'The lion is most dangerous when he is at bay,' Nafisa pointed out, 'and Menou is cornered. The Ottomans and the English must be advancing even closer to Cairo than we thought.'

'You are right, Menou fears an uprising when news of the advance is known, but he makes a great show of strength. He claimed to the diwan that the French will never leave Egypt, never abandon it, for it has become their land, subject to their rule. But the general must have seen that his words did not convince, and when we made to disperse, we were stopped at the door. We were told that, with Ottoman forces approaching, it had become necessary to detain certain dignitaries among us as hostages, as the Turks were co-religionists for whom Muslims might be expected to feel sympathy and loyalty, unlike the English.'

'Ah! So the Ottomans must be practically at the gates!' And with them the amirs, she thought: Murad – and Elfi. She turned back to Jabarti. 'But the French did not detain all of you?'

'No. They left four of us, including myself and Shaykh Bakri, to run the affairs of the city.'

'I see.' But she had almost ceased to hear Jabarti; her pulse raced with dread and relief combined. The final confrontation would come any day now. All over the city, there were women, like her, who yearned to be reunited with a husband or lover in exile; and others who dreaded the day of parting with a husband or lover they had taken among the French. There were men, on both sides, who longed to go home: the Mamlukes to their City Victorious, and the French to their land across the sea. There were those among the citizens of Cairo who chafed for the day of revenge and those who quaked at the prospect of retribution. Whatever happened, there would be winners and losers and heartache. The day of reckoning was at hand. 'May God have mercy on us all!' Nafisa prayed, and spared a special prayer for the Naqib's young daughter.

Zeinab lifted a corner of the large napkin covering the brass tray, and for the third time in an hour checked to make sure that nothing was missing for Nicolas' supper. Small dishes of olives and pickled lemons; a whole roast chicken; grilled eggplant; lentils with fried garlic and onion; creamy yogurt; thick slices of bread in the French style; and for dessert, sweet yellow plums and the first apricots of the season, carefully washed in vinegar water by her own hand, as a precaution against the plague. She added some fresh water to the basin in which the pitcher of pomegranate juice sat cooling, and curled up on the window seat looking out on the loggia and the garden. Since she had married Nicolas, she had come to think of this house, Hassan Kashif's second house in Nasiriya, as home.

Although she was not really hungry, Zeinab nibbled on an olive. The muezzin had called for sunset prayers a long time ago, and the pink and orange glow in the sky turned to purple before her watching eyes as she looked out of the window of the loggia. Nicolas must be so weary, she thought; he had been gone since daybreak, and the sound of hammering and smelting and clanging from his workshops, and the smell of the smithies, had penetrated into her bedchamber since early morning.

She adjusted the deep square neckline of her pale green dress, the one Nicolas had ordered custom-dyed just for her, the one he said enhanced the contrast between her pallor and her black hair. Eau-de-nil, he had called the subtle shade. He had studied the colours and fabric and style as seriously as he studied any of his blueprints. Nicolas had been a painter once, it was true, but she had also noticed that Frenchmen in general tended to be unabashedly attentive to the details of a woman's attire.

She remembered how she had seen Madame Verdier greet her husband when he returned from the battle of Aboukir. When she heard his firm step approaching along the loggia, she had floated gracefully to her feet, exclaiming, 'Ah, *mon ami!*' And stood there waiting, arms outstretched, her gaze holding his with a tender smile, giving him time to admire her elegant figure. Zeinab wished she could learn that kind of poise and restraint when she greeted Nicolas. She practised floating gracefully to her feet and holding out her arms with a cry of: 'Ah, *mon ami!*' Then she dissolved in giggles and flung herself back down on the couch.

A warm breeze billowing the sheer draperies around the window reminded her that it was the end of winter and soon it would be too warm to wear Nicolas' favourite dress. Would she be able to wear it next winter? Would they still be together here, like this, at the Institute? Would she be in France with him? Or would she be back in her father's house, dressed in the Turkish fashion in a tunic and pantaloons? Since the English and Ottoman advance, the ground was shifting under her feet; it was shifting under everyone's feet, but sooner or later everyone would leap to one side or the other of the gaping crevasse, and she was the one who stood to fall in the crack. Dread gripped her.

Catching a glimpse of Nicolas climbing the steps to the loggia, she jumped up, lifting the hem of her dress, and ran to meet him under the arcaded columns. He looked exhausted and dusty, his sleeves rolled up, his jacket over his arm and the handkerchief he used to mop his brow streaked with dirt. She flung herself at his neck and he held her off with his arm. 'No, *ma petite chérie*, you'll get your dress all dirty, wait till I wash off a little.'

They went indoors and he took off his shirt and washed in the basin, soaping his hands and face and neck and armpits, while Zeinab stood by with a towel and a clean shirt.

'Ah, that's much better.' He buttoned the fresh shirt. 'Now I can claim that embrace.'

'Your supper will get cold, please come eat first.' She drew him by the arm to the brass tray and uncovered the dishes.

'Whatever you say. You're very strict with me! Ah, what an appetizing chicken. Let me have a glass of that cold pomegranate juice first. Aren't you going to join me?'

'I had a bite before you came.' It was true, as far as it went; she had nibbled on a couple of olives.

Zeinab watched him eat but she could see he had no real appetite and was making an effort more for her sake than anything else. When he had wiped his mouth, and rinsed his fingers in the bowl of rosewater, he leaned back against the pillows of the window seat and spread his arms in invitation. She put away the tray and hurried to sit on his knee and nestle against his chest, smoothing his shirt and fussing and squirming till she had made herself a perfect fit.

He smiled down at her. 'Has the little bird made her nest to her satisfaction?'

She nodded, nuzzling his chest. 'What did you do today? You were gone so long.'

'I had the workshop forge a thick iron chain, a very long chain, three hundred metres long, to stretch across the Nile at its narrowest point, in the event enemy ships attempt to sail upriver to Cairo. Then I closed down my workshops, and told my mechanics to go work on the fortifications. General Belliard needs every man for the defence of Cairo.'

'Are things going very badly?'

'They can hardly go much worse. We have had news today that Menou lost the battle at Canope outside Alexandria, and retreated to the city, where he is now trapped and besieged. He not only lost the battle but he seems to have lost his head, along with his authority over the generals; several of them have rebelled against his command, and he has ordered Reynier and Damas arrested and sent to France.' He shook his head in despair. 'I tell you, *ma petite*, I don't know what will happen next.'

For a few minutes his gaze was lost in the distance. Then he seemed to remember her, curled as still as a frightened rabbit against his chest. 'But don't worry, my precious Zeinab, whatever happens, I will take care of you. *Voyons*,' he tipped her head up. 'Are you feeling all right? You're not quite yourself this evening. Is it close to being your time of the month?'

She blushed. 'How do you know these things?'

'Standard observation and deduction: you are deliciously puffy in your décolletage. Which makes me think it would be a shame to waste all that voluptuousness while it lasts . . .' He began to unbutton her bodice, and uncovered her décolletage down to the nipple; he sucked on the little pad of flesh between her breast and her armpit, the spot he had told her a long time ago was the particular object of his predilection in her whole body. 'Your magnificent eyes, of

160

course,' he had said, 'are what captivated me first, but they belong to all the world. But this sweet spot here is my own private preserve.'

Zeinab half-closed her eyes, feeling the heaviness of pleasure coursing through her limbs, when the sight of the half-moon framed in the window suddenly brought a thought to her mind.

'My time of the month – it usually starts when the crescent moon first appears in the sky, and tonight the moon is half full.'

Nicolas raised his head and frowned. 'Are you often late like this?'

Until that moment it had not occurred to her that she might be pregnant. A child, she thought, a child of his: she would have Nicolas inside her, no matter what else happened. A fierce flash of longing shot up from her lower belly. Then a wave of panic broke over her. She suppressed it; the last thing she wanted to do was to add to his worries at this time. 'I'm not sure, but not very late, I don't think. Nicolas . . . ?'

'Hmm?'

'Will you take off your eye patch?'

He hesitated. 'Why now?'

'Please.'

He nodded, and pulled it off, blinking and closing his eyes. Zeinab blew gently on the scarred and hollow lid.

'Did you lose your eye in a battle?'

'Nothing as interesting as that. It was an accident in the laboratory, a hydrogen tank blew up in my face.'

She took his face in her hands and fluttered little kisses on both his eyelids, then pressed his face against her cool breasts, to soothe the feverish eyes.

THIRTEEN

The Evacuation

I am not authorized to speak to you about the reasons for our evacuation, but only to administer the course of affairs. Everyone among
you has witnessed the friendship and brotherliness between the French
and the people of Egypt. The army and the population were like one
people . . . I hope the Egyptians will never forget this. Truly, the French
regime was just to all. What is most admired by the people is that
Frenchmen died to put an end to oppression and despotism from
which the people were suffering. Rivals, fearing that the people in the
Arab lands would submit to our rule, formed a coalition to prevent
this, yet all their efforts proved vain. Our power has asserted itself
and will remain for ever and ever.

Letter of friendship from Comissioner Estève to the Diwan,

17 Messidor, Year 9

Nafisa tried to concentrate on the accounts of her wikala at the Bab
Zuweila but the stomping and shuffling of soldiers marching to and
from the Citadel stretched her nerves till they vibrated like a plucked
lute string. In the past few months there had been a godsend for her
charities; since Murad Bey had signed the truce with them, the French
paid her one hundred thousand silver riyals monthly and that sum
she used entirely to fund the sabil and to support the blind and
infirm in the hospices.

There was a shout of warning, then a loud explosion, followed by
a crash and a cloud of dust she could see from the window: houses

were being demolished near the Gate of Victory close by. What would be left of her Cairo? She renewed her vow: when peace returned – *if* peace returned – she would complete her sabil and build a school, and then, and only then, she would erect her mausoleum. What did the scriptures say? After death, only the prayers of a righteous child, or ongoing good works, can intercede for the soul of the departed. She was childless; she had been twelve when she married Ali Bey, and the first, stillborn child she bore him nearly killed her; he had forbidden her to risk another pregnancy. When she married Murad he had had no children – not with his first wife, Abu Dahab's widow, nor with any of his concubines – so she knew from the start she would have no child by him. Good works were all she would ever have to intercede for her soul on the Day of Judgment; they were all she would leave behind for anyone to remember her by.

Perhaps, she thought, that was why the Mamlukes had been such keen builders of mosques and mausoleums and palaces at the height of their glory. When they died, their obituaries listed no place of birth, no town, no tribe, no long list of antecedents on their father and mother's side; only the name a Mamluke was given by his master, and the name of his master, and that master's master. They came from nowhere and left behind no dynasty of their own flesh and blood. Only their mausoleums and mosques and sabils, a legacy of stone and wood and marble, testifying to their time here on earth.

'Sitt Nafisa?' Her eunuch was at the door. 'There is a visitor below.' Barquq paused significantly, and she guessed immediately who it was. Nafisa felt her pulse quicken, and then her chest constrict. What could bring Elfi now, with the French in a state of such high alert?

'Ask our visitor to come up.' She draped her shawl about her shoulders, and drew the sheer veil over her head and across the lower part of her face.

Elfi strode into the room, dressed in sober clothes and a white turban, his face sombre. He stood searching for words.

Her sense of foreboding grew. 'Elfi Bey, welcome. What news?'

'I am sorry to be the bearer of ill news, but I thought it best to come myself.'

'Murad?'

'May you live a long life.' The formulaic answer told her what she had already guessed. 'Murad Bey passed away on the sixth of the month – of the plague. God have mercy on his soul. I rode south directly I was informed, and we buried him in Suhaj with the expediency that the disease imposes. But your wishes in this matter will be respected, of course, and when this is all over . . .' He gestured to the frenetic movement of troops outside the window. 'We can have him exhumed and reburied as you see fit.'

'God have mercy on his soul,' she murmured. The last time she had seen Murad, nearly three years ago, he had taken leave of her with: 'May I next see your face in good health.' She had had a premonition at the time that she would never see him again, but she had dismissed it. And here was Murad dead, and if she ever saw him again, it would be as a skeleton in a shroud.

'Sitt Nafisa? Are you unwell? Shall I call your servants?'

'Excuse me, Elfi Bey, it is nothing, only a moment's malaise.' She sat down and gestured for him to do likewise. In a minute the lightheadedness passed and she turned to him. 'God have mercy on his soul. When this is all over, as you say, there will be time to think of a proper burial. I will have a mausoleum erected for him next to that of Ali Bey. That part of the City of the Dead, at least, has been spared. For now I will order the eunuchs directly to set up a tent for the three days of mourning.'

'I will stay to pay my respects to the memory of Murad Bey, at least for the first day.'

'You have done more than pay your respects by coming here yourself. But you mustn't linger. The news of Murad's passing will soon reach the French and they will watch who comes and goes before my door. Now you must leave, Elfi Bey. Forgive me for not rising, I do not quite trust myself on my feet just yet.'

He stood up, bowed and turned to go, then turned back. 'Remember that you can count on a protector while I draw breath. When this is all over . . .' He brought his hand to his heart, in the time-honoured gesture of homage.

She thought she understood him, and nodded quickly, not meeting his eyes, to prevent him from saying anything more.

The servant knocking on the door roused Zeinab from a sweaty sleep, and she sat up, patting her damp face with the sheet. 'What is it?'

'Dr Desgenettes is downstairs, and he asks to see you urgently.'

Zeinab wrapped her large Indian shawl around her and hurried down, still groggy with sleep, to find the doctor pacing the salon.

'What is the matter? Dr Desgenettes, is something wrong with Nicolas?'

'No, not at all, he is at headquarters with General Belliard. Forgive me for rousing you so unceremoniously in the night, but I have received an urgent request from General Dugua to come to the bedside of Fatoum, his companion. She is apparently very gravely ill. It is not the plague. I need you to come with me to translate; at this hour I could not find anyone.'

'Yes, yes of course. Give me one minute to dress.'

'Thank you. But hurry, please! We may be too late to save her.'

When they reached General Dugua's house, servants were waiting for them at the door with torches in hand. They were ushered hastily upstairs and into a bedchamber where a young woman lay on the bed, her face pale as the moon against her dark hair on the pillow. Her eyes were half open.

Dr Desgenettes touched her forehead, took her pulse, lay his hand on her belly over the sheet and, when she cried out in pain, yanked the bedcovers down. She lay in a pool of blood under her hips. He turned grimly to Zeinab. 'Ask her what she's done.'

Zeinab took Fatoum's hand in her own trembling hands and asked her in Arabic:

'What happened? Fatoum, tell the doctor what happened, so he can help you.'

The girl shook her head weakly and moaned as Desgenettes touched her where the blood continued to seep like a malignant puddle.

'She was pregnant, wasn't she? Ask her.'

'Were you pregnant, Fatoum?'

Fatoum's white lips parted, and Zeinab leaned close. 'I couldn't keep the baby,' the girl whispered. 'The general will leave me behind. What will become of me? I couldn't keep it. So I tried to – you know . . . God forgive me.'

Zeinab turned to translate but Desgenettes was nodding grimly. 'She tried to abort herself. Why would she do such a thing? It doesn't matter. She's lost so much blood, I don't know if I can save her. All right, Zeinab, there's nothing more you can do. You look as if you're about to faint on me. Go now.'

Zeinab ran out the door and crumpled to the floor in the corridor outside, trembling. She clutched her arms against her belly. The sight of the blood terrified her. She would never do this to her baby. But she couldn't keep it. How could she keep it if Nicolas left? What if he asked her to do what Fatoum had done? She wouldn't tell him. But if she could not confide in him, whom could she trust? Fatoum's whisper echoed over and over in her head: *What is to become of me?*

Later that night when Nicolas came home and got into bed beside her, she pretended to be asleep. But he felt her quivering and caressed her hair and her cheek and felt the dampness of tears. 'What's wrong, *ma petite*? Have you been crying? What is it? It breaks my heart to see you weep. Tell me, what I can do?'

He turned her over to face him and enveloped her in his embrace, clasping her tight with his arms and his legs around her till she felt herself melt against him, as if her very bones had turned to liquid, and she wept into his shoulder, and let him comfort her. But when her crying had abated, and his hand slipped under her nightgown – his clever hand, his painter's hand that could blindly gauge the fullness of her breasts and belly, the fullness that might betray her – the sight of the pool of blood under Fatoum's hips rose before her and she drew away, gasping for breath. 'Wait, please. Let me get a drink of water, I'm so thirsty.'

She got up to the mashrabiyya window where the earthenware

pitcher sat on the shelf cooling in the night breeze, and lifted it as if it were empty. 'I'll go refill it from the jar in the hall.' She took her time refilling the pitcher from the big, cool jar that stood, waist-high, on a stand in the mezzanine. Then she tiptoed back and listened outside the bedroom door till she heard his breathing grow heavy and regular, and then a faint snore reassured that it was safe to go back to bed.

'Sitt Nafisa, the French doctor has sent to ask if he may come to call on you immediately after noon prayers.' Barquq stood at her door.

'Tell the doctor he is welcome in this house.' Nafisa wondered what Dr Desgenettes could want from her; surely the plague had not manifested itself again? But that was unlikely, there must be some-thing equally urgent at stake. Despite the French denials, everyone knew the last days of the French occupation were at hand. The vice was closing in on them: the English advancing from the north, the Ottomans from the east, and a sepoy force with the English army of India landing at Qusayr, the southernmost port of the Red Sea. What could the doctor want with her at a time of such crisis? Nafisa clapped for her maids and began to dress and to veil.

Her eunuch returned, his impassive manner barely disguising his excitement. 'There is news from the north,' he reported, 'I have just heard it on the street. The English and Ottoman forces have invaded Rahmaniya and seized the fortress.'

'Rahmaniya? What of Menou's wife Zubayda? That is her family seat!'

'They say Sitt Zubayda escaped on a boat with her brother, and she is now on her way to Cairo to take refuge in the Citadel with the rest of the French and their dependents.'

So Commandant Menou's wife Zubayda was safe, but what of the fate of the other women who had married or co-habited with the French? What of the naqib's daughter Zeinab, living openly with Nicolas Conté?

'There is more news on the street,' Barquq continued. 'Sitt Hawa, who was Ismail Kashif's wife, and who was taken by Bartholomew to live with him –'

Nafisa nodded. 'I know who she is.'

'She has escaped from the Citadel with her baggage, and has hidden somewhere in the city. The French are turning the city inside out looking for her; they have summoned the sectional police chiefs and ordered them to produce the woman.'

'She must have feared the French would evacuate. But how did she get away?'

'Apparently by some trick she descended from the Citadel on a donkey, with her baggage on another. In one of the alleys she paid the drivers, dismissed them, and went into hiding. When the search for her started, the drivers were questioned, they were detained, and the people of the neighbourhood where they had dropped her off were seized and imprisoned. They were pressured and threatened if the woman were to be found hiding among them. People are very worried and upset by the police search, especially by Bartholomew, who enters houses under the pretext of searching them and disturbs the owners and the women and takes their jewellery and effects.'

'Poor Sitt Hawa.' Nafisa shook her head as she adjusted her black mourning veil and pinned it into place with a ruby pin. 'Barquq, do we have any coffee left to offer the doctor?' The noise of a crier in the street made her pause and lift her hand for silence, then motion to Barquq to open the window so she could hear. The Agha was going through the streets preceded by a crier announcing: 'Do not be afraid or disturbed. Glad tidings have been received that Bonaparte has arrived with a mighty navy in Alexandria, and that the English are in retreat.'

'What fresh lies are these?' Nafisa had no time to say any more, for Dr Desgenettes was announced at her door. She went down to greet him in the inner courtyard.

'Excuse me, madame, for intruding upon you in your time of mourning.'

'You honour my house with your visit, Docteur; your good works precede you and all who speak of you invoke blessings upon your name.'

'Thank you, madame.' Dr Desgenettes hesitated, balancing his weight from one foot to the other.

'Will you not take a seat, sir?'

'Ah, yes, thank you.' He sat with his hands on his knees. Her head eunuch offered him a cup of coffee, and withdrew.

'This is a delicate matter, madame, but I count on your confidentiality. I am here today because I was but recently at the bedside of a young woman, the companion of General Dugua –'

'Fatoum?'

'Ah. You know the girl in question?'

'Fatoum was my Mamluka; I raised her from childhood. Is she sick?'

'I regret to give you pain, madame. The young woman did herself grievous harm in the attempt to rid herself of the fruit of her union with the general. I was called to her bedside and did all I could to save her, but it was too late.'

Nafisa's hand flew to her mouth. 'Poor child!'

'She feared what would become of her in the eventuality that we must evacuate. Madame, I respect your intelligence too much to pretend that her fears were fanciful.'

Nafisa nodded. 'Just now town criers were circulating proclamations announcing an imminent landing by Bonaparte. They delude no one.'

'In the event we must evacuate, then, there are many young Egyptian women who will be in the same situation as Fatoum, and I come to you to find a solution.'

Nafisa took a moment to respond. 'It was wrong of the French generals to abduct our loveliest Mamlukas, but it was not the fault of the women. As for those that freely chose to change houses, they erred, but one must forgive such mistakes. As far as I am concerned, I forgive my Mamlukas with all my heart. Any of them who wish to come back into my household will be welcome, and need fear no reproach.'

169

'I expected no less from a lady with your reputation for compassion. May I ask you to use your influence and example to negotiate a general forgiveness for these girls from other households?'

'It is not in my hands, but what I can do I will. A first step will be to enlist the support of one or two of the ulema of influence. Shaykh Jabarti I know to be a man of reason, and I will seek him out. But if all else fails, Docteur, you may let it be known that any woman who fears to return to her own mistress or household will find shelter in mine.'

'Thank you, madame. You have relieved my mind.'

He rose to his feet. 'This may be the last time we have the occasion to meet, madame. It has been an honour to make your acquaintance. Your collaboration has been invaluable in containing the spread of the plague, and now in this matter.'

'The honour is mine, Docteur. May you return safely to your home and country.'

When Desgenettes had left the room Nafisa stood lost in thought. He was the best the French race had to offer, he and the rare man like the chief engineer. Desgenettes' visit today marked the end of the era of the French in Egypt. She sighed with relief. She had managed it. She had managed to keep the thread of civility from breaking for three years now.

Even General Belliard had ridden to her door to offer his condolences on behalf of Commandant Menou, and to inform her, with regret, that the monthly payment would stop with Murad's passing away. The French had appointed Bardissi in his place, but Murad's amirs were already in revolt.

She sighed, overcome with weariness and worry at the thought of what the next weeks and months would bring. She might manage to keep the thread of civility from breaking till the last Frenchman left Cairo, but what then? What of the Ottomans, and the English, and the amirs?

Everything was up in the air. It was as if the city, indeed the country, had been picked up in the hand of a powerful Jinn and turned upside down. Nothing, and no one, occupied the same place any more. She feared there would be reprisals when the French released their grip; the city had become bitterly divided along sectarian lines during the occupation. God help them all if the country slid into civil war.

And Elfi? Where would he stand? And where should she stand, with regard to him? She could no longer pretend to be blind to his intentions. She had been a widow now, not just for the two months since Murad's death but for the three years previous. A widow for the second time: first Ali Bey's widow, now Murad's. Perhaps that was sufficient for one woman's lifetime.

She told herself this, but when she thought of Elfi, she knew she was not done yet; not done with being a woman – even if she might be done with being a wife.

Zeinab started as another burst of gunfire shattered the momentary lull. She hugged her knees as she sat in the window seat of the mashrabiyya, and rocked back and forth, rocking the unborn child within her. All day there had been shooting from the direction of Giza, where the English were advancing, but also from the east, from the Ottomans. The tambours beat continuously, and the kettledrums of the amirs boomed in counterpoint. The two armies were closing in on Cairo like the claws of a crab; the siege of the city was almost complete. Every day there was firing, and every day French cavalry units went out and there were skirmishes and they returned. There was another lull, and Zeinab waited, her nerves pulled taut.

Nicolas had gone to headquarters two days ago, leaving her at Hassan Kashif's house under the guard of the garrison of the Institute. He had been frantically busy these last few days, coming home very late or not at all. She missed him, but on the other hand, it was a relief that he was too preoccupied to notice any changes in her or to ask her questions.

This morning he had looked at her with a quizzical frown as she brought his breakfast. 'You never wear your French dresses any more?'

She had started to wear her loose-fitting Turkish clothes all the time now; they hid her form and were more comfortable than her revealing French dresses with their tight, high waists and deep neck-lines. When Nicolas questioned her, she mumbled something about the heat, not meeting his eyes. But he looked at her with that half-puzzled, half-hurt frown, the same look he gave her when she pretended to be asleep or tired every night when he finally did come home.

Whenever he looked at her that way it took all her self-control not to fling herself into his arms and beg him to hold her. But the sight of the pool of blood around Fatoum's hips would rise before her and she would turn away, finding some excuse to busy herself.

Zeinab lifted the corner of the napkin to check the tray she had prepared for his dinner: beans in oil with lemon, pickles, vegetable stew. It was the best she had been able to scrounge up: Cairo was almost completely cut off from the countryside, and for days there had been a shortage of fresh fruit, butter and cheese. The merchants were hoarding as well, exacerbating the shortages, and today her servant had come back without bread or meat. She had managed to find a melon, at three times the usual price, and it sat cooling in a basin of cold water on the mashrabiyya window seat.

The only thing that had not been in short supply at the market was talk. The maid had come back overflowing with the latest rumours and counter-rumours. It seemed that Alexandria was completely besieged, although the French were distributing a leaflet, supposedly from Commandant Menou, that claimed otherwise. Closer to home, the woman who had escaped from the Citadel, Ismail Kashif's wife, was still in hiding.

Zeinab wondered where she was, this Hawa, whom Bartholomew had taken to live with him. She'd heard that the French had searched high and low for the woman, to no avail. Zeinab remembered her sad face, when she had seen her at the Tivoli. Perhaps she really wasn't right in the head, as people said. Why had she run away from the Citadel? She must expect the Ottomans to win, and then the amirs would come back to the city, and her husband Ismail Kashif would take revenge on her for her infidelity. Surely the safest place for her was the Citadel? Bartholomew would be evacuated with the

French, that much was certain. But perhaps he would not want to take her with him? Or perhaps she was the one who did not want to leave with him. Zeinab remembered the woman as she had last seen her: hanging her head miserably as she stood behind Bartholomew's chair, while he looked every bit as brutal as his reputation. What must it be like to live with a man who relished torturing people? Zeinab shuddered. Poor Hawa. What would become of her?

What will become of me? Zeinab thought, clutching her knees and rocking herself back and forth on the window seat, what will become of me, and this child inside me?

There was a lull in the firing, as if to allow the sun to set in peace, and the sky turned lavender shot through with gold. Suddenly there was a single cannon fired, from the Citadel uphill, and this was immediately followed by the call to sunset prayers from the Citadel mosque. The chant rose faintly, then more powerfully, amplified as the other mosques around the city took up the call.

The fading notes resonated soothingly in the air, but something nagged at the back of Zeinab's distracted mind. Something was different. The call to prayer was followed by a silence so deep the twittering of the birds returning to their nests in the trees filled the air. Then a murmur arose all around the city, and then a trill of rejoicing, the *zaghruta*.

Zeinab stiffened. Suddenly she understood. The gun, the call to prayer from the Citadel! For the first time in three years. It could only mean the Citadel was in Muslim hands: the Ottomans had entered the city.

She jumped to her feet. Where was Nicolas? Was he safe?

An hour later Nicolas trudged up the steps to the loggia. He looked exhausted but managed a wan smile for her as she ran to greet him. His chin was covered in stubble, his coat lay over his arm, and circles of perspiration stained the armpits of his shirt. He wiped his forehead with his handkerchief. 'Let me get cleaned up, *ma jolie*, I stink like an old goat.'

He took off his boots and all of his clothes and washed with great splashes of water all over his face and body, then she handed him the thin cotton galabiya he sometimes wore at home in the evenings to keep cool and to save his French shirts.

'Ah.' He leaned back on the couch, and raised a hand to stop her as she was uncovering the tray. 'In a minute, *ma petite*, in a minute, I don't think I could eat just yet. But that watermelon looks so refreshing, why don't we start with that?'

She brought over the melon and a knife and he carved out slices and handed her the slice closest to the heart of the melon, where it was sweetest, as he always did. The thoughtful gesture brought tears to Zeinab's eyes. She tried to swallow, not looking at him, waiting for him to tell her what she was afraid to hear: that the time had come when he must leave.

Nicolas finished his watermelon and sat back, grim. 'It's all over. Belliard has signed a capitulation. We hand over Cairo to the Ottomans in the next few days, and the English stay on the Giza bank to guarantee our safe evacuation towards the coast. We leave on Ottoman and English ships from Aboukir. Tomorrow I must organize my remaining engineers and the more trustworthy of the servants to start packing all the instruments and tools at the Institute, and the books in the Library, not to mention all my sketches, my personal papers . . . There is so much to do, and so little time.'

The lump of dread in Zeinab's chest grew heavier by the minute. Nicolas was talking about papers and books and instruments, but what about people? What about her? Her mouth tightened and her chin lifted.

'Say something, *ma petite.*'

'I hate you!'

'Ah. That, perhaps, was not quite what I expected.' He sighed. 'Zeinab, what do you want from me? What is it you want from me?'

A burst of tears exploded from her eyes like a retch, and he reached for her but she batted away his hands and sat apart from him, her hand over her mouth, till she had swallowed the sob. She wiped her eyes with the back of her hand and clasped her arms around her middle, rocking back and forth, looking down at the floor.

'Zeinab, listen: we've negotiated that anyone who wants to

accompany us, any of the people who worked for the French or lived with them, may do so. Anyone who fears reprisals may ask to be evacuated with us. And anyone who collaborated with us but wishes to return to his former station is to be guaranteed security and safety from reprisals. So I ask you again, Zeinab, what is it you want to do?'

She stared at him. He was speaking to her as if she were a stranger to him, not his wife. 'I don't know. Can't . . . can't you stay?'

'No. Many of the troops that have deserted, or some junior officers or civilians who have converted and married in Egypt, will stay, no doubt, but I could no more stay than Belliard or Menou. I am a public man, Zeinab. My work is in France, my life is in France, my family is in France; it is out of the question.'

She winced, each word a knife thrust. She rocked back and forth for a moment till the pain passed and she could speak. 'Do you want me to come with you?'

'It's not a question of what I want. I told you that, if you were to come to France, it couldn't be as my wife. I am already married. What would I do, keep you as my concubine?'

'I could be your second wife, I would honour and respect your first wife. She would never have cause to complain of me, I promise.'

'No, I've told you, that won't be possible. I have a wife, I have three children – two of them older than you. For all I know, I may be a grandfather.'

Her face crumpled again and she bent over and hid her head in her arms, her long hair falling about her like a veil.

'Come here.' He leaned towards her and drew her in, against her resistance, gripping her knees between his, and circling his arms around her shoulders. He buried his face in her hair for a moment then tried to lift her chin. 'Look at me!'

She shook her head. He sighed. 'I've thought this over a thousand times, Zeinab, believe me. I won't leave you behind if you are afraid to stay. But you will be unhappy in France. You don't even wear your French dresses any more. Look at me, *ma petite*.' He took her head

175

in his hands and dug his thumbs under her chin, tilting her face up to force her to look at him. 'Do you even want to be with me any more?'

She closed her eyes but the tears seeped through them. Nicolas began to kiss her, gently at first, and her body responded like a creature with a mind of its own; everything in her went pliant, soft, open to him. He laid her back on the couch, and stroked her hair, and lapped her tears, and blew her face dry, murmuring endearments; he undid her sash and loosened her pantaloons and pushed them down and caressed her breasts and belly.

'Nicolas . . . ?' she whispered. She should tell him everything, he would find a way out of this terrible trap. Would he stay, if he realized she was expecting his child? Or would he ask her to do what Fatoum had done?

'Hmm?' He brushed his stubbly chin against her belly, and then he was parting her legs. What if he hurt the baby when he made love to her? The vision of the pool of blood rose before her. Her muscles tensed and her body went taut. 'No, wait, please.' She tried to push him away but he gripped her wrists and held them down over her head, and then he was inside her.

In the morning when she woke he was already up, buttoning his shirt in front of the window. She felt a vague throbbing in her breast and looked down; there was a small blue bite mark close to her armpit. 'To remember me by,' Nicolas had muttered, sometime during that night of tears and tenderness and savagery. She had cried, not because he had hurt her, but because of the finality of the words.

Zeinab stumbled out of bed, wrapping her Indian silk shawl around her, and came to stand, barefooted, behind him, as he dressed before the window. In the early-morning light she could make out the Ottoman banners flying from the ramparts of the Citadel. Nicolas turned to her with an expression she could not quite read. Was he angry with her? Sad? Disappointed?

He sat down on the bed to put on his boots and she slipped down to the floor in a pool of rose silk to help him. 'Don't,' he protested impatiently; then, more gently: 'Never mind, thank you.'

At the door he turned around. 'You have a few days to think about what you want to do, Zeinab. The plan is for the French and everyone who will be evacuated with us to leave Cairo and gather on the far bank of the Nile in Giza and on Rawda Island, under protection of the English, until such time as we head north. The Nasiriya fort will be the last place to be evacuated, so you will be safe here for a day or two longer. If you want to come with me, you must tell me. But we need to start selling everything in the house – furniture, everything.' He gestured around the room. 'I don't care to keep any of it. You can sell it and keep the money.' He tied his cravat and stopped at the door, looking back at her as if he had something more to say. Then he shook his head as if he thought better of it, and kept going.

The next day Nicolas was leafing through piles of sketches in his study, looking for one specific sketch he could not leave Cairo without, when he was interrupted by the entrance of Dr Desgenettes.

'Docteur! What brings you to the Nasiriya?'

Desgenettes sank into a camp chair with the air of a man who had been on his feet for hours. 'You should thank General Belliard, Citoyen – you and your colleagues of the Scientific Commission. He has sent me to tell you that he has managed, after a hard negotiation with the English and the Capitan Pasha, to reach an agreement for your findings and collections.'

'The Capitan Pasha?'

'The Ottoman admiral. Belliard stipulated, as per your request, that the Scientific Commission could take, as your personal property, your scientific papers, your specimen collections, and the library and scientific instruments of the Institute.'

'Ah! The Institute owes him a debt of gratitude indeed.'

'These concessions were not easy to obtain, he would have you know.' Desgenettes leaned back in exhaustion, then sat up straight again as if he were afraid to get too comfortable. 'The Ottomans and the amirs together pledged four hundred camels to carry the belongings of the Scientific Commission.'

'What of the fist of Ramses that my aérostatiers raised from

Memphis and transported with such pains to our garden here in Nasiriya?'

Desgenettes shook his head. 'They would not budge on that point.'

'Mad King George is welcome to it, then!' Nicolas tried to hide his bitterness. 'But the Rosetta Stone – that, at least, I hope our general fights for with every argument at his disposal.' Nicolas turned to the window for a moment, contemplating the Cairo skyline of minarets and towers. 'I confess, *mon ami*, that I am not sorry to see the end of this ill-conceived mission, and leave it to history to draw up the balance sheet.' Nicolas continued sifting through his portfolios as he spoke, discarding one after the other of the sketches with a quick glance.

'What is it you're looking for, my friend?' Desgenettes raised his eyebrows, his curiosity getting the better of his discretion.

'Only a sketch – it is of particular sentimental value to me, I would not want to leave Cairo without it.'

'I see. By the way, have you heard from our friend Geoffroy lately? I hear he and our colleagues who left ahead of us for the coast are in dire straits.'

'Indeed, I received a letter from him that a furious Menou accused them of desertion! Really, it makes sense to me that the work of the savants here is finished, and that they should be evacuated and repatriated to safeguard their precious collections and findings. It is entirely different for you and me, Docteur; we are indispensable to the war effort, but what could a naturalist like Geoffroy or a mathematician like Fourier contribute?' Nicolas tossed a pile of sketches to the floor and picked up another, leafing through it rapidly.

'At any rate, from what I hear, they are no better off than we are in Cairo. In fact, considerably worse, under siege in Alexandria enduring the harshest conditions. But, my dear Conté, what is this sketch that has you in such a frenzy?' Desgenettes could contain himself no longer.

'It is a sketch of Zeinab. My companion.'

'Ah, I see.' Desgenettes eyes were full of compassion. 'I take it, then, that you will not take her with you when we evacuate?'

Nicolas stopped his frantic search and began pacing up and down before Desgenettes' chair. 'I am at a loss, Docteur. It is a conundrum that tortures my mind at this time when there is so much I should be attending to. I can hardly bear to leave my little Zeinab behind, and yet how can I take her back to France with me? What of my family? Lise, my wife, is a woman of great heart; she might understand much and forgive much, but I have not seen or heard from her for three years, I cannot just land with an Oriental girl in my baggage and expect my wife to understand. We are almost strangers to each other now, Lise and I; we will need time to become reacquainted, almost as newlyweds do. How can I destroy any chance of future happiness we might have together, and alienate the hearts of my precious children? The two older ones can scarcely have forgotten me, but little Nicolas will have to get to know his papa all over again.'

'I understand. But do you believe there is no risk to the girl in leaving her behind?'

'If I thought leaving Zeinab behind would put her at risk or make her miserable, I would make sure she was evacuated with me, and find some situation for her in France. I would not keep her as a mistress, clandestine or otherwise; to do so would be an injustice to her, and my wife as well. But some situation could surely be found for her, perhaps under the kind protection of someone like Madame Verdier?' Nicolas stopped in the middle of the room for a moment then began his pacing again. 'Yet I have not the least doubt that Zeinab would be wretched enough to take her own life if I uprooted her from all she holds familiar and dear and brought her to a strange land and then abandoned her among strangers, without the one person to whom she has an attachment: the man she thinks of as her husband.'

Desgenettes nodded. 'There is no doubt it would be a wrenching experience for any girl.'

'There was a time when I might have thought she could adapt. But everything in her behaviour of late supports my impression that she would be utterly wretched in France. She seems to have lost her vivacity, and when she is not lolling in bed she drags about miserably in her harem clothing, her hair hanging down her back; she never wears her French frocks or coifs her locks in the pretty ringlets and ribbons that suited her so well.' Nicolas stopped, and dropped his voice. 'But there is more; and of graver import. She, who had been so natural, so abandoned in her transports when she lay in my arms, now seems to shy away from my caresses as if I had suddenly contracted the plague. I cannot but conclude that her attachment to me was more in the way of an immature fancy, a childish dependence; and that she might have displayed the same instinctive affection to any man who was the first to awaken her sensuality.'

'You must find this coldness on her part painful, *mon ami.*'

'It is, but it relieves my mind to think that she will not suffer as much from my absence as my vanity might have led me to suppose, and that, young as she is, she will, in time, find comfort in the arms of another.'

'In that case, we can only hope the standing and influence of her father will guarantee her safety until such time as spirits have healed and he can arrange a suitable match for her.' Desgenettes rose. 'I need to head back to the hospital at the Elephant Pond. I wish I could offer you some comfort or advice, but I can no more see into the future than you. Have you made up your mind, then?'

'Whenever I think I have, I find myself playing Devil's advocate to my own arguments,' Nicolas admitted miserably. 'If Zeinab were to ask to come with me, even now, I would, and bear the consequences. But time is running out, time is running out.' Nicolas turned back to sifting through his sketches even before Desgenettes had left the room.

PART III

The Aftermath

FOURTEEN

The Trial

'Time is treacherous.'
Arab proverb

As Elfi passed under the arch of the Gate of Victory and entered Cairo, something of the thrill that coursed through his blood must have transmitted from his thigh muscles to his horse, for it reared suddenly and the parade was momentarily disrupted as the other horses around it shied and neighed. Elfi gripped his knees and his horse responded instantly, settling down to a slow, steady pace. He looked over to his left, where white-bearded old Ibrahim Bey rode unperturbed, abreast of Tambourji and Bardissi, Elfi's khushdash.

The crowds had been lining the city walls and the streets since sunrise in anticipation of the triumphant return of the amirs and the Ottomans; houses with a window or roof overlooking the path of the procession had been rented at high rates for the occasion. Battalions of Janissaries, Albanian Ottomans and Syrian units headed the parade, marching to the beat of tambours and drums. Better to have them in front, Elfi thought; he would not have wanted to turn his back on them. Behind Elfi and the amirs came the jurists and the ulema, along with the heads of the Sufi orders and their whirling dervishes. Runners and guards scattered Istanbul coins to the populace lining the streets ahead of the Grand Vizir himself, wearing a giant turban with a diamond as big as an egg pinned to the plume.

A Turkish orchestra followed, with artillery and infantry bringing up the rear.

By the time the parade had reached the centre of the city, it was almost noon, and guns were fired from the Citadel. The Vizir, followed by the Turkish dignitaries and the amirs, stopped and dismounted at the Mosque of Husayn for the noonday prayer. The procession then proceeded to the Azhar Mosque, where the Vizir dismounted again and toured the premises before giving the order to slaughter five water-buffaloes and ten rams and distribute the meat among the attendants and servants.

Elfi willed himself to contain his impatience; he had yet to set foot in his Ezbekiah palace. He was as eager as an estranged lover to see for himself what Time, and the hands of strangers, had wrought on his beloved. But he had waited three years for this moment, he told himself, he could wait three more hours. He would take possession of his home again, and then he would call on Sitt Nafisa; there was unfinished business between them. In the three months since their last meeting, he had been able to conjure her face before him at any moment of the day or night; the time was ripe, now, to act upon his inclination. Particularly since, in this case, convention weighted the balance on the side of his desires: he was the foremost amir of her late husband, and it was his role to offer protection to the widow. He only questioned the timing of his visit; it might look unseemly, on his first day back after such a long absence, but his gut told him that time was not on his side.

On the surface he kept his face impassive, even benign; only his horse sensed his master's tension and was unusually skittish. Impatience had been one of the besetting sins of Elfi's youth, but his years in exile had taught him to tame his impatience as other men tamed their hunger by fasting.

Just when he thought he could decently take his leave, Shaykh Sadat, whose house was near the Husayni shrine, invited the Vizir to dinner, and included in his invitation the entire party: Ottoman dignitaries, amirs and ulema. There was no way for Elfi to decline without exacerbating the mutual distrust between him and the Ottomans.

By the time the banquet was over, dusk had fallen and it was by the light of the illuminations from the minarets of every mosque and nearly every house in the city that the procession remounted and escorted the Vizir up the hill to the Citadel, at the gates of which Elfi finally turned his horse's head around.

'Elfi Bey!' It was Shaykh Jabarti who now accosted him. 'May I call on you after evening prayers to congratulate you on your safe return among us?'

Elfi began to brush him off but thought better of it. In the past, he had been too often dismissive with the ulema, but he might well need them as allies now; under the French, they had demonstrated their influence over the masses. Besides, he had more time for Jabarti than for most clerics. A shrewd man, Jabarti, under his pompous airs, and Elfi had more than once consulted him on choosing books and furnishing his library. Moreover the shaykh could always be relied on to have his finger on the pulse of the city.

'You are always welcome under my roof, Shaykh Jabarti.'

Elfi turned his horse and spurred it to a flat gallop down the hill from the Citadel, then dropped to a trot as he turned into the narrow streets heading in the direction of the Ezbekiah. There was a time when, relying on the immemorial right of way of the Mamlukes, he would have cantered heedlessly through these streets while people parted before him like leaves before the wind. But this evening he slowed down, avoiding trampling so much as a rat, and looked around him as he passed, taking stock of the demolitions and constructions that had changed the city almost beyond recognition. It was a miracle that his Ezbekiah mansion still stood.

But there it was, as he turned into the Ezbekiah esplanade. Lanterns illuminated the arched doorway in the dark; the Mamlukes and servants he had sent ahead, hearing his approach, pulled open the gates. The first thing he saw as he entered the grounds of the palace was a small mosque that had not been there before, in the middle of the courtyard. The last French commandant to use the palace as headquarters, Abdullah-Jacques Menou, had built the mosque during his tenure. Elfi decided, then and there, that he would let it stand;

he would even ask the good shaykh, Jabarti, when he arrived, to say a prayer there, in gratitude for his return.

He took a torch from one of the servants and gestured to his retainers to stay behind in the courtyard and let him tour the mansion alone. Here and there he stumbled in the dark over the rising of an unfamiliar doorway, or some other modification Kléber had introduced. General Kléber had been an architect as a civilian, Elfi knew, and so he studied the changes with a critical eye, debating what he might leave alone and what he would restore to its original design. The partitions between the private and public quarters would need to be reinstated, at the very least, before he could let his Mamlukes come to live in the apartments around the courtyard.

Elfi descended to the courtyard and asked the servants to spread carpets and cushions in the receiving hall on the first floor, and to prepare refreshments. He strolled into the garden, inhaling the familiar scent of Indian jasmine and orange blossom. At the fountain he washed and then ducked his head under water and held his breath for as long as it took a hawk to circle seven times.

By the time he returned to the reception hall, several of his Mamlukes, and Shaykh Jabarti had gathered and were talking in corners. He greeted them cordially and invited the cleric to take a seat beside him on the carpet; the servants hurried to bring pipes and coffee.

'So what news of the city, Shaykh?'

'The Vizir sent out another proclamation after you left, that nobody may bring prejudice or injury to a Christian or a Jew, be he Copt, Greek or Syrian, as they are all subjects of the Sultan, and that the past should not be recalled. God willing, there will be no reprisals . . .'

Elfi took a long pull on his pipe and listened with half an ear as the shaykh rambled on, trying to pick up a pattern in the ostensibly idle gossip.

'But there are so many militias of all races pouring into Cairo in the wake of the Ottomans, Elfi Bey, it is hard to know who is who any more. All these Janissaries and Albanians . . . And they all seem bent on finding a wife. The women who ruined their reputations by cohabiting with the French, and who now find themselves in a

186

predicament, are donning the veil again and letting go-betweens make offers of marriage on their behalf to these foreign soldiers who have no idea of their past, and would not care if they knew. Nor is there anyone among the Egyptians who cares to disabuse these strangers.'

The muezzin called for prayers and a cloud of annoyance passed over Elfi's face: it would be too late to call on Sitt Nafisa this evening. Then Jabarti leaned closer.

'You will have heard, Elfi Bey, that the Ottomans intend to continue the ban on the importation of Mamlukes to Egypt? Even though the French are gone. And with the ranks of the amirs so depleted by the fighting . . .'

Elfi's ears pricked up.

'But what of the French Mamlukes, Elfi Bey? I mean, the Frenchmen who refused to evacuate with their countrymen, and are now looking to rally around a new master. I hear that, when they deliberate among themselves, there is one name mentioned – yours.'

Elfi looked at him sharply. 'You hear much, it seems to me, Shaykh.'

'Only what God gives me the ears to hear, in His compassion, to console me for the deterioration of my eyes. But indeed, any patron might find these French Mamlukes more reliable than most in the days to come, for I fear we are entering a time of even greater uncertainty and tribulation and . . . treachery.'

A bustle by the gate announced the arrival of visitors of note, and Jabarti got to his feet. 'Ah, here come your khushdash, Bardissi Bey and Tambourji Bey; I must take my leave and head home to pray. Thank you for your hospitality, Elfi Bey.'

'But the Vizir reinstated Ibrahim Bey with full powers, and gave him the title of Master of Cairo. I don't see why you are so suspicious of the Ottomans' intentions, Elfi.' Tambourji threw up his hands. 'Don't we have English guarantees from General Hutchinson? Didn't Sir Sidney write to you assuring us of protection? You are ever too inclined to distrust, Elfi. Ya Allah! Where are the women? Where are the singers? Where are the musicians? I feel we have been brought here under false pretences. Can we not rejoice, can we not celebrate, for one night at least?'

'It's not for nothing that you earned your nickname,' Elfi retorted dryly. In the ranks of his khushdash there were three Osmans, so they were known by their nicknames: Tambourji, for his expert playing of the tambour; Bardissi, after the name of the town; and Ashqar, the blond, for his fairness. Two of the three Osmans sat before him this evening, a contrast in face and mood: Tambourji smiling and light-hearted, Bardissi sombre and taciturn.

'There will be a time for rejoicing and music,' Elfi placated Tambourji. 'But it is too soon to let our guard down, and it would be a mistake to take the Vizir's assurances at face value. He is only biding his time until he makes his move against us.'

'Do you know anything you are not sharing with us?' Bardissi interjected, an undercurrent of suspicion in his tone, as he put down his goblet of pomegranate juice.

'It stands to reason. For decades now the Ottomans have longed to reinstate the Sultan's authority over this country, and for all that time the amirs before us have resisted them and offered no more than nominal allegiance; we had even stopped paying them revenues al-together. These injuries and insults have festered in their minds. Now that they have entered the country, taken possession of it, and become our masters, do you think they will leave it in our hands and go back to their own land? No. They will want clear possession of Egypt, and that means they will turn against us as soon as they are confident in the strength of their numbers. Haven't you noticed the troops pouring into the city – Janissaries and Albanians and mercenaries from all over the empire? We are exchanging one occupation for another.'

Tambourji looked worried for a moment, but then he shook his head. 'It's not possible, not after we fought beside them for three years against the French, sacrificing our lives and our property. And besides, they don't know the ways of the country or how to govern it and can't do without us.'

'Assuming there is a basis to your concern, Elfi,' Bardissi pulled at his beard, 'what do you suggest we do?'

'My advice is for us all to cross to Giza, encamp there, and make the English act as mediators between us and the Vizir and the Capitan Pasha. We should draw up mutually agreed conditions, guaranteed by the English, and we should not return to the east bank of the Nile and re-enter Cairo itself till the bulk of the Ottoman troops leave. Only those holding office, like the governor, should remain; the troops must leave.'

Tambourji objected. 'How can we show them hostility when no treachery on their part has become evident? How can we go for help to the English, who are enemies of the faith? The ulema will judge us to have committed treason against the Sultan and Islam. If we wait till the Ottomans try anything against us, then we will be taking our just revenge, and God will be on our side. And if the English then mediate between us, we will not be at fault.'

Elfi snorted in frustration. 'As for the matter of faith, the Ottomans were the first to turn to the English for help! Without their aid, they could never have expelled the French. We saw what happened last year when the Ottomans were at Heliopolis without the English. Besides, we are not asking the English for military help, only to mediate in the matter of a truce. But I warn you. If we wait for the Vizir to show his cards and act against us first, it might be too late to set matters right after the fact.'

They were silent. It was Tambourji who finally broke the tension. 'We can't settle this matter tonight, at any rate. Let's go instead to my house for some entertainment. I will send for musicians and dancers. Our first night back in Cairo . . . surely we must celebrate! Won't you join us, Elfi?'

'Not tonight.'

'You've given us much to think about.' Bardissi came to his feet. 'But I suggest we keep our deliberations to ourselves till we reach a decision.'

Elfi walked them to the gate and turned back to the courtyard. He felt suddenly very tired, but he dismissed the servants who stood ready, torches in hand, to lead him upstairs to his bedchamber. He headed for the loggia, alone, and made himself a makeshift bed with a rug and a cushion. He lay down, looking up at the stars overhead. Had he become such a wild creature that he could no longer sleep in bedchambers and palaces; that he sought the hard ground underneath and the stars overhead like a Bedouin in the desert? Three years, he thought bitterly, three years of dreaming of the first night he would spend under his own roof at the Ezbekiah mansion, and here he was, troubled by misgivings and treachery, too uneasy to allow himself to sleep soundly on soft bedding with a woman in his arms.

He would have to leave Cairo again. There was no help for it. Now that Bardissi and Tambourji had declined to commit to his course, it was no longer safe to stay. He would strike his own path.

But Sitt Nafisa? Would he have to renounce her? In his mind's eye he saw her, as he had seen her that sultry summer's day he came disguised: he had caught her off guard, in her thin rose chemise, her long honey hair loose about her shoulders, a dew of perspiration on the delicate white skin of her fine collarbone. Her face was still lovely, if no longer fresh; but her body belied her face: it was the body of a young woman. He had never dreamed to see her in this state of vulnerable intimacy, and he had hidden the stolen image deep in his mind, to be conjured in moments of solitude.

But she was far more than a woman to him. He was a man who needed women as some men needed wine, and he had never been without them, Mamlukas or Bedouin girls, he took them and kept them till he was tired of them, and then he rewarded them generously and forgot them.

Sitt Nafisa was different. It was not only that she had been Murad's wife, and the great Ali Bey's widow, as far above Elfi as the stars in the sky. When he looked into her large, hazel eyes, he sought his own reflection, the measure of his worth, in her penetrating gaze. Lady Nafisa the White, the common people called her, and there was that quality about her, a transparency, a compassion, that made him ashamed of his baser impulses.

He had lived his life by the only law he knew, the law of survival; untroubled by the suffering of others, no more going out of his way to be cruel than to be kind. But the long nights alone with his thoughts in the desert had worked a change in him, like the Sahara wind shifting the shape of the sand dunes overnight, grain by grain, till when daylight came, the dunes had moved. He had come to think that there must be other ways, and other laws; that men could live and die for greater causes and higher loyalties than their own short lives encompassed.

He kept this confusion of thoughts to himself; had it become public knowledge that Elfi was plagued by doubts and scruples he would have been cut down like a horse with a broken leg. But he believed that if he could somehow win Sitt Nafisa's trust, she could validate his faith in the better angels of his nature. Tomorrow he would go to her, and he would ask for her hand.

Zeinab looked out of the window at the preparations for the Prophet's mulid: the streets were being swept and sprinkled, the lanterns raised, the stores decorated with silk and Indian cloth in expectation of the Vizir's visit; the children played and were noisy in the streets, carrying their sugar dolls and cavaliers. How she had changed, Zeinab thought as she watched them. Only three years ago she had been a child herself, licking the sugar paste off her doll and hopping up and down with excitement as she watched the French soldiers and ladies parade on their way to the Nilometer. How carefree she had been then! Today she watched the children as a mother might, with a child growing in her own belly, and all the worries of the world weighing on her heart. Her secret grew heavier to bear with each passing day and there were moments when she had to bite the inside of her cheek not to betray herself.

She kept thinking of the last time she had seen Nicolas. As she rode away on a mule from the Nasiriya house, she had half turned in the saddle and cupped her hands on her belly, looking straight at him. He had frozen on the spot, a thousand doubts flitting over his face. She had wanted him to know, now that it was too late, or at least to wonder if he were leaving a child behind in Egypt. She had twisted around in the saddle one last time before turning the corner of the street, and Nicolas was still standing there, frozen, although he was too far away for her to read the expression on his face.

She missed him desperately. Now that they were apart, now that her dread of what he might do was behind her, she missed him with all her heart. At night, she would wake up drenched in sweat, tormented by dreams of him, a leaden pressure between her legs.

Zeinab turned back to the window. The Nile flood had been unusually high this year, so high it had exceeded the extra cubit the French had added to the Nilometer. But the Ezbekiah Pond in front of her father's house had been dammed by the French and would never flood again; this evening there would be no pleasure boats criss-crossing the water with lanterns at their prow while musicians played and syrup sellers hawked their juices.

But around the city it seemed as if all the Cairenes were feverishly catching up with festivities after three long years of abstention. Several weddings had been planned to coincide with the mulid; returning amirs were marrying the widows of their colleagues who had fallen in the fighting, and a number of the newly arrived Ottomans had already found brides among the local women.

Hearing footsteps approaching, Zeinab sucked in her belly and stood up straighter. Even though she was still flat as a loaf of unleavened bread, she was careful; as yet, even her mother had no suspicion that she was pregnant. But that could not last; and what would become of her then?

Dada came into the room. 'Sitt Zeinab, your father is asking for you in his chamber.'

Zeinab hurried; it was the first time her father had called her into his presence since she had come back under his roof. She found him standing before a mirror and winding a white turban carefully around his head while her mother stood by, holding his kaftan and sash. Zeinab quickly kissed their hands, each in turn.

'Ah, Zeinab,' her mother smiled, 'your father is preparing to go to Sitt Adila's wedding; Ibrahim Bey is giving her in marriage to Soliman, the Mamluke of her husband, who fell at the battle of Imbaba. She's been a widow for three years and now it is finally time to rejoice.'

'Her father was in a hurry to seal her marriage to an amir before one of the Ottoman dignitaries asked for her hand, knowing it would be impolitic to refuse.' Shaykh Bakri looped his turban around one more time. 'But the Turks are out to marry in Cairo, bringing prestigious positions and offering good dowries, so it is an opportunity for many . . .'

Zeinab recognized the musing in her father's apparently offhand remarks and wondered with some misgiving what he was planning.

'Did you hear,' said her mother, helping him on with his kaftan, 'Ismail Kashif has taken back his wife Hawa to live with him. Can it be possible that no one has told him of her liaison with Bartholomew? Or perhaps he knows that she was forced against her will and has forgiven her. She is not quite right in the head, poor thing.'

Zeinab breathed easier. She was glad for the woman with the sad face, but also reassured, somehow, on her own account: if Ismail Kashif could forgive his wife, it augured well for her. Sitt Nafisa had taken back Mamlukas who had been living with the French, that was true, but a freeborn woman from a notable family like Hawa would be judged more harshly than a slave girl.

'Zeinab, bring me my slippers,' Shaykh Bakri commanded as he turned away from the mirror. Zeinab hurried to bring his slippers of soft Moroccan leather and he patted her head as she bent down to set them before his feet.

'I will surely be in the company of some of the Ottoman dignitaries during the mulid procession, and later at the wedding at Ibrahim Bey's house. It would be quite natural to drop hints that I have a marriageable daughter, still only fifteen. No doubt there will be an offer or two from some well-placed Turks; an advantageous match might well come of it. Indeed, it might consolidate my position with the new authorities. But we must strike while the iron is hot, before the rumours reach them and ruin your reputation in their eyes. Under the French, I made many enemies who would seek to humiliate and injure me. Omar Makram, for one, will surely complain to the Vizir that the French deposed him as naqib to appoint me in his place. Most damaging will be the accusation that my daughter had gone over to the Franj. So we must act quickly if I am to make a match for you.'

Zeinab's mother brought her hand to her mouth and gave a little trill of rejoicing.

'Do you hear, my daughter? A match for you! May God preserve you for the good man you are, Shaykh Khalil Bakri! Zeinab, what are you waiting for, go kiss your father's hand and thank him for his concern for your welfare and your future!'

'I can't!' Zeinab's face twisted.

Her parents' consternation was complete. 'What do you mean?' her father barked.

'Zeinab, are you out of your mind?' Her mother clapped her hand to her breast. 'Forgive her, Shaykh, she doesn't know what she is saying.'

Zeinab dropped to her knees and clasped her belly. 'I can't be married, I'm – I'm with child.'

Her mother fell back on the bed, breathing in rasping gasps. Shaykh Bakri's face was a thundercloud. When he regained the power of speech, he spat: 'How far along?'

Zeinab understood. 'No, Father, not that!' The sight of the pool of blood beneath Fatoum's hips filled her mind. 'Please – you're a man of God, don't ask me to do that! Have mercy!'

His hands dropped to his sides. 'Then you have sealed your own fate,' he hissed, and turned on his heel and walked out.

Zeinab crawled over to her mother on the bed and buried her face in her lap. 'Help me, Mother, help me.'

Her mother tried to swat her away. 'Foolish, foolish child,' she keened. 'My poor child! No one can help you now. What is to become of you?'

Nicolas, Zeinab thought; Nicolas was the only one who could save her now. Perhaps it was not yet too late to run to him. There had been loud firing from the direction of the French encampment on Rawda Island this morning, and her maid said it was the gunpowder factories going up in flames; word on the street was that the French were blowing them up as they retreated. They were the factories Nicolas had set up; there was a chance he might still be there. She got up and ran to her room, calling for her maid.

'What is it, Sitt Zeinab?'

'Dada, I want you to go to the French camp at Rawda, right now, and find Nicolas. Hurry, I beg you!'

'They're gone, Sitt Zeinab. The French are all gone.'

'But the fire at the gunpowder factories this morning?'

'No, Sitt Zeinab, it turned out that it was all the doing of an idle boy who strung along with the barudis when they went to Rawda to take over the abandoned factories. The foolish boy tried to light a pipe and the gunpowder blew up and he is blown to pieces and two men with him. The French are gone, Sitt Zeinab; well and truly gone.'

Zeinab threw herself on the bed, her heart pounding. There was no one and nothing that could save her now. What would become of her?

'Welcome back, Elfi Bey. Cairo is illuminated by your presence.'

'It is illuminated with the light of its people, Sitt Nafisa.'

Elfi was dressed as if for battle, she thought: enamelled gold Turkish medals pinned to the scarlet sash of his braid-trimmed azure coat, his sword in a bejewelled silver scabbard hanging at his side, a diamond aigrette in his white turban. Dressed as if for battle – or for courting. The thought passed through her mind, returned, stood watch. Heat flooded her face at the memory of their meeting a year ago, when her emotions had overwhelmed her like a torrential rain in the desert. They had stood rooted to the spot that day, at opposite ends of the room, as if painfully shackled to the floor. Conjecture swirled in her head like a flight of birds scattered by gunshot. But this was not why Elfi was here, she reminded herself. He was here because she was Murad's widow, and he was Murad's foremost amir, and it was his place, his duty and his honour to take her in marriage. His ambition, perhaps, above all: by marrying her, Elfi would consolidate his dominant position among his peers. And Elfi was ambitious above all else. He was claiming her as his prize.

Outwardly she was composed, but glad of the added armour of her widow's black veils.

'Please take a seat, Elfi Bey.' Nafisa took her customary place on the window bench, where she would have her back to the light and her face would be in shadow. 'You must have rejoiced in spending the night peacefully under your own roof at last.'

'Yes, well . . . it is perhaps a little too soon for peace of mind. There is yet much uncertainty about the intentions of the Ottomans.'

Nafisa sighed and nodded. 'I'm afraid you are right. God forbid, if civil war breaks out . . .' She shook her head. 'What we went through with the French will pale in comparison.'

He nodded, but seemed distracted, pacing around the room. His agitation troubled Nafisa. 'Will you not take a seat, Elfi Bey?'

'Lady, there are matters of which we must speak – in private.'

Nafisa flicked her fingers and her eunuch and the two maids who had been hovering in the shadows slipped out of the room. Elfi came to stand before her.

'Forgive me, I will be blunt. If it were in my hands, if the world were different, if time were on my side – I would woo you as you deserve. Blame the uncertain times we live in for the haste of my suit. You can be in no doubt of the admiration I have for you, have always had for you. Do me the honour of taking me for your husband and protector.'

Nafisa felt herself flush, and was doubly glad of her black veil. Something in her stiffened with resistance. She had been Ali Bey's wife, and then Murad's. She was not ready, just yet, to give herself over to any man's will; perhaps she never would be again. If Elfi's offer had not been made so hastily, so inopportunely, so arrogantly . . . it might have been another matter. But he was not a man to value what he could have for the asking.

'Lady?' Elfi's face was growing sterner with every moment that passed. 'They say silence is the sign of approval, but I must ask you to speak.'

'Forgive me, Elfi Bey. You honour me with your suit. It speaks of your loyalty to my husband and to his house. But I cannot consider marriage at the moment . . . It is too soon. Forgive me.'

His blue eyes hardened. She was instantly filled with misgivings; Elfi was a proud man, and a hard man to make an enemy of.

He took a step back. 'Then I bid you farewell, Sitt Nafisa.'

'Farewell?'

'I leave Cairo this very day.'

'How is that possible, sir?'

'I have been to see the Vizir this morning, and asked him to appoint me governor of Upper Egypt.'

'And he accepted?'

'I knew he would. He is greedy, and I promised to collect considerable revenues from the estates of the Beys who died without heirs. But most of all he wishes to get rid of me: he fears me most of all the amirs in Cairo today. Sending me away accomplishes both his purposes. And as of this moment, it suits my purpose as well.'

'But – surely you will not leave today? You have spent only one night under your own roof!'

'I leave right away. The Vizir thinks I will tarry till he invests me officially with the robe and pelisse of office, but when he sends for me I will be gone. I don't trust him, even less now that I have shown my cards, and I have no doubt there are those among my rivals who will hasten to accuse me of ambition and to ask the Vizir to reconsider.' He took another step towards the door. 'I only came to know your mind; my course of action was in your hands. Had your answer been different, I would have renounced the governorship, and taken my chances with the Turks. But now there is nothing to keep me here. So I bid you farewell.'

'May God guide your path in safety, Elfi Bey.' She rose.

He stopped and turned at the door. He touched his hand to his brow, and brought it to his heart, and when he spoke again his voice and his expression had softened. 'May I next see your face in good health, Sitt Nafisa.'

The hours passed, and Zeinab lay on the bed in the darkened room, the mashrabiyya shutters closed. For her there was no sleeping nor eating nor drinking. Her maid had tried to give her a sip of pomegranate juice but Zeinab's insides were so clenched with dread that she had vomited instantly. At one point in the afternoon she had heard a stifled wail coming from her mother's room, and her maid had come to keep watch beside her, trying not to show her agitation.

'What is it, Dada?'

'Oh, Sitt Zeinab, don't ask me to speak of it. It is too dreadful.'

'You might as well tell me.'

'Poor woman!'

'Who?'

'Sitt Hawa. Her husband Ismail Kashif went to the Vizir this afternoon and asked for permission to put his wife to death. When that permission was granted, he strangled his wife forthwith, along with her Mamluka, who had borne him a son.'

'God help us! But why? Had the kashif not taken her back?'

'I don't know, Sitt Zeinab. Maybe he didn't know about Bartholomew when he took her back. Or maybe he knew and forgave her, but after a few days he could not bear to be the object of scorn and derision and winks in the street, and he decided to kill her publicly to save his honour and put an end to the talk.'

Zeinab buried her face in her pillow. The shadows lengthened in the room, and she heard her father come home; it occurred to her, in a haze, that he was home early. He had not been expected to return till very late at night after the wedding at Ibrahim Bey's palace. Lying alone in her chamber, she heard the birds twittering as they came to roost in the trees, and then the muezzin's chant, scaling the notes and rising high to hang in the air as the hush of the end of the day descended upon the city. She felt a moment of peace. The sun was setting, the day with its fears and alarms, was done; she could let her dread recede for the night.

A pounding at the gate of the house startled her and she bolted upright. The pounding and shouting continued and there were cries of alarm downstairs. In a minute her maid came to her, wailing and beating her breast.

'Sitt Zeinab, the police chief is downstairs with two of the Vizir's men asking for you to go with them right now. God preserve us from this evil!'

'Me? What can the police chief want with me? Where is my father? Call my father!'

'Your father is with them and they are commanding you to go to them at once or they will come upstairs and take you just as you are, in your chemise!'

Zeinab stumbled out of bed. 'Help me, Dada, help me dress.'

She was trembling so hard she could not dress herself, and stood shaking as the maid, weeping, helped her slip on her tunic and pantaloons, and covered her with the long black cloak. She fixed the yashmak on her face, but there was no time to comb and braid her tangled hair. Zeinab pushed her feet into the platformed wooden clogs and stumbled down the stairs, a film of terror obscuring her vision. She heard her mother wailing from her room; it sounded as if she were being prevented from coming out.

At the bottom of the stairs she found her father with three men in Ottoman livery. 'Father! What's happening?'

He neither answered nor met her eyes, and she felt her knees buckle; the Vizir's men caught her, one on each side.

'Are you Zeinab, daughter of Shaykh Khalil Bakri?' the chief of police demanded.

She nodded.

'Speak up.'

'I am Zeinab.'

'Are you the same Zeinab, daughter of Shaykh Bakri, who consorted with the French publicly and lived with them for the period of the French occupation?'

She looked wildly at her father.

'Do you deny it?' the chief of police barked.

'I repent, God help me, I repent of all my sins.'

The man addressed her father. 'What say you?'

Zeinab turned wildly to her father; surely he would tell them that he himself had sent her to the French to be married to Bonaparte? Surely he would use his influence to save her?

But Shaykh Bakri did not meet her eyes; he threw his hands up in the air. 'I wash my hands of her fate.'

199

'Father!' Zeinab screamed.

'Do what you must,' he said to the police chief, 'but do not do it here, to spare her mother.'

One of the Vizir's men threw a shawl over Zeinab's head and she felt herself lifted like a sack and thrown into a cart, and then she was rattling along in the dark, stifled by the shawl, too shocked even to scream.

The cart rolled and clattered around corners and Zeinab tried not to throw up. At some point their progress was intercepted; the cart came to a halt and she heard voices, an argument, someone saying: 'No, take her to the Citadel and wait for the Vizir there.' She moved the shawl away from her face enough to take a few gulps of air but dared not throw it off.

Then the cart started up again, veering sharply, and in a few minutes she guessed by the uphill motion that they were riding up to the Citadel. Dizziness overcame her and she barely came to her senses when she felt herself being lifted out of the cart and thrown into a cell in the Citadel prison. The door clanged shut in the dark, and she threw off the shawl and lay there in a faint.

It must have been hours later when the door opened and the light of a torch shone in her eyes. Two men took her by the arms and lifted her, feet dragging on the floor, across the courtyard and into a large hall. She blinked in the torchlight, too faint to take in the faces of the men sitting cross-legged on cushioned banquettes around the centre of the room. The policemen set her down in one corner and she collapsed in a limp heap.

'Give her some water,' she heard a voice command. After sipping a few drops she was sufficiently revived to try to raise her head and take in the room. A man in a very large, bejewelled turban, sitting cross-legged on a dais, with guards standing behind him, seemed to be presiding over the proceedings. Could that be the Vizir himself? She trembled at the thought. Of the several men to the right of him she thought she could recognize Omar Makram, the Naqib Ashraf who had resisted the French and been forced to flee; also Shaykh Sadat; and there was Shaykh Jabarti. Her teacher! Her first instinct

200

was to look to him for succour, but instantly she was overtaken by misgivings; what would he tell the court about her and Nicolas and their secret marriage? His face was as severe and impassive as ever; she could read no sympathy there. Her eyes darted to the other side of the room and she saw her father.

'Father!' She cried out, arms outstretched, and the policeman shoved her down roughly behind the gallery railing. 'Silence! Speak only when you are spoken to!'

She cringed and covered her face with her abaya, keeping her eyes to the ground. A man whose voice she did not recognize addressed the Vizir. 'We are here to ask Shaykh Bakri to answer for his conduct during the French occupation, a calamity that was only lifted from this land by the grace of God and the succour of the Sultan and Your Excellency. During the time of the occupation he insinuated himself into the favour of the French by all means at his disposal, fair and foul, and conspired with them, out of personal ambition and greed, to strip Omar Makram, the Naqib Ashraf, of his rightful title and position, and usurp it for himself.'

'There is more' – Zeinab recognized Shaykh Sadat's stentorian voice – 'he used his influence and prominence with the French to have himself declared head of the Sufi Order of the Bakris, a position for which he is singularly unfit on account of his known licentiousness and many vices, to which he added, under the French, the addiction to drink, and other comportment it is not fitting to speak of.'

'But the chief charge against him,' another voice spoke up, 'is that, in order to curry favour with the Occupation and further his aims and ambitions, he gave his daughter, the unhappy woman before you here, to the general in chief, Bonaparte. Her conduct since then, brazenly consorting with the French, has been disgraceful for a decent woman, let alone the daughter of a man who would call himself the syndic of the Prophet's descendants and the spiritual leader of the Order of the Bakris.'

Suddenly the policeman yanked Zeinab to her feet to face the dais. Then the man in the great bejewelled turban addressed her: 'What say you?'

Zeinab trembled, trying to look over her shoulder to her father. 'Father,' she pleaded in a whisper, 'Father!' He did not look at her. She turned back to face the dais, head lowered, and her voice came out low and hoarse. 'I repent of my sins.'

The great man in the turban turned to Shaykh Bakri. 'What say you?'

'I say I am innocent of her conduct.'

A murmur of astonishment and indignation rose from the benches around.

The Vizir waited a long moment, as if giving the shaykh time to recant. Then he spoke. 'Given the grievances brought to my attention, and the gravity of these accusations, I hereby strip Shaykh Bakri of his title as Naqib Ashraf, and reinstate Omar Makram in his rightful position.'

Omar Makram bowed. 'I thank Your Excellency for his justice and mercy.'

The Vizir raised his hand, indicating he wished to speak again. 'As for the position of head of the Bakri Order, is there another who is eligible?'

'There is a kinsman, Your Excellency,' Shaykh Sadat replied. 'But he is a poor man and has no means to assume such a post.'

'His poverty shall not stand in his way; the imperial purse will assume his expenses.'

Another notable Zeinab did not recognize raised his hand to be acknowledged.

'Your Excellency, I beg you to hear me. Shaykh Bakri recently contracted a marriage between his son and my daughter. I would fain spare my house the association with his disgrace, and beg your permission to annul the marriage and void the contract.'

'You have my permission to have the contract voided tomorrow at the judge's house.'

The chief of police interposed: 'With Your Excellency's permission, there remains the matter of the woman Zeinab, daughter of Bakri, who is condemned for collaboration and consorting with the French. The penalty for treason is hanging.'

The Vizir took a long moment to pronounce the sentence. 'The condemnation stands.'

Zeinab felt her knees buckle and she crumpled, but the two policemen caught her and began to drag her away.

'May I beg Your Excellency's indulgence for a moment,' a voice interposed.

Through a daze, Zeinab recognized Shaykh Jabarti as he stood up to speak in his measured tones. 'This woman may be carrying a child in her belly. A child conceived of the sin of the parents, it is true, but the child itself is innocent of all sin in the eyes of God the Most Merciful. The sentence may not be carried out on the mother until she is delivered of the child, or else the execution itself would be a crime against an innocent, and heinous in the eyes of our religion and Shari'a law.'

There was another murmur around the room, but this time one of assent. Shaykh Sadat nodded. 'We thank Shaykh Jabarti for reminding us of the mercy of our jurisprudence.'

The Vizir nodded. 'So be it. But there remains a problem. If her father himself has renounced her, there is no one into whose custody she may be remanded till such time as she is delivered, or until enough time has lapsed to prove that she is not bearing another soul within her.'

Shaykh Jabarti responded. 'By your leave, Your Excellency, I shall myself remand the woman to the custody of Sitt Nafisa the White, a lady well known to all and whose standing in this city is un-impeachable. Zeinab Bakri may be confined there till God delivers her or His will be done.'

'So be it.' The Vizir rose. Another murmur of assent was relayed around the room. Shaykh Bakri nodded his head.

'Thank God, thank God,' Zeinab repeated under her breath; she had been granted only a temporary reprieve, but her baby had been saved, and she realized, in that moment, that she would not have it the other way around for all the world.

FIFTEEN

Quarantine

'*Adieu*, Egypt! *Adieu*, Muslims! We take with us, with the memory of your country's superb monuments and its harsh deserts . . . the memory of the pains and privations that made us pay such a heavy price for the glory of having disturbed your rest and bloodied your shores.'

Commissary J.-F. Miot, *Memoirs*, 1814

Marseilles
1 October 1801

Nicolas raised his head from the letter he was writing and looked around him at the bare walls of the quarantine hospital in Marseilles. Here he was on French soil at long last, yet unable to see Lise or the children, stranded in the purgatory of quarantine for long weeks, like all the members of the expedition returning with him from Egypt. They had survived the perils of the sea voyage, beset by the English, the Turks and the Barbary pirates, only to languish in Marseilles. Right now it seemed every bit as far from Meudon as Cairo.

Would his family even recognize him if he walked in on them right now, unexpectedly? They would find him much changed, much aged, much blackened by the African sun. And what of Lise? Had she aged? Every wrinkle, every grey hair on her person would reproach him for the worry he had caused her by his absence. Had she written to him faithfully, and all her letters been intercepted by the English blockade? Had she written for a while, and then despaired when his letters – if they reached her at all – gave her to realize that he was not receiving hers? Perhaps his long absence had, at some point, estranged her heart, or tricked her memory, so that she had found consolation with another. It did not matter, Nicolas thought; he excused all and accepted all in advance. How could he not, when his own conscience was so far from clear?

And the children, how they must have changed! Pierre, a man now, matured beyond his years, perhaps; blonde Madelon, a wife, soon to be a mother; and his little Cola, old enough now to disavow his childish nickname.

Nicolas got up, looked out of the window at the brilliant blue beyond the harbour. On the other shore of the great sea, Egypt seethed in its turmoil. He was aware of a change that had begun operating in him quite independently of any conscious will the moment he had boarded ship during the evacuation: everything about Egypt remained perfectly etched in his memory, but it was as if it existed in another dimension, as with the world of the Jinn in Muslim belief. He had been told that the Jinn – supposedly beings of fire who could be good or evil, powerful or weak, like humans – were held by the Mohammedans to exist in a world quite as real as their own, yet separate, like two planets on a parallel course that never collide or intersect except – and it was a great exception – by the will of Allah. So Egypt existed for him, quite as real, but on a separate plane, a world he believed he would never visit again.

Only the thought of Zeinab tormented him. Had he done the right thing in leaving her behind? Had it really been what she wanted? Was she safe, or had she fallen victim to some vindictive reprisal? Was she in trouble and in desperate need of him at this very moment? He thought of her as he had last seen her, riding away on the back of a donkey, and that odd, pointed gesture of hers, her hands cupping her belly, and the sorrowful look she had given him over her shoulder, like a child keeping a heavy secret.

Did she mean him to understand that she was with child? But why would she keep such a secret from him in the first place?

His speculation gave him no rest, exacerbated by the enforced idleness of quarantine. In Egypt he had been used to shuttling constantly between the metalworks and gunpowder factories on Rawda Island, the textile mills in Giza, the Mint and the printing press at the Citadel, the Institute in Nasiriya, general headquarters in Ezbekiah – till he scarcely had time to sleep. Here in Marseilles he had nothing to do but sit around and wait in an inhospitable hospice with his companions, trying to entertain themselves with games and reading. But at least they could send and receive mail and news, and follow the progress and promotions of the veterans of the expedition. Bonaparte was now First Consul, truly the Sultan of the French, as the Egyptians had prophetically called him! Even General Belliard had been promoted to Minister of War. Many of his colleagues at the hospice were already writing letters to the 'Egyptian' veterans in positions of influence to petition for advantageous posts.

For his part, Nicolas found himself devoid of such ambitions. He was beset by a bone-deep lassitude such as he had never experienced in his life, and it served to reconcile him to this period of enforced convalescence. He spent his time organizing his papers and his sketches. The sketch of Zeinab that he remembered, that he had been looking for in the hours before the evacuation, still eluded him. He racked his brains for a means to obtain news of her. But they had been cut off from news of Egypt since their departure. There had been no mail or dispatches for weeks, now that the British fleet was anchored off the ports of Alexandria. But still he couldn't stop wondering: what was going on in Egypt while he was stranded in Marseilles?

SIXTEEN

The Emissary

Egypt is a theatre that must be watched; two great powers have had
a feel of it and one or the other will possess it.

Joseph de Maistre to Rossi,

March 1807

'The emissary from First Consul Bonaparte is here to see you, Sitt
Nafisa.'

'Show him into the main hall and send for Aisha. Tell her I will
need her to translate for me.'

Nafisa spoke some French, but distrusted her own fluency and
pronunciation, and could see no reason why she should put herself
at a disadvantage vis-à-vis the stranger by speaking in a foreign tongue
when he was the foreigner in her country. There was too much riding
on this meeting to take chances. The storm that had been brewing
ever since the Ottomans and the Beys had entered Cairo together,
the explosion that had been building up with the hostility between
the two parties, the treachery Elfi had warned his khushdash against
– all had finally come to pass. Most of the amirs of her husband's
house had fallen into the trap laid for them by the Capitan Pasha:
they had accepted the invitation to a 'meeting of reconciliation'
aboard a Turkish vessel off the coast of Alexandria. No sooner had
they embarked than they had been massacred before they could draw
their swords; Tambourji, Sennari the African, Ashqar the Bond, all
fallen; Bardissi somehow escaped with his life. Only Elfi had refused

207

the invitation; he had been right all along, thought Nafisa, when he had warned of the treachery of the Ottomans.

Now there would be a fight to the death for control over Egypt. The support of France, if Nafisa could solicit it on behalf of the amirs, would tip the balance in favour of the Mamlukes in their battle against the Ottomans and their rogue militias. In this delicate and secret negotiation she would call on the services of a reliable interpreter: her Mamluka Aisha – as Zeinab was known in Nafisa's house.

The night Shaykh Jabarti had brought the girl down from the Citadel, Nafisa had taken Zeinab's face in her hands. 'Poor child, you are more dead than alive. But listen to me carefully: your name is not Zeinab, daughter of Shaykh Khalil Bakri. That girl is dead. Your name is . . . Aisha.' Aisha meant 'she lives' in Arabic. 'You are a Mamluka who has just come into my household. Do you understand? Zeinab Bakri exists no more.'

The words were harsh, Nafisa knew, but Zeinab's life depended on it. Her father had betrayed her, denounced her and disowned her; she was no longer his daughter. That girl, Zeinab, had been condemned to death; Aisha had a chance to escape that fate.

The girl's arrival seven months ago had caused some curiosity in the harem, but there were three other women who had taken refuge at Sitt Nafisa's at the same time, Mamlukas who had consorted with the French, and Zeinab/Aisha had therefore been less conspicuous than she otherwise might. Most of the Mamlukas were from Georgia or Tcherkessia, which might have made Zeinab, with her Egyptian eyes and accent, the object of curiosity and petty spite had it not been for Nafisa, who made it clear she would tolerate no intrigue whatsoever among her servants.

The first few days, the girl had wept bitterly for hours on end, grieving over her father's betrayal and her lover's abandonment. On one occasion when Nafisa had come into her room and found her sobbing, Zeinab had knelt at her feet and buried her head in her lap. 'I miss him,' she sobbed. 'I miss Nicolas. Every time his child quickens inside me, I ache for him. You cannot know what it is like . . . I wish I could be like you, Sitt Nafisa, as cool as a tranquil pool.'

She thinks I am done with love and longing and the messy, bloody business of a woman's body and heart, Nafisa thought bitterly to herself; if only it were true. But her voice floated down like a chill morning mist when she answered: 'No, I cannot imagine what it must be like.' Zeinab had looked up then, and seen her cold, remote expression, and wondered if she had offended.

But Nafisa continued to be kind to her. From the very beginning, when all Zeinab wanted was to huddle on a pallet in one corner of the room, weeping until she had cried herself to sleep, Nafisa would send for her, and ask her to take dictation for the household accounts or those of the wikala at Bab Zuweila, to keep her busy and take her mind off her grief and worry.

Now she had sent for the girl to translate in this meeting with Bonaparte's emissary. Nafisa took her customary place on the couch before the window, her back to the light, gesturing to the French ambassador to take a seat, which he did, with an exaggerated bow.

'Please be seated, monsieur.'

Colonel Sebastiani patted the black curls that seemed plastered to his cheeks and forehead, and smoothed the splendid tricorn hat in his lap. He had a swagger about him, Nafisa thought, but very sharp eyes; it would be a mistake to underestimate him, and she could not afford to make such a mistake. Only the diplomatic and material support of a great European power, now, could save Egypt from the anarchy and violence of life under the Turks and the Albanians. No one was safe walking the streets; kidnappings and ransoming, rape and murder, were the order of the day, and the militias that the Ottomans had imported from around the empire were guilty of the worst abuses.

Who would have believed at the time of the French evacuation, Nafisa thought bitterly, that she would be soliciting help from their former enemies so soon? Not even she, who had kept from breaking the ties of civility to the last, could have foreseen this. But the situation was desperate, and she had lived long enough to know that enemies and allies could trade places in the blink of an eye. Old Ibrahim Bey and Bardissi had thrown their weight behind an appeal to France, but Elfi was sceptical, maintaining that Bonaparte could not be trusted and that England was the power to enlist. All, Nafisa and Elfi included, had written to Bonaparte.

At that moment Zeinab hurried into the room and stared wide-eyed at the French ambassador from behind her veil. Her eagerness quickly turned to utter dejection. Nafisa frowned. What on earth was wrong with the girl? Who had she been expecting?

'Ah, Aisha,' Nafisa patted the cushion at her feet, 'this gentleman is here from France, his visit is of a confidential nature, you understand? You will translate for me.'

Zeinab nodded and took a seat.

'Madame,' Sebastiani addressed Sitt Nafisa as he unrolled a letter with a flourish, 'allow me to read to you directly from my instructions from First Consul for Life Bonaparte: "You will convey to the widow of Murad Bey that the First Consul has received her letter, and that he has given special orders to French agents in Egypt to protect her with all means at their disposal; that he wishes that she may have nothing to fear or want, because Murad Bey rallied to the side of France in the end, and that he died with these sentiments, and that therefore the First Consul will always be the friend of his family."' Sebastiani looked up and rerolled the letter as Zeinab translated, stumbling a little.

Nafisa inclined her head in response. 'Please tell the First Consul that we receive his compliments with much appreciation and reciprocate many times over his good wishes, and pray for his continued health and prosperity.'

'Thank you, madame. First Consul Bonaparte will be pleased to hear that he is remembered with affection by his acquaintances in Egypt.'

'Do you find Egypt much changed, monsieur?'

'I have found our numbers here sadly decimated: there are only half a dozen French merchants left in Cairo. The state of insecurity is such that the few Europeans who remain are kept here only by a greater dread of prison, clamouring creditors, or miserable marriages. Indeed, madame, one cannot but be aware of the deterioration of affairs in Egypt since the evacuation of the Army of the Orient. Everywhere I go, people express their regret for the departure of the French in the most touching terms.'

Sitt Nafisa allowed herself a small, ironic smile through her transparent veil, and the ambassador seemed to feel compelled to qualify his statement.

'Well, almost everywhere! I have been received by some of the leaders of the ulema – Shaykh Fayumi, Shaykh Sharkawi. There are others, it is true, who declined to receive me. Shaykh Mahruqi in particular seems to have a regrettable *parti pris* against France. But Shaykh Bakri explained his refusal to receive me on the grounds of the very bad graces in which he finds himself among Egyptians and Turks alike, and his desire to avoid any contact that might compromise him further.'

At the mention of her father, Zeinab winced noticeably and clutched her lower belly. Nafisa tensed; was the girl going into labour that very moment? Nafisa shook off the thought and resolved to concentrate on the serious matter at hand. 'Has First Consul Bonaparte sent an answer to the letters he received from Ibrahim Bey and the amirs Elfi and Bardissi, monsieur?'

'The First Consul has indeed, madame, and he has offered the Turkish viceroy his services to mediate between him and the Beys. I have just met with the viceroy pasha at his residence in Elfi Bey's palace. But he has not authorized me to meet with the amirs and my instructions from the First Consul are not to act without the viceroy's permission.'

'The Turkish viceroy, sir, has orders from his court to wage a war of extermination against the Mamlukes of Egypt. You cannot be ignorant of the massacre at Alexandria.'

'No, indeed, madame, nor of the regrettably perfidious role of the English in that tragedy. That such an atrocity should be perpetrated so near the English camp, and against persons who were under the double guarantees of English hospitality and faith . . .'

'It is my understanding, sir, that Lord Hutchinson was as duped and outraged as anyone, and that, when he realized what was happening, it was his forceful intervention that compelled the Capitan Pasha to release the surviving amirs he held captive.'

Sebastiani diplomatically skirted the issue. 'Since I cannot meet directly with the amirs, madame, this is where your good services would be invaluable, as always, in conveying to the Beys the First Consul's good will and his continued interest in all that touches Egypt.'

Sitt Nafisa controlled her impatience. 'Thank First Consul Bonaparte, monsieur, and tell him that affairs in Egypt have come to a desperate pass, and that we need more than just his good will. In all my long years, I have seen pashas and beys and generals and armies come and go, yet I have never seen anything like the devastation and lawlessness and violence we suffer today.' She paused to give Zeinab time to catch up. 'Tell Bonaparte the chief plague of the land are the Arnaouts – the Albanian troops that the viceroy has brought to Cairo. They are ferocious beyond belief, and obey only their own chiefs.'

'Can the Turkish viceroy not control them?'

'The viceroy was a Georgian Mamluke raised in the Capitan Pasha's house and knows nothing but the cutting off of heads,' she snapped. 'He is a pawn in the hands of the militias; he cannot pay their salaries and fears for his own life. Surely, monsieur, the First Consul must see that the Ottomans cannot rule Egypt; they have just been defeated in five successive battles by the Mamlukes. France must lend its support to the amirs to reinstate the independence of Egypt from this Turkish misrule.'

'Forgive me, madame, but the state of the Beys seems to be somewhat precarious. Their numbers are decimated – down to three or four thousand, according to the best estimate – and with the Porte's prohibition on the importation of Mamlukes, they cannot recruit into their ranks. I have heard they are in such dire straits they are allowing their own sons to join, in contravention of age-old practice. In addition, there are perhaps as many as eight hundred French deserters in the lists of the various Mamluke houses, is that not right?'

'You seem to be well informed, sir. But the Beys have doubled their forces by forming alliances with the Bedouin. Almost all the Arab tribes are under their control.' Bardissi had married the daughter of the chief of the Beni Ali tribe, and Elfi the daughter of the chief of the Abbaddi tribe in the eastern desert; both were alliances of political expediency.

'Ah, but the Bedouin are notoriously unreliable, madame, is that not their reputation?'

Nafisa sat back, stifling a sigh of frustration. Clearly Sebastiani's orders were to straddle the fence while the Mamlukes and the Ottomans fought one another to a standstill. That suited France well enough; were it not for the English fleet anchored off Alexandria, would Bonaparte have sent an ambassador at all? She decided to make a final appeal to Sebastiani. 'Tell Citoyen Bonaparte – I mean First Consul Bonaparte – tell him the Albanian militias abuse the people, pillage and ravish at will, till no house and no man or woman is safe from them. If the Beys are reinstated they will at least bring security back to the country.'

'Indeed, no man can be unaware of the lack of security in the land,' Sebastiani conceded. 'I myself have been the target of certain regrettable incidents – but let us pass over those. I am sure the First Consul will be saddened to hear that matters have come to such a sad pass. He speaks often and with great affection of your beautiful country and his many friends here.'

Suddenly Zeinab interrupted in a tortured whisper, speaking in Arabic. 'Sitt Nafisa, forgive me, it is not my place to pester your august visitor with questions, but would you inquire on my behalf if there is any news of the chief engineer?'

Nafisa stared at her, taken by surprise. So that was the reason for the girl's agitation – she thought the ambassador had knowledge of Conté. But Colonel Sebastiani was leaning forward to ask a question.

'Madame, do you know where I can find Citoyen Royer, who used to be a pharmacist for the expedition and now, I understand, sells liquor to the Greek community? I have a letter for him inquiring after one of the young Egyptian women who had consorted with the French under the occupation. Do you know what fate has befallen them?'

A muffled moan erupted from Zeinab, and she clutched her belly again. Was the girl's agitation bringing on birthing pangs? Nafisa chose her words carefully as she answered the emissary. 'Five women paid the ultimate price on the same day, Monsieur. In almost every case, it was the husband who took his revenge for the dishonour.'

'And what of the Naqib's daughter? It is concerning her particular case that I have been asked to inquire.'

At that moment Zeinab abruptly doubled over, moaning out loud. Her legs were drenched in warm fluid through the silk pantaloons, and she cried out in shame and confusion. The Frenchman leapt to his feet in alarm.

'*Pardon*, monsieur.' Nafisa stood up hastily and clapped her hands for the eunuchs. 'My maid is unwell, forgive her. I thank you, monsieur, and *bon voyage* – is that how you say it? I will send you a letter for the First Consul before you depart.'

Zeinab groaned and rolled on the floor. Nafisa leaned over her. 'It's all right, child, your waters have broken, your child is ready to be born; you must be brave.'

Night came, and then day, and then the muezzin called evening prayers again, and still the baby would not come. Zeinab was more dead than alive, so exhausted from the pain and the pushing and the screaming that she lay barely conscious, without the strength to resist or even cry out as the midwife pressed on her belly to try to expel the unborn child. In the first few hours of her labour she had called for her mother, she had longed to be surrounded by her mother and her older sisters in this hour. But she had only the gruff midwife and the Mamlukas, and Sitt Nafisa who floated in and out every hour, applying a cool hand to her brow and murmuring encouragement. Zeinab prayed for deliverance; she prayed her baby would be a girl, and that she would name her Nafisa.

But as the hours passed and the pain wore her down, she no longer cared for mother or sisters; at the end she no longer cared even for her baby. 'I want to die,' she begged Sitt Nafisa. 'Please, I cannot bear it any longer, let me die.'

'God forbid, child, don't speak this way,' Sitt Nafisa soothed her.

Zeinab lay drenched in sweat, and at last she felt God was granting her wish, her life was ebbing away, and with it the pain. The contractions had stopped, and she was mercifully losing consciousness. But Sitt Nafisa roused her again with a cool cloth soaked in orange-blossom water.

'Zeinab, you need to push, one more time. You need to do it, or the baby will die inside you, and kill you with it. One more time, child, you must!'

Every instinct in Zeinab recoiled from inflicting the terrible pain on herself again, but she pushed, one last time, screaming wildly, till she passed out.

When she came to, she was aware of pain, but a dull, heavy pain, in her lower belly and between her legs. The midwife was mopping up the blood that had pooled around Zeinab's hips, and she moaned when the woman tried to turn her on her side to pull away the soaked rags underneath.

'I feel like I'm ripped up inside,' Zeinab sobbed.

'It ripped you up pretty well coming out, it did, that big head! Only let me wash you properly, or you will get childbed fever, and that'll kill you.'

Zeinab dozed on and off as she was wiped down and made to sip a little almond milk. The midwife came back with a bundle in her arms.

'Take it away, I don't want to see it,' Zeinab cried, turning to the wall.

When she woke up again it was morning. She thought she needed to use the chamber pot, but as soon as she stirred the pain made her moan. Almaz, one of the other Mamlukas, came to her bedside. 'Are you awake, Aisha? Here, let me help you.'

The pain of trying to use the chamber pot was so bad Zeinab was white in the face by the time she collapsed back on the couch. The Mamluka brought her some more almond milk but Zeinab licked her dry lips and shook her head. 'I can't,' she whispered, 'I daren't drink or eat till I heal.'

'Now be reasonable. How can you nurse your baby if you don't drink or eat?'

Zeinab shook her head and the Mamluka shrugged and left. When the afternoon shadows lengthened, Sitt Nafisa came into the room and sat beside her on the couch.

'Poor child, I know what pain you are going through. You will heal, with God's mercy, and all this will be but a bad memory. Sip only a little water for now, if that's all you can have. Don't worry about the baby. The little one will get by on drops of sugar water till we find a wet-nurse.'

Zeinab passed her tongue over her lips and turned to Sitt Nafisa. 'Is it . . . ?'

'It's a boy.'

'A boy?'

'Yes. Don't you want to see him? He is perfectly healthy, thank God. It's a miracle, after that terrible long labour.'

Zeinab nodded.

Sitt Nafisa clapped her hands and Almaz came in with a tiny swaddled form in her arms. Zeinab peered at the baby. It was very red and scrunched up in the face and had blond fuzz all over its little head, and a scaly patch on the forehead.

'That's normal.' Sitt Nafisa touched her finger to the spot on the baby's brow. 'Cradle cap, that's all. It will come off.'

The infant's eyes were scrunched up, but it blinked for a moment, and Zeinab was startled to see that its eyes were blue. She had not expected the baby to be blond; Nicolas was dark, and so, of course, was she. But she remembered that he had told her once that there were many blonds in his Norman family. Still, she had hoped, vaguely, that it would look like Nicolas. This baby looked like it didn't belong to her.

'Tomorrow we will think of a name,' Sitt Nafisa said.

A fatherless boy, Zeinab thought, he would have only a first name, like a Mamluke. Even Mamlukes took their master's name, and her child would have no father or master. Nor even a mother. Her father still had many enemies, and as long as the death sentence against her had not been revoked, Zeinab Bakri did not exist.

'Don't you want to hold him?' Almaz held out the baby.

Zeinab reached her arms out tentatively, and Almaz laid it across her chest. The baby turned his face into her breast and nuzzled, one eye scrunched up against her flesh, the other open, his little mouth twisted sideways to reach for the nipple. How did he know to do that, she wondered. He rooted around for a moment, then wailed in frustration, his face turning an ugly purple. Zeinab burst into tears. 'I don't have any milk for him!'

'No, but it will come in time, don't worry for tonight.' Sitt Nafisa nodded to Almaz, who came and took the baby away. 'Now try to sleep. It will help.'

Zeinab slept. In the middle of the night she was woken from a heavy slumber by Almaz, carrying the infant. 'This little one is hungry.'

The baby's head was turned to the side, one eye scrunched shut, the other open, his tiny mouth twisted sideways, as if ready to receive the nipple. A great burst of laughter welled up from Zeinab. 'He remembers! He remembers how to try to nurse! He remembers me!' And at that instant the baby became hers again, and she opened her arms impatiently to receive him.

'If only your father could see you!' she whispered to her infant, touching his cradle cap with a tentative finger. 'If only he knew you existed! But he will know; I will find a way to let him know. He loves us still, Nicolas, I am sure of it. I wonder where he is now, what he is doing, your father . . .'

SEVENTEEN

The Letter

'The work of the Commission of Arts will one day excuse in the eyes
of posterity the levity with which our nation flung itself, so to speak,
into the Orient. While mourning the fate of so many brave warriors
who, after glorious exploits, died in Egypt, our consolation will be
the existence of such precious work.'

Geoffroy Saint-Hilaire, in a letter to Cuvier,

November 1799

Nicolas Conté sat down at his desk, smiling to see the little bouquet
of dried lavender his daughter had placed on top of a pile of letters.
Since his return, Nicolas had found delight in the most mundane
objects and occupations, taking nothing for granted: the scent of
lavender, the slanting winter sunlight through his window, the crisp
crunch of an apple, the turning of the leaves in the autumn. He inhaled
deeply and moved the flowers aside, picking up his letter opener. It
was a gift from an admirer, and the bone handle had been carved in
the shape of an Egyptian lotus. One of the happier motifs from the
Retour d'Égypte vogue, he thought: obelisks, sphinxes, pyramids,
scarabs, chimera, hieroglyphics . . . they were popping up everywhere,
from furniture to china, from wallpaper to inkwells. Inescapable, and
often in dubious taste; Vivant Denon had ordered for himself an entire
suite of furniture 'in the Egyptian style', extravagantly carved with a
bestiary of sphinxes, swans, griffons and cow-goddesses.

Nicolas broke the seal and opened the first letter, recognizing Champy's letterhead with its pyramids, palm trees, felucca boat, crescent and a cannon, the last a reference to his role as director of munitions during the Egyptian campaign. Nicolas smiled; it did not lack originality, the vignette with the cannon! So many of the letters on his desk now were requests for recommendations from veterans of the campaign, and several of them bore letterheads piling vignette upon vignette, sometimes including entire maps of Egypt or Syria, but all incorporating either the Sphinx or the pyramids or both.

He would have to make time to write all these letters of recommendation; the network of the veterans, among the savants especially, was very strong, and he did his part, although he had no time and little interest in joining Masonic lodges. When he had first returned to Paris, Napoleon had sent General Belliard to him with a message: 'The First Consul is highly sensible of the services for which the nation is indebted to you. He says of you: "a universal man, with the passion, the knowledge and the genius for the arts, precious in a far-away country, capable of turning his hand to anything, of creating the arts of France in the desert of Arabia." The First Consul wishes you to name your own reward for your service to the Republic; there is no honour to which you may not aspire.'

'My only request is that all those who have served under my orders be promoted.'

From then onward the requests for letters of recommendations had poured in. Nicolas had asked for nothing for himself and yet had been named head of the Commission that would compile the monumental Encyclopedia on Egypt, a task nearly daunting in its scope and overwhelming in its honour. But it was his passion, his life's work, the only unambiguous legacy of an expedition that had been, in so many ways, a cruel disappointment. The annual reunion, the Banquet of Egypt in Paris, was coming up soon, and he looked forward to seeing old friends again, especially Geoffroy St-Hilaire.

His friend had shaved his moustache *à la turque* now, but had retained his wit and good humour.

He picked up the letter Geoffroy had sent him from Paris

Visited the studio of the painter Gros yesterday; he is working on an enormous canvas of The Battle of the Pyramids, *in the process of being enlarged still further by the addition of a supplementary panel to accommodate the figure of General Kléber. Never mind that Kléber was two hundred miles away, holding the fort in Alexandria at the time. We must all have our share of* la gloire. *Do you remember when Bonaparte used to refer to him scathingly as* cet allemand? . . .

Nicolas remembered when Kléber in turn had remarked spitefully, on examining the trenches before Jaffa, that they were too low to provide cover for men of any greater height than Bonaparte's own mean stature. Nicolas had seen Gros' canvas of *The Plague-Stricken of Jaffa*, and found in its glorified bathos nothing that resonated with his disturbing memories. As for Bonaparte, everywhere one turned, objects were being fashioned in his likeness – even sticks of barley sugar.

Nicolas picked up the next letter in the pile. Ah! A letter from Ambassador Sebastiani! His hands fumbled with the letter opener in his haste and he cut himself. He sucked his finger and unfolded the sheet. *I regret to cause you pain . . . five women paid the ultimate price on the same day . . . the Naqib's daughter . . . her father conspired with the police chief . . . condemned to death . . .* Nicolas covered his eyes, but he could not block the image that came to his mind: Zeinab's long, slender neck, snapped and broken; her enormous eyes dilated with terror, and those eyebrows of hers, like birds in flight – with nowhere to flee, finally.

He raged at the bigotry and barbarity of the East, at the unconscionable duplicity of that unnatural father. But however much he railed, however much he reasoned, he could not help blaming himself for not protecting the girl. Yet how could he have foreseen this dreadful fate? He saw her again the way he had last laid eyes on her, twisting around on her mule to look back at him as she rode away, and that final gesture of hers, cupping her hands protectively around her flat belly. What did it mean? Was she trying to tell him she was pregnant? But why would she not have told him earlier, if she was? It did not make sense. Had he, like so many others, fathered a child in Egypt? His mind went round and round in an infernal loop, and he paced the room, trying to shake the horrible image of that snapped neck from his head.

He had loved Zeinab; now that it was too late, he admitted it to himself, unequivocally. He had lived long enough, and seen enough of the world, to know that a heart could encompass more than one love, and that there were many kinds of love, so different that one did not constitute a betrayal of the other. The place Zeinab occupied in his memories – somewhere between lover and child, between lust and tenderness – was not usurped from Lise and his family, it was her own.

He longed to seek the relief of divulging his grief, but his liaison with Zeinab had been a closely guarded secret; only Geoffroy and Desgenettes had an inkling of it. He would have to bear his pain and guilt alone, and he would have to dissimulate as best as he could before his family and the world. But he knew he would have no rest: the bitter residue of regret would poison the sweetness of the everyday pleasures of his life: when he sniffed lavender, he would be haunted by Zeinab's attar of gardenia; when he caressed the soft, chubby cheeks of his baby grandchild he would find himself wondering if he had a child in Egypt, a child who would be toddling by now, babbling in that impenetrable language of theirs. Everything and everyone would remind him of his secret torment.

And yet this should have been the sweetest moment of his life, reaping in tranquillity the honours and rewards for his tireless service in Egypt. The story of the Egyptian expedition was being retold as a heroic legend commensurate with Bonaparte's boundless ambition, an epic in which every figure that played a part, including his own, was lent mythical proportions.

Today there were laurels aplenty to crown all heads. With bitter irony, Nicolas observed the mythical mist bathing his own head; he saw it in the eyes of the students who came to hear him lecture at the Conservatoire, or the young inventors who brought their ideas before him at the Bureau for Arts and Manufactures in the Ministry of the Interior. The Minister himself had introduced him as 'the man who fed and dressed the Army of the Orient; the man who can boast of having smelted the first steel and forged the first cannon in Egypt. The essential man.'

The words rang hollow to him now. There would be other campaigns, and other wars; it was inevitable. But not for him; he had fought his last campaign. He should be able to rest on his laurels, and sip the sweetness of life in the bosom of his family. And yet, and yet . . . the horrible image of that swan's neck that he could span with his hand, snapped and broken; that warm, live body that had folded itself into his, flung into the Nile or in some ditch.

Nicolas put down the letter, and got up from his desk. He must have it somewhere, the watercolour sketch of Zeinab he had started that day they sat under the sycamore tree in Elfi's garden, waiting for General Kléber to arrive; that fateful day when the assassin had appeared out of nowhere. Nicolas had never completed it, but he must have stashed it with his other sketches. Was it among the drawings he had brought with him from Egypt, or had he left it behind in Qassim Bey's house in the chaos of the evacuation? He was suddenly obsessed with finding it, for it seemed to him as though, were he to hold that etching in his hand, he could interrogate it over the fate of Zeinab.

EIGHTEEN

The Citadel

'Suffice it to say that since this period, the Porte has successively named and deposed Pashas, who come but to disgrace their authority; the Albanians, the main strength of the Turkish army, the support or terror of its chiefs, rendered even more mutinous by the long stoppage of their pay, plunder at will. The right of the strongest has become the law of the land. Injuries and insults with impunity have been heaped among even the most sacred characters, not sparing even European Consuls; the rights of property and personal security are trampled in the dust. And from the Cataracts to the coast, no corner has been exempt from the horrors that attend a series of ephemeral revolutions.'

William Hamilton, Esq., F.A.S., in Ægyptiaca, or some account of the ancient and modern state of Egypt, as obtained in the years 1801, 1802

'Aisha! Aisha, Sitt Nafisa wants you on an urgent matter.'

Zeinab picked up her baby and slung him on her hip with an exaggerated groan. 'Let's go see what they want of us.' She nuzzled his curls; the fine blond fuzz had given way to thick, glossy hair the colour of hazelnut shells. His eyes had turned hazel, shaded by the thick black lashes he had inherited from her; he had Nicolas' decided chin. He squirmed on her hip, trying to reach down for a toy. He was big for his age, everyone said, although he had weaned himself early.

In the end, it had been Sitt Nafisa who had named him. 'He may be a fatherless boy,' she had consoled Zeinab, 'but the Prophet too was born an orphan. We shall name him Muhammad. And further, he can be called Muhammad Muradi – of the house of Murad – since he is of this house.'

Zeinab had kissed her hand, wordless.

'Aisha!' Almaz was at the door. 'Hurry, Sitt Nafisa wants you.'

'We're coming!' Zeinab hurried down the stairs, bouncing the baby on her hip at every step to make him giggle.

'Ah, Aisha.' Sitt Nafisa looked up from the coffer in front of her and gave the boy an absent-minded smile. Zeinab could not remember when she had seen her look so troubled. 'Aisha, I need to trust you with a very delicate mission.' She hesitated. 'But I don't know, you're so young . . .'

'I can do it, Sitt Nafisa; whatever it is, I can do it. I promise you won't regret it.' Zeinab hitched the boy higher on her hip.

'All right then. Sit down and listen carefully. Some Arnaout troops abducted a Mamluka of Qassim Bey's and the son she bore him; they are trying to sell them both as booty, although they know very well that in Egypt a Mamluka who bears her master a child is a free-woman and the child is free also. There is no end to the abuses of these militias!' She shook her head and picked up a purse from the coffer. 'This is enough money to ransom the woman and the child. I need you to meet the Albanian officer and give it to him.'

'I can do that right away. Let me just run upstairs for my abaya and veil.'

'Wait, that's not all. There is more. And here I must trust you beyond, perhaps, what your years warrant, but you are such a bright girl . . .' Sitt Nafisa hesitated again, as if she were thinking better of it.

'You won't be sorry, Sitt Nafisa.'

'We must put an end to these abuses by the Albanians. They claim they plunder because their salaries are not paid, and they refuse to leave Cairo till the money they are owed is paid in full. The viceroy pasha can't pay their salaries or rein in their abuses. I need you to take the occasion of the exchange with the Albanian soldiers to ask them to take a proposal to their chief officer, Mehmet Ali. Tell him that I will undertake to pay their salaries and arrears in return for their pledge to leave Cairo. Can you do that?'

Zeinab found it difficult to breathe for a moment, as the full impact of the importance of the mission sunk in. 'I can, Sitt Nafisa. Trust me.'

'All right then. Go, get ready, and I will send Barquq with you. Call Almaz to take care of the boy.' She smiled and twirled her finger in a curl of the baby's hair. 'How big he is getting! God guide your steps, Aisha my child, and keep you safe.'

Zeinab had carried out Sitt Nafisa's instructions and conveyed her message to the Albanian chief, Mehmet Ali, who had nodded, taken the purse, and indicated he would have an answer for her mistress the next morning. That night she tossed and turned, too excited to sleep, wondering how her mission would turn out. She lay awake, watching her baby sleep with his mouth open. It was one of the many little things about him that she reported to Nicolas, in her imagination. 'Your son sleeps with his mouth open, like you, except he doesn't snore, and he rubs his ear to comfort himself.' Ten times a day she caught herself telling Nicolas about the baby, and her heart ached that he did not even know he had a child in Egypt.

When she put the baby to sleep, she would hum to him, under her breath, the French lullaby Nicolas had taught her: *Fais do-do, Cola mon petit frère, fais do-do, t'auras du lolo.* Little by little she had come to call the baby Do-do, and while others took it to be a nick-name for Muhammad or Murad, its real association was her own little secret.

That night, she lay in her bed racking her brains, as she did every night, for a way to get news of Nicolas, to let him know she was alive, and that he had a son. She had come to regret keeping it a secret from him, more than ever since Sebastiani's fateful visit; now she was convinced Nicolas was still thinking of her, asking about her, looking for her. Who but Nicolas would have asked Ambassador Sebastiani to make inquiries about the naqib's daughter? It proved she had misjudged him; he must want her with him in France. Should she join him there? Kind as Sitt Nafisa was to her, Zeinab felt trapped by her situation in Egypt, and concerned for the future of her young son.

She considered writing a letter to Nicolas and asking the new French envoy, DeLesseps – who had been calling on Sitt Nafisa regularly, if discreetly – whether he would be kind enough to relay it to France. But first she would have to muster the courage to obtain Sitt Nafisa's permission.

Dawn had been breaking by the time Zeinab finally dozed off, and when a pounding on the door of the house awoke her, the sun was streaming through the window. She sat up, alarmed. Who would dare pound on the door in this manner? She barricaded the baby with bolsters and cushions in case he turned over in bed, flung her veil over her head and hurried down the stairs. The servants and eunuchs were gathering in the downstairs hall, and the chief eunuch Barquq was standing at the door speaking to the Turkish wali, as the viceroy's adjoint was called, and the chief of police. The eunuch turned around, shaken.

'The viceroy pasha is demanding that Sitt Nafisa come to the Citadel.'

Some of the maids clapped their hands to their chests and wailed. Zeinab was too shocked to utter a sound. Sitt Nafisa unceremoniously convoked to the Citadel! The wali and the police chief at the door! Something must have gone terribly wrong with the negotiations she had undertaken for her mistress.

In a moment Sitt Nafisa came down, pale but fully dressed, adjusting her veil and holding out her arms to be helped into her abaya. 'We will see what the pasha wants.' She shot a warning glance at Zeinab. 'There is no need for alarm.'

'Sitt, let me come with you,' Zeinab begged. Her terrifying memories of the Citadel, her fear of being recognized – nothing deterred her at that moment.

'I won't be needing you, Aisha.' Sitt Nafisa drew her veil over her head. 'I will take Rokia and Munawwar.' The two maids were already dressed and veiled, muttering prayers and imprecations under their breath.

Zeinab watched them leave the house. Then she ran upstairs, grabbed her abaya, and ran down again.

'Hold on. Where are you off to?' the chief eunuch intercepted her at the door.

'To send for Shaykh Jabarti. And to warn Sitt Adila, Ibrahim Bey's daughter. Barquq, would you ask Almaz to look after the baby for me till I get back?'

Nafisa's thoughts ricocheted around her head like a panicked bird trapped in a cage, trying to find a way out of her predicament, but outwardly she was composed as she rode along the winding route through the Moqattam Hills to the Citadel, accompanied by two of her Mamlukas. What manner of man was this viceroy pasha that he would dare to humiliate the widow of Ali the Great and Murad Bey? As the popular saying went, there are those who can be intimidated but not shamed. Nafisa had no cards left to play, and she could not hope to intimidate the pasha, so she resolved to use her standing to shame him into treating her with honour. If that failed, she was lost.

But it was not her fate alone that was at stake: as she followed the wali and the chief of police uphill she could see the pasha's men fan out across the city, in search of the other wives of the Mamlukes; some would no doubt be arrested, but most, Nafisa hoped, would have been warned in time to go into hiding. What manner of dishonourable man was this viceroy, that he would take defenceless women hostage while their husbands were killed or in exile? She blamed herself for having taken the great risk of trying to subvert the Albanian militia; yet how could she not have tried to put an end to their unconscionable abuses? As she saw the forbidding Citadel walls looming before her, she closed her eyes and prayed for wisdom and strategy to guide her in her confrontation with the viceroy.

Now she had arrived at the foot of the towering walls of the Citadel, and her cortège passed through the Gate of Torment flanked by its red-and-white striped twin towers. The local inhabitants of the fortress town gathered in the streets, wailing at her passage, and even the muezzins suspended the call to prayer from the minarets of the twelve mosques within the walls.

Sitt Nafisa was led to the viceroy's palace within the northern enclosure and brought into his presence. The pasha, a short man in a voluminous turban, rose immediately in deference and asked her to be seated; she took heart at this gesture, but as soon as she had taken a seat on the divan he leaned forward and levied his accusation against her in the starkest terms.

'Is it true that your Mamluka Aisha has been speaking with Mehmet Ali the Albanian officer and telling him that if he works on behalf of the rebellious Mamlukes, she will be responsible for the soldiers' back pay?'

Nafisa hesitated. The viceroy had mentioned the name 'Aisha'; which meant that he knew, or thought he knew, the identity of the Mamluka who had been the go-between with the Albanian. What would his spies find out if they dug a little deeper? Nafisa had never lied, and she would avoid doing so now if she could; but her over-riding concern must be to shield Zeinab. So she chose her words very carefully as she answered: 'If it is proven that my Mamluka said so, then I will bear the consequences. She should not be held responsible.'

A hateful look of triumph passed over the pasha's face, as if he had trapped her into a confession. 'Proof? You want proof?' He took a paper out of his pocket and pointed to it. 'This is proof.'

Secure in the knowledge she had sent nothing in writing to Mehmet Ali, Nafisa immediately called his bluff. 'What is this piece of paper? Show it to me – I can read Turkish – so I may see what is in it.'

Realizing that he had been foiled, the viceroy put it back in his pocket, and she used his momentary discomfiture to press her advantage. 'As long as I have lived in Cairo, my standing has been well known to all, great and small alike. The Sultan in Istanbul and his dignitaries and their wives know me better than I know you.' She let the implication sink in; the Sultan's possible displeasure would be the one thing the viceroy would dread. Then she pressed on, hoping to arouse in him some sense of shame. 'The nation of the French came and went, and though they are enemies of the faith, yet they treated me with honour. As for you, Pasha, your conduct is unworthy of your nation or of any other.'

He was clearly stung. 'We do only what is proper.'

'Is it proper to order me to be escorted by the wali like a criminal?'

'I sent him only as my chief aide, as a mark of respect for you.'

'If that is indeed so, then ask him to accompany me back to my house.'

For a moment he hesitated, then his eyes narrowed in cunning, and she knew she had overreached. 'You will be my guest in the Citadel a while longer, Sitt Nafisa, until this matter is resolved. You will be taken to the house of Shaykh Sahimi, here in the northern enclosure of the Citadel, where you will be treated with all honour and dignity, and will be guarded at all times by my own men.'

At Shaykh Sahimi's house the bewildered cleric and his family fell over themselves to make her welcome, torn between expressing the great honour her visit bestowed on them and lamenting the circumstances that brought it about. By then the news of her arrest had made the rounds of Cairo and a groundswell of anger rose like an ugly haze from the city. Within the hour a delegation of prominent jurists and ulema had ridden to the Citadel to speak to the viceroy and demand to see with their own eyes that Sitt Nafisa was unharmed.

Nafisa met the delegation in the reception hall of Shaykh Sahimi's house. The chief judge, the naqib, and several of the shaykhs were there, all visibly disturbed and unusually determined to take action; Jabarti in particular looked incensed at her mistreatment. The viceroy made his appearance in short order, a sign that he had been made aware of the popular resentment brewing in the Citadel and in the city below.

'As you can see for yourselves, shaykhs,' he hastened to reassure them, 'Sitt Nafisa is safe and unharmed, and the guest of your colleague Shaykh Sahimi. But her intrigues warrant her detention to put an end to her sedition. She tried to subvert some of the high officers of the Albanian militia to the cause of the rebellious Mamlukes, and promised to pay the soldiers' salaries. If she can indeed afford to pay the militia's salaries, then she should be forced to pay them.'

Nafisa's heart sank. If the pasha was intent on a ransom, he would not be deterred. She countered nevertheless. 'There is no basis for the pasha's accusations of collusion with the Mamlukes. I have no husband among the amirs that I may put myself at risk for his sake. If the pasha's intent, as it seems, is to extort money from me, I have nothing left and many debts.'

Shaykh Jabarti spoke up. 'Pasha, by your leave. This matter is highly unseemly and much evil will come of it, and the people will blame us if we allow it to happen. If you pursue this action we will have nothing to do with it, or with any matter from now on, and we will leave the city in protest.'

The jurist paused to let the full effect of his ultimatum sink in: if the ulema left the city in protest there would be no one to prevent the people from rising in anger against the viceroy and his men. Jabarti rose to his feet, gathered his robes, and headed with all deliberation towards the door; the other jurists followed suit. The viceroy watched them filing out, and called them back as they reached the door.

'There is no need for that, shaykhs. I will release the lady; she may leave the Citadel under your protection and return to Cairo. But in return I must have assurances that you undertake to raise a levy of eight hundred purses from Sitt Nafisa and the other wives of amirs.'

Jabarti nodded. 'We stand as her guarantors.'

As the pasha stomped out, the shaykh turned to Nafisa, his dour face bitter. 'And to think that at the beginning of this viceroy's reign, the thirsty thought he was water itself! But what matters is your safety, Sitt Nafisa, *salamtek* a thousand times.'

Not her safety alone, thought Nafisa. Zeinab's safety was equally at stake, and no ultimatum by the ulema would intervene to guarantee it.

*　　*　　*

230

When Sitt Nafisa returned to her own home two days later, Zeinab had never seen her look so pale and drawn, even if her composure remained unshaken. Her maids hovered about her as if she were ill: preparing her bath, rubbing her feet, bringing mint tea.

When she had bathed and changed and taken to her bed, she sent for Zeinab.

'Ah, Aisha . . .' She sipped from a cup of mint tea, and reclined against the bolsters. 'Come here, child.'

'*Hamdillah salama*, thank God for your safe return. I am so sorry, Sitt Nafisa.'

'You did nothing wrong. If anyone took a risk, it was I. But now I am worried for you. The viceroy pasha is angry that he had to bow to the ulema's ultimatum to let me go, and I don't doubt that he is biding his time to get revenge. A hawk that is frustrated of its original prey falls back on smaller game. Do you take my meaning? He might turn his wrath on you, as the instrument of my intention.'

Zeinab's head spun. Sitt Nafisa frowned. 'Did you tell the Albanian officer your name was Aisha?'

'No, I gave no name, as you instructed.'

'Precisely. Yet the pasha knew the name you go by, so his spies must be making inquiries. So far he knows only that you are a Mamluka by the name of Aisha; at any minute he might discover who you really are, and that there is a death sentence hanging over your head – and when he does, I cannot protect you.'

Zeinab swallowed. 'I see.'

'I am so sorry, child, to have put you at risk like this. I should never have sent you to negotiate with the Albanian.' She shook her head.

Zeinab slipped to her knees by the bed and kissed Sitt Nafisa's hand. 'I owe you my life, and my child's life. You were a mother to me when my own father denounced me and my mother abandoned me. Whatever happens, I will still be in your debt.'

Sitt Nafisa stroked her hair. 'Sweet girl! But we must make sure you stay safe, for your own sake, and your little boy's. You must go away, where no one can find you, and you will come back when it is safe.'

231

'I must leave you?'

'Yes. But you must also leave your baby.'

'No!' Zeinab clapped her hand to her mouth. 'Why can't I take my baby with me? Where am I going? How long will I be gone?'

'I can't tell you, child, except that where you will go it is not safe to take your child. You must trust me. Will you trust me, Aisha? I swear by God that I will take care of your boy as if he were my own grandson, till you come back.'

'You have been kindness itself to him. But can't I please take him with me? I can't bear to be parted from him!'

'For your own safety, and his, it's best that you don't. You will understand. Now collect your things – only what you strictly need – and be ready to leave tonight with Barquq.'

'Tonight?'

'Yes, you will understand why. You must hurry. God bless you, child.'

Three days had passed since Zeinab, under Barquq's protection, had embarked on a felucca headed downriver from the port of Bulaq. When she woke that morning she sniffed the air; a fresh breeze was blowing and there was a tang to it that she could not identify. 'What is that?'

'That?' Barquq smiled. 'That is the smell of the sea. Have you never been to the sea before?'

'Never! Where are we?'

'We are approaching Alexandria.'

'Alexandria? Is that where I will be going?'

'You will board a ship in Alexandria – if it has not left already.'

A ship? Zeinab's head reeled. She had never seen the sea, except in books and in Nicolas' sketches. Where would the ship take her? She missed her little boy desperately, imagining him every moment of the day: how he rubbed his eyes when he woke up, and how warm and fragrant he was when she picked him up in the morning, like a toasty roll of bread fresh from the oven; how he rubbed his ear to put himself to sleep at night, and how he slept with his mouth open. She knew he would sleep as easily in Almaz's bed as in her own; in the harem the baby was everyone's pet and everyone's business, handed from one to the other of the women as if they were all his mothers. If he had a favourite, it was Almaz. Zeinab trusted implicitly Sitt Nafisa's promise to keep an eye on his care as if he were her own flesh and blood, but she missed her little Do-do.

In the next few hours the felucca reached the great port of Alexandria, and Zeinab could hardly take in all the novel sights and smells and sounds. She had imagined the sea to be a very large lake, but it was incomparable. It was as vast and alive as the sky, undulating and sparkling in the sun, rushing in small white waves to slap and splash against the breakfront, over and over, with a dull roar. And the ships! Nothing like the river flotillas she'd seen. These ships were like tall palaces on the water.

'English ships,' Barquq told her. 'They evacuate today. We are barely in time. I will leave you here, sit on the pier and don't move or speak to anyone till I get back, I must make inquiries and arrange for your passage.'

Zeinab sank to the ground, overwhelmed, staring at the square white fort gleaming at the tip of a promontory, and the tall ships flapping their flags in the breeze. She would be leaving on one of these ships? On an English ship? In a daze she stared at the sailors bustling back and forth between the docks and the ships, and listened to the cacophony of foreign tongues: Turkish or English she recognized without understanding, but there were other languages she could not even hazard a guess at. The tangy salt breeze whipped the sails and drummed on the masthead flags and snatched at the ends of her abaya.

Barquq came back and hurried her down the dock to a boat that rowed them out to a great ship, and she clung to his arm as they climbed on board the floating palace. She followed him to one side of the vessel, where a large group of men were standing together, their backs to her, looking out to sea; their dress and deportment set them apart from the English officers and motley sailors.

'Mamlukes!' Zeinab turned to Barquq in wonder. 'What are they doing on an English ship?'

'Hush!' He approached a man in an azure turban who was unmistakably the amir, and handed him a letter. The Bey read it, and turned around to glance at Zeinab. He had a greying blond beard, an arrogant mouth, and sharp blue eyes under fierce brows. He brought two fingers to his eyes, nodded to Barquq and turned his back to her again.

'God be with you.' The eunuch handed her the baggage. 'I must go back to my mistress. You are under the Bey's protection now.'

'Who is it?'

'Don't you recognize him? That's Elfi Bey. Godspeed.'

PART IV

The Journey in Reverse

NINETEEN

A Rock in the Middle of the Sea

'As the Bey's consideration is high with both Mamlukes and Arabs, he might be a forcible instrument in the hands of government in the event of those occurrences against which it had expressed such desire to be prepared, and at the same time counteract any project of the French to build a rival interest with those parties, in their disappointment at our departure.'

Lord John Stuart to Lord Hobart,
28 February 1803

Malta. A handful of rocks flung into the sea. An island you could cross on horseback in less than a day, an island like a prison. All these people babbling in a language that was a maddening mix of the familiar and the foreign, like a child playing hide and seek. All summer long Elfi had been detained here, looking out to sea for the ship that would finally carry him away to England, just as the boy Shamil had peered from the heights of his Caucasus Mountains at the glittering Black Sea. He felt the same frustration, the same powerlessness as he had then; the same sense that the world was moving on without him while he was forced to wait. Elfi had not felt so much at the whim of others since he had been manumitted, and the rage burned silently inside him.

He did not blame Sir John Stuart. He understood how these matters stood. When the French learned of his embarkation, they would inevitably put the most damaging construction on it to alarm the Porte, and the Porte in turn would protest vigorously to the Court of St James. Stuart had acted on his own initiative and must have subsequently received counter orders. 'I will clear up this matter directly, my dear Bey,' he apologized as he left without Elfi. 'And you will follow on the next ship; only let me prepare the ground so that your reception in London will be everything that you could hope.'

Elfi had come to believe this voyage to London was necessary ever since he had received a report from Sitt Nafisa following on Sebastiani's visit. 'The French will not act,' she had told him. 'You are right to try your chances with the English.' But the English were as reluctant to take sides as the French, playing the Mamlukes against the Turks. Only a personal appeal on Elfi's part to the king himself had any chance of succeeding, and so he had set sail with Sir John Stuart when the British fleet evacuated.

That had been back in March, and it was now almost autumn. Elfi had spent the entire hot, baking summer on this God-forsaken rock in the sea, as the begrudged guest – prisoner, more like – of Sir Alexander Ball, English governor of the island, with no better company than his own restless Mamlukes.

A red shawl agitating at the bottom of the cliffs below him made Elfi squint to make out the small figure picking its way up the rocky incline towards him. It was the woman called Aisha. From time to time she stopped to wave her shawl and call out to him, her words unintelligible at that distance. What was it that was so urgent?

Elfi turned his gaze to the ships in the harbour. While he remained stranded on this rock, events in Egypt were unfolding without him. News had reached him of the arrest and ordeal of Sitt Nafisa and the other wives of the amirs, taken as hostages; indeed, the viceroy pasha had sent a threatening letter, reminding the Beys that they had wives and children in Cairo. Elfi had written back in a fury:

You sent to us warning of the Sublime Porte's displeasure,
offering as guidance the divine saying: 'Obey God, and obey
the Messenger and those in authority over you.' But you did
not cite to us any verse showing us how to get out from under

*the sky, nor one indicating that we should cast ourselves with
our own hands to destruction! You told us our womenfolk and
children were in Cairo, and that as a result of the hostilities
some harm might befall them. We were astonished to hear this,
since we had left our households behind in good faith, believing
them to be in your custody and protected by your honour, on
the grounds that manliness precludes the thought of lifting one's
hand against women, for men should fight with men.*

Shaykh Jabarti had later written to him that when the letter was
read, the hearers marvelled, as though they were looking beyond the
veil of the Unseen. Elfi smiled grimly, recognizing Jabarti's disguised
sarcasms. The same boat had also brought the news that the viceroy
and his troops had been besieged and massacred by those same
Arnaout mercenaries he had refused to pay. In the confusion that
followed, Ibrahim Bey and Bardissi, at the head of the Mamlukes,
had entered Cairo and taken possession of it. Now all of Egypt was
theirs, with the exception of Alexandria, which was still held by the
Turkish garrison. The news would tilt the balance in favour of his
being allowed to continue his journey to London: it must have
reached England by now that the Beys had entered Cairo in triumph.

The girl stopped halfway up the winding path on the cliff, clutching
her side and catching her breath. Elfi turned back to his sombre
thoughts. His palace in the Ezbekiah – having survived three successive French commanders, two insurrections, not to mention the
bombardments during the repressions that followed – had been
destroyed in the Albanian uprising against the viceroy pasha. Elfi
counted the nights he had spent there: sixteen nights before Bonaparte
took it over; one night on his return to Cairo. He would never walk
its halls again, he would never duck his head under the fountain and
hold his breath underwater for as long as it took a hawk to circle
seven times. He shook his head now, like a dog shaking off water;
it was only a house, he reminded himself, only stone and wood; he
could build another.

The small figure on the rocky path was drawing closer, and even at this distance he could discern her excitement. She waved her shawl at him again and shouted his name. He raised his hand briefly to acknowledge that he had seen her. Sitt Nafisa's letter had told him the sorry story of the girl who had been Bakri's daughter and, once, Bonaparte's bride. Sitt Nafisa had explained the girl's predicament to him, and appealed to his chivalry. 'She is in your hands, from your right hand to your left,' she had written. And he had given his answer to her eunuch in one sentence: 'Tell your mistress the request is a small thing and she who makes it, dear.' He touched two fingers to his eyelids as he spoke, and he knew the eunuch would relay the wordless gesture.

So, in keeping with his promise to Sitt Nafisa, Elfi tried to be patient with the girl, after his fashion. What to do with her once he reached England was a problem, but the least of his worries. Here in Malta he let her spend her time learning English from his dragoman Vincenzo Taberna; for one thing it distracted her, and when she was not distracted she was inclined to mope after her child; and for another she might well prove a valuable interpreter one day in England, should he find himself in need of someone whose loyalty was less questionable than Vincenzo's.

'Captain Vincenzo speaks Arabic, and Turkish too, and Italian. How comes an Englishman speaks Arabic so well?' the girl had asked Elfi once.

Elfi had snorted. 'He's no more an Englishman than I am.' Vincenzo was Piedmontese by birth, and had spent twelve years as a Mamluke in the household of the Capitan Pasha before enlisting under Murad and Elfi in the Upper Egypt campaigns against the French. Now he worked for the English, passed for a dashing Englishman, and had been assigned to Elfi as dragoman.

The girl climbing the rocky path had come within earshot of Elfi, and stopped to catch her breath, clutching her red shawl to her panting chest, strands of dishevelled hair blowing about her face. 'Elfi Bey,' she panted, 'Elfi Bey, the ship has come, the order has come – we are to leave for England tonight!'

TWENTY

The Great Metropolis

'The extraordinary embassy of one of the principal Beys in England, the retinue and state deployed in London by a party in open revolt against the Sublime Porte, the welcome he receives from the ministers of his British Majesty, no longer allow for any doubt as to the policy of England toward Egypt and the Ottoman Empire.'

Foreign Minister of the French Republic Talleyrand to
the Ottoman Ambassador in Paris,
11 November 1803

Zeinab sat on a bench on Rotten Row in Hyde Park and watched the Englishmen walk by. No one else walked quite like a certain type of Englishman. They held themselves very tall, very straight, yet perfectly easy; brisk yet unhurried, looking straight ahead, as if they never had to watch their feet; smiling vaguely at no one in particular, as if they knew the whole world must part to make room for them. No one walked like an English lord. Not the French, with their forward-tilting, impetuous energy; not the Turks, with their heavy gravity; not the Beys, with their cavalier's swagger – how often, at their passage, had she heard Shaykh Jabarti quote reprovingly from the Koran: 'Do not tread pridefully on the Earth.'

The English rode well, too, but it was the horses that fascinated her. She had never seen such great big horses, with their brushed manes and their glossy black coats, standing so high she thought she would need a ladder to climb into the saddle. She never tired of sitting in the park and watching the king's cavalry guards parading in their bright red uniforms, their pony-tailed helmets and silver shields reflecting the sun, their huge black horses snorting white plumes in the frosty air.

Everything in this country was built to a bigger scale than she was used to: the horses, the people, the streets, and especially the palaces. The palaces here were like the pictures she'd seen of the Sultan's Top Kapi in Istanbul.

The thought of the Sultan in his palace brought a frown to her face. The Porte was creating endless difficulties for Elfi Bey, insisting that he not be formally recognized at the court of the English king. Zeinab sighed; there were days when Elfi Bey was in a foul mood, and days when he threatened to turn right around and go back to Egypt, even though the seas had been so choppy on the voyage from Malta that it made Zeinab ill just to think of getting onboard a ship again. She missed her baby boy desperately, but she had come this far, and she would not go back till she had carried out the plan that had formed in her mind. Ever since her son was born she had racked her brains for a way to get news to Nicolas; to let him know she was alive, and that he had a son. The hand of Providence had placed her on the ship to Europe, and Zeinab saw this as a sign. She would find a way to reach Nicolas in France – but for that she would need Elfi Bey's help.

She expected him to arrive in the park at any moment, with an escort of four of the seventeen Mamlukes who had made the voyage with him. But Zeinab was finding it very difficult to get a moment in private to confide in him; during the day he was occupied with matters of state, and in his few hours of leisure he was taken up with the English lady he had met two weeks earlier, at a ball hosted by Sir John Stuart in one of those grand houses with liveried footmen and blazing chandeliers. The lady had been quite openly curious about Elfi Bey's party, but then everywhere they went, in the street and in the park, people stared and children pointed, crying, 'Look at the Mamlukes!' till Elfi would glower and mutter: 'By Allah, you'd think we were trained bears in a mulid parade!' Once or twice, Amin Bey and some of the younger Mamlukes lost patience and drew their swords and feinted a charge; then the children squealed and the ladies pretended to faint.

This lady, though, didn't seem the fainting type. Her back was one straight line from her lofty neck down her sloping shoulders and long torso to the tapering waist of her pale pearly dress. Her hair was of a fox-fur red, and she had very fair skin that flushed a hectic pink when she was dancing. In between dances she sipped goblet after goblet of the punch her partners brought her. She had seemed fascinated by the Beys at the ball, returning to their side of the hall between dances, and sending sidelong smiles in their direction from behind her fan. She kept up a running commentary to her lady friend in that clear, carrying voice that Englishwomen had.

'He cuts rather a fine figure, don't you think, the Bey? Were it not for that positively ferocious expression . . . *Quelle manière de dévisager les gens!*'

Zeinab had noticed that English ladies often dropped French expressions into their speech; but even without that, her lessons with the dragoman had borne fruit, and she was able to at least catch the gist of much of what she heard in English. It amused her that the lady, oblivious, was speaking about her practically to her face.

'And that girl – what extraordinary eyes! Much too dark to be fashionable, of course, but still, those eyes . . . and what exotic dress! Quite the thing in Paris, that cunning little turban, apparently, the French are wild about everything that is *retour d'Égypte.*'

Zeinab felt self-conscious, suddenly. She was wearing her eau-de-nil dress, with a gold-embroidered amber and green turban wound around her head, her curly locks spilling down her neck and shoulders. Her only adornment were dangling pearl earrings that were part of the wedding jewellery her father had given her when she was wed to General Bonaparte; it seemed so long ago now.

The English lady saw Sir John headed in their direction and caught his eye. 'Ah, Sir John! Will you not introduce your guest?'

Sir John strode over, smiling. 'With pleasure. Lady Cecilia, may I present Elfi Bey's er . . . ward, miss . . .'

'Madame,' Zeinab interrupted on impulse. She raised her chin and set her mouth. 'Madame Conté.' Her face flushed at her own nerve.

Sir John seemed taken aback for a moment but quickly recovered his aplomb. 'I beg your pardon, madame. Allow me to present Madame Conté, Lady Cecilia. Will you excuse me? A host is never master of his own leisure!'

'Of course, of course.' The lady turned to Zeinab. '*Vous parlez français?*'

'*Oui, milady.*'

'And Monsieur Conté? He is an émigré? He is here?'

'I am a widow,' Zeinab replied in French, at the same time muttering *Allah forbid* under her breath, to ward a bad omen off Nicolas. God willing he was alive. But an émigré, her Nicolas, the fervent Republican? What an idea. She knew better than to say as much, however; she found the English to be sympathetic to French émigrés, of whom there were many, but highly suspicious of 'Jacobins', who would be subject to arrest as spies if they dared set foot on English soil.

'I am a widow myself,' the lady commiserated. 'But you, my dear, are so very young to have lost . . .' She was distracted, glancing in the direction of the Mamluke group. 'And which of these gentlemen is Elfi Bey? No, let me guess, it can only be the gentleman in the blue turban.' She gestured to where Elfi stood, spread-legged, tossing back a glass of punch. 'He seems to have developed a taste for our milk punch. Does he not ever smile? Surely it is his own fault if he cannot find entertainment in such pleasant society! Might he be prevailed upon to dance, do you think?'

'*Non*, milady, *il ne danse pas.*'

'A pity. There is much one would like to ask about Egypt and its mysteries. Mr Hamilton has been entertaining us all with tales of his trip up the Nile, the monuments, the mummies . . . Does the Bey speak French?'

'*Non*, milady, *il ne parle pas français.*'

'More's the pity. Well, perhaps he might be prevailed upon to go for a ride in the park? He does ride? Of course he would, how silly of me, he's a Mamluke. Good! I recommend Hyde Park, I enjoy nothing better myself than a ride in the Park at this time of year. Particularly of a Sunday afternoon.'

The lady had met them in the park that Sunday, and several times since then, in various homes and public assembly rooms. She rode side-saddle on the tall English horses with as much ease as if she were sitting on a chaise longue; but then it was true that these English beasts were as steady in temperament as they were intimidating in size. Zeinab wondered which of her elegant riding habits the lady would be wearing today; she had one of black velvet, and one of crimson red, both with matching tall hat and veil.

A sudden gust of biting wind came whirling like a dervish down Rotten Row, tossing the fallen leaves in the air, and Zeinab leapt up and began stamping her feet and clapping her gloved hands till the gust had passed. She had never known cold like it. In Egypt, even in winter, the sun warmed the roofs and the courtyards, and when night fell and temperatures dropped, a brazier of perfumed sandal-wood chips sufficed to make a room cosy. Here in London, the sun, like the Sultan, had no empire; it was weak and timid and dared not show its face even during the day, and half the trees lost their leaves and shivered to death. Indoors, great fires were lit in every room, but the icy draughts, like evil Jinn, lurked in the hallways waiting to seize Zeinab as she passed from room to room.

'It will snow,' Elfi Bey had said that morning. 'I can smell it in the air.'

Zeinab was excited at the prospect of seeing snow for the first time, but Elfi just said that, growing up in his mountains, he had been snowed in so often, for days and weeks at a time, that he did not care if he never saw snow again in his life.

Several ladies passing by in cloaks and fur muffs smiled as they watched Zeinab's frenzied little dance, and she smiled back, abashed, and began a more sedate pacing, to and fro in front of the bench. It was far too cold to sit down again. She kept a wary eye out for the wind that was frisking in little waves across the lead-grey pond. It reminded her a little of the Ezbekiah Pond, except that there were no pleasure boats; only the geese and the ducks would venture on the water in this weather.

Where, she wondered, was Elfi Bey? She had yet to find the opportunity to disclose her plan to him. She saw less and less of him these days, as he was gone much of the time to meetings with British officials, and in the evenings Lady Cecilia would send a carriage for him and he usually returned very late or not at all. Lady Cecilia had even prevailed on him to be fitted for English clothes and boots, and today she was to meet him in the park and accompany him to the tailor. Where was Lady Cecilia?

Zeinab wondered what time it was; she found it difficult to keep track of time without the muezzin's call for prayers punctuating the day. She strolled a little way down the path, blowing on her gloved fingers, vaguely looking around for the younger Mamlukes, who had not accompanied Elfi Bey to Westminster and were riding in the park. Suddenly she saw a man in black clothes standing behind a tree and staring at her intently, motionless, as if he had been there for a while. She stopped short and caught her breath. A swarthy, stubble-jawed man with a thick neck and muscular build, awkward, somehow, in his very ordinary English clothes. Zeinab had the impression she had seen him somewhere before, but she could not place the face, only a vague sense of menace she associated with it. He continued to stare at her, very deliberately, and that unnerved her. She turned away and looked up and down the path for Elfi Bey.

She heard horses coming down the carriage drive to the south of the park, and peered in that direction; it was Elfi and Sir John Stuart, followed by four of the Mamlukes. Elfi and Sir John dismounted and walked in Zeinab's direction, deep in conversation, Captain Vincenzo between them, translating.

'My dear Bey, I urge you to be patient. I thought the meeting at Westminster today went quite as well as could be expected.' Sir John raised his hat to Zeinab as they approached, and went on in reassuring tones. 'Lord Hobart seemed quite receptive to your arguments.'

'It is to your king himself that I should be making my arguments.

246

I have written to your grand vizir but have received only polite excuses in response.'

Zeinab noted that Vincenzo translated Elfi's 'grand vizir' to 'prime minister'; so that was what he was called in England. She availed herself of every opportunity to improve her English, in case Elfi Bey ever had need of her services as an interpreter. Something moved behind a tree, a glimpse of black, and she was distracted for a minute, but turned her attention back to the conversation.

'I am sure Prime Minister Addington is giving your letter careful consideration, and indeed I have written him myself to second your argument. I have a copy with me right here.' Sir John brought a letter out of the inside pocket of his coat. 'Let me read the most relevant passage to you: "The Bey expressly stated that his object in coming to this country was not to urge on the British Government points which might tend to involve it in fresh conflicts or disputes with foreign powers, but to clear his own and his friends' characters from imputations of rebellion as well as to prove the justice of the foundation upon which they built their pretensions to the protection and countenance of their country."' Sir John folded away the letter.

The black shape moved again behind the tree and Zeinab was sure it was the man who had been staring at her earlier. She looked to Elfi Bey to catch his eye, but he frowned, and she held her tongue; he did not like to be interrupted.

'Sir John, I need to know how things stand with your government.' Elfi sounded grim. 'I am not asking them to send English troops, only to give us the arms and support to fight the Albanian militias ourselves.'

'My dear sir, I would never abuse your good opinion of me by deceiving you in the slightest. The government is of two minds about your delicate situation, or rather, it is of two minds on any given day, depending on the news from the Continent. On the one hand, there are those, like myself, who hold that the renewed threat of a French invasion of Egypt can only be forestalled by strengthening the hand of the Beys. On the other hand, the Porte has expressed great uneasiness as to the objects of your voyage, so there are some at Westminster who believe it prudent to allay these fears by treating you as a distinguished visitor to whom the common laws of hospitality extend, but no more.'

Zeinab's eyes darted again to the tree. Now the man had disappeared from view; he must have hidden behind the broad trunk.

Elfi snorted impatiently. 'Then perhaps I should travel to Istanbul and pledge myself and my brethren to recognize the sovereignty of the Sultan, and defend Egypt in his name, if he in turn allows us to secure our lives, the lives of our families, and the return of our properties.'

'I cannot dissuade you from travelling to Istanbul, Elfi Bey,' Sir John shook his head. 'And I will not deceive you, there are those in Westminster who would encourage such an endeavour on your part, to extricate the government from a delicate situation. But as your friend, I must warn you that you would be taking a grave risk.'

Elfi nodded. 'I know. It would not surprise me if the Capitan Pasha has sent assassins after me all the way to London, let alone Istanbul.'

'There he is!' Zeinab exclaimed in Arabic, unable to restrain herself any longer.

'Who?' Elfi turned around.

'There, behind the tree, there was a man, a man in black, he was staring at us . . .'

'Staring at us? Are you out of your mind, girl? Who does not stare at us in this country?'

Sir John looked concerned. 'My dear young lady, what can have alarmed you so?'

Elfi shot her a warning glance and she shook her head. 'It is nothing, forgive me, Sir John.'

'I am glad to hear it. Ah, I see Lady Cecilia's carriage approaching. I will leave you to pleasanter occupations. Speaking of which, I am to convey to you an invitation from the Prince of Wales to dine with him tomorrow evening at the Union Club House, as Carleton House is undergoing major repair. A carriage will be sent for you at seven. Clarence and Cambridge – the Prince's younger brothers – are to be of the company as well. Elfi Bey, you will have your audience with the king very soon, depend upon it.' Sir John bowed and took his leave.

Elfi squared his shoulders and rested his hand on the hilt of his sword as he watched the carriage approach down the south carriage drive at a brisk trot, a coachman at the reins of the matched pair, two footmen standing behind.

'Elfi Bey, listen to me, please,' Zeinab caught his arm. 'This was different. This man, I think I've seen him before; he was watching us as if he was following us . . . what if he is an assassin?'

'Is it this talk of assassins that is rattling you? Then from now on don't wander about on your own. I will speak to Amin Bey and tell him to keep an eye on you when I'm not around.'

'But Elfi Bey, I need to speak with you about something import-ant, I –'

'You must tell me later. Here comes the lady.'

The coachman brought the purple carriage to a halt, the white satin curtains with silver fringe parted and Lady Cecilia's long face with its pointed chin and bright eyes appeared in the window frame; she was wearing a green velvet hood trimmed with sable. 'Good after-noon! It is much too cold today to ride. Do get in, Elfi Bey, I am longing to see you in your new boots!'

One of the two white-wigged footmen, in livery matching the carriage, climbed down and opened the door. Lady Cecilia slipped a hand out of her fur muff and beckoned Zeinab with a gloved finger. 'And little Madame Conté! Will you not come with us? No, no, Elfi Bey, I will not hear anything against it, I am determined she must come with us. Besides, think of it, she will be a capital little dragoman between us and we will not need the services of Captain Vincenzo.'

Elfi shrugged, and Zeinab followed him into the carriage; at a signal from him, the four Mamlukes mounted and fell in along-side. Zeinab sank into the quilted white satin upholstery and Lady Cecilia drew part of the fur throw that covered her lap over Zeinab's knees.

Zeinab peered out of the silver-fringed curtains of the window.

249

She recognized Pall Mall, and noticed every head turning to stare at the four Mamlukes on horseback flanking the carriage.

'We shall be the talk of the town tomorrow,' Lady Cecilia sighed unconvincingly. 'Quite the scandal, I'm afraid, driving down the Mall with a Mamluke escort. We might even eclipse reports of Lady Emma Hamilton's latest dinner party at Merton. But then, you are in the papers already, Elfi Bey, did you know that? Look, here in the *Gentleman's Magazine.*' She brought out one of those English newspapers that had clever, grotesque drawings. 'It says that you have a suite of seventeen . . . that you drink two bottles of champagne or burgundy after dinner – now that is positively libellous; I have never seen you drink more than a bottle and a half myself! Ah, now this is delicious: it says you are fascinated with everything . . . especially with the ladies. Is that true, Elfi Bey? Do you have eyes for more than one lady?' she teased, and he smiled back, and was silent. Zeinab suddenly wished she were not in the carriage, and turned away to look out of the window.

The carriage was now passing through narrower, shop-lined streets, and Elfi Bey, seeing a sign on a shopfront, suddenly stuck his arm out of the window and rapped sharply with the hilt of his sword on the side of the vehicle. The startled coachman reined in the horses, and the Bey jumped out and headed towards the shop.

'But this is not the street we want,' Lady Cecilia protested. 'And if we stop we shall be late for the theatre – oh, never mind.' She shrugged with a smile at Zeinab. 'We might as well go down, my dear, he will do whatever enters his head anyway.' She lifted her skirts and let the coachman help her out, Zeinab close behind her. They followed Elfi Bey into a shop that had a harpsichord on its sign. He was looking around the instruments in the crowded shop, lifting the tops, and fingering the keys, somewhat to the alarm of the shopkeeper, a small bespectacled man.

'These are not as fine as the ones I've seen. Tell him I want a finer one,' Elfi instructed Zeinab.

'*Il veut un plus beau,*' she translated to Lady Cecilia.

'Is it a pianoforte he has in mind?' She raised her eyebrows.

Zeinab had heard the lady play this amazing instrument more than once in the drawing room of her house; the first time, Zeinab had clapped so hard she had drawn attention to herself. Elfi had not clapped, but he would sit perfectly still whenever Lady Cecilia played, and whenever she looked up and put her hands in her lap, as if to stop, he would nod to her, in a silent plea, and she would lift her magic hands to the instrument again.

She looked at Elfi now with an exaggerated frown.

'My dear Elfi Bey, be reasonable, you cannot decide to buy every telescope and microscope and musical instrument you set eyes on!'

Zeinab resisted adding, on her own behalf, what Elfi had said when they had visited the giant telescope aimed at the heavens, outside of London. It was an instrument so large she could stand upright in it. Elfi Bey, who was fascinated by the study of the stars, had spent hours examining it and asking questions. As they left, Zeinab had overheard him tell Amin Bey that he would buy every instrument and every book he could, and recreate the Institute of Egypt in Cairo on a grander scale even than the French. There would be peace one day, he said, and then he could hire scientists from England or France or wherever he could to staff it and instruct Egyptians in all the arts and sciences.

'But a pianoforte!' Lady Cecilia was protesting. 'Would not a harpsichord do? Whatever would you do with a pianoforte?'

'Tell her it is for Egypt, I will take it back with me.'

'But you don't play!'

'I will pay for someone to play.'

'Does anyone play these instruments in Egypt? Never mind. Tell the Bey he shall have a pianoforte, if his heart is set on it, but we shall have to order it from Broadwood's, and it will cost him a great deal. Now do let us get on with our errands, or we shall be late for Drury Lane.'

At the boot maker Elfi Bey tried on the new boots that had been made to measure for him; they were knee-high, of soft black leather, and required a special contraption and the help of the apprentice to pull on. Elfi stood up and stomped about in them, then nodded, and brought out his purse. He barely glanced at the bill the man presented, took out a handful of coins and tossed them on the counter, and left. By the shoemaker's surprised but pleased expression, Zeinab suspected he had overpaid considerably.

The next stop was the tailor, where it was unseemly for ladies to accompany him, so Elfi entered with the Mamlukes. Zeinab sat looking out of the window at the bustle of the street, trying to distinguish the cries of the street vendors hawking their wares. One of the little urchins called chimney sweeps passed by, with such a cheerful grin on his soot-blackened face that she fumbled in her reticule for a coin to toss him. Every child she saw reminded her of her own baby; she fretted that he might be forgetting her. Whenever she weakened with homesickness for him, she reminded herself that she was abroad on a mission, for the boy's own sake: to find his father. But if she was to put this plan in motion, she must enlist Elfi Bey's help – and when would she ever have an opportunity to speak to him alone?

'Tell me, my dear,' Lady Cecilia leaned back in the carriage and snuggled into the sable-lined hood of her cloak, 'you seem so distracted this afternoon. Is everything all right? Are you still mourning for Monsieur Conté? But he must have been very much older than you?'

'He was, yes.' Zeinab nodded and changed the subject: 'And yourself, milady? Have you been a widow long?'

'Goodness, yes, for a great many years now. I was married very young myself, a *mariage de raison*, as the French say. Sir Ambrose was older than my father, but a pleasanter husband one could not wish for – when he was not in his cups, and that was every evening. He finally succumbed at the age of sixty, leaving me with no desire ever to marry again, and, thankfully, the wherewithal never to be constrained to it.' A sign on one of the shops in the street attracted her eye. 'Oh, there's a little curio shop on the corner, shall we have a look round?'

She got out of the carriage and picked up her skirt to cross the slushy street. Zeinab started to follow when a movement caught her eye and she stopped. It was him again, the swarthy man in black, ducking into a shop; she was sure of it. She took a step or two in his direction, then hesitated in the middle of the street. Should she follow him? Elfi Bey had told her not to wander off on her own. Should she tell Elfi? But what would she tell him, exactly? She crossed the street and idled in front of the shop windows. Which door had the man entered? The one with the pipes in the window, or the one next to it with men's hats?

She shuddered in the chill air and drew her cloak closer around her; soft white flakes were drifting down silently in the grey twilight, and the shopkeepers were lighting the double-branched street lamps. Snow! So this was what it was like? She held out her hand and caught a flake and tasted it. She had seen frost, every morning since they had come to London, but this was the first time it had snowed. Down the street, Lady Cecilia was being helped back into the carriage and Elfi Bey was striding out of the tailor shop, brows lowered, followed by the shopkeeper, who seemed to be protesting volubly. Zeinab hurried back to the carriage.

'Ah, there you are, my dear, I was wondering what had become of you.' Lady Cecilia made room for her in the carriage. Elfi Bey shrugged off the protesting tailor and climbed in, while the Mamlukes swung themselves up into the saddle.

'But, Elfi Bey, whatever can be the matter?' Lady Cecilia raised her brows.

'I will not wear those clothes, and that is all there is to it.'

'I can't imagine why not, I am sure you would look very fine in a proper riding coat and breeches. No? Well, at any rate, we must pay the tailor – the clothes are bespoke; whether you wear them or not, you must pay for them.'

Elfi looked astounded. 'I pay for what I buy. I do not pay for what I do not want to buy.'

'But you must, that is the way it is here. Never mind, I'll ask the tailor to send the note on to you. I'm sure once I explain this to you properly . . . but we must be off now, it will never do to be late for the curtain, the king and queen are expected in their box tonight.

And then we are invited for a late supper at Ranelagh with Lord Elgin; he has promised a spectacular exhibition of mummies brought back from Upper Egypt by Mr Hamilton – you remember Mr William Hamilton? He speaks very highly of you and of the protection you extended his little party on their archaeological expedition up the Cataracts. But whatever is the matter with little Madame Conté? My dear, you're shivering, you must borrow my muff – no, I insist.'

Zeinab buried her hands in the soft muff and leaned back in the shadow of the deep seat. She would not have a chance to speak to Elfi Bey this evening about the man who had followed them. He would be off to another dinner, and then the theatre, and she would be left to wonder when she could speak to him alone again. She sighed and leaned her head against the window, soothed by the steady clip of the horses, the bright busy lights of the great city outside sieved through the soft, light snowfall. She wished she could tell Nicolas that she had seen snow, at last; she remembered how he had once tried to describe it to her. Was it snowing where he was now, in that France so near and yet so far away? When could she tell Elfi Bey of her plan to try to find Nicolas? When could she see her husband again?

TWENTY-ONE

The Spy

As he had done every day since receiving Sebastiani's letter, Nicolas Conté went to a trunk in a corner of his study and brought out piles of sketches and aquarelles, skimming through them and stopping every now and then to examine a watercolour he had forgotten: a waterwheel with pots, turned by a buffalo; the obelisk of Cleopatra in Alexandria; a glass-blower's mean, hole-in-the-wall workshop; the painting of one of the interior courtyards of Hassan Kashif's house, with the sundial Nicolas had set up on the southern wall over a mashrabiyya window, and the Nubian doorkeeper looking up at it. Nicolas could not remember, now, if he had included the figure of the man for scale, or if he had really been present.

There were sketches for engravings as well: street hawkers bent under the weight of the huge water jugs on their backs; women in black abayas or in Turkish harem dress: a headscarf wound about the forehead, a thin chemise, a sash . . . How he had reproached Zeinab for reverting to that manner of dress during their last weeks together; and yet now he found a certain charm even to this.

Ah, here it was, finally! The sketch he had made of Zeinab, sitting under a tree, dappled with light and shade. Daubs of colour: the violet touches on her white dress, her black curls slipping out of the pale green ribbons, her dark pools of eyes shaded by the long, thick lashes. She was holding her hat in her lap as carefully as a child with a precious toy, and that detail touched him to the quick: there had been so much of the child about her. That, and the way she carried her head, as if it were almost too heavy for her long, slender neck . . . the image of that slender neck snapped, broken, rose before him. With a supreme effort of will Nicolas shoved the sketch back into the portfolio and returned everything to the trunk. He could not allow himself these black reveries. He should be occupying himself with the hundred matters that claimed his attention, and he should start with his mail.

He picked up the next letter in the pile and slit open the seal. It was a letter from Bartholomew, the man Bonaparte had appointed chief of police in Cairo. Nicolas frowned, surprised. Why would Bartholomew be writing to him? He had not seen the fellow since the evacuation, when they had embarked for France on different ships. Since then Nicolas had vaguely heard that Bartholomew had joined a 'Chasseurs d'Orient' corps expressly created to regroup the various elements, from renegade Mamlukes to Copts and Greeks, who had served in some military capacity under the French and had evacuated with them. But why would Bartholomew write to him? Nicolas read on: he was requesting an interview, at a time and place to be nominated by Citoyen Conté. He claimed to have urgent information that concerned Conté personally.

Nicolas leaned back in his chair. What could the man possibly want with him? A recommendation for some post, no doubt; but surely he would do better to petition one of his military patrons if that were the case? Still, Nicolas could not refuse to see him; he felt he owed that much to a man who had served the French cause with loyalty and personal courage. Yet he was reluctant to admit the former police chief into the sanctity of his home – a reluctance he traced to the disturbing, indelible memory of Bartholomew torturing Kléber's assassin with a relish that went beyond the call of duty. No, he would not introduce that smell of sulphur into Lise's lavender-scented drawing room; he would meet Bartholomew at a tavern in town. He picked up his pen to respond, suggesting a rendezvous at the Moulin Gallant in Meudon.

Nicolas walked to town, conscious, in a way he would not have been before his three-year absence, of the invigorating chill and the pale winter sun, the broad trees, the orderliness and familiarity of the streets and houses along the way. The brisk walk helped to chase away the melancholy that descended upon him when he was alone with his thoughts. He entered the Moulin Gallant and nodded to the tavern-keeper's wife, who greeted him effusively and started to clear a table close to the fireplace. A swarthy, muscular man rose to his feet and came towards Nicolas. Wthout the beard, the red-plumed hat and the ceremonial fur pelisses, it took him a moment to recognize the former police chief.

'Ah, Bartholomew! Well, we are a long way from Cairo, are we not! Take a seat.'

'Some mulled wine to warm you, Citoyen Conté?' the hostess offered with a smile, adjusting her shawl over her large bosom.

'Just the thing, citoyenne, just the thing. With some of your excellent cheese, perhaps? Does that suit, Bartholomew?'

'Thank you.' Bartholomew sat down opposite him, stroking his stubbly jaw with that unconscious gesture that betrays a man who would never grow accustomed to having shaved his beard. He fixed his eyes on his host with an uncomfortable intensity. The tavern keeper brought them mulled wine in pewter cups, a slab of mature cheese, pickles, and crusty bread. Nicolas raised his glass.

'To your health, Bartholomew. Tell me, what news of the Chasseurs d'Orient?'

'Papas Oglu was appointed commander – do you remember him? He used to be Murad Bey's captain, and after the invasion he commanded the Nile flotilla under the French.'

'Of course. Are you still attached to the Chasseurs?'

'More or less. Our duties are largely ceremonial; we are present at all the parades. The Mamluke Corps, they call us.'

That could not be enough, thought Nicolas, for a man as active as Bartholomew had been in Cairo. Rather than wait for his guest to broach the purpose of his visit, he brought it up himself. 'What can I do for you, Bartholomew?'

'It is rather I who wish to render you a service, Citoyen Nicolas.'

'I see. Or rather, I confess I do not see how . . . ?'

'Presently. First I must explain that I have returned but recently from across the Channel.'

'You have been in England? For what purpose? It must be very dangerous, surely, if you were caught?'

'Indeed. But as it was, the false papers with which I was supplied passed muster. I was sent to England on a secret mission for the Republic, by General Belliard – I should say Citoyen Minister Belliard.' He paused, puffing out his chest. 'You have heard that Elfi Bey is in London? I was sent to follow him, and to report on his movements: which ministers and princes he met with, where he was received. You can imagine that this is of interest to those in the highest quarters – not only in Paris but in Istanbul.'

'Yes, I see.' Nicolas nodded. 'Did you find him?'

'Of course. Not that he makes any attempt to keep his movements secret or to disguise himself. He goes everywhere with a Mamluke escort, trusting no one but his own men. He has always been wary and distrustful by nature. But his instincts are slipping . . . the Elfi Bey I knew would have sensed that he was being followed. I was one of his artillerymen before the French invasion, you know.'

'Didn't he recognize you?'

'He never got a good look at me; I was careful always to keep at a distance.'

'I'm sure you performed a very valuable service, Bartholomew, and France is in your debt. But, forgive me, I fail to see why you would come all the way to Meudon to speak to me of your mission?'

'Ah, but I am not done.' Bartholomew leaned closer, fixing his eyes even more intently on Nicolas. 'Elfi Bey had his Mamlukes about him, but he was also accompanied by a young woman. A young woman who calls herself the Widow Conté.'

Nicolas jolted his cup down and drops of wine spattered the table. 'What is this talk?'

'The Widow Conté, that's the name she goes by. Of course, perhaps it's not so unusual a name – I am not familiar with French names. But what a coincidence, that she should be in Elfi Bey's retinue, come all the way from Egypt! I found this most intriguing. You see now why I thought you should hear of it.'

Nicolas saw the look of satisfaction in the other man's eyes, and sensed that whatever practical consideration motivated him to bring this news, it was secondary to the enjoyment he was deriving from Nicolas' disarray. He tried to compose himself.

'A young woman, you say? What did she look like?'

'Young, small, slender. Black-haired, dark-eyed. She spoke French, but I doubt she was a Frenchwoman.'

Nicolas picked up his cup, exerting all the willpower he could muster to keep his hand steady. 'Did you speak to her?'

'No. Not directly.'

'Did you inquire about her?'

'I did indeed, from the chambermaids. They say they overheard the Mamlukes call her by a different name.'

'Yes?' Nicolas' breath caught in his chest.

Bartholomew looked at him for a long moment, eyes narrowed; then he leaned back in his chair. 'Aisha. It sounded like Aisha.'

'Ah.' Nicolas exhaled, feeling a sinking in his stomach, as if he had fallen from a height.

'Yes. Well, I just thought you would want to know, Citoyen Conté.'

'Yes, yes, of course, I am obliged to you.' Nicolas roused himself from the turmoil in his head. 'Much obliged. You have come a long way out of your way, and must be considerably out of pocket for the expenses of the trip. You must let me make good your trouble.' He fumbled in his pocket and brought out his purse.

'You have my address, in case you need to reach me, Citoyen Conté.'

They parted at the door of the inn, and Nicolas strode away, his head abuzz with speculation. Could Zeinab be alive? Could she be this mysterious Widow Conté? But Bartholomew had said the woman was called Aisha. Curious that it should have been Bartholomew, of all people, who would intervene in his life in this unforeseen way! The man had no cause to lie, and yet . . . he had been holding something back, Nicolas was almost sure of it. As police chief, Bartholomew had known everyone's business in Cairo. He must have heard rumours, at least, that Shaykh Bakri's daughter was living with the chief engineer, and going about publicly with him, boating and riding, and to the Tivoli and to the Republican New Year festival. Yet he had not mentioned any of this to Nicolas. Out of discretion? Hardly.

But Bartholomew's motivation did not matter. What mattered was that Zeinab might still be alive. Nicolas' elation, his relief, was overwhelming; the burden of guilt and grief lifted from his heart like a Montgolfière cutting its moorings and rising in the air. The next moment his euphoria plummeted. Was it truly her? And if so, what was she doing in England with Elfi Bey? He must find her, he must get to the bottom of all this.

He had been so lost in his thoughts that he was startled to realize that he was nearly home. He slowed down and took a detour to buy himself some time. If Zeinab reappeared in his life, what explanation could he give Lise? A wiser man would leave the past alone, surely. But he could not; he must at least satisfy himself that she was alive, that she was well, that she was not in need of him, and that the child . . . Was there a child?

The chill of the night air piercing his lungs finally drove him indoors to his hearth: the cosy fire, Lise raising her face from her mending and tucking a lock of greying blond hair into her lace cap; Cola looking up from his book, the dog roused from his dozing. While his wife went off to fetch him a hot toddy, his son relieved him of his overcoat and hat, and sat him down in the rocking chair by the fire with the protective, bullying manner that cherished younger sons take with an ageing father.

'You were late, Papa, we were starting to worry.' The boy knelt to help Nicolas remove his boots, and the gesture reminded him, with a pang, of Zeinab kneeling before him for the same purpose, the scent of gardenia wafting from the parting in her black hair. He patted his son's dark head as the boy carried away the boots; immediately the dog came and lay across Nicolas' stockinged feet to warm them.

Lise came in with a steaming cup. 'What is it, *mon ami*?' She sensed his mood; he could never hide his emotions from her.

'Nothing, my sweet. I am a man who has more blessings than he can count, that is all.' And a man, he thought ruefully, who was capable of putting this blessed life at risk to lay a ghost, once and for all.

TWENTY-TWO

Windsor Castle

'The arrow that struck the eagle was an arrow made of an eagle's feather.'

Murad Bey to Sir Sidney Smith, in a letter
2nd April 1801

Nafisa hesitated, pen in hand, choosing her words carefully. She was distracted by the sound of Vincenzo Taberna's boots as he paced back and forth in the courtyard below; he was waiting to carry her letter to Elfi Bey. What she had to say would pain Elfi, alone and far away in a strange land, but it must be said: things were going very badly in Egypt; the new Turkish viceroy was even more of a tyrant than the last, but even he was only a puppet in the hands of the Albanians. And now Mehmet Ali – that same Arnaout officer who had betrayed her to the Turkish viceroy when she had tried to bribe him into evacuating Cairo – was now professing friendship towards the Beys while playing them off against each other. Some of the Mamlukes were rallying the French, some the English, all switching camps until any trust that existed between them was destroyed.

Beware Mehmet Ali, she wrote to Elfi, *he sows envy and fear of your ambition among your brethren, and spreads rumours that you intend to use your English connections to take all of Egypt for yourself. Meanwhile he takes advantage of the*

reigning anarchy to promote his own interests with the Porte; a
horsetail medal has arrived for him from Istanbul.

A horsetail medal! Nafisa snorted. It was unheard of for a simple Janissary officer to be so honoured; three horsetails made a pasha. Her thoughts were interrupted by the entrance of Barquq.

'Sitt Nafisa, Captain Vincenzo begs you to remember that he must set sail before the tide turns.'

'Tell him I am almost done.' She picked up her pen again:

Without your steady hand at the reins, your khushdash are in
disarray. Your first lieutenant, Elfi the Younger, is abusing the
power you have placed in him; he is unjust towards the people
and disrespectful of his elders, even of old Ibrahim Bey, who is
in the position of his grandfather. The odium that should land
on his head is being laid at your feet, for he acts in your name.
A runaway horse must be reined in, and this horse can only be
checked by his master.

Elfi the Younger . . . people had called him that almost from the day he entered the ranks of Elfi's Mamlukes. Everyone pointed out the resemblance between them, the fair colouring and square face so typical of their Tcherkess mountains, but the similarity went deeper, to something intangible in their spirit. The young Mamluke was fearless, he was loyal, and those were the qualities that mattered most to Elfi, so he had made him his lieutenant and set him up in his place before he left for England. Given time, she believed, Elfi would have tempered his protégé's violence and his excesses, but the acceleration of events before his departure had denied him that time. No one dared defy his lieutenant, for the awe in which he himself was held, but the blame for his surrogate's injustices fell on Elfi's head.

Whatever the success or failure of his mission in England, Elfi was needed back in Egypt and he must return soon, else it would be too late. Nafisa knew she was the one person from whom Elfi would never ignore an appeal. And yet . . . was she recalling him into a trap? Would his life be in danger if he returned, with no one he could trust among his envious brethren?

Barquq came upstairs again. 'Sitt Nafisa, the captain says he must leave now.'

'Yes, yes, one moment.'

Remember that the arrow that struck the eagle was an arrow made of an eagle's feather

The final sentence written, she signed and sealed her letter. Elfi would understand.

Elfi looked uneasily out of the window of the coach that was carrying him, with all the speed of three matched pairs, to meet the king of all the British. A coachman sat up front, and a postillion rode the lead left horse. When Elfi had first arrived in England, the notion of men riding in carriages like women in palanquins had seemed effeminate to him. But he had quickly come to appreciate the skill and daring required to handle one of the rapid, open carriages pulled by two horses that were so fashionable in this country. At Lady Cecilia's urging, Elfi had ordered a phaeton, as they were called, to be delivered in spring. 'Just in time for the fine weather,' she had promised. 'Ah, Elfi Bey, an English spring! You have never seen anything so enchanting. Nor have you seen me in my spring bonnets. I have ordered a quantity of muslin frocks, and a chip hat so cunning . . . only wait and see!'

Wait and see. Wait and see, everyone repeated. But he was not so sure that he would indeed stay long enough to experience an English spring: it all depended on how this audience with the king went. And as he rode along in the fast-moving coach, Elfi was uneasy. He felt trapped in the quilted blue velvet and gold fringe accoutrements of this grand conveyance, and longed for the freedom and familiarity of a horse's flanks between his thighs, like an extension of his own body, responding instantly to his every instinct, whether to advance or to flee. Not that he feared treachery on this mission to meet with the sultan of the English; only he was a man who hated to feel trapped, under any circumstances. Six of his Mamlukes on horseback flanked the carriage on either side; he had insisted upon it. Sir John Stuart and Vincenzo sat across from him in the coach, smiling and chatting as they pointed out the features of the landscape.

From time to time he felt the leather folder tucked into his sash; it contained the letters Vincenzo had handed him just before they got into the carriage. 'Letters from Cairo, Elfi Bey, important letters . . . there is much to tell you,' he had whispered, although none of the English could have understood Arabic anyway, Elfi thought irritably. He had sent Vincenzo on a mission to Egypt and the man had only just returned. Elfi was annoyed that he had not had time to debrief him about the situation there in order to prepare himself before this crucial meeting with the king.

'I only landed yesterday,' Vincenzo explained, 'and took a post chaise for London; we drove through the night and here I am.'

But Elfi had had no time to read the letters, and he did not want to do so in the carriage under the eyes of Sir John. He had glanced briefly at the seals and the writing as he tucked the slim leather folder into his sash; one of the missives was from Sitt Nafisa.

Sir John interrupted his thoughts. 'It is a signal honour that the king will give you an audience in the more informal setting of Windsor Castle, Elfi Bey. That is where he and his family reside.'

Elfi did not comment. It was no secret that the king's bouts of debilitating illness were the cause of his lengthy confinements at Windsor, far away from the eyes of London society. Elfi had been warned against the king's illness, a madness that came and went, so that one day he was frothing at the mouth and restrained in an iron chair, and on another he was as sober as a judge. He had been told that the king had not had a major bout of illness for some time, indeed he had reasserted his powers recently against Parliament, as they called their diwan. A month earlier Elfi had been at the theatre when everyone suddenly came to their feet and clapped and looked up in the same direction, and he realized that the king and queen had just entered the royal box.

'Rather plain and Germanic, isn't she?' Lady Cecilia had whispered slyly under cover of the applause. 'But His Majesty is very faithful to her. You have met the princes; there are also several princesses, all unmarried, and likely to stay that way, I'm afraid.'

Elfi had kept his thoughts to himself; it surprised him, certainly, that the king would be faithful to only one woman, and such an unprepossessing one at that; but he found it even more inexplicable that the daughters of such a powerful sultan would not find suitors, no matter how plain they might be. But there were many things he found inexplicable in England, and he made it a policy to hold his tongue and wait for the moment of illumination. He wondered whether the king had liked the gifts he had sent ahead, in Mamluke style: jewel-encrusted gold daggers, caskets intricately inlaid with mother of pearl, solid gold and silver candelabra, a five-foot long pipe studded with diamonds . . .

'Windsor Castle.' Sir John touched his arm and pointed to the forbidding walls and crenellated towers of the castle as they came into view. 'Nothing remotely like the Top Kapi Palace, eh, Elfi Bey? Nor must you expect the extravagance, the splendour of the Sublime Porte. This court makes a virtue of plain simplicity.' Lady Cecilia had been less tactful. 'Frugal to a fault,' she had once remarked to Elfi about the English sovereign.

Still, when Elfi was finally admitted to the king's presence, at the end of a long walk through chilly, austere corridors lined with halberd-bearing guards and white-wigged footmen, down draughty passages and cold stone steps that resonated with the sound of boot heels as he strode along – Sir John beside him, his Mamlukes behind – past a succession of curtained antechambers to a lofty hall, finally, where they were asked to wait – still, when King George came into the hall surrounded by his entourage, Elfi was taken aback by the simplicity of the king's appearance and demeanour: a sallow, sickly old man, whose hand, when he extended it, smelled strongly of a mustard poultice applied to draw out the 'ill humours', as the English called them.

'Good trip? Cold, what? How many seasons do you have in your country? How many crops can you rotate?' Fixing Elfi with his large, protruding eyes, the king peppered him with questions through the dragoman. He spoke in a jerky, disjointed manner, interrupting and repeating himself, and constantly interjecting 'What, what'. But his questions were perfectly shrewd and his manner alert and fully engaged in the conversation. Vincenzo strained to keep up with the translation.

Elfi was astonished at the king's interest in agriculture, his knowledge of crop rotation and irrigation, but it was a subject on which he himself happened to be well versed, by virtue of his vast sugarcane estates in Esna, so he was able to give a detailed description of the manufacturing process, to which the king listened with keen attention.

'And the by-product? What do you do with it? Molasses, what? Good, good. And the tough fibre from the cane, after it has been pressed? Mixed with mud for thatching?'

The audience went on in this vein for longer than Elfi had been given to expect. He could find no trace of the majnoon in this sultan, and was beginning to develop the disquieting impression, from his pointed questions, that the English king might well have designs on Egypt for himself. 'God forbid,' Elfi muttered under his breath.

Just when Elfi felt that the moment had come to plead his suit, the king seemed to tire and lose concentration. Elfi had no choice but to press on, trying to make a case for the need to bring order and peace to a country rampant with chaos and violence, and to expel the foreign militias of the Ottomans.

'I do not ask that Your Majesty commit a single English soldier to Egypt; all I ask is for is the support, tactical and diplomatic, with which to defend ourselves.'

He prepared to speak of the reforms he himself intended to bring to his country. But the king was growing increasingly agitated, chafing with some sort of physical discomfort, getting up and sitting down again abruptly, and the courtiers around him exchanged concerned glances.

266

'Yes, yes, we shall speak of this at another time, what?' And with that the king rose, indicating the end of the audience. 'Meanwhile welcome to England, sir.' At the whispered prompting of one of his courtiers, he added: 'And thank you for your presents. Very fine, very fine.'

Sir John bowed, and began backing out of the hall; Elfi, frustrated, had no choice but to follow suit, adding a salam for good measure and bringing his hand to his heart. The king strode out of the room, followed by his entourage.

In the carriage on the ride back to London, Elfi was silent, seething with disappointment and frustration. For months his hopes had been pinned on this audience with the king only for it to prove inconclusive. And he was beginning to understand that another audience would advance him no further. He did not believe it had been deliberate evasiveness on the king's part; but even if it were, it made no difference. This king's power waxed and waned, and when it waned, the Prince of Wales and his Whig coterie, Parliament with its many factions, were on the ascendant. There was no one man who could give Elfi a definitive answer. Meanwhile he was wasting his time here. He felt the folder of letters again through his sash.

'I thought the audience went very well, didn't you?' Sir John's soothing voice cut through Elfi's glum absorption. 'His Majesty looked well, I thought, and was most gracious.'

Suddenly feeling a rush of restlessness rise in him like a fever, Elfi stuck his arm out of the window and rapped on the side of the carriage, bringing it to an abrupt halt; the Mamlukes riding alongside reined in their horses sharply and drew their swords.

'Elfi Bey, what is it?' Sir John looked alarmed.

'Excuse me, I need air.' Elfi jumped out of the carriage and signalled for Amin Bey to dismount. Waving the disconcerted Amin to take his place in the carriage, Elfi leapt into the saddle and spurred the horse into a gallop.

'No, he is not the grand vizir at the moment, that would be Mr Addington, whom you have met, but it might be of greater use to you to meet Sir William Pitt. He was prime minister for many years – until two years ago, in fact, when he fell out of favour with the king – and everyone believes he will be prime minister again very soon. It might well be to your advantage to make his acquaintance. Are you paying me any attention at all, Elfi Bey?' Lady Cecilia tapped his arm with her fan. They were in her sitting-room; she had left her guests in the drawing-room and come to persuade Elfi to join the company.

Elfi made a gesture of impatience. He had lost interest in meeting Lady Cecilia's illustrious guests. How long did they expect him to wait around in London, while governments and ministers changed, and their policies with them, as the winds of war on the Continent blew this way and that? His hopes had ridden on the audience with the king this morning, but nothing had come of it; only more half-promises and postponements. He was wasting his time here in London, while all hell broke loose in Egypt. The news he had received in the letters from Cairo could not be more urgent or troubling.

When Vincenzo asked to be excused and left the room, Lady Cecilia came to sit beside Elfi on a gilded chaise longue upholstered in rose silk 'Now, Elfi Bey, do try to be agreeable.' She slid a satin-gloved hand down his arm. 'You will come into the drawing-room and meet my guests?'

She fixed him with her bright eyes, her long, elegant white fingers fiddling on his arm. Elfi took his pipe out of his mouth and held her gaze. Not for the first time, he wondered whether or not to take the lady at face value: was she as she appeared, forthright and light-hearted and spontaneous? Or was she in league with Sir John, instructed to humour Elfi and report on his activities and his state of mind? Were her feelings towards him genuine? Had they started that way and then changed into something else? Or was it the other way around?

She met his eyes guilelessly, her bare shoulders rising creamy white from the bodice of her pale yellow gown, the tiny freckles dusted here and there on her collarbone like rose petals scattered on snow. His doubts did not matter, Elfi decided, he could refuse her nothing when she smiled at him in just that way. He sighed and nodded his assent.

So he found himself again sitting in her grand drawing-room, at a card table blazing with candelabra, while Hamilton – the same Hamilton who had put his small archaeological expedition to Upper Egypt under Elfi's protection – carried on about Elfi's camp at Aswan to a rapt audience that had gathered around them. Elfi tossed back two glasses of burgundy and pushed back from the table, slipping a finger inside the tight collar of his tunic. He felt hot and hemmed in, suddenly, in this brilliant, gilded salon. His head was in turmoil ever since he had read the letters Vincenzo had brought back from Egypt this morning. He needed to be outdoors, he needed to clear his head; he suddenly had an overwhelming urge to be on a horse, riding flat out across the desert.

He strode out of the bright room and crossed the long hall, past the footmen with their white wigs, not stopping to take his leave of anyone, not even his hostess Lady Cecilia; he had glimpsed her at the other end of the room, whispering behind her fan to a man he did not recognize. He would never understand her sort of Englishwoman, he thought, any more than he would ever learn to speak English without an accent.

At the outside gate he found Amin and five of his Mamlukes milling about with the horses, smoking Turkish pipes and making desultory remarks to each other, their voices carrying in the chill night air. They came to attention when they saw him, gauging his mood instantly. Amin wordlessly unhitched his horse and handed him the reins; Elfi leapt into the saddle, and set off, the packed snow on the ground muffling the clatter of the horse's hooves.

When he felt the city close in on him like this, in Cairo, he had but to canter through the streets, shouting ahead for the gate-keepers to fling the gates open before him, and then he was outside the walls and out in the desert, and he could gallop till he had outrun his demons and the night, and only return at daybreak. Here in London there were laws about that, there were laws about everything. At first he had found these laws irksome in the extreme, and he and his

Mamlukes had left a wake of dismayed pedestrians and protesting shopkeepers wherever they went. But now he had come to a revelation: it was their laws – even more than their science and their arts of war – that made the English great.

He had come to England with one thought in mind: to discover and appropriate the secret of British power and prosperity; and to that end he had bought every instrument he could lay his hands on, every book he saw or heard of. He had gone everywhere to observe their industries: from the great looms and mills and foundries to the meanest blacksmith. He had been to the hospitals, and watched the surgeons cut up cadavers. He had sat in on the sessions of their parliament, and on the sessions of their court; and it was there that he believed he had discovered the secret. The secret of their prosperity: on the farms where the udders of the fat cows were bursting with milk; in the city, where the wheels of industry ground day and night; the secret of their power on the sea, where their great ships denied passage to all others. The secret was justice.

If the poor man could be certain that he would enjoy the fruits of his labours, and that he had recourse against the grandee who would confiscate them, he would strive to better his lot and that of his family. So it was with a people. If you had a cow, and you tended it well, feeding it the best of clover and letting it rest, it would produce a generous return of milk; but if you mistreated it and starved it and beat it, you would have nothing for your pains. So it was with a province or a country.

Elfi headed for the park, the only place he knew in London where he could break into an all-out gallop. Lady Cecilia had warned him that cutthroats lurked there at night, and that he should avoid it when unescorted, but he scoffed at the notion that he might prove unequal to any band of ruffians. Besides, he did not fear death at the hand of an assassin, only the ignominious death of plague or illness.

Ah, here was Hyde Park; finally he could give his horse its head. Ice frosted the stripped branches of the trees like glass bottles hanging on twigs in the moonlight. The cold air driving into his lungs braced him, but in his head he worried over the letters from Cairo – and

270

Sitt Nafisa's, in particular – like a dog worrying a bone, trying to extract the marrow. *Remember that the arrow that killed the eagle was an arrow made of the eagle's feather*, she had written. Who had she meant to put him on guard against? His own khushdash?

Elfi turned his horse and took another lap around the pond at a gallop. He was coming to the bitter realization that it was time for him to go home, empty-handed.

What good would it do to stay on here? He could get no assurances of logistical help from the English. Their government was divided among itself on the matter of the 'Sick Man of Europe', as they called Turkey; they were holding Elfi like a card in reserve. One day he was neglected, and the next, if news from Egypt came that the Mamlukes had the upper hand, he was fêted and his credit was extended with merchants.

The first few months here, he had been fascinated with everything; there was so much to discover, so much to learn, so much to acquire. There were pleasures he had not dreamed of: the theatres, the balls, the music, women. A lifetime would not be long enough to see everything there was to be seen and do everything there was to do. But now disenchantment had set in, a growing certainty that he did not belong here. Here he was but a pawn on a gigantic chessboard; at least in Egypt he knew the layout of the chessboard, and he had an outside chance of making a play for vizir.

By the time Elfi had ridden back to the house he was renting in London, the sweat had frozen to icicles around his horse's nostrils and on its withers. He handed the reins to the English groom, who made disapproving noises under his breath as he began rubbing the horse down, and crossed the courtyard to the fountain. Seized by a sudden impulse, he smashed the crust of ice over the fountain with the hilt of his sword, removed his turban and his tunic, took a deep breath, and plunged his head into the freezing water. The shock numbed him for a moment, but he held his head under while he counted, slowly, picturing the hawk circling in his mind's eye. Once . . . twice . . . three times it circled, and his lungs began to burn. Four times, five . . . He came up gasping and sputtering. For the first time in his life, he had failed the test. Either the air in this country had damaged his lungs, or his years had finally caught up with him.

Shaking his wet head and wiping his face and neck with the folds of his turban, Elfi climbed the steps to his room, hurrying now, as he felt a chill fall upon him. In the corridor that led to his room he was surprised to find Aisha waiting; Amin Bey stood guard at the door, arms crossed.

'What is it?' Elfi snapped, resisting the shiver that was coursing from his wet head to his chilled feet.

'Elfi Bey, I must talk to you.' Her fine brows took flight over her wide black eyes and her soft mouth quivered at his tone, but she set her chin.

'Can't it wait till morning?'

'Now is the only time I find you. Please, I've sat up all this time waiting for you.'

'All right. Call the servant first to get the fire going in the room.'

'Let me do it, I know how, from watching the servants.'

Elfi shrugged. He went into his chamber and found a fur-trimmed cape to wrap round his shoulders, and sat down to take off his boots in a chair before the fire. The girl followed and knelt in front of the hearth, raking up the embers with tongs, carefully fanning the flames with the bellows. Then she sat back on her haunches, poking at the fire that was starting to blaze in earnest; the flames threw shadow and light on her face. It occurred to Elfi, for the first time, that she was truly lovely.

He had not paid Sitt Nafisa's protégé much attention, beyond making sure she had what she needed and that she was safe: one of his Mamlukes was always within calling distance if she needed him. As for the conduct of his own men, he could answer for it unreservedly; he knew their dread of him, even more than their loyalty, was sufficient guarantee that the most foolhardy among them would not attempt to take advantage of her by so much as an untoward glance. The girl had enough to keep her entertained, surely, he thought, with the occasional ball and the outings in the carriage and the kind attentions of Lady Cecilia. What did she need to tell him

272

that could be so pressing? Was she homesick for Egypt and her little boy? He could tell her that they would be going back soon, at any rate. At that moment he knew his decision was made, and that it was irrevocable.

She looked up from the fire and blurted: 'Elfi Bey, I want to go to France.'

'What?' That was the last thing he had expected to hear. 'Don't you realize that England is on the verge of war with France? Why would you want to go to there anyway?'

'I want – I want to find my husband. I'm not really a widow, he is alive.'

'I know. Sitt Nafisa told me your story in the letter she entrusted to Barquq.'

'You know?'

'Yes. I know who you are, and what that Frenchman was to you. But who is to say that he is still alive, your chief engineer? There were many who did not survive the crossing. And even if he is alive, how will you find him? France is a big country. Do you know where he is?'

'No. But he is an important person, if we make inquiries, surely someone will know of him . . .'

He shook his head. 'Do you think France is like Cairo, where everyone knows everyone? How will you go? Alone? And how do you propose to get there? On a magic carpet? You will need one to cross the water, with English ships blockading the Channel. Besides, girl, be reasonable. He left you behind; he could have taken you with him, but he didn't. What makes you think he would be happy to see you again?'

For the first time, his words seemed to have touched her to the quick: her eyes filled with hot tears and she turned to look into the fire.

'I believe he sent to inquire after me. At any rate, I have to try to find him, Elfi Bey, I have to try. He has a son.'

'There isn't time. We're going back to Egypt.'

'Oh!' Her eyebrows took flight. 'When?'

273

'As soon as I can get Sir John to arrange for a ship.'

'Please, Elfi Bey, give me time to try!'

'I leave on the next ship to Malta. If you want to come with me, you have only until then. What monies you need for your search, I will give you. But time is the one thing I don't have. Now, go to bed, and let me get some rest.'

But when she had left the room he did not rest. He brought out his astrology book from the trunk, sat down by the hearth and opened it across his knees. For a long while he studied the dates and the times and the tides, but however he calculated it, the signs were inauspicious for his making a voyage.

Wait and see, everyone repeated. If he left now, he would never know what an English spring was like; he would never drive the phaeton he had ordered, he would never see Lady Cecilia in her bonnet. Lady Cecilia . . . he thought of her fingers flying over the keys of the pianoforte. She would not forget him, that much he knew, just as he knew that she would cease to regret him the moment the door closed behind him. He would take the pianoforte with him to Egypt, though, that he would take, no matter what else he would have to leave behind.

Finally he closed the book. The stars were against his making his voyage home, but sometimes a man had no choice but to play the hand he was dealt.

TWENTY-THREE

The Hand of Providence

Zeinab lifted her mask for a moment and fanned herself, dizzy from the crush of the masqueraders whirling around her in the vast Soho assembly rooms. So this was what they called a masquerade! The first, and no doubt the last, she would ever attend; Elfi Bey had told her that morning that the ship bound for Malta was now in port, waiting for a favourable wind, and that he would be leaving the next day for Folkestone. If she wanted to go home, if she wanted to see her child, she must leave with him. Every day their voyage was delayed increased their chances of getting caught in an outbreak of hostilities, for war with France was now inevitable. This masquerade would be the last for some time, according to Sir John Stuart.

But you would never have guessed that the shadow of war loomed over the boisterous crowd in the assembly rooms this evening – or perhaps it was that very shadow that lent a heightened frenzy to the merriment. A burst of laughter by the door drew Zeinab's attention: a party of mock shepherdesses with crooks were making an entrance, one of them actually carrying a live white lamb. They were followed by three Dominoes and a Punch. Zeinab had noticed several people, men and women both, dressed in what they called 'Indian dress' or even 'Mamluke style', with veils or turbans, but it was easy to pick out the real Mamlukes, Amin Bey and two of the younger amirs, wearing their own clothes. Underneath her velvet cape, she herself had donned the ordinary clothes she wore at home in the harem: Turkish-style wide-legged pantaloons and a tunic tied with a wide sash at the waist. Her hair hung loose down her back, a sheer white yashmak across the lower part of her face and a small black mask covered her eyes – her only concession to the masquerade.

Elfi Bey – himself engrossed in preparing for the voyage, supervising the packing of the precious instruments, telescopes and microscopes and pianoforte – had given Zeinab permission to attend, with Amin Bey as chaperone. Partly, she suspected, to distract her from her disappointment: she had made no headway in finding Nicolas. As the bitterness of February turned to the mildness of March, Zeinab had seen time run out on her efforts to locate Nicolas.

She had tried, discreetly seeking out French émigrés in London, to ask if they perhaps knew of the chief engineer of the balloonist corps, Nicolas Conté – a distant relative of her own late husband. But none of the émigrés was able to give her a useful lead, apart from the location of the Institute, in Meudon. She contemplated simply travelling to Meudon and asking about Nicolas there, but who would be willing to accompany her to France on the eve of war? Certainly not an Englishman, nor a bitter and fearful émigré.

Night after sleepless night she had racked her brains, to no avail. Yet she was loath to give up her quest, loath to put an ocean between her and Nicolas when all that now separated them was the English Channel. Yet that narrow body of water seemed no less of an obstacle than the Indian Ocean. And now she had run out of time. Tomorrow she would have to prepare to leave with Elfi Bey, or stay in a country where she was a stranger, and worse, a foreigner, with no prospect of finding a man who might no longer be alive; at any rate, a man for whom she was already dead.

All around her, as if to sharpen the sting of her isolation, the masqueraders were making a game of recognizing friends, carrying them off to one or other of the rooms for supper or dancing. Suddenly, at her elbow, she heard a whisper:

'Zeinab.'

A chill ran down her spine and she spun round. A black Domino stood beside her, facing forward. She stared at him but he paid her no attention. Was her mind playing tricks on her?

Then the grating whisper came again. 'Zeinab. No, don't turn to look at me, you are being watched. Face forward. Now, I must speak to you. Follow me to the veranda when you can get away unnoticed.' He spoke in French with a thick accent.

'Who are you?' she breathed.

'It does not matter. You can trust me. Nicolas Conté sent me.'

She turned involuntarily and he admonished her again, 'Don't!' before turning and disappearing into the crowd.

Zeinab made a move to follow him but she saw Amin Bey frowning at her from across the room; the Mamluke started to weave his way through the revellers, trying to get to her.

There was a great burst of screams and laughter from the direction of the door and the crowd parted as a man entered with a live bear on a chain, hobbling upright on two feet. Zeinab saw her chance and ducked sideways along the wall and into the next room, and through the French windows to the terrace. She looked around her; black Dominoes seemed to be everywhere; she hesitated before the balustrade, looking down at the winter-forlorn garden. Then a black Domino stepped out of the shadows at her elbow.

'Zeinab, your husband sent me. He wants to see you, he is waiting for you.'

'Where?'

'On the coast. He has come at great risk to himself, just to see you. You must come with me right away.'

'Right away? But I must go back first, I must tell –'

'You must tell no one. You come with me now.'

Zeinab's head whirled. 'But who are you? How do I know I can trust you? How do I know Nicolas really sent you?'

'I know who you are, is that not proof enough? Do you want to see Citoyen Conté or not?'

Zeinab glanced back over her shoulder. Through the bright windows she caught a glimpse of a grim Amin Bey forcing a path through the throng; he must be looking for her.

'Let me at least send a message to Elfi Bey, he will worry!'

'No, come with me now.'

Zeinab hesitated, torn with misgiving. But she had come so far, she could not let slip this chance of finding Nicolas, no matter what the danger. She flung her cape on and pulled the hood over her head, then followed the black Domino as he grabbed her hand and dragged her down the garden steps and around the corner, into a waiting sedan chair. It took off instantly, and they wound down alleys and back streets till they stopped before a nondescript house where a coach stood waiting, the horses snorting and snuffling in the night air.

The Domino took her by the elbow and helped her into the coach. 'You will find a dress and hat and ordinary clothes in there,' he said. 'Change into them – you're too conspicuous in that costume. When you're ready, let me know.'

Zeinab found a small leather valise on the seat and closed the door of the coach behind her, drawing the curtains shut tight. She took out the clothes: a teal velvet dress, high-waisted in the French style; a creamy lawn shawl; high-heeled buttoned boots; tan gloves; a small-brimmed hat with teal feathers. Whoever had prepared this outfit had thought of everything; it seemed to her that she could detect Nicolas' hand in this, and it reassured her. Still, if she could only get word to Elfi Bey . . .

An impatient rapping at the door made her part the curtains. 'I'm ready.'

The man who came in and sat down beside her as the coach set off at a brisk trot, the man she thought of as the Domino, was no longer wearing his black mask. He was powerfully built, swarthy, stubbly around his square jaw – she recognized him immediately: it was the man who had been watching her in the park.

Zeinab woke with a start, and looked around her, for a moment completely disoriented. Her throat was dry, every bone in her body ached from the rattling of the carriage, and she did not know how long they had been travelling or where they were or what time it was. They had driven through the night, changing horses twice. She realized that the motion of the carriage had finally put her to sleep, a fitful, nightmare-disturbed sleep that left her even less refreshed when she woke.

She looked at the man opposite her; his eyes were bloodshot from lack of sleep and his jaw was covered in stubble like a magnet covered with iron filings. She could not help feeling a clutch of apprehension in her chest; she should be grateful to this stranger, surely, if he were leading her to Nicolas; but there was something about him that she mistrusted, and a nagging feeling that she knew him from somewhere.

She licked her lips and sat up, arranging the shawl over the low-cut décolletage of her dress and tucking tendrils of dishevelled hair under her bonnet. She parted the curtains just enough to look out, but the fog outside was impenetrable.

'Where are we?' she asked.

'Almost there. We're close to the coast. Thirsty?'

He held up a jug of what turned out to be mulled wine and she took a sip or two from a pewter mug.

Nicolas. All she could think of was that she would see Nicolas any moment now. After two long years . . . how would he look? She realized that she could not remember his face as a whole, only fragments of him, like an image in a shattered mirror: his one good eye, his ear with the eye patch looped over it, the whiteness of his chest under his shirt contrasting with the brown of his sunburnt neck; his clever hands as he sketched.

She was seized with a sudden doubt: how would he find her? How would she look to him, Nicolas the painter? The black hair and dark eyes that had enchanted him against the brilliant blue of the Egyptian sky, how would they look against this muted English palette of grey sky and smoky fog? Would she look dark and dull to him, like tarnished silver? She smoothed the shawl over her bosom. Her body too had changed, now that she had borne a child: slender still, but more womanly. But her hair! Her hair was wild with the mad flight, and Nicolas preferred her with her hair done up properly. She hugged her arms about her to quell the shaking, but it was not the damp sea air blowing off the cliffs that made her shiver, it was the thrill of anticipation one moment followed by the chill of doubt and apprehension the next.

What would she tell him of his son, the son who knew nothing of him? Her little Do-do who must have grown, now, in the year since she had left him in Sitt Nafisa's arms. Would he even recognize his own mother? She should have been leaving with Elfi Bey this very day for the ship that would carry them home to Egypt. She doubted the amir would wait for her if there was a favourable wind. Every day brought England closer to a declaration of war with France, and Elfi could not take the risk of any delay, for fear of ending up trapped for the duration of the hostilities.

Zeinab heard seagulls crying and parted the curtains again. She could barely make out cliffs in the distance, and a lighthouse perched on the tip, with, in the foreground, a small, single-storey building. The sea beyond was lost in the fog.

'Nicolas is waiting for you there,' the man pointed to the house.

'Oh!' After two years of waiting and longing, it was too sudden; she wished she had more time to prepare herself.

But the coach was rattling on the path leading uphill to the house, and within minutes they had rolled to a stop. It seemed to be the sort of inn that catered to travellers waiting for a boat to cross the Channel or just arrived from the opposite shore, one of those discreet safe houses she had heard about, used to smuggle émigré refugees at the height of the Terror. Zeinab alighted, dazed, feeling her legs wobbly from the long ride.

'Wait for Citoyen Conté inside,' the man instructed.

She went in, drawing her cape close about her, and nodded to the lighthouse keeper, who apparently kept the inn as well. A fire crackling in the hearth lit the room dimly; there were three other travellers, two men sitting at a wooden trestle table, blowing into their steaming cups, and one standing by the hearth, leaning one arm on the mantelpiece. They had kept their travelling capes and their hats on, perhaps because of the cold, or more likely, thought Zeinab, to keep to themselves; no one wished to advertise his business travelling to or from France in these dangerous times.

Zeinab found a chair in a corner and sat down facing the door, hugging her cape about her and wiggling her toes to stay warm, her eyes fixed on the doorway through which Nicolas would appear, any minute now. She put a finger to the base of her throat and felt her pulse jumping.

The man who had been standing by the fire came around to her corner. 'Would you care for a hot rum, mademoiselle?'

She ignored him, but he leaned closer and removed his hat; it was then that she saw the eye patch. It was Nicolas! It was Nicolas, but she could barely recognize him in this older man, his curly hair infiltrated with grey, his face pale as she had never seen it under the fierce Egyptian sun. And in the same instant she realized that it did not matter: it was Nicolas' face, inexpressibly dear in its familiarity.

He looked at her with his one good eye, quizzical, and she knew that he had read her thoughts as they flitted across her face.

'So, you find me changed,' he murmured. 'But then, I was never much to look at.'

She beamed at him, speechless with the joy of beholding him before her, and he smiled back. He was the first to break the spell, and took her by the elbow, looking around them. 'Come, I've reserved a little corner where we can have some privacy.' He lowered his voice. 'I am sorry to bring you to such a den of thieves, but it has the advantage of being known only to smugglers, spies and émigrés.'

She followed him behind a partition through a low archway into another, even smaller room, where an adequate fire burned in the hearth, and two rough wooden chairs were drawn before it.

'Ah, that's better. Let me look at you.' He drew the cape off her head gently. 'My little Zeinab! Quite the woman now, and so very lovely.'

'How did you know I was in England? How did you find me?'

'Providence, in the unlikely form of Bartholomew – the man who brought you here. He saw you with Elfi Bey. Did you not recognize him? The chief of police in Cairo?'

'Of course! Fart Rumman! I thought I had seen him before.' She remembered him now as she had last seen him at the Tivoli: black-bearded and sinister, with the poor sad Hawa, Ismail Kashif's wife, in tow. The sight of him had always chilled Zeinab. To think her deliverance had come at his hands!

'Ah yes, Providence works in mysterious ways.' Nicolas ran a finger down her cheek, and brushed a strand of hair off her brow. 'I thought you were dead. God, how I suffered! I can hardly believe that you are standing here before me. I need to feel your dear little body solidly against mine to truly believe it.' He drew her towards him impulsively but she stepped back and held him off with her gloved hands against his shoulders.

'You left me behind,' she blurted, all the hurt of the past two years rising in a flood of bitter tears. 'You didn't care, you left me to my fate!'

'That isn't fair. I left you because I thought it was best for you, I thought it was what you wanted. You were so withdrawn and unhappy, you couldn't bear to let me touch you, the last few weeks before the evacuation . . . How else was I to interpret your behaviour?'

The lighthouse keeper's wife came in with a pitcher, cups, and a plate of shortbread. 'Here's the hot cider you ordered, sir. Is the young lady all right?' She eyed Zeinab warily as she set the tray on a stool before the fireplace.

Zeinab nodded and wiped her face with her hands. The woman left them alone in the room.

Nicolas poured a cup of cider and handed it to Zeinab. 'Drink that, please, you will feel better and it will warm you. Sit down,' he brought the chair closer to the fire for her. 'I am not making excuses. I had told you I would protect you, and I failed you, I know. Believe me, it has haunted me. Thank Heaven you are alive and I will have a chance to redeem myself.' He remained standing, his hands behind his back. 'Don't you think I've tormented myself every day since I left? All I can say in my own defence is that I did what I believed was right at the time. There were no easy answers, Zeinab, can you at least grant me that? There were no easy answers.'

He paced the stone floor behind her chair, speaking as if to himself. 'Looking back now . . . there are so many regrets. Perhaps this whole expedition was misconceived from the start. And yet, and yet . . . we set off with such high aspirations! Such arrogance, such ignorance on our part, we French, to think we could remake the world in our image.' He shook his head. 'However a man parses his own conscience, sometimes he cannot distinguish what part of his actions was driven by good intention, and what was driven by his own desires . . .'

He came and stood before her and crooked his finger under her chin. 'Look at me, Zeinab. Perhaps I should have left you alone from the beginning. Is that how you feel, *ma petite*?'

She looked up at him then, pondering his question. What if she had never known Nicolas? What if none of it had happened? What if the French had never come, what if Zeinab Bakri had remained that child of twelve, waiting, unquestioning, for her father to make a match for her? What if she had never met Bonaparte and never known Nicolas? If she had been spared the torment and the horror that followed when he left her?

'I don't know,' she admitted, finally. 'It's like asking someone who was born blind and then briefly had the gift of sight only to lose it again, whether they think they'd have been better off never knowing what it was they lacked.'

If she had never known Nicolas, if she had never had her child . . . at the thought of her child, she blurted, 'No, I'm not sorry to have known you. I'm not sorry for that.' She smiled at him then, all the warmth of the fire reflected in her eyes.

He grabbed the chair opposite her, with the impetuous gesture she remembered, and took her hands in his, and kissed her palms. 'You forgive me then?'

She let her hands lie in his, feeling the familiar firm, warm touch. And yet, something between them had changed, something ineffable she could not grasp in the heat of the moment, like a snatch of a tune that she knew but could not immediately identify.

'Is that why you came to London? To find me?' Nicolas insisted. 'Yes.'

'My brave little girl! You must come back with me, you will get to know France.'

'But what shall I do in France?' She looked him in the eyes, serious.

'You will do very well. Just look at you: such poise, such carriage, and how you carry off that hat, as grand as any English lady. Why did I ever doubt that you would be able to adapt to life among the Franj! Do they still call us that in Egypt?'

She did not hear him say she would be his wife, or that her son would be his – the son he did not know existed, the son she could not leave behind. 'I can't come with you, Nicolas. I must go back to Egypt.'

'Then why did you come all the way to find me? Zeinab, look at me.' He took her face in his hands and pressed his thumbs under her chin to tip up her face. 'Was I blind? Were you with child? Do I have a child in Egypt?'

She met his eyes, speechless, but it was enough for him.

'Why did you hide it from me? How old? A boy or a girl?'

'He will be two this month.'

'Ah! Is he a big boy? Does he look like me?'

'A little; he has your chin. And he sleeps with his mouth open, like you.'

He threw back his head and laughed. 'What's his name?'

'He is called Muhammad Muradi.'

He frowned. 'What sort of name is that? Never mind. That can be changed later. You must bring him to France, he must be raised as a Frenchman, he must be educated.' He began pacing the floor again, with the vigour and lightness of tread of a much younger man. Then he stopped in his tracks. 'There will be no time to bring him over, though, before war breaks out. It is inevitable now, *ma petite*, and it will be a long war, and no corner of Europe will be spared. No, you must wait to bring him till it's safe, safe for you both.'

Zeinab listened to him making plans for her, for their child. Was this what she had been hoping for? And yet . . . she had not heard him say she would be his wife.

They heard heavy steps approaching; it was Bartholomew rapping on the door. 'The lookout says he sees men heading this way, riding hell for leather. We must leave this instant, Citoyen. If we are caught without passports . . .'

Nicolas cracked open the door. 'Give me a moment.'

'I am going down to the boat and will wait for a few moments only. I must warn you, Citoyen, I will leave without you if you delay.' Bartholomew stomped off.

'Nicolas, you must go!' Zeinab jumped to her feet. 'Please, I couldn't bear it if anything happened to you.'

'Not without you. Not this time, not until I know what will become of you.'

'You know I have to go back to Egypt, to our son. I have no choice. Just as you have none. But I'm not sorry I came, truly. I needed to see you, to speak to you, to understand . . .' She wasn't sure she understood, even now; all she knew was that she had needed to see him again, that her life had been suspended from the day he left her until this moment.

They could hear the horses drawing steadily nearer. Zeinab turned to him in a panic. 'You should go now!'

'I can't just leave you here, where will you go?'

She looked out the window at the four horsemen coming around the bend at the bottom of the hill; something about the way they sat in the saddle, even at a distance, made her press her face against the thick glass and peer intently. 'Those aren't Englishmen!' She turned back to Nicolas in relief. 'Those are Mamlukes, I'm sure of it. Amin Bey must have followed me. Don't worry, no harm will come to me. But you had better leave; they must think I was kidnapped. Go now, leave it to me to explain.'

'All right. But remember – as soon as it's safe, I will send for you, and you will bring the boy and come to France.'

He was making a promise, she thought, that neither of them might be able to keep. She took a step closer, touching his grizzled sideburns with her fingertips. 'And you?' she whispered. 'You are content? And your family? Your children? All well?'

'Well, yes, all is well,' he gave a twisted smile. 'Content . . . ?' He shrugged.

'Then may I see your face in good health, Nicolas.' She lifted the hood of her cape over her head and brushed past him out of the small room. She stumbled out of the inn and stood in the lifting fog, hardly able to make out the approaching horses through her tears. It had taken all her resolve to tear herself away and now she felt a sick wrenching in her guts.

She closed her eyes, willing herself to stay upright until the horses had galloped to a rearing halt in front of her. Then she opened her eyes to see the outstretched hand of the lead horseman, ready to swing her up into the saddle behind him. 'Come, hurry, we must sail before the tide turns; Elfi Bey is waiting,' Amin urged her as she grasped his hand.

TWENTY-FOUR

The Eagle's Feather

'There can no longer be any doubt today that Elfi Bey has been carried
back to Egypt on a warship . . . The purpose of England is . . . to tear
your Empire apart piece by piece. It is in her interest that you be no
longer that ancient Muslim people, that heroic people that the universe
admired. She divides you to ruin you. Look what she has done to
Egypt. If the Ottomans triumph, she favours the Beys; if the Beys
hold power, she sets the Ottomans against them. When the Beys and
the Ottomans are near united, she finds the Arnaouts to create eternal
anarchy.'

French Ambassador Brune to the Reis Effendi
(Ottoman Prime Minister), in Péra, 12 March 1804

Zeinab woke to the motion of the ship rolling gently beneath her;
the wind had picked up, they were moving again. She wrapped her
cloak about her and came up on deck, disoriented for a moment by
the bright Mediterranean moonlight casting long shadows across the
ship. She looked about for Elfi Bey and found him standing by the
railing with his back to her, his gaze fixed on the rolling horizon,
the tension in his square shoulders betraying the intensity of his
anticipation.

She went to stand beside him; he did not turn around though she
knew he sensed her presence. 'Elfi Bey, how long now before we reach
Alexandria?'

'It depends on the wind, but not long now. Not long.' He took a deep breath and was lost in his thoughts. Then he turned to her. 'Zeinab, have you given any thought to what you will do when you get to Egypt?'

'Only that I will be reunited with my child.'

'Yes. But there is so much turmoil in the country, such lawlessness. I don't know if even Sitt Nafisa can protect you now. You would be safer if you were under the protection of a husband to answer for you and for your son. Tell me this, Zeinab, are you free to remarry? Or are you still attached to the father of your child?'

Zeinab caught her breath. She understood his question, and pondered her answer. She had had weeks onboard ship to relive every minute of the hour she spent with Nicolas at the inn, to parse every phrase and sift every emotion. She had been overjoyed to see him, but even in the thrill of the moment she had realized that something elemental had changed between them. It was only later that it struck her: what was missing was the overwhelming urge to run across the room and fling herself into his arms; when Nicolas took her hands in his, her skin had not tingled, her pulse had not leapt in her throat. The tremor, the passion had burned out; the bonds of the flesh between them were irrevocably broken. She was not free of the wrench of parting; not free, even now, of a dull ache whenever she thought of him. She would always conjure his face in her mind, inexpressibly familiar and dear, and she would always wish him well. Nicolas was the man of her life, the father of her child; she would never love another, she would never give herself body and soul in the same way again.

But she was free of Nicolas, free in a way she had not been before they were briefly reunited at the inn; he had no claim on her now that she could not in good conscience bring to a union with another man. She thought of herself as Nicolas' wife no longer; she was free of the hope of a reunion and reconciliation; when the war was over, she might take his son and go to France to live, but she would never be his wife, she knew that now.

She looked Elfi straight in the eye when she answered: 'I am free.'

'Then it is best if you arrive in Egypt under the protection of a husband. There is one whom you have come to know over the past months in England . . .'

'Yes?' She had not thought of remarriage. Was Elfi Bey doing her the unimaginable honour of asking for her hand?

'Amin Bey,' he continued.

'Oh!'

Elfi frowned at her disconcerted expression. 'Amin Bey is a Mamluke of courage and honour. I intend to settle property and houses on him as soon as we are re-established.'

Zeinab straightened her back and raised her chin. 'He is everything you say, and more. But . . .'

'Land ho!' The cry floating down from the top of the masthead startled them. Elfi rushed to the railing and peered intently at the horizon. And as if that cry had been the cry of doomsday that raised the dead, all about them the ship suddenly came to life and swarmed with English sailors and officers.

Captain Hallowell came striding across the deck in Elfi's direction. 'Sir, I came looking for you. We have sighted land.'

'Yes, I must get ready.'

'But I came to warn you, Elfi Bey, that you must not think of disembarking when we land at Alexandria. It would be by far the more prudent course of action to stay offshore while we send an advance party to discover the situation on the ground. I am duty bound to warn you, in the strongest terms, of the reports of a conspiracy to assassinate you the instant you set foot on Egyptian soil. Osman Bey Bardissi is said to have dispatched assassins to every port with instructions to kill you on sight.'

Elfi shook his head. 'No! My khushdash would not betray me so basely. This must be a plot of Mehmet Ali's.'

'No doubt. Nevertheless, your brethren, or at least Bardissi, have a hand in it. I warn you, sir, these are not reports to be trifled with. You should not have refused Governor Ball's offer of English troops when *The Argo* was in the port of Malta.'

'I never wish to see an English soldier in my country. English

289

arms, yes. I would be glad to encourage the importation of English-manufactured weapons, but I never again wish to see a foreign soldier in my country.'

'Then you will bear the consequences, sir.'

Elfi nodded. 'I thank you. But I wish to put into port as soon as possible.'

Captain Hallowell threw up his hands. 'Sir, I have done my duty to discourage you with every argument at my disposal, but I cannot keep you against your will. We will drop anchor off Aboukir in a few hours. I cannot answer for the consequences.' He turned to give directions to his officers.

Amin Bey and the other Mamlukes had gathered on deck, hastily winding turbans and girding swords. Elfi gestured to them. 'Come, we must prepare for landing. There is much to do. The matter of the instruments in particular, they must be unloaded with the greatest care.'

'Elfi Bey!' Zeinab tripped after him as he headed below deck.

He turned to her for a moment. 'There will be time to speak of this later, God willing – or not, if He has other plans. But do not dismiss it lightly; you need protection for yourself and your son, and Amin Bey is an honourable man.'

Zeinab watched him as he descended the stairs, Amin and the other Mamlukes close at his heels, and turned back momentarily to stare at the horizon. The thought that she would soon be reunited with her child chased away all other thoughts, like a powerful wind blowing through her mind, lifting her spirits till they soared as high as the great sails above her head. She rushed down to her cabin to change into her Turkish clothes and pack her few belongings.

When she returned to the deck an hour later she found Elfi Bey, in his azure turban and his English boots, surrounded by the Mamlukes, all glittering in full regalia, from their diamond turban pins to their jewel-encrusted scabbards. To a man they scanned the horizon, gripping the railings in their excitement as the thin line of green sketched the shore. But it was Zeinab's sharp eyes that glimpsed it first, the squat, stark white fort, like a child's sandcastle, advancing to greet them as the ship cut through the water. 'The fort! Qait Bey Fort! I can see it! Alexandria! We're home!'

The Mamlukes shouted with joy, and some even fell to their knees in a prayer of gratitude. All of them, even the sternest, even Elfi, wept. But they composed themselves and took up their watch again as the English sailors hurried back and forth on the deck, shouting commands and pulling ropes, raising and lowering sails.

When they were close enough to make out the banner whipping in the wind over the fort, Amin Bey muttered: 'Turkish flag.' Elfi only nodded.

Zeinab shaded her eyes with her hand and peered at the shore, picking out orange and turquoise-painted sailboats bobbing in the marina; figures small as ants clambering about the docks; men on horseback bustling about. The inhabitants of the city had seen their approach, and were coming out to greet them, gathering on the docks. A small felucca bobbed in the waves, heading towards the ship. When it had reached hailing distance, it pulled alongside.

Captain Hallowell reappeared, smartly dressed in his winged admiral's hat and a tight coat with braided epaulettes and brass buttons. 'Elfi Bey, there is a courier asking permission to board. He insists his business is with you personally.'

Elfi nodded. 'I will speak to him.'

As soon as Zeinab laid eyes on the man she recognized the familiar, impassive Nubian face. 'Barquq!' The eunuch allowed himself the merest nod in her direction before turning to Elfi with a bow. 'Elfi Bey, I come to warn you: your enemies have crossed the Nile, surrounded your house in Giza and massacred many of your Mamlukes.'

'My lieutenant?'

'Elfi the Younger survives, and is gathering the remainder of your men to come to your defence. But you must not land – your enemies have spread a wide net stretching east and west of Alexandria, that you might not slip through its meshes, whether you land in Rosetta or Aboukir or any port in between.'

'Who has done this? Mehmet Ali? Osman Bardissi, my khush-dash?' He looked disbelieving.

291

'My mistress sends you this –' Barquq handed him a letter in silence. Elfi broke the seal and carefully unfolded the fine parchment. It was utterly blank. But a single eagle's feather rested in the fold. Elfi studied it for a long moment, his face like that of a man who feels the earth shaken under him. Then he put it carefully in his pocket.

'By God, sometimes I think there is no room for me on His wide Earth, now that I have become one man among thousands of enemies. Here are my own kin and companions, my khushdash, who abandon our cause and attack me for no fault of mine or trespass against them. In bringing me down they will hand over the country to my enemy and theirs.' Elfi looked out to sea, adrift in his thoughts. Then he remembered Barquq. 'Thank the sender for the message,' he instructed him and turned to summon his Mamlukes.

Barquq bowed in Elfi's direction and headed for the gangplank.

'Barquq, wait – how is my boy?' Zeinab caught his arm.

'The child thrives.'

Suddenly, as if seized by an afterthought, Elfi called, 'Wait!' Then he turned to Zeinab. 'You will go with him, it is safer. Don't argue, I have no time for explanations. Collect your things as quickly as you can and leave with the eunuch.'

Zeinab's heart quickened at the prospect of being reunited with her child, and Sitt Nafisa, sooner than she had expected. But Elfi's grim face worried her on his account.

'Elfi Bey, may I see your face in good health,' she ventured as she turned to follow the eunuch.

'Go in safety, Zeinab, *bilsalama.*'

But she could see his mind was already on other matters. Elfi's preoccupation, Barquq's grim demeanour, everything pointed to danger on the approaching horizon. They had crossed the great sea and left war and exile behind in Europe, and here was war and treachery awaiting them on this other shore. For a moment she felt the weariness of despair grip her; was there no peace to be had anywhere? How long must her fate be suspended while she was buffeted this way and that by the winds of history?

Then she took a deep breath and set her chin; her son, her future, for better or worse, waited beyond the white fort of Qait Bey, and she was home, come what may.

Nicolas Conté sat at his desk, absently turning the pages of the *Description d'Égypte*. The first volume had been published, the volume he had anticipated with all the more eagerness knowing that he would not see the complete works in print during his lifetime. The monumental task would take decades, and in the meantime there were wars to wage, and kingdoms to conquer: Napoleon had launched his conquest of Europe, and the attention of the country had shifted. But when the *Encyclopedia of Egypt*, ancient and modern, was finally completed, it would be the greatest work of its kind, and he must derive his satisfaction from this posthumous prospect.

And yet he felt a taste of bitterness now as he stroked the rich vellum of this first edition. Who was there to share his triumph? To whom could he confide his frustrations and his sorrows? Lise had passed away a month ago, of the same illness that had carried away his brother earlier in the year. Pierre, along with Madelon's young husband, was away fighting for the Emperor somewhere on the eastern front. Only Cola, mercifully still too young, was by his father's side. Nicolas' eyes rested on his son's dark head as he sat by the fireplace with his book, petting the dog with an idle hand. He wondered, sometimes, if his Egyptian son looked like Cola. Would he ever set eyes on the boy, or see Zeinab again? He had pretended to her that all was well in his life, to spare himself the look of commiseration in her eyes, for he well knew her ready tenderness and did not think he could bear it at their moment of parting.

A parting that he had sensed, even then, might be final. There was a sea between them now, and long years of war ahead, more perilous an obstacle than any ocean. He was no longer a young man. He rose and stood by his window, breathing in the whiff of heather carried over the fields beyond the town. Would he live to see peace return? Would he live to see his Egyptian son in France, studying at the grandest institutes?

The great work of the *Encyclopedia* would outlive everyone who contributed to it, that much he knew; it would outlive his children and his grandchildren. He closed the precious book and smoothed the leather binding. No matter how much the *Description* encompassed – data and illustrations, flora and fauna, history and geography, topography and mineralogy, ancient monuments and modern peoples – it could never truly tell what it had been like to be flesh and blood in those three heady years. The thousands of pages of facts and figures would be stripped clean of the passion and despair that were the messy lot of the human condition. There were so many stories left untold, and his story with Zeinab would be one of them.

Epilogue

Cairo
March 1826

'Is this the day then, Mother? Will you finally tell me who my real father is?'

Zeinab reached up and smoothed her son's thick dark hair and took his face in her hands. He smiled, and rubbed his cheek against her palm, but she could feel the tension and impatience vibrating in him, so like Nicolas, taut as a plucked lute string.

'You promised,' he prompted. 'If I studied, if I was selected for this trip to France, you promised to tell me why it was so important. What has this to do with my father? I mean, the man you call my real father? I always thought Amin Bey . . .'

'Amin Bey – may God have mercy on his soul – raised you as his own, but you are not his son.' Amin Bey had indeed raised her Muhammad Muradi as his own, from the day he had taken Zeinab for his wife till the day he died in her arms, a year ago.

'Was it the famous Elfi Bey? You accompanied him to England . . .'

'No, no, it wasn't Elfi.'

'Who then, Mother? Is he alive?'

'I don't know. He may still be alive. You will find out – when you get to France. It was his dream for you: that you should one day go to France to study. It is for this, all these years, that I have been speaking to you in French, teaching you what I know of the language, pushing you to study and become a scholar, when all you wanted was to learn the ways of war. I told you that one day you would understand.'

How strange the ways of Providence, that it should be Mehmet Ali, the great enemy of the Mamlukes, who would now be her son's benefactor! The viceroy had announced that four of the Azhar University's finest students would be sent to study the arts and sciences of France at the university in Paris, led by a chaplain, Rifaa Tahtawi, who was himself scarcely older than his charges. The young scholars would study abroad for many years, and return to lead the movement for progress in their native land. Muhammad Muradi had entered the competition and been chosen for his academic brilliance and his fluency in the French language.

Here before Zeinab was her Do-do, bearded and turbaned like an Azharite, about to cross the sea and set foot on European soil, reversing the journey his father had taken a quarter century earlier. She could hardly believe it. He would be gone for years, for a decade, for an eternity, it seemed to her mother's heart. The thought of parting with him caused her such anguish that she set it aside as one sets aside private mourning until the public rituals of burial are accomplished. What would her days be like, bereft of her reason for rising in the morning? She would run her household; she would busy herself with the supervision of Sitt Nafisa's sabil and her school for orphans; she would visit her two married daughters – Amin's daughters. She had tried, but never could she love them as she loved her first-born.

Yet she had striven for this day, had prepared Nicolas' son for this journey, this parting, all his life; she had only failed to prepare herself for the sacrifice.

Was Nicolas still alive? If he were, his son would find him. That Nicolas would welcome his estranged son with open arms she had no doubt; even after all these years, she knew him well enough to know that he would not have changed in that regard. She still dreamed of Nicolas, dreams that came when she least expected them, when she had not consciously thought of him for months, it seemed, and then there he would be, every detail so real she could feel the texture of his skin, hear his voice, smell the hollow of his neck, as if she were snuggling against him on the window seat in Hassan Kashif's house. In her dreams now he was always smiling, benevolent, encouraging, and she awoke comforted rather than unsettled.

'My soul,' she smiled at her son now. 'You really are my soul, you know, it is not just an endearment. You must tell your father, if you find him, that I have sent him my soul.'

'But where is he? Who is he? Was he a warrior or a scholar?'

'Both. But a scholar first, and a warrior only by default. He was a genius. I will tell you everything as we ride towards Bulaq, but let us hurry, all of Cairo will be coming to see your ship sail!'

It took an effort of will, and extraordinary circumstances, for Sitt Nafisa to muster the courage and strength to ride across the city at her age, but the departure of the ship carrying the Egyptian delegation to France was an event she would not miss She, who had been there at the beginning to witness the arrival of the French, would be there today to see the circle closed.

There were so few who still remembered, but to her it seemed like only yesterday that the French general – Bonaparte, he was then, before his rise and long, long before his fall – had sent his stepson to her house as emissary; yesterday that she had made her vow to keep the thread of civility intact between her and the Franj until the day the last Frenchman left Egypt. She had kept that vow, as she had kept her vow to complete her sabil and her school for children, against great odds. She had seen the forces of occupation come and go, first the French, then the Turks, and now the Albanians. Several years ago she had prepared a marble tomb for herself, in the burial grounds of the Mamlukes, beside that of Murad Bey. Now she waited, neither reluctant nor impatient, for her rest and her reward.

But today, as she rode towards Bulaq, Sitt Nafisa felt the years weighing her down. What had it availed her to have lived so long if it were only with hindsight that she could recognize her errors in judgment? She thought of the men in her lifetime in whom she thought she had seen Destiny, only to be cheated; and the men of Destiny she

297

had met and not recognized until it was too late. Bonaparte, of course, but also Mehmet Ali – should she have foreseen that the Albanian officer would one day become sole master of Egypt?

And Elfi. She had seen in Elfi a promise she had seen in no other of her caste since Ali Bey the Great. She had recognized the uncommon will, the energy and ambition in the young blond Mamluke brought home by Murad. But it was when Elfi Bey returned from England that she had seen in him a man tempered, humbled and inspired by his experience. 'If God gives me power over this country,' he had pledged to her, 'I will prevent the abuses we were raised to commit. I will make justice prevail, so the land will prosper, the cities grow, the people thrive, and it becomes the best of God's countries!'

She had believed in him but Elfi's stars had been against him in the end. Mehmet Ali had been under no illusions as to the danger his adversary posed: 'As long as this Elfi lives, I will have no ease. He and I are like two acrobats walking a tightrope, except that he has wooden shoes on his feet.' When Elfi was killed, his death marked the end of the Mamlukes; he was the last of his caste, they never raised their banner after him.

As Sitt Nafisa crossed the Ezbekiah esplanade towards Bulaq, it seemed to her that half the citizens of Cairo must be thronging the road in their excitement to see the Azharites' ship set off for the land of the Franj. She recognized Shaykh Jabarti on his donkey, led by his apprentice. The old historian was almost completely blind now, yet still writing and revising the four-volume history of Egypt that was his life's work. His journal of the French occupation, his chronicle of the lives of his contemporaries – Ali Bey, Murad, Elfi; Nafisa herself, no doubt – would never be published in Jabarti's lifetime, thought Nafisa. Certainly not while Mehmet Ali was in power, and Jabarti was an old man now, older than she.

As she passed, Jabarti's apprentice tugged his master's sleeve and whispered, 'Sitt Nafisa the White.' The old man reined in his ass and bowed blindly in her direction. She slowed down and inclined her head in return, even if he could barely make out the gesture. Their paths still crossed sometimes, the old historian and the White

Lady, in this their ancient city: two ghosts, out of favour and forgotten. She would ride before him on the street, an old lady in her veils, and he could not see her, but he would stop and bow in her direction, and she would acknowledge his homage in return, acknowledging the memories they alone shared that the world around them had forgotten, and the secret they had conspired to keep: the story of the Naqib's daughter.

GLOSSARY

Agha: chief of police.

Amir: commander, prince; title given to top Mamluke commanders (see Mamluke, below).

Ardab: measure of weight equalling fifteen thousand tons.

Arnaout: Albanian contingent in the Ottoman army.

Bey: highest Ottoman rank given to Mamluke commanders.

Capitan pasha: Admiral of the Ottoman fleet.

Daftardar: treasurer.

Diwan: council of ulema.

Elfi: he of the thousand, from the Arabic *elf*, one thousand. Elfi Bey was bought for one thousand ardabs of wheat, hence his name.

Grand vizir: prime minister to the Ottoman Sultan.

Kashif: title given to Mamluke governor of a province, below Bey in rank.

Khatkhuda: intendant, secretary.

Khushdash: brothers, expression used to refer to Mamlukes of the same generation trained in the same house.

Kuttab: Koranic school.

Mamluke: literally, Arabic for 'one who is owned', i.e. slave. Designation of a military caste of slaves from the Ottoman Empire trained as cavalry, then manumitted and often promoted to rule provinces of the empire. In Egypt in the period covered by the book, the Mamlukes were largely of Georgian or Circassian origin, from the Caucasus Mountains. (See historical note.)

Milayya: black sheet worn as outer garment by women.

Naqib: syndic or head of guild.

Naqib Ashraf: syndic of the descendants of the Prophet Mohammed.

Majnoon: madman.

Ottoman: Ottoman Turkish empire. At the close of the eighteenth century, the empire extended across the Middle East from Tunisia to the Arab Gulf as well as across much of Central Eastern Europe. Its capital was Istanbul.

Pasha: title given to Ottoman governor or viceroy.

Sabil: public waterworks, comprising wells and fountains, often funded by benefactors, where the public could fetch water for drinking, bathing, and cooking.

Sabil-kuttab: a public waterworks with a school built over it, a common combination.

Sahlep: powdered root of orchids, used to thicken milk for a creamy hot drink popular in Turkey.

Sick Man of Europe: euphemism for the Ottoman sultan.

Sublime Porte: the Ottoman court, and more particularly the Foreign Ministry, when referred to by Western diplomats.

Tcherkess: Circassian, of a region of the Caucasus Mountains.

Ulema: scholars and jurists.

Wali: representative, in this case representative of the Turkish governor of Egypt.

Wikala: a caravanserai or covered market place with an inn for merchants and pilgrims. Most wikalas specialized in specific goods and were located near one of the gates of a city for the convenience of traders and travellers.

Yashmak: sheer white face veil worn by women as part of Ottoman dress.

Yussef Saladdin: the Mamluke sultan Yussef Salah-eldin, the Saladin of the Crusades.

HISTORICAL NOTES

I was first intrigued by a passing mention of **Zeinab El-Bakri** in French sources. Napoleon, we are told, had several Circassian slaves presented to him, whom he found too plump and perfumed for his taste; then Zeinab, daughter of Shaykh El-Bakri. The young, chubby Zeinab did not please Bonaparte, who kept her as his mistress for only a few days; but when the French evacuate, a number of women accused of 'horizontal' collaboration pay with their lives, among them El-Bakri's daughter. For the details of the trial and execution, French sources rely on the account of Abdel-Rahman El-Jabarti, the Egyptian historian who kept a daily chronicle of his times, an indispensable primary source for all historians of the expedition.

I followed up this intriguing footnote of history in Jabarti's chronicles in the original Arabic and in translation. Jabarti speaks of the collaborationist Shaykh Bakri, who sought to curry favour with the occupation and whose daughter consorted with the French at his instigation. In another entry, without mentioning names, Jabarti lambastes the base ambition of many an Egyptian father who drives his daughter into an alliance with a Frenchman; the latter, having no religion of his own, according to Jabarti, has no compunction about going through the empty rituals of an Islamic marriage. Since Bonaparte was known to have made deliberately ambiguous claims to having embraced Islam, it seemed to follow, for me, that any liaison with Shaykh Bakri's daughter would have been conducted under the fig leaf of 'marriage'.

After the evacuation, Jabarti goes on to tell us, five women faced reprisals on the same day for going over to the enemy; Shaykh Bakri's daughter was one of them. Her father, fearful of being held to account for his own collaborationist role, disavowed her, claiming: 'I wash my hands of her fate.' Moreover, Jabarti tells us, with evident indignation at the father's perfidy, Shaykh Bakri 'had his daughter killed by the hand of the police chief.' He adds: 'They snapped her neck.'

The sad fate of this young girl inspired me to rewrite her story with a happier, entirely plausible ending. It is one of two liberties I have taken with history in this novel. The other is the liaison between Zeinab and Nicolas Conté; there is no record of it, but it is entirely plausible, again, in the context of relations between the French and local women at the time. Frenchmen, from Commandant Menou to naturalist Geoffroy St-Hilaire, took Egyptian wives and had children with them.

The fate of other women in Zeinab's situation who did follow their husbands and lovers to France is instructive. When the French evacuated, **General Menou** took his wife Zubayda El-Rashidiya with him. According to Shaykh Tahtawi, travelling to France a quarter century later at the head of an Egyptian student expedition, Menou converted back to Christianity, while his wife remained Muslim for many years; when she gave him a son, he insisted on having the boy baptized against her resistance, persuading her that all scriptural religions are true and valid in the eye of Islam. In the city of Marseilles, Tahtawi tells us, he found many Egyptian Copts and Syrian Christians evacuated with the French, but few Muslims among them; those who had been Muslim, 'the Georgian and Circassian Mamlukes in particular, and the women who in their youth had been abducted by the French,' had converted to Christianity.

The French expedition spelled the beginning of the end for the centuries-old **Mamluke system**. The name in Arabic means 'one who is owned' and is different from the term for slave ('abd). In fact since Mamlukes were recruited to form a military caste and were eventually manumitted, their situation was far closer to indentured servitude than traditional slavery. Originally recruited from prisoners of war by the sultans of the Abbasid and Ottoman empires to form an imperial guard with loyalties undivided by allegiance to tribe or clan, the Mamluke system had evolved considerably over the millennium that preceded the French expedition.

That evolution in Egypt had taken the form of an independent Mamluke dynasty (1250–1517), founded by Salah-Eldin Ayyubi (the Saladin of the Crusades) and lasting for nearly three centuries till the Ottoman Turkish invasion. The Mamlukes of Egypt progressively reasserted their power against the Ottomans till, by the time of the French invasion, the Beys were paying only lip-service and the occasional tax tribute to Istanbul.

Most of the 8,000 or so Mamlukes in Egypt at the time of the French expedition had been recruited as boys from poor families in the region of the Caucasus Mountains, Georgia and Tcherkessia, although there were Mamlukes from every corner of the Ottoman Empire and beyond, like Murad Bey's Sudanese Sennari, or Elfi Bey's interpreter the Piedmontese Vincenzo Taberna.

Once a boy entered a Mamluke house, he was given a Muslim name and rigorous training in the arts of cavalry and war, along with rudimentary instruction in Arabic and religion. A code of honour based on loyalty to his overlord and his Mamluke 'brethren' was also inculcated, although not always observed. The most capable of each generation of Mamlukes rose to the ranks of kashif, or governor of a province, and then amir, or commander. In Egypt at the time of the French invasion, the top positions of power were held by the 'Master of Cairo' and the 'Prince of the Pilgrimage', posts occupied by the two senior Beys, Murad and Ibrahim.

The Mamlukes drew their wealth from tax-farming, and were resented by the peasants and the general populace for their tax exactions and undeniable arrogance and abuses, but after the evacuation of the French, Lord Hutchinson, the British Commander in Egypt, faced with a choice of two evils, found that: 'The Mamluke system . . . is toleration and mildness when compared with that of the Turks. It has the advantage, moreover, of being the one to which the inhabitants had become used . . .' Perhaps even more telling, Egyptian historian Jabarti was of the same opinion; critical as he was of the Mamluke regime before the French invasion, the anarchy and violence unleashed by the Turkish militias in the aftermath of the evacuation had him nostalgic for the antebellum years and even for the French!

In the power vacuum that ensued after the French evacuation, the Mamlukes and the Turks struggled for power, with the French and the British favouring both sides of the conflict, often simultaneously, all the while claiming neutrality. In this power struggle **Muhammad Bey Elfi**, 'the rebel amir' who travelled to England, played a controversial role. The French, naturally, put the worst possible construction on his voyage to portray him to the Ottoman Sultan as the tool of British ambitions in Egypt. History is written by the victors, and as Mehmet Ali was finally victorious over the Mamlukes, whom he exterminated in a massacre, it is to be expected that the reputation of Elfi, his great rival, would be blackened under the Mehmet Ali dynasty for 150 years. Subsequently, under Nasser's Arab nationalism, the Mamlukes were reviled as foreigners, and Elfi in particular tarred as the traitor who invited the British to invade Egypt in 1807.

Historical record disputes these allegations. To begin with, we have contemporary British accounts, which make it clear that his English interlocutors never regarded Elfi as sold to their side, and that although he lobbied for Britain to exert her influence on behalf of the Mamlukes, and for British arms to help drive out the abusive Ottoman militias, the British were convinced he never wished to see them established in his country. For French and British views on the occupation and its aftermath, we have the dispatches from the Foreign and War Office records of both countries. Elfi cut a rather dashing figure in London society, according to the society magazines of the period, and memoirs by contemporary intimates of the Prince of Wales. In his account of an Upper Egypt expedition under Elfi's protection, William Hamilton writes that, in comparison to Mamlukes in general, 'Elfi indeed had been more fortunate than most of his brethren. His mild manners and liberal disposition had gained him many friends, who had shared his fate and fought in his cause amid mountains and deserts, in poverty and defeat. He had likewise in his better days distinguished himself above the rest by spending very considerable sums of money in improving his lands and the lot of his peasants, digging canals, repairing dykes and punctually executing other duties of a landlord.'

The account of another of Elfi's contemporaries, the Egyptian historian Jabarti, is particularly interesting in its evolution. It follows the development of Elfi's character from an arrogant and abusive Mamluke to a man tempered by adversity, and enlightened by his voyage to England, 'during which his character was refined by his experience of the architecture of (British) cities, their well-designed laws, their wealth, prosperity, manufacturing, and their justice to their subjects.' If we are to believe Jabarti, 'on his return, Efi pledged: "If God gives me control of Egypt and power over this country, I will prevent the abuses we were raised to commit. I will make justice prevail, so that the land will prosper, its cities become populous, its inhabitants thrive, and it becomes the best of God's countries."' Jabarti concludes in his necrology of Elfi in 1807: 'In short, he was the most gallant, energetic, and perspicacious of the Mamlukes who were our contemporaries. He was one of a kind, unique among the men of his caste.'

There is still a street in Cairo named after Elfi Bey, and 'Elfi' is the family name of a numerous clan in Egypt today.

Abdel Rahman Jabarti died in 1826; his voluminous Chronicles were published in Arabic in Egypt sixty years after his death, and widely translated and disseminated. In France, under the title *Journal d'un Notable du Caire*, they form an integral and essential reference for all accounts of the period of the French expedition in Egypt.

Sitt Nafisa the White's sabil-kuttab, charitable waterworks and school, still stands on Sugar Street, close by her wikala, the caravanserai market at the Gate of Zuweila. The sabil-kuttab was recently restored by the American Research Center in Eygpt and re-opened to the public in 1998.

Nicolas Conté died December 6, 1805, on the day of the victory of Austerlitz, a year after the death of his wife and his brother. The twenty volumes of the *Description of Egypt* was published incrementally from 1809 to 1822, and sold out immediately at each printing. It remains a landmark work. In 2007 the complete web version of the *Description* was made available, free of charge, by the Bibliotheca Alexandrina in Alexandria, on the web site http://descegy.bibalex.org/

The **Ezbekiah**, dubbed 'the Champs-Elysées' of Cairo in Napoleon's day, is now a crowded, low-income neighbourhood in the heart of Cairo. Elfi Bey's palace in the Ezbekiah, completed in 1798 and almost immediately commandeered by Bonaparte as headquarters for his French army in Egypt, was later badly damaged in the fighting of 1803. In the neighbourhood of **Nasiriya**, where the French set up *L'Institut de l'Égypte* in Hassan Kashif's house and Qassim Bey's garden, the only Mamluke residence restored and open to the public is that of Ibrahim Sennari, Murad Bey's Sudanese Mamluke, which was commandeered by the French as a residence for their savants. It is on Monge Street, so called after Gaspard Monge, the first president of the Institute; Nicolas-Jacques Conté was its last president.

The **Citadel of Cairo** still dominates the skyline over the Mokkatam hills, but many of the original buildings and the mosque built by its founder, Sultan Salah al-Din (the Saladin of the Crusades), were destroyed and replaced by the grand mosque of Mehmet Ali. Of the original houses from the time of the French occupation that remain within the Citadel complex, the house of Shaykh Sahimi, where Sitt Nafisa was briefly incarcerated by the Turkish viceroy, is restored and open to the public.

Mehmet Ali, the Albanian officer who rose to power after the French evacuation, made a move to consolidate his sole mastery over Egypt in 1811 by eliminating the last of his Mamluke enemies in a massacre known as the Massacre at the Citadel. Mehmet Ali invited the Mamlukes in exile to come to a banquet at the Citadel, then once they were inside, locked the gates and set his archers upon them. According to reports, all perished but one, Amin Bey, who leapt from the ramparts of the Citadel on his horse. Mehmet Ali died in 1849 and his dynasty went on to rule Egypt until the last descendant, King Faruk, abdicated under pressure in 1953.

Cairo, described by Bonaparte's French expedition as 'an immense city', had a population of some 275 thousand in 1798. The population of Cairo and Giza in 2008 is estimated at some 16 million, and counting.

AUTHOR'S NOTE

In the transliteration of Arabic and Ottoman names, I have not followed strict rules, but rather the spelling most likely to be familiar to the reader. So Ezbekiah, from French sources at the time of the expedition, rather than El-Azbakiyya; and Elfi, the common spelling in English and French diplomatic dispatches in his day, rather than El-Alfy. Mehmet Ali's name is spelled phonetically according to the Turkish pronunciation, which he himself would have used, rather than the Arabic Muhammad Ali.